GREEN DAWN AT ST ENDA'S

TRACEY ICETON

Published by Cinnamon Press,
Meirion House,
Tanygrisiau,
Blaenau Ffestiniog,
Gwynedd
LL41 3SU
www.cinnamonpress.com

ISBN 978-1-909077-99-7
British Library Cataloguing in Publication Data. A CIP record for this book can be obtained from the British Library.

Designed and typeset in Garamond by Cinnamon Press. Cover design by Adam Craig, from original artwork 'Green Dawn at St Enda's' by Tracey Iceton, © Tracey Iceton, showing the Hermitage, St Enda's Park, Rathfarnham – once St Enda's school; now the Pearse Museum. Artwork digitised by Mike Walker Photography www.mikewalker-photography.com

Cinnamon Press is represented by Inpress and by the Welsh Books Council in Wales.

Printed in Poland

The Publisher acknowledges the financial support of the Welsh Books Council.

Acknowledgments

This book owes its existence to the following people:

Those who best remain nameless who advised me this project was too epic or who otherwise tried to steer me from the folly of it; your doubt made me determined; your rejection gave me resolve.

Brian Crowley, curator of the Pearse Museum in Dublin, who provided practical support through access to museum archives and his very helpful book *Patrick Pearse: A life in pictures*, and who encouraged the writing of *Green Dawn*.

Dr Elaine Sisson for both her book *Pearse's Patriots*, which gave me a fantastic insight into the world of St Enda's and the man who ran it, and for her kind supportive communication with me.

Michael and Larry of Teach an Phiarsaigh (Pearse's Cottage) Rosmuc, Galway who welcomed me on each of my three visits (in a single week) and who answered my many odd questions about Pearse's cottage and rural life in Connemara. Also their colleague, Máirtín Ó Meachair, who was kind and generous enough to correct my use of Irish throughout the novel. Go raibh maith agat!

Danny Morrison for his eleventh hour read through that addressed some crucial issues and for his extremely generous words of praise for the novel which mean so much, coming as they do, from an author and a Republican.

Fred Gardner who kindly read an early draft of the book and delighted me by saying he had learned a lot about the situation in Ireland from so doing.

Clare Wren who not only read and praised the novel but who let me bend her ear over lengthy lunches as I battled uphill into a gale to see the book in print.

Natalie Scott, friend and fellow writer, whose long standing support and encouragement helped me to keep faith with the sometimes frustrating and dispiriting profession of writing.

Laura Degnan of Writers Block NE, Middlesbrough, who guided me through some detailed early edits of the novel, without which I may not have caught the attention of Cinnamon Press.

Dr Jan Fortune at Cinnamon, who saw the potential of this book and who shared my vision for it. Without her belief in the project, her passion for it and her fantastic editorial guidance this book would still be a 'loose baggy monster' left to languish on my laptop. I can never thank her adequately for her utter faith in not just *Green Dawn* but my entire Irish Trilogy, books two and three of which to follow under the Cinnamon imprint in 2017 and 2019.

Clíona Colum Ní Shúilleabháin and the Estate of Padraic Colum for generously allowing me to reproduce, without charge, extracts from her great uncle's book *A Boy in Eirinn*.

My family, Johnsons and Icetons. Without their unconditional acceptance of my dream to be a writer I would never have dared to dream, much less write.

John, my husband, who, if I had to thank only one person, would be that one. Throughout my writing career he has been everything from (in no particular order); bankroller, therapist and talking dictionary to research assistant, sounding block and cheerleader but most of all he has been himself; patient, supportive, understanding and caring. If not for him it is no lie to say this book would not exist.

And finally, I cannot in good conscience end without thanking Patrick Pearse himself. Although, as I hope this book goes some way towards testifying, not the only person of his generation who showed extraordinary faith, dedication and courage in acting as his conscience dictated, "in defence of some true thing," it was Pearse who spoke to me and Pearse I must thank for living as he did and sacrificing himself as he felt he must, "for Ireland and for freedom."[1] It has been a privilege to have spent so much time in his company and to have made even so small a contribution as *Green Dawn at St Enda's* can offer to keeping alive his legacy.

---

[1] Quoted from a letter dated 3rd May 1916 written by Pearse from his cell at Kilmainham Prison to his mother. (*Last Words* ed. Piaras F. MacLochlainn, 1990)

Author's Note

In 2003, while teaching World War I literature to sixth formers, I came upon David Lloyd George's 'The Great Pinnacle of Sacrifice' speech. In it he justifies Britain's entry to the conflict with the following statement, "if we had stood by when two little nations [Serbia and Belgium] were being crushed and broken by the brutal hands of barbarism [Germany], our shame would have rung down the everlasting ages."

Later that summer I visited Dublin and, taking the Kilmainham Gaol tour, first learnt of the 1916 Dublin Easter Rising. We stood in the stonebreakers yard, under the Irish tricolour, where fourteen leaders of the Rising were executed for their act of 'treason': trying to free their own "little nation". Lloyd George's hypocrisy was a bullet in my chest. I whispered to my husband, "Don't let them know we're English!" I wasn't joking. What had happened in Ireland in 1916 was, to me, a more insidious crushing than that on the continent. And at British hands. It haunted me. I knew one day I would have to write about it, if only to exorcise my own demons.

For this exorcism I had a simple plan: to write a novel based on real events so potent they overwhelmed me. For me it had to be a novel, not only because I'm not an historian but because I believe in the power of novels to take readers on impossible journeys, losing themselves in other worlds, befriending people they would never otherwise meet. I boldly embarked on my task, researching and drafting; well-meaning souls tried to deter me, saying the project was too ambitious. Their pleas were quickly drowned by a new voice, that of a fellow writer and teacher. A voice wholly Irish and wholly Gaelic. A voice silenced by a dawn firing squad. A voice I listened to with growing fascination and a voice I felt deserved to be heard again: Patrick Pearse's voice.

At first I thought to make fact and fiction meet in that mysterious realm of historical literature by playing with the truth. As it turned out, I didn't need to: the story was already there, a narrative so finely and tragically crafted that it needed little more than typing up thus *Green Dawn* doesn't stray far from the facts as found in scholarly works. Actually, it uses as many of them as I plausibly could, including, in places, the actual words attributed to or written by those for whom the Easter Rising was not a story to be told but a life to be lived. Critics and readers may argue all they please over how believable is the story of the Easter Rising, the events that led to it and its poignant ending. It happened. *Green Dawn*, in the main, tells it as it was. Any deviation from the facts is deliberate on my part to enable me to tell *my* Easter Rising story which, though differing little from *the* Easter Rising story, is nonetheless a facsimile such as can only be written by a novelist.

On *Green Dawn's* cast list, all the boys at my St Enda's are fictional characters. The adults, with the exception of Finn's parents and a few minor players, are all men and women who really lived and died, written as I imagined them from what I have read of their lives and transformed here into literary characters.

Finally, in vindicating *Green Dawn*, I would point out that history is not more, or less, than story. While somewhere out there truth may exist none of us can say for certain that we've found it, or, if we have, that we are repeating it accurately. Anyway, I wanted, hoped, to write something purer than truth: a fascinating story, one I felt was well-overdue a retelling. One I think Pearse himself would have told if only he'd lived to see a free Ireland and one I couldn't have told without his help.

Tracey Iceton, 2016

I care not though I live but one day and one night
if only my name and deeds live after me.
Cúchulainn, An Táin

Green Dawn at St Enda's

September 1911

Ahead of them William's father cut a swathe through the crowd, snarling and shoving. He cursed the steerage passengers who didn't know to step aside for him; glared at the second class upstarts who stopped to ogle him; nodded to the gents and ladies who recognised an eminent man. William felt himself towed along by his father, though it was his mother's hand that tugged gently at his.

William was worried about his mother. Her eyes were red and her cheeks pale. He hoped she wasn't getting a fever like the one she had last winter. There'd be no one to look after her this time.

'Hurry along, William. Greta, you're slowing us down, so you are. I'll not have us miss the sailing for your dawdling.'

William peaked up at his father. The fedora was pulled low; William could only see his nose and the bushy black moustache which covered his mouth but couldn't muffle the bellow in his voice. William's eyes watered. He told himself it was the stinging wind. His father ploughed on. His mother squeezed William's hand.

His father halted at the gangplank.

'This is us. Say goodbye to your mother and be quick about you.'

William longed to throw his arms around her, losing himself in her soft fur coat. Instead, he held out his hand.

'Goodbye, Mother.'

'Is that all I get?' she teased, trying to smile.

William let himself be pulled into a hug, melting against her.

'Greta, don't fuss the boy. Jesus, he's twelve. William, now.' His father's hand stamped down on William's shoulder, dragging him backwards.

His mother dabbed a handkerchief to her eyes. 'Goodbye, Michael. Take care of yourselves. Wire when you arrive.'

His father removed his hat and pecked his mother on the cheek.

'I'll be back by the fifteenth. Be sure to forward any urgent correspondence.'

His mother nodded.

'Now, get along with you, woman.'

She rested her hand one last time on William's arm. The warmth soaked though his coat and into his skin.

'I expect a letter from you every week. I want to hear all about your adventures.'

'I promise, Mother.'

She withdrew her hand. William's father jerked him towards the queuing passengers. William watched as the crowd surged around his mother, drowning her. The warmth on his arm faded.

'Come on, lad.' William's father set the fedora back on his head and pulled it down over his ice blue eyes.

Case in one hand, the other balled in his pocket, William trudged up the gangplank in his father's long black shadow. On deck William stood on tip-toes. Around him people waved; he clutched the railings with whitening knuckles. Horns tooted their farewells. The ship began to drift from the dock and skirt Liberty Island. William thought of those times his mother had taken him on the ferry to visit Lady Liberty. Up the hundreds of steps they toiled, his mother telling him how Lady Liberty had been gifted to New York as a symbol of the freedom won by France and America through hard-fought revolutions. William let go of the railings and waved frantically at Madam Liberty as they sailed by her.

He stayed at the railings until the whole of Long Island was reduced to a pin-prick on the horizon, recalling his father's words, 'You're going home, home to Ireland.' William ground his top teeth into his bottom lip as he watched his real home falling into the sea. He was blinking away tears when his father came to take him down to their cabin where, for the next six nights, William lay restless on the narrow bunk listening to his father snoring six inches above him as the ship groaned and heaved around them like a great stomach. The days were no better; William stood on deck, eyes on the horizon as his father commanded, the only help for William's sickness. How he wanted his mother's ginger tea to sip and her cool hand caressing his stomach.

'And, don't you dare be sick in the cabin, laddie, or I'll rub your nose in it,' his father warned.

The dock at Liverpool was a mirror image of the one in New York. Dragging his case, William swayed and staggered down the gangplank behind his father and struggled after him through the hurly-burly.

'Michael! Michael Devoy, would that be yourself?'

A man with an accent more lilting than his father's was calling to them. His father stopped. William crashed into him.

'Jesus, William, watch where you're going!'

'Wheesht, Michael,' the stranger exclaimed, 'So this'll be the wee man? He looks a grand fellow, Michael, the spit of your father.'

'Aye, Sean,' his father mumbled, 'Good to be seeing you again.' He extended a hand.

The stranger grasped it and pumped his father's arm with a force that seemed impossible for so sickly a-looking man. He was pale, the shock of dark wavy hair and the heavy eyebrows making his complexion seem whiter. He had sticky-out ears and a half-hearted dimple in his chin. William noticed he lent heavily on a walking stick. The man transferred the stick to his right hand and William noticed his left now hung stiffly at his side.

'So it is yourself, Michael, mighty good after all this time. You look fine.'

'You're not looking too badly done by yourself,' his father replied.

'Keeping up appearances. But it's not been easy. Who'd be eejit enough to be an Irishman in these parts?'

William saw the wink and the grin.

'William, this is Mr Sean MacDermott. Say 'hello'.'

William stepped forward. Mr MacDermott crouched down, ending up head and shoulders shorter than William.

'Mr MacDermott is an old friend.'

'Pleased to meet you, sir.'

'And you, William. You must be tired and hungry after your journey.'

William nodded.

'Then we best see about something to eat and a bed.' Mr MacDermott struggled up, 'Just the one night you're staying is it, Michael?'

'I've tickets for the Dublin boat tomorrow. I'm taking William to school.'

'That'll be that new school run by our Mr Pearse, will it?'

'It will. St Enda's.'

St Enda's. William cursed the name, the place and his father for sending him there. He'd gone on and on, proclaiming, 'A boy needs an adventure. My father had his; I had mine and my son will have his too.' William's innards somersaulted.

Mr MacDermott glanced at William. 'We'd better be getting along,' he turned to William's father, 'I've some friends eager for a word with you.'

'Indeed,' his father replied through clenched teeth.

The three of them boarded a tram into town. His father stared out of the grimy window with a stone-faced expression. Mr MacDermott made small-talk. William listened but was glad to be able to keep his replies to 'yes, sir' and 'no, sir'.

Mr MacDermott lived in a narrow house. It stood in a row with a dozen identical houses running the length of the street. They had to walk the last two miles and William was lagging behind when they reached the door.

'William,' his father bellowed.

'Bejesus, let the boy alone,' Mr MacDermott said, 'He's done in. It's a fair way we've walked today, isn't it, William?'

'Yes, sir.'

'Is that what you want, Michael? To wear him to the bone? Come on, William, I think I've some barmbrack. We'll have ourselves a thick slice with a cup of tea and you'll be right.'

William followed Mr MacDermott inside. It was cold and smelled of soil after rain. He sat at the table as Mr MacDermott set the kettle to boil, unwrapped a loaf and, picking up a dull-bladed knife, hacked at it, before dumping slices on a plate.

'Help yourself, William.'

'Thank you, sir.'

William ate the barmbrack, which was only sultana bread but not sweet like his mother's, and sipped the tea which tasted of dishwater. He would rather have had cocoa. The two men hunched up at the other end of the table, talking in low voices. William heard unfamiliar names. Some his father growled, others he spat and a few he hummed. When the plates were cleared and the cups drained Mr MacDermott showed William to a bedroom. It was colder than the kitchen. Two beds were pushed against opposite walls. William took off his shoes and climbed between the rough sheets. He knew his mother would be cross with him for getting into bed dressed but she wasn't there and the stale air was too cold for fumbling into his pyjamas. He rested his head on the pillow, moved away from a lump, closed his eyes and fell asleep.

When William woke he was in the ship's belly again. Everything was still. The ship must have sunk to the ocean floor. Any minute icy water would rise around him. He would shiver and drown. William sat up with a jolt. Seeing the empty bed opposite he remembered where he was. He got up, crossed the room and inched the door open. From downstairs he heard his father's voice, the boom reigned in to a dull rumble. William shuffled onto the landing, fearful of creaking boards, and crouched down, peering between the wooden railings that edged the staircase. He caught the reassuring tinkle of Mr MacDermott's voice. William tiptoed to the bottom.

The kitchen door was open a crack. Light, dimly yellowed as though old and tired, seeped out. William stepped into a puddle of it and held his breath.

Now there was a third voice. Not loud, but crisp and sharp. William flattened himself against the peeling wallpaper, eyes screwed closed.

'I'm telling you, Michael, it's no good at all. Redmond's an Asquith puppet. He'll fall in with whatever crock of shite the establishment sets out. Home Rule's a pipedream. We need a return to action. This 'wait and see' policy is fecking useless and I don't intend to be lying on my death bed with Ireland still in shackles. We must act.'

The voice turned William's legs to sand. He opened his eyes and found himself slashed by the narrow chink of bleeding light, looking into the kitchen at the back of his father's coal-black head. To his left at the table was Mr MacDermott, in profile. Of the third speaker there was only an arm visible.

'Away, Tom. You're making a complicated matter over-simple. Jesus, there's more to it than you're thinking,' William's father said.

'And you're making a simple matter over-complicated. Sure, all we're needing's some fire power, a return to the campaigns of '81 and blow the feckers to Kingdom come,' the man replied.

William checked his escape route but was held back by his father's next words.

'And what the fuck did we achieve with that? By Christ, you've some strange ideas, Thomas Callan, especially for one who would've done fifteen years hard time if not for my efforts. If action's required then we'll be the first to take it. But we must be cautious. And be warned, Tom, if you take matters into your own hands it won't end well for anyone, least of all yourself.'

'Would that be a threat now?'

'Just a statement of facts.'

'Facts, eh? So you're willing to take action against your own but not the enemy?'

'I've said what my plans are. We wait.'

The Tom man made a rude snorting sound.

'You're a fucking impostor, not the Michael Devoy I knew. Not Daniel Devoy's son, the bold lad that set out for Fremantle, the man I was proud to serve with. You've gone soft. You're a fucking…'

There was a swoop, a raven diving. William's father launched himself over the table at the Tom man. The arm disappeared from view. Four legs, tangled up, rolled on the floor. Mr MacDermott vanished, reappeared, vanished again. William heard three hard whacks, bone pounding flesh, then a muddle of grunts, scrapes, cries, bangs.

'Now, gents,' Mr MacDermott's calming voice pleaded.

Rooted where he stood, William saw one of the pairs of legs scramble up. Silence teetered for a moment. A door slammed. A hand righted the fallen chair. The other pair of legs got up.

'Tom, you eejit,' Mr MacDermott said, 'It's lucky he didn't take a shot at you.'

William now had a clear view of the table. On it tea things lay tumbled and broken and in their midst, shiny and cold, was a pistol. The kitchen door closed with a soft click.

William fled back upstairs, diving under the blankets to lie trembling. He listened but it stayed quiet and his terror drained away. He dreamt of his father pointing a gun at him.

In the morning William found Mr MacDermott alone in the kitchen. The savoury smell of frying sausages filled the room. Everything was tidy. The pistol was gone. William wondered if it had been a nightmare. Mr MacDermott turned from the stove. His eyes were bloodshot.

'Ah, William, you look well this morning. You must have slept like the angels,' he blinked and rubbed his raw eyes, 'I thought you'd best have a proper breakfast to see you on your grand adventure so I've done you a couple of bangers. I hope that'll be fine with yourself?'

'Thank you.'

'No trouble at all. Help yourself to bread and butter. These'll be ready in a flash.'

William pulled out a chair, catching his hand on the jagged edge of a crack. He scanned the kitchen and spotted three dark splotches on the floor.

'Where's my father?'

'Running some errands. He said you're to be ready by ten.'

Mr MacDermott set the sausages in front of William. Their skins were shiny and tight. William stabbed one with a fork; grease gushed out.

'What's Home Rule?'

Mr MacDermott turned from the sink. 'Why would you be asking about that now?'

William stared into the shimmering sausage juice on his plate.

'Happen you didn't sleep so well after all,' Mr MacDermott mused, 'And I'd best tell you a thing or two but you've to let me give you a wee bit of advice first.'

William nodded. Mr MacDermott sat opposite him.

'Don't be seeking out trouble. It'll come to you, sure enough. Do you understand me?'

'Yes, sir.'

'Grand. Now, Home Rule: that's a thing the Irish have been wanting a canny long time. See, William, Ireland is her own land; she belongs to her own people: me and you, all us Irish folk. But years ago the British stole Ireland from us. They rule us and most of them'd prefer to keep it that way. Now there's one or two ready to see sense and they've been trying to get Ireland Home Rule. That means Ireland would make her own laws. Sure, it's not a good thing, having someone else tell you what to do, especially when what they're telling you isn't fair.'

'I don't want to go to school but I have to because Father says so.'

'Aye, well, it's different for you, William. You're only a wee man. Your father's a grand fellow. Haven't I trusted him with my life? You'll not go far wrong if you turn out half the man he is.'

William scowled and jabbed at a sausage.

'As for Ireland, she's a good bit older than you; she knows what's right for her and there's men like your father, and myself, going to help her get it.'

'Why?'

''Tis our duty as Irishmen. Now, enough blether, your breakfast's going cold.'

The boat to Dublin was small and the crossing short. William strode along the deck on his new-grown sea legs, watching Liverpool sink into the sea and Dublin rise from it. His father sat in the salon with his gloves on, not drinking his coffee.

They docked and disembarked. A short train ride took William and his father into downtown Dublin. They stood on the platform. A sharp wind skirted them. A patrolling policeman passed. William's father pull his fedora over his eyes and flipped his collar up, glancing around. William looked too but saw nothing.

'William, over here, lad.'

William turned and found himself facing a young woman in a long grey skirt and coat. A plain hat perched on a mass of wild hair.

His father stuck out a gloved hand. 'Miss Pearse?'

The young woman smiled. 'Miss Mary Brigid, aye.' To William's amazement and delight she shook his father's glove robustly, nearly pumping his arm loose.

'And you'll be Mr Devoy, if I've my wits. Pat sent me to meet you. And this is himself, our William that's to be?'

William took his turn shaking her hand which was fire-side warm despite the cold wind.

'A pleasure to meet you,' she said, 'You're joining us at the Hermitage, I'm told.'

William frowned. 'I'm going to St Enda's.'

'Aye,' she said with another smile, 'St Enda's is at a place called the Hermitage. I'm to take you both there.'

'Apologies, Miss Pearse,' his father cut in, 'I must beg your pardon. I have urgent business. Would you take William to school and give Mr Pearse my regrets? I'm keen to make his acquaintance but other matters are pressing. I hope to visit him before returning to New York.'

'That'll be fine,' Mary Brigid replied, 'We'll have ourselves a grand time on the ride. I'll show you the sights, William.'

'Thank you, miss.'

'I have the boarding fees.'

His father passed Mary Brigid an envelope which she stuffed inside her coat.

'Thank you.'

His father turned to him. 'Mind what I've said. 'Tis a grand school you're away to, run by a grand man. You're to learn everything he teaches you. I don't want any complaints about your behaviour. Make the most of this opportunity, as my father did his and I have mine. Mark this, William, men may or may not make opportunities but opportunities, when seized, always make men.'

'Father?'

'The devil, I've not time to explain it.'

William dipped his head and pictured the gun on Mr MacDermott's table.

'Goodbye, William.'

'Goodbye, Father.'

He snatched at William's hand, let go again and stalked away down the platform.

'Here you go.' Mary Brigid waved a handkerchief.

'I'm not crying.'

'Good for you. But keep it for later, in case you have need of it, to blow your nose or the like.' She smiled.

William, dry-eyed, took the handkerchief. Mary Brigid swung his case onto the waiting trap then swung herself into the driver's seat; William climbed up beside her. As she geed the reins William glanced behind. His father was gone.

The horse clipped down the road. William's eyelids threatened to droop then actually drooped. He forced them open and watched the scenery rolling by. Houses straggled further apart. There were more trees. They pointed bare limbs at the grey sky. Ahead mountains, darkly purple, rose up. William shivered.

'It's a cold one,' Mary Brigid said.

'Not as cold as New York.'

'Gets colder than this, does it?'

William nodded, 'So cold that in winter the ponds freeze solid. Sometimes it's cold enough that you can turn on the outside tap and the water runs to ice.'

'That's plenty cold enough. And what'll you be doing in the midst of this arctic freeze-out? Staying in where it's warm?'

'No, miss. I clear the sidewalk and run messages for my mother. One year she fell so Father said I was to take the messages in winter. When she's well we go to the park and skate on the lake.'

'Aren't you the gent, taking such care of your mother? It sounds like you have yourselves a grand time together.'

William went back to staring at the fields that were rolling away from them on all sides, punctuated by cottages and presided over by the mighty mountains. Mary Brigid clicked to the horse; it stepped out with more vigour and William was jolted on his seat.

'Is it so different here?'

'Everything's very short,' William replied.

'Aye, we've a bit of growing to do yet,' she laughed and the sound tickled William's ears, 'I'd like to see New York one day. Perhaps when you've finished school and gone home I'll be able to pay you a wee visit.'

William couldn't think that far ahead. He checked Mary Brigid wasn't looking and rubbed a sleeve over his face.

'It's a long way from home you are,' she said, 'But it's a fine place you've come to. I've to admit that your da's right: Pat's a grand teacher. Who's to say what wonderful things you'll do because of what you learn here? But,' she smiled at William, 'it's not wrong for you to be sad; if anyone tells you differently you can send them to me.' The words were stern but she winked as she spoke.

William smiled back.

'Sure, that's better,' she said.

'What's it like, St Enda's?'

'See for yourself.' Mary Brigid gestured with her head as she steered them off the road.

Ahead was a cinder track sheltered by dense undergrowth and roofed with the bent branches of sycamores and birches. Hooves and wheels crunched. With each crack and pop William felt better. Any place with a Mary Brigid couldn't be all bad.

The trees thinned, revealing a large square building. Three rows of windows marked the rooms. Steps led to an entrance flanked by four tall pillars. On top of the pillars was a slab roof. It was engraved with the words 'The Hermitage'. The whole building was grey and stout, a hefty block that could have been hewed from one solid piece. The track wound around the front. Mary Brigid hauled the horse up at the entrance.

William swivelled on the seat and dangled his legs over the side, ready to charge the building and become what his father wanted him to be: a St Enda's boy.

The double green and glass doors swung open. A man stepped out and waved.

'Hallo, Mary Brigid. Will you be needing a hand with the horse?'

'Hello, Con. I will, please.'

The man sprang down the steps. William stayed in his seat, gawping. The man was small, thin and wiry, clean shaven with short neat hair. The top half of his dress was normal; a jacket, collar and tie. But instead of trousers he wore a knee length skirt with pleats around the back, finished with knee socks and shiny brogues. The man whisked the reins from Mary Brigid's grasp; his sharp movements and darting dark eyes made William think of a sleek stoat.

'This'll be our Master Devoy, will it?' he said, 'Haven't we been full of ourselves since we heard you were joining our band.'

Mary Brigid glowered at the man and made a strangled shushing sound. 'William, this is Mr Colbert, one of St Enda's masters.'

She climbed down from the trap and William followed, trying to keep out of the glare of Mr Colbert's staring eyes.

'Is your da not with you, William?' Mr Colbert probed, 'I was looking forward to shaking his so fine hand.'

'Mr Devoy had business,' Mary Brigid said in a clipped tone.

'Aye, fair play. There's much to be done by a man the likes of him,' Mr Colbert continued, 'And won't I be as well shaking his son's hand. Come, William.'

William's cheeks blazed. 'Pleased to meet you, sir,' he stammered.

Mr Colbert seized his hand. 'Ah, William, the pleasure's mine.'

'That's enough, Con,' Mary Brigid snapped, 'Where's Pat?'

'In his study. He said for you to take William in. I'll see to the old boy.' Mr Colbert slapped the horse's flank.

'Thanks, Con. Come along, William.'

Mary Brigid climbed the steps; Mr Colbert walked the horse off. William hung back, staring at the retreating Mr Colbert, trying to make sense of what he had said, before chasing after Mary Brigid.

'Please, miss…'

'Now William, it's Mary Brigid you're to call me. And don't be worrying, William, all will be well.' She rested a hand on his shoulder. William felt the heat of her hand through his coat. It reminded him of his mother's touch. 'You can find me later if you're wanting a-thing.'

She reached for the door. William plucked at her sleeve.

'Mary Brigid,' her name filled his mouth, 'Please…why did Mr Colbert say those things, about my father?'

'It's nothing for fretting on,' she said and hurried inside.

William watched her disappear into the darkness. Annoyed she hadn't answered him, he trudged inside.

In the entrance hall William was confronted by a large fireplace. Mounted above it hung a painting of a boy with a greying cloth wrapped around his waist and fallen to his bare feet. His arms were stretched out so he made the shape of a cross. His fair hair was circled by a halo. He stood in a grove of fruit trees with hills behind him. There were words at the boy's feet but they were alien to William. It looked like paintings he'd seen in churches, except they were of Jesus: this was a boy.

Mary Brigid had crossed the hallway and was knocking on a panelled door.

'Who is that in the painting?'

'Íosagán.'

'Ee-sag-awn?' William repeated.

Mary Brigid nodded. 'Pat'll be telling you about him,' she added, 'It's a grand story but you'll be sick to death of it before long.' Her laughter was still twinkling when the door opened.

'Mary Brigid, what the devil's the cause of this hilarity? You'll have the boys thinking there's fun to be had at St Enda's.'

'Pat, you made me jump,' she said, 'I've brought you William.'

'Thank you, a dheirfiúir bhig*.'

William gaped at the strange words.

'Mr Devoy asked me to pass on his apologies. He's some business in the city but he's hopes of seeing you before he sails.'

'Fine, Mary Brigid. I think Mother'll be wanting you in the kitchen.'

Mary Brigid cast William a concerned glance. His stomach rumbled.

'We'll not be long, a wee chat and we'll join you.'

'Fine, Pat, but see you do.' Mary Brigid winked at William and headed out by a door to one side of the fireplace. As William watched her go his eyes fell on the painting over the mantel again. Something about the calm stillness of the boy made William want to know him.

'It's a good painting, is it not?'

William nodded.

'Wouldn't you know there's a canny likeness between you and my little Íosagán. You have his fairness, or he yours. Now, William, come in and let us be acquainted.'

The interview with Mr Pearse was short, as he promised. He explained that his school was for boys like William, whose families wanted their sons to have an Irish education. William wasn't sure what that meant or why his father wanted it for him. Mr Pearse spoke quietly but firmly. He was nothing like William had imagined. He seemed young to be a headmaster although his hair was thinning. There was a softness in the round lines of his face and a kindly glow in his eyes. William studied him and decided that, if he didn't yet like Mr Pearse, he didn't have to fear him.

'Sure, I hope you'll be happy here,' Mr Pearse continued, 'but more than that, I hope you'll learn a lot, about Ireland and what it means to be an Irishman like your father.'

William dropped his eyes to the floor. His face, foreshortened and distorted, was reflected up at him in the varnished boards. What sort of an Irishman was his father?

'Would you tell me what you dream of, William?'

---

* little sister

'I don't know, sir.'

'What do you long to do?'

William's thoughts were of the heroes in his comic books who strode out into the world, righting wrongs and living courageous lives.

Mr Pearse said, 'When I was a boy I wanted to be a hero.'

William nodded his agreement.

'Like Cúchulainn. Do you know who he is?'

'No, sir.'

'Cúchulainn was perhaps Ireland's greatest hero, yet he was a boy. I wanted to be like him because he performed the most fantastic feats, was brave and protected his people, doing things grown men were afraid of,' Mr Pearse's eyes lit up as he spoke, making his face seem younger, 'But William,' William's heart pounded, 'there's many a-way to be a hero. It's my hope you'll learn them all at St. Enda's. Now we best get our tea or that terrible Mary Brigid'll be after me.'

William remembered her conspiratorial wink. 'What'll she do, sir?'

'The worst of punishments, feared throughout the land: a double dose of the castor oil!' Mr Pearse smiled at William and patted his shoulder. There was reassurance in the touch. Maybe even a trace of camaraderie.

They crossed the entrance hall. William glanced again at the painting. He wanted to ask Mr Pearse more about Íosagán, and Cúchulainn, but his stomach was complaining. He put his hand in his pocket and stroked the soft fabric of Mary Brigid's handkerchief; the boy in the painting looked on until William was out of sight.

Six long tables filled the basement dining room. At each table sat half a dozen boys. Cheerful chatter bounced off the stone walls. Mr Pearse paused in the doorway. Some boys at a nearby table noticed him and fell quiet. The silence spread out. All eyes turned to them. The boys, William noticed, made do with a quick glance then back to their dinners but the masters who ranged around the room let their gazes linger. As the room hushed William caught a snippet from two masters who stood nearby. One was pointing towards William and Mr Pearse.

'...be Michael Devoy's lad.'

'A grand thing, to be having a Devoy back in Dublin.'

'Not before time, but it's the father we need.'

William fidgeted, hoping they didn't know he'd heard. Mary Brigid came over and the chatter rose up again.

'At last, Pat, I was after sending a search party. Poor William, how hungry you must be.' She swept William along, setting him down at a table in the corner, 'I'll bring your dinner. It's stew tonight, I made it myself and a fair offering it is. Help yourself to water.' She indicated the jug.

William nodded but sat paralysed. He longed to check if he was still being watched by the masters.

'William.'

He flinched at the sound of his name. It was Mr Colbert.

'Boys,' Mr Colbert addressed William's table, 'this is William Devoy. Fresh from New York, he hails from grand Irish stock.' Every face at the table twisted in William's direction. Every hand arrested the progress of fork to mouth. Some mouths gaped. 'Close your mouth, Barrett, you look like a trout.' The mouths snapped shut. 'William is joining us and a welcome addition he is. I've a mind he's in your dorm, Barrett, so make him feel at home. As you were, boys.'

Mr Colbert strode off. Now ten eyes were watching; five mouths remained tight lipped. Panic fluttered in William's chest. The boy called Barrett stood up and held his hand out.

'Welcome to St. Enda's,' he said in a voice with a crisp English accent.

William took the hand. Even with his mouth closed William saw Barrett's resemblance to a fish. He was about William's age with a mop of ginger curls and a sprinkle of peppery freckles over his flat nose. His eyes, under their pale brows and lashes, bulged a little.

'I'm Charles, Charlie to my friends,' Barrett spoke in a grown up way, 'This is Henry O'Hanlon,' Charlie indicated the boy next to him, dark haired, dark eyed and with a square face and jaw. He stood now, towering over the table, and offered William his hand.

'Call me Hal,' he said. His words were thick with a hard accent that mocked the lilt of the other Irish voices William had heard. His grip, when William gave over his hand, was crushing.

'That's Stephen and James Harley,' Charlie pointed at two identical boys, skinny and with sharp narrow faces under light brown hair that swept up from high foreheads. Their pale eyes twitched; neither offered a hand.

One of them said in a reedy voice, 'No, I'm James; that's Stephen.'

Charlie rolled his wide eyes. 'Don't try that,' he warned, 'Twins.' He tutted and the brothers scowled at William. 'Stephen has a mole on his cheek. Remember that and they won't fool you,' Charlie advised, 'and over there is Freddie Blackwell.'

The last boy, seated at the end of the table, was hunched up, shoulders drawn to neat ears, glossy black head bent low over the book spread in front of him. He raised a winter-white face to William and peered at him through wire-rimmed spectacles. His arched brows furrowed at the interruption, his green eyes read William's face, he nodded once and went back to the pages, flicking them with slender fingers, the index of which was stained with blue ink.

William was about to say, 'nice to meet you' when Stephen or James spoke.

'Why'd your da call you William? Not an Orangeman, is he?'

William hadn't the faintest idea what that meant; he blurted out, 'He's a doctor and I'm named after my grandfather.'

There was some sniggering.

'So it's your grandfather who's the Prod,' the twin declared, 'So much for Colbert's grand Irish stock.' He elbowed his brother.

Charlie barked, 'Shut up, Stephen,' and glared at him.

William, still mystified, replied, 'He was German,' adding, 'My mother's father.'

'It's Wilhelm you'll be,' Freddie said, keeping his eyes on his book, the light winking off his lenses.

William was about to say yes, that was his grandfather's name.

'Have you introduced yourselves, boys?' Mary Brigid was back with William's stew.

'Aye, Charlie's done it, miss,' Hal said.

'Glad to see your manners are so impeccable, Charlie,' Mary Brigid replied, 'Now eat up, William.' She turned to Charlie. 'When you've finished, would you show William around the school before bed?'

'Yes, miss.'

Mary Brigid touched William's arm, 'Mind you show him where he can find me and Miss Margaret if he needs anything,' she instructed before leaving.

William looked to Charlie.

'Miss Margaret is Miss Mary Brigid's older sister. Mr Pearse's sister too of course. They live here and help out. Mrs Pearse too. That's her there.'

William swivelled round and saw an older woman, dressed in black, her face lined and her grey hair scraped into a bun. She wore a severe expression and an old fashioned mop cap. Her brow creased as she inspected the room of chattering boys. Her grey eyes homed in on William. Mr Pearse sidled up to her and bent his mouth to her ear. She listened, her eyes never straying from William. When Mr Pearse had finished she nodded and her face relaxed into a thin-lipped smile.

'Is she married to Mr Pearse?' he asked Charlie.

Hal made a gulping noise. James, no Stephen, leaned over and whacked him on the back. Charlie smiled then straightened his face.

'Mrs Pearse is Mr Pearse's mother. Mr Pearse is not married.'

'Oh.'

'Don't worry,' Charlie said, 'I'll fill you in.'

After they cleaned their plates they trooped up to the dorm. William paused on the threshold to study the nameplate. It said 'Colm Cille N'.

'What's that mean?'

'It's some saint. All the dorms are named after one,' Charlie said.

Inside William saw his case and satchel at the foot of the bed nearest the door. He wandered over to his things, sneaking glances at his new home. The room was cosy. Six single beds, three under the windows and three opposite, lined the walls. Next to each metal bedstead was a small bedside cabinet. William noticed several boys had a photograph of their family in a plain frame and resolved to ask his mother to send one of herself. Like the others, he also had a wooden chair at the foot of his bed. There was a large chest of drawers inside the doorway and each boy had a drawer for his clothes. A wash stand was next to the bureau with a large jug and bowl; a mirror hung on the wall above. The fire place was at the opposite end of the room. William's bed was furthest from the fire.

Seeing him gazing at it Charlie said, 'Sorry but if you come last you can't expect to sleep by the fire.'

William nodded and began to stow his clothes and the comics and storybooks his mother had helped hide in the trunk. Then he removed a small bundle, wrapped in last week's *New York Times.* He peeled back the paper, hoping his three secret treasures had survived the journey.

'What's that you've got?'

Hal's loud voice with its harsh syllables made William flinch.

'Things from home.' William showed the three precious items.

Hal reach out. 'What the bejesus is this?' He turned over a six inch horn shaped thing, creamy in colour and decorated with intricate carvings of a battle scene.

'A whale's tooth. I found it on the beach.'

'Let's see.' Freddie put down the book he'd read throughout dinner. 'Looks like it's from Orcinus orca, the killer whale. A lucky find.'

The Harley twins and Charlie clustered round. Hal spotted the second treasure and pounced.

'Whoa, would this be a bullet?' He held aloft a twisted metal cylinder an inch and a half long, 'What's this it's stuck to?'

'The button from a Confederate soldier's uniform,' William said, 'I reckon it saved his life. See, the bullet's hit him here and welded itself to the button.' He took it from Hal and held it up.

'Let me see.' Charlie stuck out his hand.

'What about this?' James picked up the final treasure, 'Did you make it?'

'Yes,' William said, his chest swelling as James rolled the smoothed handle of William's catapult between his fingers before passing it to Stephen.

'Pretty neat collection,' Hal said, patting his shoulder. His words didn't seem to grate so much.

William grinned.

'We'll take that tour now,' Charlie offered, 'You'd be as well to put your togs here,' he indicated the chair at the foot of William's bed, 'That way you're not fumbling around too long in the cold tomorrow.'

'Thanks.' William took his advice and the two of them left the dorm, the others marvelling over William's thrilling hoard.

William and Charlie rambled about the rooms and corridors. Charlie gabbled as they strolled.

'When Father died last year Mother moved us back to Ireland, so she could be nearer her people. That's when she sent me here… This is the chem lab…Of course it took some getting used to, Hampshire to Dublin, a bit of a shock… Maths and geography in there, history, lit and Latin here… So I know what it's like to be a stranger. Don't worry though, we're a friendly bunch, mostly… More dorms up there… You won't get much out of Freddie when he's got his nose in a book but he's handy if you're stuck with your prep. And he's a Dubliner so he knows the short-cuts to town… Here's the study hall, prep and assemblies in there… Don't mind Hal, he comes off big and scary but he's a decent stroke, it's because he's from the north; they breed 'em tough up there… The chapel, prayers and that guff… But keep your eye on the twins; wily as thieves those two… Now this, this is hallowed ground.' Charlie had stopped in front of a closed door. 'This is where the Pearses hide themselves. They've got a nice set-up from what I've seen; parlour, sitting rooms, all that.'

As though they'd uttered a magic word the door swung back; Charlie and William froze. A tall slim man emerged.

'To be sure, Mother.' The words were directed at someone in the room. Then the speaker caught sight of them. 'Hello Charlie, what are you doing wandering the school at this hour?' The voice was firm, not cross.

'Miss Mary Brigid asked me to show William around, Mr Pearse. Sorry if we disturbed you, sir,' Charlie said. William noticed his accent stiffened when he spoke to a grown up.

'Not at all, Charlie. I'm just surprised to find you roaming the corridors but if sister Mary Brigid gave you permission who am I to cross her?' He laughed and his young serious face broke wide open. 'You'll be the William I've heard so much about? William Devoy of New York and now, grand for us, of St Enda's.'

'Yes, sir.'

''Tis always good to be adding another member to our family, especially one of such auspicious lineage and with so fine a name.' This second Mr Pearse winked at William.

The words of the Harley twins came back to William: Orangeman, Prod. The meanings had eluded him but not the tone.

'I'm named after my grandfather. My mother chose it for me, sir.'

'And my father it for me,' Mr Pearse replied, 'and a grand name it is too. Didn't Pat tell me your mother's people hailed from Frankfurt? But with a bit of luck there's more of you that's like your da's folks.'

William was struck mute.

'I don't think you should be much longer, Charlie. You've a full day of lessons tomorrow and I wouldn't want you falling asleep in the burnt umber. You'll never be the next Rembrandt like that.'

This second Mr Pearse grinned and ran a hand through the sea of dark waves on his head. William saw the same light in his eyes that he had noticed when the first Mr Pearse had talked about Cúchulainn. He realised now that the two Mr

Pearses were each other's compliment; the first older, shorter, rounder, more serious and the second younger, taller, more angular and lighter of heart. The first loved stories and the second loved pictures. They both loved St Enda's.

'Yes, Mr Pearse,' Charlie said and moved off. William stayed, spellbound by the dark dancing eyes.

Mr Pearse glanced down.

'Do you like art, William?'

'I like drawing and making things. Mother and I did a lot of that.'

'Grand,' Mr Pearse said, 'I'll be looking forward to seeing some of your artistic talents in my class tomorrow.'

William nodded.

'Óiche mhaith dhuit*,' Mr Pearse said then seeing William's confusion added, 'That's 'goodnight' but you'll soon be picking up the lingo.'

William ran after Charlie.

'That was Mr Pearse the younger,' Charlie said needlessly, 'Mr Willie Pearse. He's a painter. And a sculptor. Went to a fancy art school. He's pretty decent.'

But William had already worked that out for himself. And the second Mr Pearse was a fellow William.

Lying in his new bed, listening to the snores and snuffles of his five roommates, William wished he could wake in the morning to the waving blue cornflowers on his nursery walls and his mother calling him to start morning lessons.

He tried to sleep but things nagged him; odd words, nosy stares. He cursed himself for asking Freddie what, 'auspicious lineage' meant. 'It means you've a lot to live up to. Is your da a big man?' William didn't know. The dorm room curtains were thin and moonlight shone in. He sat up. A draught blew under the door; he pulled at the blankets and drew his knees to his chin. He wanted to know.

William got up, wrapped himself in his dressing gown, tiptoed across the room and out.

---

* good night

He descended to the ground floor where he strained his ears in the dark hush. When he was sure it was safe, William made his way to the entrance hall and stood in front of the picture above the fire. He reached out a hand to the boy, Íosagán, but couldn't bring himself to touch the boy's peaceful face.

As he crept through the house William noticed more paintings like those he'd seen in churches. William counted half a dozen of the Virgin Mary; he didn't understand why the Pearses would have so many paintings of her. Others showed crosses, angels, a fruit tree with one ripe red apple hanging from a low branch. William thought of the apple tree at home. The one he had climbed up, swung from, hid in: Robin of Locksley, Young Jim Hawkins, Huckleberry Finn; he played them all from early spring until the boughs were heavy with fruit. Then he and his mother would pick the apples, coat them in toffee or pack them away for bobbing come Halloween. He knew the story of Adam and Eve but he'd never considered picking fruit a sin. His mother, after they'd read it, had said the story wasn't about eating apples. She hadn't said what it was about. William moved on, heading for the Pearse family rooms. If there was an answer to be had about his father it lurked in there.

William edged up to the door and let himself through, into a sitting room. Three easy chairs were settled around the fire; a rug sprawled on the floor. In one corner a glass cabinet housed the Pearse best china. On a low sideboard, sitting on a doily, was a fat serving bowl with the same flower pattern as the cups and saucers in the case. William slid open the top drawer but found only cutlery. The one below it was stuffed with table linen. He crossed to the bookcase and scanned the shelves but there was nothing interesting there either.

Ahead was another door. William dared himself through it. It led to the family dining room identified by the round table and six chairs in the bay window. In one corner was a piano, in another an upright frame with strings laced from top to bottom. William raised a hand to pluck one but, noticing the third inner door, had second thoughts. Voices drifted through.

'It's certainly a coup for you, Pat, and for St Enda's. The son of Michael Devoy.' It was Willie Pearse.

William wondered if Mr Pearse kept a belt for boys caught creeping around at night. He hadn't seen one in the study and decided the risk worth taking.

'I dare say he was thinking of his son,' Mr Pearse replied.

'Pah!' Willie Pearse snorted, 'There's many a fine school but none so finely Irish as ours. Why else would a noted Fenian send his son thousands of miles if not to show his support of your vision for St Enda's and Ireland?'

'Perhaps.'

'And others will come. I'm certain of it, Pat,' Willie Pearse continued, 'The lad's arrival is a rallying cry.'

'And behind whom are we to rally, brother?'

'Behind Ireland, Pat, as you've long spoken of.'

'There's time aplenty for that,' there was a pause, "'Tis late. I'm away to bed.'

William bolted for the door and dashed through the sitting room. He yanked back the outer door, tumbled into the hall and closed it behind him, his heart thrumming in his ears, his narrow escape spurting hot fear through him.

'Sweet Mary, it's yourself, William.'

William, cringing, peered up. Mary Brigid, still dressed but with her hair flowing in heavy auburn curls over her shoulders, stood over him. She recovered the tray loaded with three mugs that had nearly leapt from her hand.

'Are you ill?'

William shook his head.

'Too tired for sleep, then?'

He nodded.

'You're in luck. I've some hot milk here. Would you take a cup with me?'

William nodded again and Mary Brigid led him into the room he had just fled. She sat on one of the easy chairs. William shuffled forwards.

'Don't be standing there out of place,' she teased and pointed to a chair.

William sat. The inner door swung back, revealing Mr Pease. On seeing William he stopped.

'Look, Pat, I've met a wee man having trouble sleeping. I reckoned a drop of warm milk would help.'

William thought there was a glow of pink in Mr Pearse's cheeks but the light was dim and it was hard to be sure. When he spoke the words were too bright.

'The very thing for a restless mind.'

'I'll away to make up another mug.' Mary Brigid stood.

'No need, sister, I'll not take a cup tonight,' Mr Pearse replied, making for the door, 'Don't be keeping William late.'

'Aye, Pat.'

'Óiche mhaith dhuit.'

'Goodnight.'

Mr Pearse backed out. Mary Brigid handed William a mug.

'I'll give Willie his,' she said and slipped next door.

William, aware he was drinking milk meant for his headmaster, found the mug heavy in his hands. He blew on the frothy liquid and sipped. Mary Brigid returned.

'Perhaps if you can't sleep you might try reading.' She picked a little hardback from a shelf and held it out to William. He read the words, '*Íosagán and other Stories* by P. H. Pearse'.

'Yes, miss, Mary Brigid, miss. Thank you.'

They drank their milk in silence. William forced down the hot liquid, not caring that it blistered his tongue.

'Are you done?'

'Yes, Miss Mary Brigid. Thank you.'

'Then you best be off to bed.'

'Thank you, miss.'

'And William.'

'Yes, miss?'

'Haven't I told you to stop calling me 'miss'?'

'Yes, miss.'

William darted from the room, mounting the stairs two at a time.

Back in bed he closed his eyes and repeated Willie Pearse's, 'noted Fenian,' until the phrase was stowed amongst the odd assortment of facts William had collected in the last few days. He was disappointed with it. It was another question.

*

The first lesson was history with Mr MacDonagh. William straggled into the room behind Charlie and Freddie. At breakfast he had been too filled with dread to eat as his new friends listed the ferocious strictness of the master: talking forbidden; scrupulous inspection of work; detention for incomplete tasks; lines for messy work; caning for any mischief whatever. William expected to see a fire-breathing monster in black teacher's robes, swishing his cane through the air. Instead, smiling at him, was a youngish man of average height with a friendly face, dark wavy hair that he ruffled with a nervous movement of his hand and warm brown eyes. His ears stuck out, giving him a comical appearance and the yellow bowtie at his neck completed his jester's costume. He nodded at William. William smiled back. The boys took their places and the lesson began.

William listened, copied from the board in his neatest script and did his best to catch the facts fired out. The topic was Irish history and he quaked at the thought of being picked to answer a question. He only started breathing evenly when there was less than a quarter of an hour left.

'Right, lads, I think we may put aside our books,' Mr MacDonagh announced, 'As you'll have realised, we have a new fellow, Mr William Devoy, and I thought to finish we would ask him to tell us something of his history. For what is it, boys, that I'm always saying?'

'History is his story,' the class chorused.

'Excellent! William, if you'd come here.'

William pushed back his chair, which screaked along the wooden floor, and started the long walk between the rows of desks. When he reached the chalk board Mr MacDonagh spread his hands.

'Away you go, William, tell us of your fine Irish history.'

William gulped and faced the class, made up of the boys from his and two other dorms; eighteen faces stared back. Charlie, who was in the front row, grinned. Hal and the twins looked bored. Freddie kept his eyes on his book. If only William knew what was so great about his family history. All he had was the story his father made him learn by heart. Since coming to St Enda's he felt it was missing the last page.

'My father's father was a County Wexford man. His family worked the land in peace until the blight came. The blight killed the potatoes. Without the potatoes there was no food in his village so he was forced to leave for America. He arrived in 1847 with his wife and child. The child perished a week after their arrival. My grandfather thought he and his wife would soon follow. Then some kindly New Yorkers, who were really Irish like him, saved them, giving my grandparents shelter, food and comfort in their grief. My grandfather regained his strength, found work and was able to care for his family. Then my father was born and,' William stumbled over the ending, 'they lived happily ever after.'

Collective tittering invoked the sharp eye of Mr MacDonagh.

'Now, boys. Thank you, William, that was well recited. Fair play to you for giving it a happy ending. There're some things best not dwelt on. Aye, fair play, indeed.'

William caught the Harley boys exchanging smirks. One scribbled something in his exercise book and slid it over for the other to read. They grinned malevolently. The bell clanged and class was dismissed. On the way out William found himself jostled and thought he heard the words, 'fair play' hissed behind him. He span round and saw the Harleys wearing matching expressions of innocence. Charlie took William's elbow and steered him outside.

'Did you hear that?' William asked when they were under a grove of trees in front of the building.

'Hear what?'

'One of the twins, I think, saying something about 'fair play'.'

'So?'

'It sounded like they were making fun of me.'

'You've not been to school before, have you?'

'My mother taught me at home.'

'I wouldn't spread that around,' Charlie advised, 'Ignore it. It'll be forgotten by lunch.'

'But it was alright, wasn't it? What I said?'

'Word perfect.'

They stood under the trees. It was cold and William shivered as the day's fine drizzle soaked through him.

'Look out,' Charlie hissed.

Crossing the grassy space between them and the school was a group of five boys, all of whom had been in the history lesson and heard Mr MacDonagh's, 'fair play' comment.

'See him, the tall lanky boy with the hook nose? That's Richard MacDonnall,' but before Charlie could say more the boys reached William and Charlie, surrounding them.

'Now, Ginger,' Richard said, stepping forwards, 'Found yourself a new pal.'

'Hallo, Richard,' Charlie said, eyes on his shoes.

'Sure, that was a pretty speech you gave. What was it MacDonagh was saying there, boys?'

'Said, 'fair play', Richard,' one piped up.

'Aye, that's right. Fair play to you for your fairy tale ending,' Richard said, eyeballing William and slapping his tongue down on the word 'fairy'. He was a head taller than William, lean and strong. His light grey eyes were colder than the sky. 'And that's fair enough, isn't it, lads?'

William's gut knotted.

Richard turned to the boys behind him and poured out a rapid torrent of alien words. William looked to Charlie whose face drained of colour word by word.

'That's not fair,' Charlie blurted out.

Richard wheeled back and Charlie's face coloured to match his hair. Richard howled with laughter and the rest of his mob cackled in chorus.

'I think it's very fair,' he replied and repeated some of the foreign words. 'I see you've not got the Gaelic,' he said to William, 'That's too bad because it was a grand joke and so nice of your pal here to add the punch line. Not fair! Genius. From now on I think we'll be calling you Finn. Aye, Finn the Fair. A damn sight better than William. Your da must be soft in the head, naming you after that Orange git,' Richard's voice became cruel, 'Bollocksed if I'll call you by that bastard's name. So Finn it is. There's a favour for you, Finn-boy,' Richard patted William's cheek, the third tap crisping to a slap, 'a new name, one that's not treasonous. Come on, lads, don't want to be late or we'll cop the cane.'

Richard swaggered back across the lawn, flanked by his posse. William stared after them. Charlie became fascinated by a rotten chestnut at his feet.

'Sorry,' he mumbled.

'What did he say?'

'Nothing.'

'But...'

'It was William of Orange who beat the Catholics in 1690.'

'What's that got to do with me?'

'Nothing. But it's bad luck, you being called after him.'

'I'm not. My grandfather…'

'You said,' Charlie muttered.

Awkwardness hung in the damp air.

'What was that they were speaking?'

'Irish. Gaelic,' Charlie said, 'We learn it here. Some, like Richard, already know a bit. Pity he uses it for such, well, never mind. Don't worry. Mr Pearse'll give you lessons.'

'Finn. Why'd he call me that?'

'Means fair in Gaelic.'

For the rest of the day the new name dogged William. Charlie tried to cheer him. Lots of the boys had nicknames. Freddie was 'Bookie' because he was always reading. That was fine, William thought; it suggested intelligence. But Finn the Fair? Girls were fair. Or the weather. Sailors hoped for a fair wind. Fair of face meant pretty. Men were supposed to be dashing. His blonde curls didn't help. Any attempt to reassert his own name rewarded William with a whoop of taunting howls and the words, 'it's not fair.'

The next day William resolved to follow Charlie's advice. Seeing Richard in the corridor, William walked passed, head up.

'Orange boy,' Richard hissed and kicked out, catching William's shin. Surprised, William tumbled to the floor. Richard bent down, hand raised to strike.

Mr Willie Pearse emerged from a classroom. 'What's going on?'

'Devoy tripped, sir. I was helping him up.' Richard uncurled his fist.

Mr Pearse hovered in the doorway, brows arched. 'Don't be late for lessons.' He slipped back into his room.

Richard's fist reappeared. He landed a punch on William's arm and threw him back to the floor. 'Whore's melt,' he spat and stalked off.

By the end of the day William was exhausted. At teatime he took the same seat at the end of the table and kept his head low. Freddie was opposite William tonight, his head also down, bent over an exercise book that he scribbled into between bites. William was glad not to have to talk.

'Doing your prep?'

William and Freddie looked up. Freddie resettled his glasses on his nose and squinted through them. Sean O'Malley, one of Richard's pals, was standing over them, his mousy hair ruffled and his tie on the slant.

'I am.'

'Gis a look. I'm stuck.'

Sean snatched the book, his hand flying towards William, colliding with William's cup of tea. It toppled with a clatter and a quick brown torrent gushed over the table and into William's lap. William leapt up as the hot liquid stung his legs.

'Bejesus, William, what a mess,' Sean mocked, 'You should be more careful.' He dropped Freddie's book into the puddle of tea and wandered off.

Freddie rescued his dripping work, muttering under his breath. William span round. Sean was by Richard and the others, sneering at him. Richard pointed and they broke into laughter. Mrs Pearse flashed a glare on them and they fell quiet. She didn't look in William's direction. Nobody looked tonight. William dashed for the door, his legs burning, his whole body shaking and tears brewing.

Alone in the dorm he inspected his thighs, which were bright red and throbbing. Using water from the washstand, he bathed them while his trousers hung drying by the fire. When his roommates returned he was dressed again and lying on his bed, pretending to sleep. They were talking as they entered but stopped at the sight of William's curled form. He stayed as still as he could even when his bed sagged.

'You alright?'

William opened his eyes and saw Charlie sat there.

'Fine.'

'It was probably an accident. He's a clumsy bugger, Sean. But listen,' Charlie went on, 'You mustn't say anything, to any of the masters, I mean. It'll only make things worse.'

That night, as William lay in bed with his legs throbbing, he mulled it over. The bruises and burns would fade; he knew now the name wouldn't. He didn't want to be Finn. He was William Devoy of 42nd Street, New York City. He slipped a hand into his bedside cabinet, groping around until his fingers touched the smooth handle of his catapult. He held it up, studying the black Y of it against the whitewashed ceiling: the last letter of his real name. The one that could help stop it being erased. He slid the catapult under his pillow.

'Finn-boy! How's yourself? Fair to middling?'

The day was bright. Wind stripped the trees. William's hair danced as he span in the direction of the jibe. Richard and his gang were almost upon him. Apart from Freddie, who was under a tree with a book on his lap, William was alone in the park that surrounded the school. He cursed Charlie for getting a detention. Scanning the ground, he swooped on a round pebble the size of a dollar coin.

'What about this grand Irish weather? It's a fair day today, isn't it, lads?' Richard crowed. His followers chortled. 'I bet it's fairer here than in Yankee land this time of year,' Richard went on.

In his pockets William balled his fists around the pebble and the catapult.

'Wasn't I asking you a question, Finn? It's rude not to answer. Didn't your mammy tell you that, Finn?' Richard stopped and leaned over so his face was inches from William's.

'My name's William.'

'Did you hear that, lads? He's saying his name's William. But that's a lie, Finn, because I've been calling you 'Finn'. That's your name. Why would I be calling you a thing if it wasn't your name?'

'You know it's not my name.'

Richard laughed. 'What are you after changing your name for, Finn? What's wrong with 'Finn'? It's better than that of the bastard murdering Orange king.' Richard spat. William felt the gob on his cheek, warm and sticky. 'Now Finn's a fair name for such a fair laddie.'

Richard rumpled William's hair. William jerked backwards, whipped out the catapult, loaded the stone, stretched back the elastic and let go. The rock hit Richard on the forehead. For one moment time stopped. Then Richard's knuckles powered into William's mouth and the taste of nickels bloomed on his tongue. William toppled backwards, blinded by starbursts of pain.

'That was an eejit thing to do.'

William felt the catapult snatched from his hand and heard the crack of it snapping.

'It's Finn you are and Finn you'll stay,' Richard snarled, 'We'll not have any fecking Orangemen around here. Isn't that so, lads?'

The cheering posse, led by Richard, strode away through the trees. William picked up the two pieces of his catapult. Freddie had been dragged from his book by the fracas. They stared at each other. Freddie went back to reading. William, licking blood from his lips, dropped the broken weapon to the grass and struggled to his feet.

The dorm room door opened.

'Ah, William, I've been hunting for you.' It was Mr Willie Pearse. 'Your father's here... Goodness, what's happened to your face?'

'My father?'

'Aye, but your face?'

'I fell.'

Mr Pearse scrutinised William's bruise. 'Hmm. Well, come along.'

William clambered off the bed and they descended.

'How are things?'

'Fine,' William lied.

'I remember when I was first away to school. Wasn't I hating it? The teasing when you're the new boy.'

William wondered how old Willie Pearse was.

'How did you say you hurt yourself?'

Miss Margaret opened the door to the family quarters.

'Willie, are you busy?'

'No, Maggie,' casting him a sidelong glance, Willie Pearse said, 'Are you right to make your way to the study, William?'

'Yes, sir.'

William scuffed along the hall. In the entrance the painting of Íosagán caught his eye. He hadn't been able to read the book Mary Brigid had given him. It was in Gaelic.

From behind the study door his father's voice boomed.

'Mr Pearse, my apologies for not coming sooner. The price on my head drives me to the shadows in my own city.'

William had all but forgotten the mystery of 'noted Fenian' in the midst of his troubles with Richard but his curiosity spiked now.

'I am appraised of your situation, Mr Devoy, and 'tis an honour you have the time to visit.' Mr Pearse spoke softly, his words floating, dandelion clocks in the wind.

'Please, call me Michael.'

'Pat.'

William tried picturing the two men, his father tall and dark; Mr Pearse smaller and lighter, shaking hands.

'And my thanks too for sending us your son.'

'It's time the boy had a proper education. His mother has been attempting, shambolically, to education him. Women! She has covered the basics but my wife is not Irish so is without a proper grasp of Irish history and culture.'

'I understand your difficulties. My father was English. But my mother is Irish and, like yourself, keen that Willie and I be educated in the traditions of Ireland. Faith I can pass some of it to the boys in my care.'

'Aye.'

William felt tension across his back pulling him upright.

'For too long our culture has played second fiddle to that of the English who think they are kings of the world,' William's father said.

'There we agree.'

'That we've allowed those devils to maintain their stranglehold on things they've no goddamn right to…'

'I understand there is concern in America for the current situation,' Mr Pease interjected.

'Some feel Mr Redmond will make the difference.'

Recalling that Mr Redmond featured in the row at Mr MacDermott's, William added his name to the growing mystery-list.

'May I counsel your opinion on Mr Redmond?'

William held his breath; his father was silent a moment.

'Redmond, like others, serves the crown and the half-crown. Nevertheless, I am resolved we should wait. He may yet succeed where others have failed.'

'Home Rule?'

'Perhaps.'

'And if not?'

'We return to the ways of our forbears. Rest assured, you have more than one powerful Fenian friend across the water. And, by God, we're ready to act.'

'You have no fear of such steps?'

'I do not.' His father's voice was loud and determined.

An image, of his father brandishing a pistol, overwhelmed William. He staggered back from the door, his foot catching the curling corner of the rug. He stumbled, fought for balance and landed on his backside. The office door swung open. Mr Pearse smiled down on him.

'Ah, it's yourself, William.' He came forwards, offering a hand up. 'Are you alright?'

'I tripped, sir.'

'I meant your lip.'

'I tripped then too, sir.'

Mr Pearse frowned but said no more as he steered William into the office.

Inside his father reclined in the chair in front of Mr Pearse's desk. There was no gun.

'William,' his father said, remaining seated, 'I have been discussing with Mr Pearse how you've settled into his fine school.' His eyes fell to William's plum-purple lip. He snorted. 'I see you're getting acquainted with the other lads. Boys will be boys, will they not, Mr Pearse? And so they make men of each other.'

Mr Pearse sank into his chair. William remained standing, thankful his throbbing lip had been dismissed. His father continued speaking about William as though he were not present. Mr Pearse tried to include William.

'I understand, William, that you have no knowledge of Gaelic.'

'No, sir.'

'In that case I'll be ensuring you master the language personally. I teach the boys the purest form I can, Mr Devoy, the Gaelic of Connemara, and have written some, I feel, helpful texts. *Íosagán and other stories*, has, if I may say, proved popular. I'll get you a copy, William.'

'I have one, sir. Miss Mary Brigid loaned me it, sir.'

'You see, Mr Devoy, you need have no worries for your lad. He's keen enough. All bodes well for him.'

William thought of the book cast to the back of his locker and hung his head.

'Well, William, I must be off,' his father said, not offering a parting hand. 'Remember who you are, from whence you hail and take care to finish your fights.'

Íosagán, William learnt, was the son of God. He helped the old man Matthias to be welcomed into the arms of God upon his deathbed. Íosagán was a boy pure of heart and soul. His concern was to ensure that those who needed it, received his help. William had never read any story like it. Íosagán. He rolled the word around in his mouth. Íosagán was a hero cut from a silken cloth and although Íosagán was only a character created by Mr Pearse, this didn't stop William wanting him to appear with his halo and lend a hand; Richard had discovered the joy of getting William into trouble. His prep would go missing; the masters concluded he hadn't done it. His socks developed holes; Mrs Pearse scolded him for not taking care of the things his mother provided. In Mr Willie's art class, William's favourite, his pot of dirty water would tumble, spoiling the work of his neighbour. For these things and more William was punished: lines; detentions; no pudding; no supper; extra chores; long stints holding a heavy book at arm's length.

William didn't know how he could finish the fight, as his father demanded, without help. But Íosagán refused to show himself.

Hilary Term 1912

Dear Mother,
I am returned safely to school and continuing my studies. Mr Pearse has praised my progress in Gaelic and says the extra work I did in the holidays has made a difference. He is impressed I can read so well now.

This term we are to have some half-day lectures as well as our regular lessons. I am looking forward to that and to the things that will keep me busy. I will, as Father suggested, try out for one of the sports' teams.

The bell for supper will be sounding soon so I must say goodbye.
Your ever loving son,

William set down his pen and rubbed the achy spot above his eyes. A glance at the clock confirmed he'd been working on this letter for an hour and it was still terrible. His mother had chided him for the sparse nature of his correspondence but what could he do? His real news was a list of injuries and punishments courtesy of Richard. Already he had a red welt on his arm and had been bawled out by Mr Colbert for being late to physical education because his kit had disappeared. As if games wasn't enough of a torture without invoking the wrath of the games master who was disappointed that William, with his grand Irish stock, was useless at hurling and Gaelic football.

William was equally clumsy in both sports. Once he'd got the rules, he improved a little but as the season wore on Richard had taken advantage of the opportunities to whack William's shins with his hurley stick or aim the heavy football at William's head. For this Richard was praised as a courageous player by Mr Colbert who drilled the boys rigorously. William might well be Finn now though his life was anything but fair.

'Alright, lads. Good Christmas?' Richard leant against the doorframe with familiar smugness.

William covered his letter with a textbook.

'Not bad,' Hal said gruffly. The Ulster in him made him big enough to shrug off Richard.

'Good man, yourself, Hal,' Richard said with a respectful nod, coming into the dorm, 'Bookie, Ginger. Eh up, lads.'

Charlie and Freddie muttered greetings.

'James, where's your other half?'

'Hallo, Richard. Downstairs. You want me to fetch him?' James jumped up.

As bad as it was having Richard for an enemy, William reflected, it wasn't worse than having him for a friend.

'Finn, was I hearing you've a bit of trouble with Colbert already?'

William kept his head down, hoping Hal's watchful eye would be enough to hold Richard back.

'So lads, what did old Saint Nick bring you? Get a stocking full of oranges, did you, Finn?'

'The usual,' Charlie said, trying to cover Richard's taunt.

'Get a load more new tomes, Bookie?' Richard moved over to Freddie.

'An interesting one about Genghis Khan.'

'Want to see what I got?'

Hal sat up. 'Bet you'll show us even if we say no.'

Richard rolled back his left sleeve and held his arm out.

'Needed a new one, did you?' Hal barked. 'Pity he didn't bring you the right, as that's your pitching arm.' He laughed; Richard's face darkened. William saw what Richard had come to show them.

'The watch,' James yelped. He scurried over to Richard, 'Must've cost your folks a packet.'

'I'm worth it. Solid silver and accurate to a minute a day. They got it from a Swiss watchmaker my father knows.' Richard came over to William, his arm outstretched, light glancing off the watch's chain-link bracelet. 'Bet you wish you had one, eh, Finn?'

Afraid of saying no, William murmured, 'Yes.'

'I'd be careful about showing it around,' Charlie said.

'Why's that, Ginger?'

Richard strode up to Charlie and held the watch under his nose.

Charlie inched back. 'Someone might pinch it.'

'They'd bloody better not. Right, lads, be seeing yous later. Welcome back, Finn-boy.' On the way past, Richard slapped William's foot.

'Blowhard.' Hal slumped against his pillows.

'Bet they got it from a pawnshop,' Charlie said.

'Did not,' James chirruped, 'You heard him, Swiss.'

'Aye,' Freddie said, picking up his book, 'Probably made from cheese.'

William folded his letter. There was nothing to add.

For a full week Richard strode the halls with his sleeve rolled up, an infraction of the uniform code, displaying his prize possession and offering everyone the time of day.

'Finn, Mr Pearse is asking for you.'

William looked up at the name that wasn't his but that he had accepted.

'Mr Pearse?'

'Mr Willie Pearse,' said James, 'You better hurry, Finn.'

William tucked *Íosagán* under his pillow.

'Did Mr Pearse say why he wanted me?'

James shook his head.

On the stairs William saw Sean O'Malley. He hugged the wall but Sean passed by, apparently oblivious. Relieved to have dodged trouble with Richard's second in command, William skipped down the remaining stairs. He was sure Mr Pearse could only want something good.

'Steady, there, William. There's not a fire, is there?' Mary Brigid called.

William skidded to a halt, pleased to see her and hear her laughing voice.

'No, Mary Brigid.'

'That's as well because you're headed in the wrong direction for rescuing me,' she teased.

'Yes, miss.'

'You would come and rescue me, wouldn't you, William?'

'Yes, miss.'

'Aye, well, off you go. But slowly, William.'

William arrived at the art studio and knocked on the half open door.

'Hallo?' Mr Willie Pearse was at an easel, brush in one hand, paint speckled pallet in the other.

'You wanted to see me, sir?'

Mr Pearse laid his head on one side and studied William.

'Alas, William, you've been given a false message.'

James had fooled him, probably at Richard's suggestion. When he returned to the dorm he'd find his things ransacked again, William thought.

'Still, you're here. Why don't we crack on with that new masterpiece of yours?' Mr Pearse set down his brushes and replaced his painting with William's.

Pushing aside his worries, William stepped forward.

'I don't know what you've in mind but I've been thinking you could do with a bit of something in the foreground here.'

William listened, nodded and, under Mr Pearse's guidance, painted for two happy hours.

When William returned to the dorm he was surprised to see his slice of it as he had left it. Perhaps Richard was getting bored, would pick a new victim this term. William lifted his pillow to retrieve *Íosagán*. The book wasn't there. William flung the pillow down and wrenched open his bedside locker to see what else was missing. *Íosagán* was inside. He withdrew the book, examined it and found no damage; he must have put it away without thinking. The tea bell sounded. William tossed the book back into his locker, hoping his torment was over.

Sunday tea was a pleasant affair. As Mr Pearse liked to remind them, God had rested on the seventh day and they were as well to do the same. William helped himself to a thick slice of soda bread which he liked and a mug of tea, which he could stomach now. Charlie plopped down opposite William. His cheeks were reddened by the chill air and his hair had been blown wild across his forehead. He swiped a piece of bread and started to chew.

'What've you been up to?'

'I went to see Mr Pearse. We worked on my painting.'

'So you haven't heard?' Charlie confided, his eyes widening. 'Richard's moaning to everyone that he's had his watch pinched.'

'His watch?'

'Serves him right. That's what you get if you keep bragging. Anyway, I reckon it isn't stolen. He's lost it and knows his father'll give him hell so he's cooked up this story about it being pinched to save his backside.'

William nodded.

Noise rose to a raucous level as dozens of boys gossiped and munched. It had been a good day, William thought, and now this business of Richard's watch. It would keep his attention away from William. William was musing on this when Charlie nudged him and William saw Mr Pearse by the door with a grave expression on his face. William gulped down the mouthful he had and didn't take another.

'Lads,' Mr Pearse addressed them, 'Apologies for interrupting your tea but a serious matter has come to my attention.'

The room fell silent.

'It appears one of you has been the victim of that most abhorrent of crimes: theft. While I am confident that no one here would deliberately deprive his fellow of a prized possession there might be occasions amongst you when the borrowing of things occurs. However, it is vital that possessions be returned to their rightful owners and I request that if one of you has borrowed something from a fellow that it be returned before sunset and no more will be said.' Mr Pearse swept the room with his steady eyes, touching each of them. He cleared his throat, 'Now to the borrower let me speak directly; if you return what is not yours I'll hold true to my promise but if you do not I will be forced to take action. I'll search every dorm until the item is found and punish you for your wilful act of thievery.'

William's stomach flipped over.

''Til sunset, lads,' Mr Pearse warned. He turned on his heel with a military step and marched from the room.

From his bed William watched the falling sun paint the sky with reds and oranges. He wished he had the skill to copy such a scene. As the light melted into the horizon William returned to the book on his lap. Leaving *Íosagán* in his locker, he was reading a story the title he translated as, 'The Thief,' from another of Mr Pearse's collections: *The Mother and other stories.* It was a tale about a boy, Anthony, who stole a doll for his poorly sister because he thought it would make her better. Instead of being punished, Anthony was forgiven his sin because, although he did a wicked thing, he did it for a good-hearted reason. It was funny, William mused, that Mr Pearse thought it was fine to steal if there was reason enough. He hoped whoever stole Richard's watch had a good reason, then he might avoid being expelled.

'Stand to your beds, boys.'

Mr Colbert was in the doorway flanked by the two Mr Pearses and Mary Brigid.

Charlie, Hal, James and Stephen stood to attention. Freddie got up but kept the book he was reading pressed to his nose. William set down his book and stood.

Mr Colbert spoke.

'I am sorry to report, boys, that despite Mr Pearse's speech the missing item is still, er, missing. So we're searching the dorms.'

Mr Colbert took one side and Mr Willie Pearse the other. Mr Pearse and Mary Brigid stayed by the door. William caught her eye; she gave him a limp smile.

Mr Colbert started on William's side of the dorm, moving down the line to Stephen's bed, then to William's. He opened the door of William's nightstand, rummage around and straightened up with a bundle in his hand.

'What's this, William?'

William blushed as he recognised the yellowed pages of the *New York Times* that still protected his two remaining treasures. After the catapult's destruction the whale tooth and bullet-button had been cast out of sight in shame.

'Mementos from home, sir.'

Mr Colbert unwrapped the bundle.

'Pat.'

Mr Pearse peeked over Mr Colbert's shoulder. His face paled. His eyes flitted between William and the bundle three times. Willie Pearse, noting his brother's pain, came up.

'Whatever is it, Pat?'

William rushed his words. 'They're just things I found.'

'Found? Where?'

'On the beach and…'

'Beach?' Mr Pearse repeated, 'Sure, we're finding ourselves at crossed purposes.' He reached into the bundle, 'This, William, where did you get this?' He withdrew a familiar silvery chain-link bracelet.

No one spoke for five seconds. William glanced to Mary Brigid but there was no catching her eye now.

'Devoy?'

William had nothing to say.

'Thank you, Con, for your help,' Mr Pearse said, 'You may tell the others the search is ended.'

Mr Pearse strode from the room. Mr Colbert followed. Willie Pearse laid a hand on William's shoulder.

'Come along, William,' he said brightly, 'We'll see if we can't clear up this puzzle.'

William straggled along, piecing it together as he went. Richard had got Sean to plant the watch. That explained the fake message from Mr Pearse, passing O'Malley unharmed on the stairs and *Íosagán* making his own way into the nightstand. None of the masters knew of the war Richard had been waging on him. Richard was the victim and William the perpetrator. If he told the truth now he wouldn't be believed. But if there was a reason for him taking the watch...

William stood before Mr Pearse's desk.

'Thank you, Willie, I'll deal with this.'

'I'll stay, Pat.'

Mr Pearse frowned but didn't challenge his brother. He laid the watch on his desk.

'I'll not have thieves in my school, Devoy.'

'Yes, sir.'

'Why did you take the watch?'

William gulped. Half a story formed in his mind.

'For a dare, sir.'

'Pardon?'

'Sort of a game. We see if we can sneak in and get things out of each others' dorms.'

'And who would it be that dared you to take Richard's watch?'

'I'd rather not say, sir.'

Mr Pearse's brow creased. 'Your silence does you no credit. Why do you partake in these dares?'

'I thought it would help me make friends, sir.'

'Have you not friends already, William?'

'Some, sir, but I still get teased a bit.'

'Teased how?'

'They call me Finn, sir.' It was all he dared say.

'And for this you create such a disturbance in my school? Did you not think to return the watch after supper?'

'I forgot, sir.'

'Do you understand the seriousness of this, William? We've ransacked the school in search of this blasted watch all for a foolish dare!'

'Sorry, sir.' William bowed his head.

'You've been at St. Enda's but a term, William, yet surely you realise this is not how things are done here. I'm disappointed. I'll have to wire your father. I cannot tolerate this behaviour. By rights I should be expelling you.'

William jerked his head up. Willie Pearse's eyes were on him but he stared through William, fixed on something far away.

'Pat,' he murmured. William held his breath and waited to hear what might be said in his defence. But Willie spoke in an incomprehensible tongue. Some of the words were Gaelic, fewer English, the rest sounded like baby-babble. William caught his own name and Richard's but little else. Mr Pearse interrupted twice; Willie talked over him and on until he'd said his piece.

'William, you are fortunate. I have been persuaded your crime is not that most heinous one of theft but rather of boyish high spirits. Your punishment will be six strikes, two months' extra chores and isolation. You will also write an apology to Richard. And, most importantly, you will attend confession and tell the priest of your sin,' Mr Pearse listed.

'My father, sir?'

'I have been convinced not to involve him but if more incidents the like of this arise I will not hesitate in asking him to remove you from St Enda's.'

'Yes, sir.' William exhaled deeply.

'Willie, if that's all?' Mr Pearse said.

'I think so, Pat,' his brother replied and slipped from the room.

William hadn't had the cane before. His father used a belt across the backside. Mr Pearse caned him over the palms of his hands, leaving glistening welts on each hand. William was shaking when he left the room.

The school was in darkness now. William had a foot on the bottom stair when a soft voice called out.

'Have you a minute to be sparing me, William?'

Mr Willie Pearse led William into his studio. Ghostly moonlight illuminated the easels, making them appear like spiky alien creatures. At first neither spoke then both spoke at once.

'I know you didn't…'

'Thank you, sir, for…'

'I beg your pardon, William. Perhaps you'd allow me to speak first.'

'Yes, sir.'

'I know you didn't take that watch. You were with me all afternoon. Plus, I think you're canny enough to hide it somewhere safer than your bedside locker, even if it was a dare. Why did you lie?'

William didn't answer.

'You've been reading Pat's stories, Mary Brigid says. Got to 'The Thief' yet?'

The question wrung a nod from William.

'And you thought it best to give a good reason for the watch being found in your things and hope for mercy?'

'Yes, sir.'

'Well, William, perhaps you'd do me the courtesy of telling me the truth, seeing it was myself that saved you from expulsion.'

William studied the streaks that crisscrossed his palms. The floor was spattered with black droplets.

'Come, let's look at those hands and you can tell me about it.' Mr Pearse crossed to the sink, putting on the light as he went. He held William's hands under the cool water.

'Someone put Richard's watch in my locker, I suppose,' William admitted, watching his blood running down the drain, imagining it to be scarlet watercolour.

'And why would this mysterious someone do that?'

'I don't know, sir.'

'If it was to get you into trouble it worked a treat.' Mr Pearse tore up some strips of cloth and bound William's hands. 'I'm no Mary Brigid,' he mused, 'but I think that'll do.'

'Thank you, sir.'

'Sit, William.' Mr Pearse steered him to a stool. 'Pat would be upset if he knew lads at his school were not showing Christian compassion to each other. William, you can tell us.'

The beatings he'd taken, the cuts and grazes that scarred his arms and legs, the chipped molar that hurt when he ate: they would be nothing to what he'd get if he grassed.

'It's what I said, sir. Some of them still think of me as the new boy and they tease me, call me Finn, get at me. But it's fine.'

'Truly, William?'

William clenched his teeth and nodded. Mr Pearse retained a sceptical look.

'You shouldn't be minding the boys calling you Finn. 'Tis a grand Irish name. Your father would approve. Here,' Mr Pearse reached up to a shelf and retrieved a sheaf of lose pages, 'It's called *A Boy in Eirinn* by Mr Patrick Colum. He's a friend of mine and Pat's. He's hoping to publish it but he lent me it first. Guess what the hero is called?'

'Finn?'

'So he is! And he's an adventurer, does things that would terrify other lads. They scare him too sometimes but he does them anyway. That's what I think being brave is; feeling scared and doing the thing anyway. Do you understand, William?'

'I think so.'

'You'll like it.' Mr Pearse pressed the pages into William's bandaged hands. 'There's no shame in seeking help, William. Sure, we all need it sometimes.'

'My father says real men don't; they fight for themselves.'

'Aye, there's something in that too. If the Bible tells us to turn the other cheek it teaches us also to right the wrongs we encounter.'

Back in the dorm the ball of newsprint sat on his bed, emptied of treasures. William rooted around inside his locker but the whale tooth and Confederate button were gone. He hurled the paper ball at the bin. It missed. He left it on the floor and crawled into bed.

William slogged through his punishment. During prep, lessons and assemblies he had a seat away from the others. He ate alone, supervised by a master. After lessons William was set to work scrubbing floors, sanding graffiti from desks, possing dirty laundry. At night he slept in a windowless cubby on the top floor. Only in games did he have contact with the others, with Richard. In those two months William suffered a broken thumb, a sprained wrist, two bumps on the head, four black eyes, three fat lips, so many bruises that his body became an aching patchwork quilt. He also lost the slack molar and had another broken.

But the silence hurt most. Whether his friends believed he had stolen the watch and snitched about the bullying to avoid being expelled or because they guessed the truth and were ashamed they hadn't helped him, William wasn't sure, but they wouldn't speak to him. Between his friends' silence and the masters speaking to him only when they had to, William was alone with the echo of his father's voice: 'Finish your fights.' The voice never said how.

A Boy in Eirinn sat unread in William's locker. It became the daylight outside his prison cell. If he made it through he'd allow himself to peer into a world where Finn was the hero.

The door opened at last. William found himself at large in the school. He was welcomed back from solitary like a stoic prisoner of war. But so much time in his own company had armoured him. The time was coming when he would finish the fight. Then Richard's parents sent for him, an illness in the family, and he stayed at home for the rest of the term, leaving William's resolve cooling, molten steel tempered and unbreakable.

Trinity Term 1912

William was among the handful of boys who stayed at school for the Easter holidays. He spent the long bright days wielding a hurley or kicking a football at an empty goal and the dull drizzly ones painting and studying. He helped with the chores he had become accustomed to doing during his punishment and was rewarded with pleasant evenings in the Pearse family room, listening to Mr Pearse reading his stories or Mary Brigid playing the piano or harp while everyone else sang in a mixture of heavenly and heathenish voices. He also began reading *A Boy in Eirinn*.

Finn O'Donnell, the book's hero, was teased for his name, but, unlike William, he didn't mind because he was named after Finn MacCoul, the great Irish warrior who captained the Fianna of Ireland, a band of soldiers who valiantly defended Ireland. Both Finns were the kind of lad William wanted to be: bold and adventurous. MacCoul was a brave warrior who proved himself leading Ireland's most fearless band of men. William thought that was the reason Mr Pearse had given him the book. He had a duty to live up to his name's sake, the honourable Finn, not the cowardly William. It was what his father expected too.

Before he returned the manuscript, William copied the passage describing how Finn MacCoul conquered the goblin that threatened the High King of Ireland, earning himself captainship of the Fianna. He read it aloud, repeating the word 'Fianna'. Buried within it he heard that secretive, mysterious word 'Fenian'. He determined to root out the connection. But first he'd finish his fight with Richard.

On Good Friday the family and boys went to church for high mass. On Sunday, in celebration of the Lord's resurrection, Mrs Pearse laid on a grand spread attended by many friends from Dublin and beyond.

'William, there's someone I'd like you to meet.' Willie Pearse beckoned William. 'This is Patrick Colum. Pat, this is the lad I lent your book to, Michael Devoy's son.'

'Indeed! A pleasure to meet you,' Mr Colum said, his brows arching in surprise as he extended slender fingers, the index and thumb stained with violet ink.

'And you, sir.'

'Has your father plans to pay us another visit soon, do you think?'

William's grip failed him.

'I don't know, sir.'

'Well, let's be hoping so, eh, Willie? Now I suppose I shall have to ask the question all writers fear,' Mr Colum continued, 'What did you think of my wee book?'

'I thought it was very good, sir,' William stammered.

'Do you think it's something other boys would enjoy?' Mr Colum pressed.

'Yes, sir, I should think so.'

'I hope you don't mind, William, but I told Mr Colum how some of the boys have a mind to call you Finn,' Mr Pearse said.

William blushed. 'But I would have liked it as well if the character had some other name. It's grand, sir.'

'I'm glad you enjoyed it, William,' Mr Colum said, 'Perhaps I may come to you for a recommendation? The word of a Devoy is worth much in these parts, is it not, Willie?'

Mr Colum nudged Willie and winked. William could only manage a half-hearted smile before Miss Margaret came up and whisked her brother and Mr Colum away.

In bed that night William took the pages onto which he had copied Finn MacCoul's defeat of the goblin.

'And before dawn something that had the appearance of a bull with eyes blazing like torches tried to rush past him. Finn struck the thing on the forehead with the magical spear-head. It changed and became a great serpent that tried to crush Finn with its coils. Again Finn struck it with the spear-head. Then the thing became an eagle that rose with blazing wings towards the roof of the mansion. Finn hurled his spear and pierced its wing. It fell to the ground...And so the youthful Finn MacCoul became head of the noble Fianna of Ireland.'

William dreamt of himself standing at a fork in the ford. To his left the water was stagnant, scummy and dank. To the right it flowed clear with frothing white crests. He stepped into the surging right-hand burn. He would become a hero.

It was a wild, windy Saturday two weeks into term and cold for the time of year. William was digging the vegetable garden because on Tuesday Richard had landed a paper aeroplane on William's desk during prep, on the wings of which was a rude caricature of Mr MacDonagh, including bowtie. The master was not impressed by William's stoic silence and his punishment had been a Saturday of chores. He was turning over the cloyed earth before mulching in the contents of the compost heap. His hands were so numb he felt he would be able to snap each finger off like the twigs of frost-bitten rose bushes. The shovel slipped in the palms of his wet hands and blisters swelled, burst and swelled again. Mud coated his boots and he felt the pull of it as the ground tried to gobble him up.

From through the trees a troop of muddied and bloodied boys emerged, their hurleys over their shoulders like swords. Their laughter reached William and he glanced up. Richard was in front, bragging. William shovelled another clod and saw something glistening in the dull brown earth. Spearing his spade into the mud, he slid his fingers into the slimy earth, mud oozing through his fingers.

'Look, lads, Finn's having a bath.'

Half a dozen pairs of brown-spattered legs came into view.

'At least he's down in the shite where he belongs, eh lads? Where all Proddie swine belong. How's it down there, Finn-boy? Right enough for you, you Orange whore's son?' Richard cackled and raucous laughter swung back and forth.

William plucked his hand from the soil but before he could examine his find Richard called out, 'I've something for you, so I have.' William's whale tooth hit the ground. Richard toed it onto the stone slabs that edged the veggie patch. 'Go on, take it.' He moved his foot aside.

William clutched the creamy canine.

Richard raised his boot. Stamped down, pulping William's fingers under the sharp studs and shattering the tooth.

William snatched his hand back, cradled the bloodied mess and trapped a yelp of pain behind his teeth.

'What's the matter, Finn, lost your tongue? Dropped it in the muck have you?' Richard howled, 'Let me give you a hand.'

Richard tugged the spade free and cracked it across William's back.

Pain tightened his chest and William felt himself falling, his face crushed into the festering mud that pressed into his ears, up his nose and under his eye-lids.

'He hasn't got a close enough look, has he, boys? Let's help him. Want to give him a 'fair' chance of finding it, eh?'

A heavy weight jammed down between William's shoulder blades, driving him deeper into the mud. Air rushed from his lungs. He tried to fill them; globs of soggy earth and veggie peelings wormed further up his nostrils. The weight stayed on his back. He was drowning, thrashing now, a fish in a rapidly draining pool. The more he struggled the more the weight bore down. It moved to his neck, strangling, suffocating, choking. William wriggled and squirmed. His lungs screamed. He didn't know if his eyes were open or closed. He was going to die.

'He'll asphyxiate if you don't let him up.' The voice was quiet and distant.

'What are you going to do about it, Bookie?'

'I'm just checking you understand the fundamentals of human respiration,' Freddie said in the same neutral tone. 'Of course if you do want to kill him you're doing a grand job.'

Sean O'Malley spoke. 'Let's go, Richard.'

The cleats of Richard's boots bit harder into William's neck. His lungs flamed. His heart tore at his chest. Then everything stopped.

William opened his eyes. He was on his back, rain pattering on his cheeks and forehead. Freddie's face loomed into view. He offered William a handkerchief, reburied his nose in his book and walked away. William sat up, Freddie's handkerchief clutched in his throbbing hand. He gulped air and waited on his backside in the dirt as wetness crept through his trousers and the woozy feelings in his head faded. Then he uncurl the fist that still clutched the object he had plucked from the ground. Its surface was worn smooth and, as he cleaned it, he could feel the cold glossiness of thousands of years. The fragment was triangular, about three inches across the bottom edge and five to the point. William ran a finger along each dulled edge, sure he could sharpen it, restore it to the deadly spearhead it was once. Like that Finn MacCoul had used on the goblin. William folded the treasure in his palm: the ideal replacement for his broken catapult.

Richard,
Come at three o'clock. The grove behind the school. Come alone so I know you're not a coward.
F.

William set off towards the trees beyond the stream that ran through the school's woodland grounds. It was the place Richard used for fights, out of earshot of masters. As William jogged over the footbridge he appealed to his new hero, Finn MacCoul, for the strength to finish this fight.

Calling him a coward had worked. Richard was alone.

'Finn the Fair. Didn't I think you wouldn't show?'

William held his ground.

'You're not wasting my time, are you?' Richard snarled, 'Don't want to have come here not to knock your block off.'

William gave his answer by charging Richard, barrelling him off his feet and getting in several quick punches. Richard pulled himself together and William felt hands gripping him, flinging him backwards. He landed heavily, breath rushing out. Richard was up already, taking his stance again.

'You need to learn a few manners, Finn-boy. I've tried to teach you, so I have, but it hasn't got through your thick Orange head. This time I'll beat it through.'

Richard hauled William to his feet and punched him in the stomach. William lashed out with a foot, striking Richard's knee, which buckled. Richard swore and staggered but was on William again in seconds. They rolled on the ground, raining blows on each other. Richard pelted William's head, chest and stomach. William blocked what he could and tried to jab with his elbows, hitting mostly air. Richard got him on his back and sat on top of William, punching him twice hard in the face. Blood pooled in William's mouth, gagging him. Battered and beaten he lay vanquished, Richard on his chest, crushing the fight out of him.

'Don't think you can beat me, Finn-boy. Bollocks you can. Know why?'

When William didn't reply, Richard slapped his face and gripped his cheeks in one powerful hand, shaking William's head until his eyes rolled like dice in a cup.

'Because I'm the king. There'll be no King Williams at St Enda's. I'll slay every single miserable fucker. What's that you say, Finn? It's not fair? Sure, that's too bad.' Richard flung William's head to the ground where it bounced off the hard earth. 'Because I'm the fecking king here and you'll bow to me, if you want to live.'

Richard's laughter echoed, filling the grove with an army of crowing, tyrannical Richards. He got up and William felt stiff boot leather plunged into his side. He rolled over and threw up as Richard strolled towards a spot under a chestnut tree. William dragged himself onto his hands and knees. Bursts of light popped before his eyes. The whole world jigged. The only solid thing was the sharpened flint blade, buried in his pocket. He locked trembling legs straight out beneath him and turned in Richard's direction.

Up ahead a lumbering figure made off through the undergrowth, hunched and gnarled, walking with a monstrous gait, its arms swiping from side to side. Familiar taunts called out to William. Wounds old and new throbbed through his body. Hot terror beat in his chest as he stood again before Mr Pearse, Richard's watch in the headmaster's hand. There would be no end unless he brought one. His father's voice bellowed, 'Finish your fights, boy. Be about it, you cowardly wee shite.' William chased down the monster ambling away from another conquest, saw the flash of the beast's white throat, and slashed out with the hand that gripped the spearhead. The white skin split neatly in two. Red filled the gap and flowed free. William staggered away, tripping on a tree root. Splayed on his back, pale blue sky filled his vision, washing away the red that had flooded in, scaring him.

'William.'

It was his name but it sounded odd; wet and bubbly, as though it was being said under water.

'William. Le do thoil*.'

This time his name was a gurgle, as though from the mouth of a sludgy river. He sat up.

Richard was swaying on his feet, his eyes pleading. He raised a hand to his neck and felt the groove carved there. He opened his mouth to speak again and red frothed out.

William lurched to standing. Richard crumpled. The grass under him was scorched with blood. His eyes rolled back, showing only the whites. The hand that had been clawing at his throat shivered and fell limp.

William was confused, stunned, horrified. He'd been on his hands and knees, puking and wretched, his eyes filled with starbursts, his head full of pounding pistons. His father had been yelling at him. Then he was staring at a cold sky. Now he was up and Richard down, a new smile etched into his neck. And clutched between William's fingers, in drying-to-sticky blood, was the spearhead. He was sick again, spewing a lumpy hot mess on the ground. William crawled away through the briers and sat, his back braced against a tree, waiting for reason and sense, shouting voices, ringing bells and trampling feet: the end of his world. But there was no alarm and no bell. No one came. Nothing moved except a raven, its feathers glimmering with a green sheen in the slanted sunlight. The raven hopped over to Richard and pecked at the bloodied ground. It cast an unblinking eye on William, cawed a two note call and flapped away.

He hadn't meant to but if not this, then what? He had to stand up for himself; it was what his father expected, what Finn MacCoul would have done. But he hadn't just beaten; he'd killed.

William studied Richard through the raven's eye. What had happened? Richard had been robbed; murdered by the robber. William stumbled over and squatted down to lift Richard's sleeve. The skin was warm. Fingers fumbling, William undid

---

* please

Richard's watch. The glass was cracked and the hands frozen. Fiddling with the pin, William wound the hands on then lobbed it a little way from Richard. He remembered his note. Retching, William thrust his hands in every pocket. He found his last lost treasure, the bullet-button, and slipped it into his pocket where it clicked against the flint, but not the note. Maybe Richard had already scrapped it. At least it wasn't signed, not properly. There was nothing William could do except hope.

He brushed leaves from his trousers. The raven fluttered back down to inspect the scene. It winked a yellow eye at William. William trudged to the stream and washed his hands and face. His reflection showed smears of purple and red; evidence of his guilt or his innocence? He dropped the bullet-button into the lapping waters where it blended into the pebbly bottom.

When he emerged at the back of the school Sean O'Malley and a few others from Richard's gang, were perched on the wall surrounding the terrace, their heels kick-kicking the bricks, a football on the ground beside them. William gauged the distance. In his head a starter's whistle blew. William leapt forward, sprinted hard, raising his head once to check his course, and clattered into Sean, shoving him backwards off the wall. Sean landed with a crack but was up quickly. He threw a punch at William who made sure it cracked against his cheekbone. He grappled with Sean and they rolled around in the gravel. The glass door onto the terrace flew open.

'What the bejesus is going on?' Mr Colbert hollered, stepping into the fray and scruffing William and Sean like feral cats. 'Devoy, O'Malley. Have you eejits lost your minds?'

'He started it. He pushed me off the wall, sir.'

'It was an accident,' William lied, 'He punched me first.'

'Enough, so,' Mr Colbert barked, 'Let Mr Pearse hear it.' With a boy by the collar in each hand, Mr Colbert backed through the door and spun in the direction of the headmaster's office.

Mr Pearse, unable to distinguish victim from perpetrator, sent both boys to their dorms for the rest of the day.

*

By half eight, when his dorm mates returned from tea, William was a mass of nerves and emptiness. His stomach was chewing on itself and his head hurt. Only after Hal announced the mysterious disappearance of Richard MacDonnall was William able to sit up without pain searing behind his eyes.

Charlie bounced down on William's bed. 'I smuggled this out for you.' He dropped a squished soda farl on the counterpane. 'What do you make of this Richard business?'

William stuffed his mouth with bread.

'I reckon he's done a runner,' Charlie carried on.

'Why would he be doing that?' Freddie asked, staring at William.

Charlie shrugged.

'What are they going to do?' William asked.

'I heard Mr Plunkett say they were after searching the grounds.'

James interrupted William's thoughts. 'Where were you all afternoon?'

William crammed the last of the bread into his mouth.

'Busy kicking shite out of Sean O'Malley, I heard,' Hal said, patting William's leg, 'But you don't look to have come out of it so well.' Hal studied William's face.

'I'm fine. And call me Finn.'

'But I thought…'

'I'm sick of William. It's a no-good name. Call me Finn. All of you. It's Finn I am now.'

So it was Finn who lay tossing and turning in his bed that night, tangling himself in the sheets and waking from half-sleep, cold sweat coating his back.

It was Finn who got up in the dim dawn and examined the bruises on his chest as he dressed, staying silent when Hal remarked on what a pasting he had taken from Sean.

Into the dining hall for breakfast went Finn, following in the wake of his friends, in his pocket the fatal flint he was afraid of keeping and terrified of losing.

And Finn it was who sat during morning assembly as Mr Pearse made the solemn announcement that Richard

MacDonnall was dead, murdered, it seemed, by a villainous robber.

Finn MacCoul Finn MacCoul Finn MacCoul.

Finn Devoy Finn Devoy Finn Devoy.

Finn Finn Finn.

The school was silenced by the news. Steeped in a potent mixture of fear and thrill no boy could bring himself to speak of what had happened. Lessons were trudged through. At break they roamed the Hermitage making dumb comments. At lunch they ate their colcannon with the ruminative concentration of cows. Finn caught Freddie watching him and fretted as Freddie stared through his spectacles with penetrating eyes before going back to scanning his pages. All day, whenever he glanced up Finn's eyes found Freddie's, his gaze quick and glassy.

As they filed out of the study hall that night Freddie snaked up alongside Finn.

'William.' Willie Pearse called to him.

Relieved, Finn stepped out of the line and over to the master.

'Please, sir,' he said, 'It's Finn I'd like you to call me.'

'So you truly enjoy *A Boy in Eirinn*?'

'Yes, sir.'

'This mind for calling yourself Finn, I hope that's what you want?'

'Yes, sir.'

Mr Pearse searched Finn's face. 'I've been thinking, maybes I put you on the spot, introducing you to Mr Colum. I hope your change of mind over the name isn't because of that.'

'No, sir.' Finn shuffled on his feet.

'You look as though you've been in the wars.' Mr Pearse's steady eyes fixed him in place. 'You're a bright lad, Finn,' he said, stressing the new name, 'Bright enough, I've a hope, to know what's worth fighting for.'

'Yes, sir.'

Mr Pearse sighed. 'Very well. Goodnight, Finn.'

'Óiche mhaith dhuit, sir.'

Finn didn't want to go to bed for another sleepless, sweat-soaked night. Inside him was a prickly, hollow feeling he couldn't name. He slipped outside, his feet wandering and his mind dodging thoughts he wanted to hide from. He ended up crossing the bridge and heading for the grove. The stream's silvery voice formed slow drifting words that floated up and burst with a soft fssst by his ear. 'You thought it would be as easy as that? Slay your enemy and rise triumphant? You thought yourself as great as Finn MacCoul, your cause as righteous?' Finn pressed his palms to his ears and turned his back on the mocking water.

Memories of the previous day flickered in the dying light. Was it a sin, killing the enemy? Finn MacCoul would say no and Anthony, the boy who stole for his sister. His father was always charging him to fight for himself. Alone in his dissent stood Íosagán, the boy who was pure, holy and innocent.

Finn sank to his knees, clasped his hands and peered up through naked branches. He tried to pray but no words came. Instead he sobbed, choking on tears and self-pity. He flung himself facedown. Sodden leaves clagged to his cheeks and salty grit pricked his skin.

Wrung dry, Finn sat up. Scrabbling on hands and knees, he crawled to the chestnut marking the spot where Richard had fallen. From his pocket Finn pulled the spearhead. What was done would have to be carried all his life. Using the flint he scored four letters into the trunk. Then, raising his arm, he pitched the flint hard and far. It fell beyond reach. He studied his handy work, a single word: F I N N. Himself alone.

The dorm was dark and silent. Finn dumped his clothes over the chair and slipped between the covers, bumping into a lumpy bolster.

'William?' a voice hissed.

Finn held his breath.

Charlie sighed. 'Finn,' he corrected, ''sthat you?'

'Yes.'

Finn heard the rustling of bedclothes, the rasp of a match and smelled burnt sand as the flame flared up. Charlie held the yellow flicker to a candle and a pool of light tripped out across the room.

They stared at each other.

'Where've you been?'

'Walking.'

'I put a pillow in your bed case anyone checked.'

'You didn't have to.'

Freddie stirred, raising his dark head. He saw Finn and bolted upright. Without his spectacles his eyes were wide and fixed, the candlelight making them gleam like a raven's. Finn stared back.

'Do you think the police'll come?' Charlie asked.

'Aye, they will,' Freddie said, his eyes shifting not a quarter inch from Finn's, 'And they'll be speaking to anyone who might've seen Richard. Did you see him, Finn?'

'I was in Mr Pearse's office.'

'I expect they'll ask his friends,' Charlie said, 'Wonder what he was doing in the woods.'

'Maybes he was meeting someone.'

Finn didn't flinched and didn't look away.

'Oh,' Charlie said, 'Do you think he knew whoever…?'

Freddie said, 'What're you reckoning, Finn?'

'I reckon it serves him right,' Finn said.

'He was a proper git,' Charlie conceded.

'And that makes it alright?' Freddie challenged.

'He got what he deserved,' Finn snapped.

Freddie blinked, his eyes staying closed too long. When he opened them again he looked to the ceiling. 'Did he, so?' He laid down, pulling the bedclothes over his head.

Charlie threw a perplexed glance at Finn but Finn shrugged it off and settled on his pillows. Charlie puffed out the candle and moments later there was the gentle murmuring of his snores interlaced with Hal's piggish grunts.

Finn counted to twenty then said, so anyone who might be listening, 'He did deserve it.'

*

The police came. They talked to those boys who were friendly with Richard. A few had seen him heading into the woods but they either didn't know or wouldn't say why. Finn's note had vanished. He wasn't suspected. No one questioned him so he was saved from lying. The police left. Details filtered through the school; Richard's pockets had been turned out, his watch was thought to be missing, then found broken. His throat had been cut. This was a sensation and facts about this technique of dispatching a man circulated: it took five minutes for someone to bleed to death if their jugular was sliced; no, it took three; there would be a six foot arc of blood; your tongue would flop out the gash in your neck; you wouldn't be able to speak. Finn listened, sickened.

There was an inquest and Mr Pearse shared the verdict with St Enda's to quell speculation: death caused by person or persons unknown. The police would continue investigating but it was accepted that the murderer was a vagabond now lost to the wild Wicklow mountains.

On an errand a day later, Finn passed a fair lady with red-rimmed eyes, clinging to the arm of a tall man with a pinched face. Soon a hush ran around the building: Richard's folks are here. Later, from his dorm window, Finn watched the rounded black dome with the haze of a veil thrown over it and the delved crown, shiny in the grip above a curved brim, as mother and father stood on the steps of the Hermitage, shaking hands with Mr Pearse.

On the day of the funeral lessons were cancelled. A procession of boys sporting black armbands was led by Mr Pearse to the waiting hearse. There were two carriages for the MacDonnall clan; the school fell in behind them. The chief mourner, his tails flapping like limp wings and his top hat under his arm, set off on a sombre march. The horses, their coats silky in the sunlight, followed sedately. The carriages creaked and groaned. Sixty pairs of feet clap-clapped behind.

Finn sat in the darkened church, his head bowed and his mind shut. He lost himself and was surprised to emerge into midday sunlight. The march back was led by Mr Colbert who pushed them along at a brisk pace. On arrival they were ordered to occupy themselves with some quiet activity. In the art room Finn filled two pages of his sketchpad with incoherent doodles. He sought out Mrs Pearse, hoping for chores but she chased him. He drifted into the chapel at the back of the study hall, perched on a pew and gazed at the round window set high in the arched wall until his restless mind bade him move again. He found himself in the empty dorm. A letter from his mother lay on his bed. After three attempts he knew he couldn't reply to her that day. Throwing his pen into his locker Finn saw his copy of the crucial pages from *A Boy in Eirinn*. Taking them up, he read to the end.

'Then the King was satisfied that the goblin had been overcome, and he held Goll MacMorna to the word he had spoken as Captain of the Fianna of Ireland – that he would give his allegiance to Finn MacCoul as Captain of the Fianna.

And so the youthful Finn MacCoul became head of the noble Fianna of Ireland, and while he lived our country had strength and prosperity.'

The words taunted him, 'See what happens when you listen to us, see what you've done.'

Behind him the door clicked. Finn spun around. Freddie was there. Finn crumpled the tormenting pages in his hand.

'What're you doing?' Freddie asked.

'Nothing.' Finn held on a moment longer then yielded. 'You know, don't you?'

'This is yours, isn't it?' Freddie took two cautious steps towards Finn and held out his missing note. 'Did you do it?'

'Are you going to tell?'

'I'm no grass, but, Finn, why?'

Finn drew a deep breath. 'We were fighting. I knew if I didn't do it… I'd had enough.'

Freddie dropped his eyes to the note. 'I'm sorry.'

'What?'

'I knew what he was doing to you. The others did too but they didn't see him that time when he had you in the mud.'

'You saved me.'

'Richard got scared, that's all. I should've helped you. It's my fault.'

'No! It was me did it. I shouldn't have.'

'Maybe you had to.'

'Does that make it not wrong?'

They stared at each other, each wishing they had the answer.

'We should've stuck together,' Freddie said at last, 'Isn't that what friends do? Here.' He held out the note. 'Get rid of it.'

Finn crinkled the paper between his fingers. 'It didn't seem real, like it wasn't me. I don't know…'

'It doesn't matter. We should forget it. I want to forget it.'

'Alright.'

Finn turned to the fireplace. He took a match from the bundle on the flagstones, lit one and touched it to the note. The paper curled and crisped as the flame gobbled it. Finn dropped it into the grate before it nibbled at his fingers. The match still glowed in his hand. He set alight the pages of *A Boy in Eirinn* and watched as the words he had copied burned.

'What's that?'

'Nothing,' Finn said. He offered his hand to Freddie and hoped he would get his tongue around the word properly. 'A chairde*?'

'Aye,' Freddie replied, taking Finn's hand, 'Friends.'

---

* friends

Michaelmas Term 1912

'Hallo, Finn. Didn't think you'd be here yet.'

'We had a good tail-wind; crossed in record time. Might have even been a blue ribbon sailing!'

Charlie came over and shook Finn's hand.

'Who else is in here?' Finn asked, indicating their new dorm.

'Hal and Freddie. Not the twins.'

'Oh.'

'Word is their mother asked for them to be moved. We've got Sean O'Malley, worse luck, and some new chap. Don't know his name.'

Finn's hands coiled into fists at the mention of O'Malley.

'Is he here yet, Sean?'

'Comes tomorrow, I think.'

Finn nodded determinedly.

'Have you heard?' Charlie was on to something new.

'What?'

'There's a Dublin Juniors Hurling championship this year. All the schools are putting up a team. Will you try out?'

'Yes.'

'Good. Me too.'

They hadn't seen each other for two months and both were a head taller than when they had left in the summer. Finn wondered what else had changed, making the reunion harder than he'd expected. He pushed the feeling down.

'I'll unpack later. Let's get in some practise.'

'Grand idea.'

Mr Pearse made his inaugural address to the school on the first day of term proper. Finn, Charlie, Hal, Freddie and the new boy, Alasteir Keane, filed in with the rest of the school to take up chairs laid out in the study hall. The walls had been repainted over the summer in a deep shade of evergreen. With the dark wood floor varnished to a high sheen and the cloud-cream ceiling, Finn felt he was in a shady forest.

Chatter died away as Mr Pearse took the stage. Finn thought the master looked tired but happy: glad to have his boys back.

'It's good to see so many familiar faces and to welcome the newcomers. We hope you'll find happiness at St. Enda's, as well as learning, growing and becoming men ready to go out into the world and play your part for Ireland and God.' He let the words settle before continuing, 'This year, with your help, shall be the most triumphant in St. Enda's short history. Grand things are planned, only some of which I'll share with you now for the day is too bright for boys as fine as yourselves to be in this dusty old hall listening to this dusty old man.'

There was light chuckling at Mr Pearse's description of himself as he stood so upright on the stage, his sparkling eyes scanning them. Finn scanned too. He was looking for O'Malley.

'Of the many great things in store, the first we shall embark on is the Dublin Junior Hurling championship. I am sure some of you will be eager to represent your school in this new and most prestigious competition. Mr Colbert will be in charge of team selection and will be looking for twenty-five boys of exceptional agility, skill and speed to do battle on the pitches of Dublin. I urge all of you to take what part you can. While some of you will be our champions all of you should be our supporters.'

Finn and Charlie exchanged grins.

'The usual lessons will continue and I plan more guest speakers this year. Countess Markievicz has kindly consented to return and I have secured talks from the great poet W. B. Yeats, Sir Roger Casement, Irish nationalist, who will lecture on historical Ireland, and Mrs Margaret Hutton, who has written a beautiful translation of the classic text *An Táin*. As some of you know, St Enda's has a fine reputation for amateur dramatics here and at the Abbey Theatre. This year we'll test our mettle by staging a magnificent pageant in celebration of all things Gaelic and Irish. This will take place at the end of the year and involve every one of you.'

Mr Pearse paused. A tiny flutter of nattering rose up like a flock of disturbed starlings; this would be a glorious year at St. Enda's.

'Before I'm releasing you into the sun I want to finish by saying that I believe in you, in your potential, your beauty and your hopefulness. Boys in circumstances far less auspicious have accomplished great things. Here I cite Cúchulainn as an example. It is with this great Irish boy warrior in mind that I first founded St Enda's for I wanted to ensure the future of an Ireland that will stand triumphant over her enemies. It is through you boys of Ireland that such victory will be achieved. The future of our nation, the future of our lives, rests in your hands. Do all you can to meet the challenges, overcome the difficulties and rise up against those who repress our sense of ourselves as wholly Irish, wholly Gaelic.'

The room filled with the buzz of dozens of boys imagining themselves battling enemy after enemy and beating them in single combat. Riotous applause broke out. Mr Pearse smiled and gave a nod of his head as Mr Willie Pearse, Mr Plunkett and Mr Colbert began signalling the boys to file out.

Their merry band of five slipped away from the Hermitage. Finn wasn't conscious of leading them until he realised they were crossing the bridge over the stream and heading into the grove of trees that was sacred ground to him. He dropped onto the grass. Charlie, Hal and Freddie followed. Freddie pulled a book from his pocket, pushed his glasses up his nose and began reading. Alasteir stayed standing. He was a thin boy, tall enough to be taken for a fifth former, with limp sandy hair and sharp features. His nose was hooked and he had a scrawny neck. Finn thought he looked bird-like, a gangly stork darting glances at them, waiting to peck out their eyes.

'Sit down, eejit,' Freddie mumbled, 'You're blocking my light.'

'Sorry.' Alasteir shuffled to the side but stayed standing.

'That was a fine speech, so it was,' Hal said, stretching out his muscled limbs.

'Aye,' Finn agreed, leaning back on his four letter name, slightly smoothed now by summer rains, 'It's going to be a good year. What do you think, Freddie?' Finn slapped Freddie's ankle.

'Sounds like old man Pearse's not leaving much time for reading.'

'You read too much,' Charlie moaned, 'Don't suppose you'll try out for the hurling?'

'Sure.' Freddie shot his eyes to the heavens.

'Me and Finn are, aren't we?'

'Damn right.'

'Finn. 'Sthat your real name?' Alasteir spoke so unexpectedly that even Freddie put his book down.

Finn's jaw tightened.

'Yes.'

'Isn't it Gaelic for fair?'

'It's after Finn MacCoul.'

'So you're Irish?'

'My father is.'

'You don't sound Irish.'

'My grandfather moved to New York during the famine,' Finn snapped.

'So you'll be Michael Devoy's boy.'

Finn sat up. 'What's that to you?'

'An American,' Alasteir went on.

Finn got to his feet, aware of having to look up at the curiously tall Alasteir. 'I'm as Irish as anyone here.'

'As Irish as me, for sure,' Charlie said with a laugh that fell over itself.

'I'm Irish on both sides,' Alasteir said, 'Where's your mother from?'

Finn felt a lie on his tongue. He rolled it around his mouth for a moment then swallowed it. 'Germany.'

'So how'd you end up being Finn? You should be Hans or Wilhelm or something.'

It was a lucky guess. Finn screwed down his grip on himself.

Hal got up. He was almost as tall as Alasteir and made up the deficit with brawniness. He stood at Finn's side, his broad frame fattening the air.

'If you're Irish you'll know about Finn MacCoul and how he defeated the goblin that threatened the high king.' Hal spoke purposefully. The threat was clear. Alasteir stepped back and made the sound of a bird trying to get a stuck worm down.

'No offence,' he said to Finn. 'I just thought it an unusual name.'

Finn and Hal waited until Alasteir sat down before sitting themselves. For a moment the only sound was Freddie's page flicking. Alasteir looked around but avoided Finn's eye. It occurred to Finn that Alasteir didn't sound all that Irish himself and he wished he'd said so, but the moment was gone. The rasping of a match being struck pulled his attention away. He turned and saw Charlie with a cigarette between his lips.

Charlie, feeling himself ogled, blew out a cloud of smoke and grinned. 'What?'

'Where'd you get that?' Hal asked.

Charlie shrugged. 'Want a go?' He offered the cigarette to Hal.

Hal hesitated then took and raised the cigarette to his lips, sucking hard. Not knowing what to do with the smoke, he puffed out his cheeks and stored it, like a squirrel with nuts, until his face got red and his eyes bulged worse than Charlie's.

Charlie whacked Hal on the back, making him belch smoke.

'You're supposed to breathe out.'

Hal coughed and rubbed his watering eyes.

'Let me try.' Freddie threw his book aside.

Hal passed the cigarette on. Freddie took an elegant sip at it.

'Very nice,' he spluttered.

Finn sat up. 'My turn,' he demanded and Freddie, little finger extended, passed it over. Finn put the now soggy end in his mouth and drew on it like he was drinking through a straw. A flavour worse than burnt toast filled his mouth. He swallowed and when he opened his mouth only a few faint wisps of smoke escaped. Charlie laughed.

'You're all useless. Like this, see.' He demonstrated his prowess with one deep breath in and out, letting off a cloud of white-grey smoke that reminded Finn of the steam from trains.

'Let's have another go,' Hal barked, determined he wasn't going to be beaten by so spindly an opponent.

Charlie pulled out a packet and offered them round.

'No, thank you,' Alasteir said in a clipped voice.

Charlie returned the pack to his pocket. 'Suit yourself.'

He shared out matches and they sat guzzling on cigarettes.

After three puffs Finn cracked it by pretending he had a blocked nose that made him breathe through his mouth.

'I've got it,' he announced.

'That's it,' Charlie said, 'Go on, Bookie, you can do better. Hal, not going to be beaten, are you?'

The challenge was set. Finn sat crossed legged on the ground. He pictured himself in a ceremonial headdress of eagle feathers, holding a long thin pipe. He was Sitting Bull and Charlie his Indian Brave. Freddie and Hal could be Nez Purse. Alasteir, he decided, was a pesky pale-faced interloper.

They smoked until Charlie was satisfied they'd mastered the art. When they headed back for tea Finn felt light headed and elated.

Mr Colbert organised hurling trials on the first Saturday of term. Finn, Hal and Charlie lined up on the pitch. Freddie sat behind the goal with a book on his lap, occasionally glancing up and cheering as forty boys thundered back and forth, their hurleys raised, tossing the sliotar.

The wind lifted Finn as he ran the length of the pitch. He was nimble and swift, dodging and twisting, a swallow in flight. Mr Colbert tried each of them in different positions and watched as they passed, tackled, scored and saved. He carried a clipboard and a stubby pencil. Whenever Finn caught a break in the play he would steal a glance at Mr Colbert. Once or twice he caught the master's eye but mostly Mr Colbert was bent over his clipboard, pencil twitching between his fingers.

Sean O'Malley was at the other end of the pitch. The sliotar was in play following a throw-in. Finn ran to take possession. Sean ran too, his hurley raised. Finn stretched out to catch the ball and play it back to his team. He was within reach when he was jolted from behind. He stumbled, his hurley flew into the air and he missed the sliotar. He whirled around and saw Sean, his hurley held high.

'You did that deliberately.'

'Did what?' Sean asked.

'Made me miss.'

'Sure, I did not.'

'You did.'

'If you missed it's because you're shite at hurling,' Sean snapped.

'Better than you.'

'How many goals've you scored today?'

'More than you,' Finn sneered as he retrieved his hurley.

'Catch yourself on.'

'Least I'm not a cheater.' Finn spat the word in Sean's face.

'Think I don't know how to 'play fair', so?' Sean retorted. 'But you are the expert in what's fair, aren't you?'

Finn drew back his hurley and whacked Sean's ankle. Sean yelped and struck back. A jagged spasm raced up Finn's leg, through his body and out the top of his head. He retaliated with another crack at Sean who screamed, dropped to the ground and rolled around, clutching his leg.

'What the bejesus is going on?' Mr Colbert charged across the pitch.

'It was an accident, sir,' Finn muttered.

'He hit me, sir,' Sean moaned.

Mr Colbert knelt down.

'Let me see, O'Malley,' he ordered, yanking Sean's hands away from his ankle and prodding the skin that was purpling.

Sean screamed again.

'Stop that,' Mr Colbert barked, 'You're making out it's worse than it is.'

'It hurts, sir,' Sean insisted, 'He hit me twice, sir.'

'Twice?'

'It was an accident,' Finn repeated.

Mr Colbert scanned the pitch. 'O'Hanlon, get up to the school and bring Miss and Mrs Pearse and a stretcher. Barrett, did you see what happened?'

Every boy on the field clustered around a trembling Finn, prone Sean and the kneeling Mr Colbert. Charlie pushed a shaking hand through his red hair, spiking it in sweaty tufts on his head.

'I was on the other side of the pitch, sir.' Charlie shot Finn an apologetic glance.

Hal, who hadn't heeded the order to fetch help, butted in, 'If Finn says it was an accident then an accident it was.'

'O'Hanlon, I told you to fetch a stretcher,' Mr Colbert roared.

Hal scowled and tramped off.

'While we're young, O'Hanlon,' Mr Colbert yelled and Hal broke into a lethargic jog.

Alasteir, who had come to spectate, spoke up. 'I saw what happened.'

Finn's heart banged against his ribs.

'Well?'

'It looked, sir, like Sean accidentally bumped Finn. Then Finn said Sean was cheating and started hitting him.'

'Is that what happened, Devoy?'

Finn screwed his mouth into a pout; Freddie spoke.

'It was never an accident, sir. O'Malley was cheating. He wasn't even aiming for the sliotar.'

'I was.'

'Then you better not let him on the team, sir, he's the worst shot ever.'

Sean groaned and rubbed his ankle.

'It hurts, sir. I think it's broken.'

'Jesus, Mary and Joseph.' Mr Colbert got to his feet. His small, round face was red, ready to pop. 'Trials are over. All of you, back to school. Except you three.' Mr Colbert swept his arm in an arc that gathered up Finn, Freddie and Alasteir. Finn fidgeted. Maybe Freddie had seen what happened. Or maybe he was doing what he hadn't before: standing up for Finn, friends together.

They stood before Mr Pearse's desk, three bottles balanced on a wall. Finn felt ready to topple, a single word would do it. Mr

Pearse drummed his fingers on his writing pad, looked between the three of them and back at Mr Colbert.

There was a timid knock on the door.

'Aye?'

The door opened and Mary Brigid slid into the gap.

'Come to let you know, Pat, the leg's not broken.'

'Thank you.'

The door closed again. Finn went back to studying the floor.

'I am entirely unsatisfied by the accounts given me,' Mr Pearse said, 'Blackwell, you claim it was a deliberate foul by O'Malley to provoke Devoy and you, Keane, say the opposite. Both cannot be true.' Mr Pearse sighed.

Mr Colbert whispered into the headmaster's ear.

'Blackwell, Keane, you are dismissed,' Mr Pearse ordered.

Alasteir made for the door. Freddie caught Finn's eye. Finn shook his head. It was his own fault for letting himself be riled. Freddie left too.

'Do you have anything to say, Devoy?' Mr Pearse asked.

'I was wrong to hit him but O'Malley was cheating; it was a deliberate foul.'

'And that upset your sense of honour?'

Finn wasn't sure he had such sensibilities but, guiltily, nodded anyway.

'Finn, you must learn,' Mr Pearse groaned, 'There are many ways to be a hero. Haven't I said as much before? None of them requiring you to batter a fellow pupil with your hurley. At least it was no serious harm. However, you disgraced yourself and that cannot be tolerated.' He paused. 'Mr Colbert was telling me what a skilful hurler you are, which is a pity, Finn, as, sure if I'm not going to have to ban you from representing St. Enda's.'

'Sir, please.'

'The matter is settled, Devoy.'

Finn skulked from the room.

Finn brooded over the punishment. He would have taken the cane or any amount of extra chores. This was a death blow to his hope of triumph in St Enda's name.

'You don't seem to be making much progress with this painting.' Mr Willie Pearse was at Finn's elbow, appraising his still life. 'Maybe you should try a different subject if your heart's not in fruit.'

The awkward silence was filled by the lunch bell, the clatter of chairs pushed back and the clap of easels folded away.

'Boys, make sure you've washed your brushes.'

Finn stood to leave. Mr Pearse laid a hand on his shoulder.

'Wait a minute, Finn.'

Finn sighed and sank back down. The rest of the class filed out.

Mr Pearse took the seat opposite.

'Finn, are you going to tell me whatever it is that's got a look on your face that would frighten the devil himself this morning?' Mr Pearse asked.

'Nothing, sir.'

'Could it be to do with this hurling ban I've been hearing of?'

Finn acquiesced with a glum nod.

'I see. You'll be thinking it's not fair?'

Finn shook his head.

'So it is fair?'

'I suppose...'

'But you wish it wasn't so?'

'Yes.'

'Would I be right in thinking Mr O'Malley was a friend to Mr MacDonnall and therefore an enemy of yours in days past?'

Finn's dropped gaze answered for him.

'Sure, I've some advice for you, Finn: keep your friends close and your enemies closer. If you can, make friends of your enemies and avoid repeating past woes.'

The clock ticked. From outside Finn could hear boys' laughter and the crack of a sliotar whacked by a hurley. Sweat pricked his forehead and his stomach bubbled as he recalled Richard's last smile, the one carved in his neck.

'Take heart,' Mr Pearse added, 'things that hurt us don't come but they go too.'

'Not in time for me to play in the championship, sir.'

Mr Pearse chuckled. 'We'll see. Now, are you dining or staying to try to make something of this sorry bowl of fruit?'

He smiled and Finn couldn't help smiling back. He picked up a brush and pasted it on the green block of colour that would perfectly match the apple if he could wash it right.

Sean was back from the school infirmary when Finn came up from prep that night. Hal and Charlie were in the dorm too. Sean was on his bed, Charlie pinning him down. Hal had Sean's crutch raised over his shoulder, about to drop the chopping blow.

'You did it on purpose, ya wee shite,' Hal was saying, 'Admit you did it to get Finn into bother or I'll knock shite out of ya, so I will.'

Sean's eyes were wide, his pupils large. In them Finn saw Hal's towering form, armed and ready to strike.

'Stop it.' Finn rushed into the room, slamming the door behind him, charging at Hal, snatching the crutch and flinging it across the room.

'What're you doing that for? He was gonna admit it,' Hal raged.

Finn said, 'You'll make things worse.'

'How can they be worse?' Charlie demanded, 'You're not allowed in the team because of his cheating. You should've broken his ankle, then they'd have to let you play; there'd be no one else.'

'It's too late.' Finn flopped on his bed and stared at Sean, still pinned by Charlie. Sean's eyes fixed on Finn. 'You're right,' Finn spat, 'I am an expert in what's fair and I'm being fair to you now. You better bloody remember this.'

Finn turned, saw Alasteir opening the door, heard the sound of a palm slapping flesh and a yelp that was Sean's. Alasteir stared at Finn.

Mr Pearse introduced Mrs Margaret Hutton in Irish. She was visiting St. Enda's to read from her translation of the *Táin*. Mr Pearse had insisted the lower school boys attend and opened the half day lecture up to the rest as an optional extra. Finn hadn't weighed the choices long; he could listen to the talk or sit on the sidelines, watching Charlie, Hal and the others charging about in a vigorous battle for the sliotar. The first round of the competition was being staged the following weekend and they were training hard. Besides, Finn's father had never read him the Cúchulainn sagas. All Finn knew was that Cúchulainn was a boy warrior, the greatest in Irish history. Cúchulainn was also Mr Pearse's special favourite; reasons aplenty to resign himself to the study hall on a sunny day.

Mrs Hutton laid a thick green book on the lectern. She was a youngish woman, small and delicate, with dark hair tied in a bun and glasses perched on her nose.

'Thank you, Mr Pearse. 'Tis a pleasure to be here at St. Enda's.' Speaking in Irish her voice was melodic, the phrases rippling out hypnotically. Then she switched to English and some of the music vanished from her words. 'I'm going to read from a section of the *Táin* I hope will interest you: The boyhood deeds of Cúchulainn, in particular, how Cúchulainn came to be so called.'

She turned a few thick pages and began to read. Finn listened as the story of Cúchulainn's first triumph unwound. In her stirring verse Mrs Hutton recounted how Cullan, the smith, invited King Conor to a great feast. On his journey there Conor encountered the child Setanta playing against fifty opponents and thrice gaining the goal. Impressed, Conor bade Setanta to attend the feast with them but, not satisfied his game was done, Setanta offered to join them later.

When the king arrived at the poor smith's house, Cullan asked whether all the party had arrived for he wished to loose his hound, a fearsome, savage creature which he kept to protect his meagre livelihood. Forgetting about Setanta, Conor bade Cullan to release his beast.

When Setanta arrived at the smith's doon* it was the furious hound that greeted him. But so skilled was Setanta that he killed the hound, throwing his playing ball into the dog's mouth with such force it tore through his body, allowing Setanta to hurl the hound against a stone pillar, slaying it. Hearing the fight, Conor, Cullan and the Ulster warriors

* fortified residence

hurried forth. Cullan, seeing the beast slain, bemoaned that he was now without protection. Realising his deed's consequence, Setanta vowed to raise a hound as savage as that he had killed and, until such a hound was trained, he himself would guard Cullan's property. King Conor declared this a just undertaking, adding:

> Hence, from this hour, I thee will designate
> *Cucullin, Hound of Cullan.*' 'Nay, not so,'
> Besought the child. 'I like my own name more,
> Namely, Setanta son of Soo-altim.'
> But Cathbad spake. 'O little lad,' he said,
> 'Reject not this. It is thy hero-name.
> The men of Erin and the men of Alba,
> Telling their famous tales, shall speak that name.
> Long as the wave-great sea shall girdle Erin
> Men's lips shall speak it; yea, the mouths of men
> In Erin and in Alba shall be full
> Of that renownéd name.' 'Then,' said the child,
> 'I take the name. I take it willingly.'
> And so it came to pass that from that hour
> Wherin he slew the hound, there clung to him
> This most distinguished name, Cucullin.

Mrs Hutton closed the book with a thump; applause rang out.

Mr Pearse rose. 'A thousand thanks to Mrs Hutton for reading so beautifully from such an eloquent translation of *An Táin*. We hope this will not be your last visit to St Enda's. And lads,' Mr Pearse's glance settled on Finn, 'you'll be glad to know we've purchased copies of Mrs Hutton's book; any of you wishing to read her full translation can collect one from me.'

Mr Plunkett began emptying the hall. Finn dawdled out, dazed by the revelation that Cúchulainn too had fought against having his name changed and, like himself, had come to embrace the new name which promised such greatness: the hero-name. Finn wanted to hold the book in his hands, be united with the legend of Cúchulainn but to do that he would have to visit Mr Pearse.

*

Finn loitered outside. He owed his mother a letter but wasn't in the mood. Hurling practise would be over soon; the players would troop back, their faces red, hair plastered to their foreheads, Charlie looking like he had a giant tomato for a head. It wouldn't make Finn laugh today. He kicked a pebble.

Mary Brigid appeared, a wicker basket balanced on her hip.

'Have you nothing better to do?'

Finn shrugged.

'Will you not give me a hand with the laundry, so?' she teased.

Finn hung back.

'You could at least offer to carry it, you so strong and me so weak,' she chided.

Finn squinted up. The sun was behind her and loose strands of auburn hair shimmered like wispy flames. He held out his arms for the basket.

They walked towards the outbuilding that housed the laundry.

'Did you hear Mrs Hutton?'

'Yes.'

'Well?'

'It was good,' Finn said in a hollow voice.

'I don't much care for the *Táin* myself. The women folk in it come off rather badly for my tastes. Of course it's an important part of Irish culture and Cúchulainn was a brave warrior but…'

'It's not fair,' Finn broke in.

'What's not?'

'How can I be a hero when I'm not allowed to play?'

'So it's a life-time ban he's given you?'

Finn avoided her probing eyes. Mary Brigid felt like a friend but really she was the sister of his headmaster.

'Sure, you should plead your case.'

Finn shook his head.

Mary Brigid reached out for the basket and set it down.

'I'll tell you a sisterly secret. Mind, this is just for yourself,' she cautioned. Seeing Finn nod she went on, 'Pat's impressed by people who fight their corner. He believes if you want a thing it's for you to make it happen. Do you see?'

Just like my father, Finn thought as he said, 'Yes.'

'Right,' she swept up the laundry. 'I think you'll find Pat in his study.' And off she went, swinging the laden basket like it was empty.

Finn knocked on the door.

'Aye.'

Mr Pearse was behind his desk.

'Finn, what can I be doing you for?'

Finn's courage buckled. 'Can I have one of Mrs Hutton's books, please?'

'You can, Finn.' Mr Pearse picked one from a stack.

'Thank you, sir.'

'Tá fáilte romhat*.'

Finn lingered.

'Is it something else?'

'He was a great hero, wasn't he, Cúchulainn?' Finn stammered.

'I think so.'

'Good at hurling too.'

'A champion, surely.' Pause. 'As you could be.'

'I don't think so, sir.'

'You have the skill and speed on the pitch. Haven't I seen it myself?'

'If I was that good I wouldn't have behaved in a way that's stopped me from playing, sir.'

'It's an awful thing, isn't it, Finn, to love a thing yet be kept from it?' Mr Pearse added.

'Yes, sir.'

'Tell me why you want to play.'

Finn gathered together the feelings that hurtled around inside him when he flew up the pitch, hurley in hand.

'When I play I feel like a hero,' he said at last.

'Being a hero isn't just grand fun, Finn. Heroes have responsibilities.'

---

* you're welcome

'I know, sir. I'm sorry I let you down. It won't happen again. Give me another chance and I'll prove myself to you.'

'You need only prove yourself to yourself,' Mr Pearse replied. 'A great man, one who leads others, is someone who does things for the right reasons and knows with certainty what those reasons are. He regrets nothing.'

'Like Cúchulainn. He had to kill the hound but when he saw he'd hurt someone he made it right.'

'Just so,' Mr Pearse agreed. He put his elbows on his desk and touched the tips of his fingers together; his eyes were unwavering. 'If I'm not letting you back in the team, won't I be hearing of it from now until I go to the grave, from Con, Willie and Mary Brigid too. And I'm especially afraid of Mary Brigid,' he added with a wry smile. 'You may rejoin the team, Finn, but as a reserve only. I don't think it fair to depose a fellow from his hard-won position, do you?'

'No, sir,' Finn said but the words tasted bitter.

'Perhaps you could inform Mr Colbert of this development.'

'Yes, sir. Thank you, sir.'

The referee blew his whistle and tossed the sliotar between the teams. Charlie won it for St Enda's and set off down the pitch, passing to Hal who returned it. Finn gripped the edge of the bench with straining fingers. Beside him Mr Colbert sat bolt upright, muttering the instructions Finn had heard him bestowing on the team in the dressing room, 'Play an attacking game, fight for possession, work as a team, go for goals, not points. Play cleanly.' Finn prayed to Cúchulainn they'd win. Charlie was running down the goal. He caught a pass Hal sent his way and flung the sliotar into the net. The goalie stood, arms outstretched, twisting his head in search of a ball that had already beaten him. Finn leapt off the bench and cheered as the score board flipped round.

Watching as one of the team was better than being a mere spectator and Finn hoped Mr Colbert might sub him on, only not for Charlie or Hal. If he played he'd rather it was with them, so they could share the victory. The game ran through his head the way he wanted it to go. He gets the sliotar, passes to Charlie who catches it high in the air, bringing it under control as Hal surges forward, snatching Charlie's pass on. Finn dodges around his opponents, taking up position in front of the goal. Hal flings the sliotar to him. Finn watches it falling, falling, straight to him. He scoops it out of the air, hurling it towards the goal seconds before the opponent's number fifteen is tackling him for a ball he no longer has. The sliotar flies straight. Cúchulainn himself couldn't have sent a truer shot on its way. It bounds into the goal as the referee blows his whistle and the scoreboard shows St Enda's as victors. That was how it should go.

By half-time it was clear St Enda's was the superior team and at full time Finn stood from his warm spot on the bench to slap his team mates on the back as they strolled by. He changed alone while Charlie, Hal and the others loudly relived their glory under the steamy spray.

Mr Colbert entered the changing room.

'We won, sir.'

'And in fine style.' Mr Colbert strutted around. When Finn said nothing more he halted in front of him. 'You're a might disappointed you didn't play.'

Finn avoided Mr Colbert's piercing eyes.

'Don't fret, Finn. We've a long way to the final yet, and, mind, I aim to get us there. Happen we'll be making use of you.'

St Enda's won their next three matches. Then they drew and had to replay. After a tense stand-off lasting for fifty-three of the sixty minutes, St Enda's took the lead and, with skill and daring, held their opponents at bay. Finn had played in two earlier matches, substituted at half-time to 'keep his arm in' as Mr Colbert put it, but in neither match did he score the winning goal. In the rematch he didn't play at all. But his team had made it to the semi-finals and he practised every spare minute.

The semi-final between St Enda's and Dublin Grammar was in November. The rain had been relentless the week before the match and when the boys took to the pitch grey clouds dowsed them in thick torrents that soaked their jerseys, leaving them chilled and shivering. Finn paced the sidelines, hugging himself and trying to keep his mind off the ice-sheet that clung to his back. On the field mud-caked figures sallied back and forth with no gusto. At half-time Mr Colbert reprimanded them, commanding them to play as if the wind was lifting them to victory.

'I wish the wind'd lift him somewhere,' Charlie grumbled in Finn's ear. 'It's not him out there half drowned. Jesus, I'm so cold I can't feel my feet.'

'At least you're playing.'

'Maybe someone'll get injured and he'll put you on,' Hal offered.

'No chance of you shamming a sprain, is there?' Finn half joked.

Hal laughed.

'You're better off on the bench, Finn, it's God awful out there,' Charlie moaned.

The chuntering boys trudged back into the deluge. Finn took up his spot on the bench again. He longed to don his duffle coat but, as Mr Colbert sat only in his kilt and school jersey, Finn daren't show his own weakness. He didn't imagine Cúchulainn ever wore a coat.

After an agonising thirty-four minutes St Enda's fired two shots in quick succession over the bar, putting them five points in the lead and the opposition relinquished the task as futile. When the referee blew his whistle thirty relieved boys squelched off the pitch. Finn was still at Mr Colbert's side when the master from Dublin Grammar joined them.

'That was a top match your boys played,' he said in a raspy voice.

'Yours too,' Mr Colbert replied, 'You were unlucky to lose.'

The master shook his head. 'The weather didn't help, but your lads had more spirit. I'm not ashamed to have lost because I'm certain I've lost to the winners of the Dublin Junior Hurling championship.' He extended his hand.

'We'll look forward to a rematch next year,' Mr Colbert said.

The master nodded and followed his bedraggled team into the changing room.

'Do you think that's right, sir? Are we going to win?'

Mr Colbert, who was not much taller than Finn now he'd starting growing, met him eyeball to eyeball. Finn felt the excitement of shared realisation.

'By the grace of God, Finn, I think we will.'

'He's got it!' Charlie bounded into the dorm, his tie swept over his shoulder, and plumped down onto Finn's bed.

'Who's got what?'

'Sean and mumps.'

'Oh.' Finn wanted to add 'good' but he'd forbade himself to wish evil on his enemies in keeping with Willie Pearse's advice.

'So that means you're in.'

'In what?'

'The team, you ass. Colbert's going to tell you so look surprised.'

Finn pushed aside the letter he was writing.

'We're going to be in the final together,' Charlie crowed.

'We're going to win together,' Finn corrected.

The morning of the final Mr Colbert paraded the team in their team colours and with their hurleys over their shoulders, ready for Mr Pearse's inspection.

As he crossed the study hall, his hard-soled shoes rapping on the floor, Mr Pearse swept his gaze over them, admiring his fine St Enda's boys turned out ready for the fight. Then he cleared his throat.

'No words can describe the pride I feel towards you as you hover on the edge of victory. For, win or lose, the victory is yours because, in playing a Gaelic sport you align yourselves with heroes past and ensure you become heroes of the future. Boys as brave, strong and true as yourselves will one day be heroes for Ireland.' Mr Pearse tipped Mr Colbert a wink and added, 'Of course, I hope you win. Ádh mór oraibh, a stócaigh*.'

A great crowd gathered for the match. Staff, students and parents from both teams filled the rickety wooden bleachers that had been erected around the pitch. Finn watched boys waving to their people who had turned out in their best winter coats on this crisp December afternoon to will their sons to victory. Banishing thoughts of his father, Finn moved to his attacking position.

The referee sounded a shrill note. The sliotar rolled between the two captains, Hal and a stocky boy with fierce eyes in the number five jersey for St Patrick's College. Hal was quickest, pouncing on the ball and flicking it behind him with barely a glance over his shoulder. Finn followed its trajectory, grinning as the sliotar fell to their waiting player, a wiry boy called Benson from Cork. The play was on. The battle begun.

Play was fast and ferocious. Frost had hardened the ground, making it slick with ice. Twice Finn fell and was left winded and with the cold sting of frozen grass on his legs. He pulled himself up and continued his rampage down field, up field, left, right, chasing the wily sliotar that flew a jagged course around the pitch. He tackled, took possession, passed, ran, tackled again, losing himself in wingless flight. After twenty minutes St Enda's were seven points ahead.

'Boys, you're playing well,' Mr Colbert said at halftime, 'but keep your guard up. Don't let them sneak through at the back. To lose from where we are now would be a shame. Stick to the set pieces, that's where you're strongest. Work together and they'll not break through.'

Finn chewed his orange segment. Sticky juice ran between his lips. He licked it up and swallowed the pulp. They marched back onto the pitch. Charlie flanked him on one side and Hal on the other.

'This is grand, isn't it?' Charlie said.

'Be grander if we win,' Hal barked.

'We will,' Finn replied.

---

* Good luck, lads

They lined up. The whistle peeped. The ball rolled between the captains but this time the keen-eyed number five swooped it up and set off at a gallop for the St Enda's goal. Three quick passes later and it was in the net, leaving Patrick Healy, their goalie, dazed. St Enda's lead was reduced to four points but four was plenty. They played on, the sliotar swapping sides half a dozen times in ten minutes but not making it into either goal. Finn didn't worry; they were leading. He dived into the fray, coming up with the sliotar this time. He twirled on the spot, searching for someone to pass to. Benson was to his right, close but with an opponent shadowing him. Charlie was open but a long way off. Finn wasn't sure he could throw that far. He played it back instead. The opponent saw the move and darted for the sliotar which was heading towards the St Enda's goal. Finn started a charge after it. His legs pumped like steam-powered pistons and his heart hammered; he chugged out clouds of frost-white breath. Keeping the enemy in his sights, Finn scooped up the ball and span round to find himself attacked from two sides. He had four seconds to release the sliotar. He scanned the field. Three seconds. Hal and Charlie zigzagged through the throng of green-shirted boys that surrounded them. Two seconds. The greenshirt on Finn's right was getting closer. Finn sprang into a run but the enemy stuck out his hurley and Finn tripped. The sliotar flew up over his head. Finn clattered to the ground, face first. Over the thunder of blood in his ears, he heard the piercing peep peep of a whistle and a scrum of voices cheering and jeering. He rolled onto his back. Hal's face hove into view.

'That's bloody torn it.' He offered Finn a hand and hauled him to his feet.

'What?'

'An own goal.'

Finn twisted round and saw Healy on his backside, having dived for, and missed, the sliotar which lay behind him.

'But he tripped me.'

'Try telling the bloody ref that.'

'That's not…' Finn stopped. He pulled away from Hal and took two steadying breaths.

'Fine,' he faced Hal, 'There's still one point in it and time for a brace of goals. Let's beat these cheaters fair and square.'

Hal grinned.

There was a throw-in. A greenshirt got there first but Charlie tackled him, won the sliotar and set off. After a quick foray through the St. Pat's half, Charlie knocked the ball over their goal but it was disallowed. There was another throw-in. As St Pat's fussed over who would take it Finn fidgeted, shifting his weight onto his right ankle. Pain raced up his leg. Balancing on his left foot, he bent down, digging his fingers beneath the sock bunched around his ankle. Pain on pain dizzied him.

'Finn, look about.' Benson, engulfed by greenshirts, was aiming the sliotar at him.

Finn snatched his hurley. The sliotar fell against it and Finn juggled the ball down before lobbing it to Charlie. Then Charlie to Hal, Hal to Benson, Benson to MacLeish, MacLeish to Jacobs. Jacobs was caught out by a greenshirt but Hal dealt with him. Finn hurtled down the pitch, every other step firing sharp spasms through his ankle. Hal flung the sliotar at him. Finn got enough touch on it to direct it at the St Pat's goal. It sailed in, a hawk diving on its prey, and the crowd erupted. There were four points in it again. Charlie and Hal crowded around Finn.

'That's it, the winner I'm sure,' Charlie said, slapping Finn's back.

'Hope so,' Finn said grimly.

'You alright?' Hal asked, seeing the whiteness around Finn's lips.

'Ankle hurts. I'm fine though.'

'Do you want to go off?'

'No!'

Five minutes of play remained. Finn hobbled about, counting down the seconds as waves of agony heaved his stomach and drench him in sweat. For one horrible moment St Pat's fought back with a flurry of passes and Finn feared they'd score, forcing extra time but the referee blew his whistle: St Enda's had won.

The team rushed Finn. Hal and Charlie hoisted him onto their uneven shoulders as a torrent of St Enda's boys flooded the pitch. Hands grabbed at Finn, pulling his legs, arms, shirt, as if touching him gave them a share in his triumph. Finn smothered a yelp and brushed aside another rip of pain when someone yanked his injured ankle. They'd won!

Finn admired the trophy, a gilded cup engraved with the figure of Cúchulainn, hurley raised. On the base was etched 'St Enda's – 1912', the first team to win. He leaned on his pillows with a sigh. His ankle was too sore to bear weight; Mary Brigid had diagnosed a bad sprain and while her tender ministrations were welcome her prescription of bed rest wasn't. Finn wanted to be sharing the glory of their triumph instead of languishing alone in the dorm. At least he had the trophy.

'Hallo Finn, how's the ankle?' Charlie appeared, a grin tattooed on his face.

'Alright, thanks.'

'Brought you something.' Charlie presented him with a square of folded card.

Finn opened it. Pasted inside was a photograph of the St Enda's hurling team, leaning on their sticks, still begrimed with the muck of their glorious battle. Finn scanned the image: Charlie and Hal: the victors. The heroes.

'It's great,' Finn said, returning it to Charlie.

'That's yours. We've all got one. I'm sending mine home. Reckon Mother'll be surprised. What about you?'

'I'll hang on to mine,' Finn said, setting it on his nightstand.

'And don't think you're keeping that.' Charlie pointed to the cup.

'I know.'

'Still, without you, we wouldn't have it.'

'We did it together.'

'Yeah. Next term's going to be a drag now the tournament's finished.'

'I'm sure there'll be something else,' Finn replied.

'Hope so.' Charlie raised his arm as though holding a sword, and yelled Cúchulainn's battle cry, 'All play! All sport!'

Hilary Term 1913

Dear Mother and Father,
I hope the new year has started well for you. Thank you for the presents. I have been inundated with requested from the other boys to borrow my annuals and the candy you sent was equally popular and is eaten up already. I will have to procure a vast supply to bring back next time I visit.

When the presents arrived Finn had imagined his father ranting about a thirteen year old being too grown up for Christmas gifts. But his mother, bless her, had won through so Finn hadn't spent the holidays without some home comforts.

He'd been relieved when his father ordered him to remain at St Enda's for Christmas. Finn wrote to reassure his mother that, as the Pearses lived at the Hermitage, he would have a family Christmas, with his school family.

Mrs Pearse had cooked a splendid dinner while Mary Brigid and Willie Pearse had conspired to provide each boy staying with a gift. Mary Brigid told Finn how she and Willie had disagreed over his present most. Willie had won with his gift of a new set of brushes so Finn could complete his latest painting, depicting Cúchulainn slaying Cullan's crazed hound. Mary Brigid promised Finn her present of a new copy of the *Táin*, his being dog-eared now, when she could find one she thought he'd like. Finn was glad the brushes had triumphed when he learnt this.

It had been a grand Christmas but Finn was eager for term to start. He willed the days to pass until his friends would return and the four of them could strut around their castle. Unfortunately the wind that blew them in would also bring Sean O'Malley and Alasteir Keane but Finn vowed to follow Cúchulainn's example and be jovial to them.

After adding his letter to the pile for posting that day, Finn slipped outside, heading for his spot amongst the grove of trees.

As he cleared the last tree obscuring his grove from view, Finn was surprised to see a girl sitting in the midst of his kingdom. She was at the foot of his chestnut, her back pressing his four letter name, her knees drawn to her chin, an open book resting on them. Finn watched as she pressed back pages flicked by the wind, smoothing them before retracing her place with a finger, juicy pink lips moving silently.

Finn shuffled his footing. A dry twig snapped under his boot. The girl raised her head. Her eyes met his. They were light hazel and framed with arched brows in a deep mahogany that matched her hair. Her features were dainty; a small upturned nose, a neat chin, creamy skin and, when she smiled, even, white teeth.

'Who are you?' he blurted.

'Cathleen Murphy. Who are you?' She spoke in Gaelic even though Finn had used English.

'Finn Devoy,' he replied, switching to Irish, 'What are you doing here?'

'You speak Irish?'

'I'm the best in my year, Mr Pearse says.' Finn took a step towards her, trying for a stern expression. 'Only teachers and pupils are allowed here.'

'Is that right?' Her eyes flickered over him and settled on the book. Her finger hovered a moment then jabbed the page. She turned to Finn.

'If you're so smart you can tell me what this says, Mr 'I'm-top-of-the-class'.'

Finn didn't move.

'I don't bite,' she teased, keeping to Irish.

Finn stepped forwards and read upside down, the word her finger underlined.

'It says, 'paradise'.'

'Paradise,' she repeated, 'What does it mean?'

Finn sat in front of her and spoke in English. 'It means heaven.'

'Well, why isn't he just saying neamh*?' She scowled. Her English was as fluent as Finn's but her accent made the words dance.

'It's not the same.'

'How?'

---

* heaven

'It just isn't.'

'That's stupid.' She tossed the book aside.

Finn picked it up. *A House of Pomegranates* by Oscar Wilde.

'It's stupidly hard,' she informed him.

Finn skimmed down the story of *The Young King*.

'Not as hard as reading *Íosagán* in Gaelic,' he said, holding the volume out to her.

At his confession she smiled and took the book.

'I didn't think you were a native Irish speaker. Still, you're pretty good.'

'As good as you in English?'

'Of course not.'

'So why don't you speak English all the time?'

'I've been living in Westmeath with my aunty since my mammy died. She only speaks Irish.'

Finn tore up a handful of grass. 'Oh.'

'It's alright, it's a while she's been dead.'

'Why are you here now?'

'I'm starting at St Ita's this term. Mr Pearse arranged it for my father. He's Michael Murphy.'

'The gardener?'

'Aye. So I've as much right as you to this spot,' Cathleen replied.

'Sorry if I was rude. I wasn't expecting to see anyone here,' Finn explained.

'You're back early, aren't you?'

'I didn't go home. My family's in New York.'

'America?' Cathleen's eyes brightened, 'What's it like?'

'Not that different to here but bigger, taller. I like here better, though.'

'Why?'

'It's my home.'

She studied him.

'I bet you didn't like it at first. I don't. Nobody likes change. Especially when things get changed for you.'

'I suppose,' Finn agreed, 'But once you've made friends you'll be fine.'

'Will you be my friend?'

'Well...'

‘Or don’t you want a girl for a friend?’

‘That’s not…’

‘If I can beat you at something, sure, you’ll be my friend?’

‘Beat me at what?’

‘Bet I can climb this tree higher than you.’ Cathleen smacked the bark of the chestnut. ‘Unless you’re afeared of heights.’

Finn jumped up. ‘Course not.’

Feet scraping the bark and hands scrabbling for grip, Finn hauled himself from branch to branch. Cathleen was above, racing to the top. Finn hadn’t climbed a tree since he’d scaled the little apple in their New York garden. Now, half way up the chestnut, Finn realised that was a sapling compared to this redwood. He didn’t remember any stories of Cúchulainn climbing trees but he was sure not even a giant sequoia would have been too tall for him. Finn charged himself with not looking down. Overhead, Cathleen clambered monkey-like, merry laughter and the sound of rustling skirts drifting down to him. Finn forced himself higher, ignoring the splinters piercing his palms. He dragged himself over a fat branch.

Cathleen’s hazel eyes greeted him. ‘I won’t have you beating me.’

She stood on tiptoes, reaching for the branch above. The breeze gusted. The navy wool of Cathleen’s skirts billowed like sails then whipped back with a clap. She tottered, fighting for balance. Her feet slipping, she tumbled, a starfish of arms, legs and tendrils of hair. Finn squeezed his eyes shut and waited for the thump of her body breaking below. When he heard nothing he made himself check. Cathleen was dangling from the branch they were on. Her face, flushed with thrilling peril, gazed up. She swung there, her legs kicking, a swimmer propelling herself to the surface.

Finn grabbed her wrists.

‘What’re you doing?’

‘Helping.’

‘You are not.’

She pulled free from his grasp, hung one-handed, reached out and took a new grip further along the branch. Her legs stopped treading air; she hung motionless, her eyes shining, her mouth shaping a smile. Finn sat back. Cathleen flipped her other hand over and glanced down. Finn followed her gaze, gauged the drop to be twenty feet.

'Let me help.' This time he only offered his hand.

'And have you win?' She began to swing her legs, this time together, with increasing rhythm. After a few swoops she used the momentum to haul herself up, getting her elbows on the branch and hooking her arms over it. She pressed her weight down through her wrists and locked her arms, lifting herself waist-high to the branch. She flung a leg over and sat straddling the bough.

'You're looking pale, there.' She covered one of his hands with her own, 'Are you alright?'

Finn felt a tremble fluttering through her cold fingers.

'Are you?'

'Aye, course.' She snatched her hand off his.

'We should get down.'

'Not 'til I've beaten you.' She stood, stretched again for the bough overhead, and, walking her feet up the trunk while hanging from the branch, scrambled onto it, some half squirrel-half bat creature.

'Alright,' Finn called, 'You win. Let's get down.'

'After you,' she shouted, 'Unless you're needing my help.'

In answer Finn started down, checking every foothold and digging his fingers deep into cracks scoring the bark. When he reached the bottom he watched as Cathleen hopped from bough to bough, hand and toeholds opening up in the trunk wherever she put her feet or fingers. At the last fork in the trunk she held out her hand.

'You can help now.'

She was three feet off the ground.

Finn took her hand and she sprang down.

'Thank you.'

Finn craned his neck. Through the maze of branches he traced a path that led to where Cathleen had tumbled, snapping twigs and making a gap that she left behind like part of her still hung there.

'You'll be my friend now.'

Finn's words were sharp. 'You should've let me help.'

'Didn't I do just that?'

'Only when you didn't need it,' he huffed.

'What do you suppose would happen to me, if I was forever being helped, when there wasn't someone to lend his hand?' Cathleen shook her head, her hair whipping her cheeks. 'It's not a laoch♣ I'm wanting but a cara♦. There's a difference like your paradise and heaven. Will you be walking me home now?' She set off, her question unanswered.

They strolled through the park, Cathleen leading, Finn feeling less cross as his eyes tracked the hypnotic swish of her glossy hair. They stopped at the gardener's house by the west gate.

'Are we friends, so?' This time her voice was softer.

Finn noticed there were gold flecks in the hazel of her eyes.

'Finn's got a girlfriend.'

'Haven't.'

'I saw you talking to her,' Charlie accused.

'She's not my girlfriend.'

'Who is she, then?'

'A St Ita's girl.'

'Who is?' Hal sat at the table and started shovelling in porridge.

'Finn's girlfriend,' Freddie explained, not taking his eyes from his book.

'You've got a girlfriend?' Hal spluttered through a mouthful of oaty mush.

'No!'

'I saw you talking to her,' Charlie repeated.

'I was saying hello.'

'Came to see you specially, did she?' Charlie laughed.

'Cathleen's father's the gardener. She came to see him after church.'

'Oh, aye, on first name terms with her,' Hal teased.

♣ hero

♦ friend

'I met her before term started and...'

'Now she's your girlfriend,' Charlie deduced.

Finn banged his spoon down.

Freddie said, 'He's only jealous; there's no one eejit enough to fancy him.'

'Not true,' Charlie snapped.

'Something putting you off your porridge, boys?' Willie Pearse had crossed the dining room at the sound of raised voices and was at Finn's elbow.

'No, sir.' Finn slunk into his seat.

'Then eat up. You'll need your strength if you're after joining the Fianna Éireann. Mr Colbert won't be taking weaklings, to be sure.'

Mr Pearse moved into the background and Finn, grimacing at the lumpy bowlful, plunged in his spoon.

'So you're joining?' Hal asked.

Finn said, 'Can't think of anything else to do now the hurling season's over.'

Alasteir, who sat with them despite their efforts to shrug him off, butted in.

'Is that the only reason you want to join?'

Finn hesitated. 'It'll be a gas.'

'It's just the Irish boy scouts, isn't it?' Charlie joked, 'You'll be spending your time tying knots.'

'I've heard it's quite military. Are you getting ready to join an army when you finish school?' Alasteir persisted in his squawking voice.

Finn gulped down his porridge.

'An army? What…?'

'You can't if you join the Fianna,' Freddie interrupted. 'You have to vow never to serve in the British Army, who oppress nations like Ireland to maintain their empire. That lets you out, Charlie.'

Charlie bristled. 'Doesn't. Fecked if I want to join the bleeding army.'

'I thought your father was…'

'So what?'

'Well, I'm with you,' Hal said, slapping Finn's back, 'All that shooting, hunting and camping. What a lark.'

Freddie snapped his book shut. 'Yous don't know a thing. It's not a lark.'

'Course not,' Finn fudged. Like Hal, he'd pictured himself trekking through the mountains, working up the skills Cúchulainn had mastered before the age of six.

'What then?' Charlie demanded.

'A boy who joins the Fianna Éireann pledges his life to freeing Ireland. He declares himself strong, true and pure, like the real Fianna,' Freddie paused, 'It's a great honour and a lifelong commitment.'

Charlie barked, 'Where do I sign up? Anyway, how'd you get to know so much about it?'

'Reading. Really broadens the mind. Try it. Yours could do with a stretch.' Freddie strode off.

'What's bitten him?' Hal asked, spattering porridge everywhere.

'He's keen is all,' Finn defended. Out of the corner of his eye he spotted Alasteir reaching for Freddie's book. He slammed his hand down on the cover and drew it towards himself. Alasteir's hand skulked back under the table.

The book was the *Fianna Handbook* by Constance Markievicz, the countess who gave half day lectures at St Enda's. It was she who had founded the Fianna movement. Finn studied the cover; his mind was made up. It would be the start of a new adventure.

The Fianna Éireann met in the gymnasium, a converted stable that sat square and squat behind the Hermitage. Mr Colbert greeted them in military fashion. Towering beside him was an almost unrecognisable Madam Markievicz. Finn gaped. Her usual elegant crepe dress with ruff sleeves, lace trim and detailed embroidery had been replaced by a uniform of trousers, tunic and brat, topped with a slouch hat. The only nod to her gender and social standing was the feathers that adorned the hat's brim.

The Countess was flanked by David Reddin and Michael Western, seniors, sixteen and with only two more precious terms at St Enda's. Both wore the Fianna Éireann dress uniform of dark green kilt, saffron cloak and green jersey and sported the Fianna Éireann badge, a flaming sun pierced by a rapier. The words, 'Fianna Éireann' and the motto, 'Strength in our hands, Truth on our tongues and Purity in our hearts' encircled the sun. They stood as guard of honour to the Countess, their founder and ultimate leader. Behind them, pinned on the back wall was the Fianna Éireann flag, a vivid blue with the same flaming sun motif, this time rising from a corner, as the boys in the Fianna would rise for Ireland.

Mr Colbert spoke. 'Welcome to An Fianna Éireann. By committing yourselves to the Fianna you dedicate yourselves to a noble cause, one for which you must be willing to fight with your dying breath, as past legions of Fianna have done. Before we begin Countess Markievicz wishes to address you.' He stepped aside.

'Thank you, Mr Colbert,' she nodded, 'Boys, I'm sure you know of the Cúchulainn legend and it was with that in mind that I founded the Fianna Éireann for I believe the strength, courage and devotion of the boys of Ireland will bring freedom and peace to its people. In fighting for your land as Cúchulainn did, protecting it from enemies without and within, you do Ireland the greatest of services. And be not mistaken, boys: we will be fighting.'

The Countess whipped a pistol from her belt and held it overhead. There was a gasp from those who hadn't had the privilege of encountering a battle-readied Countess. Seeing the gun, Finn remembered the incident at Mr MacDermott's house and a thrill of fear ran through him.

'Thanks to my papa I'm a dashed good shot and I'll be making sure all of you are too.' She holstered her weapon and gestured to David Reddin. 'I'll now ask Mr Reddin, your school captain and captain of the Fianna at St Enda's, to speak. David.'

David Reddin strode forward. He was a tall, lean lad with a man's shoulders already. His jaw set firm and his blue eyes fixing the assembled boys with a steady gaze, he commanded easily. Finn had been at the assembly last term when Mr Pearse announced the results of the election that won David the school captaincy for a second year. David was the most senior boy in the school, one to respect from afar; Finn had never spoken to him. Now, as he looked over the gathered recruits, Finn felt David's eyes settle on him.

'Grand to see so many of you eager to join the Red Branch, our band of the Fianna Éireann. Your willingness and enthusiasm is, as Madam Markievicz has said, what makes Ireland great and by joining the Fianna you'll ensure she becomes even greater, as well as having some fun,' he winked at Finn, 'I'm sure you'll want to know what you're letting yourselves in for so I'll tell you what we're about and what we've planned this year.'

They would be drilled, David explained, like real soldiers, using rifles, the mention of which making Madam Markievicz nodded gleefully. Their eyes would become keen, their bodies strong and their minds resolute. Finn listened to the promised adventures, picturing himself, haversack on his back, knife strapped to his waist, running through the hills, a cross between Sitting Bull and Cúchulainn.

'You should only join if you truly believe this is for you,' David finished, bobbing his head to Finn.

There was some applause then Mr Colbert invited them to inspect the equipment laid out to illustrate the skills they would master during their expeditions with the Red Branch. Hal and Charlie wandered over to examine the kit. Finn hesitated a minute, watching the Countess bent in discussion with Mr Colbert, wondering at the two so mismatched sides of her life. Only when she had taken her leave did Finn join his pals by the display of equipment.

There were knives, axes, flint fire lighters, cooking pots and mess tins, tools, tents and bed rolls. A rifle was propped up in the corner. Its barrel gleamed blackly and the butt was the warm brown of wood worn smooth.

'What d'ya think, Finn?' Hal asked.

Finn eyed the gun. 'Definitely. Charlie?'

'Why not?' Charlie said.

'Where's Freddie got too?' Hal wondered.

Finn swivelled his head and saw Freddie chatting with David Reddin.

'Since when's he so chummy with our Dave?' Charlie muttered.

Finn crossed the room. As he approached he caught the end of Freddie's sentence.

'…return to action and see the English off.'

David slapped Freddie's back and chuckled but straightened himself when he caught Finn staring. Freddie took off his spectacles and made a show of polishing them.

'Finn Devoy, our junior hurling champ,' David said, offering his hand, 'Hope we'll see you in the seniors next year.'

Finn's face heated up as he pressed his hand into David's and squeezed hard enough, he hoped, to show David he was ready for senior hurling and the Fianna Éireann. 'If I'm picked.'

'There's no doubt,' David returned, 'Freddie was telling me you hail from New York.'

'Yes.'

'Your father's Michael Devoy?'

'Yes.' Finn searched David's face. 'He's Irish, though.'

'Isn't he, just,' David replied, then hurried on. 'So are you with us?'

'Absolutely.'

'Grand. It's the likes of you we're wanting.' David shook Finn's hand again, 'Excuse me, I must have a wee word with Mr Colbert.'

'What were you jawing about?' Finn demanded as David moved off.

'Nothing,' Freddie said.

'Why did he ask about my father?'

Freddie shrugged. 'No idea.'

Needing extra money for his uniform and kit, that evening Finn wrote home of his plans to join the Fianna Éireann. He mentioned David Reddin too, asking, 'Did Father know of him?' and posted the letter before curfew.

Finn lay awake, listening to Hal snoring worse than a horse with a cold and brooding over a dread he couldn't pin in place. To his left Sean slept and snuffled. Since Finn had stopped Hal braying him, Sean had given up his grudge, become half friendly, even going with them to the meeting and saying he would pledge to the Fianna. Alasteir, however, had been strangely absent when they'd set off for the gymnasium. Finn sat up and studied the greasy blonde hair flopped on Alasteir's pillow. He was polite, but there was always a sneer in his words and a coldness in his eyes. At least with Richard it had been open warfare. Alasteir was more like the enemy within that the Countess had spoken of.

Finn transferred his gaze to Freddie's bed. What had he been talking to David Reddin about? The phrase 'return to action' hummed in Finn's brain as he recalled the guilty red flush on Freddie's face.

A book sat on Freddie's nightstand. Finn crept out of bed. It was the Fianna handbook. Finn pictured the Countess, her gun drawn, as he angled the book into a shaft of moonlight. Freddie had it open at an essay on the organisation's aims. There were pencil underlinings: 'At your feet, you, the best and noblest of Ireland's children, is laid the task of winning freedom for Ireland. This one true goal of the Fianna Éireann must be achieved, and I believe, will be achieved, no matter if the price be suffering and pain.'

The words 'freedom for Ireland' had been double-lined. Finn returned the book, crawled into bed and remained awake until dawn.

His mother's reply came. She enclosed a banker's draft signed in his father's hand, for his expenses with the Fianna Éireann. She begged him to be careful. He must follow instructions and not wander off when trekking. She pleaded with him to be wary of the guns. And no, his father didn't know of the Reddin boy. Perhaps the connection lay with David's father, was he also a doctor? Cheque in hand and determined to get a better answer, Finn went scouting for Mary Brigid.

It was the slack time of the day, when most of the boys were doing prep so she was in the family room. Finn heard the sweet sound of a harp. He waited for a break in the music before tapping on the door.

'Come in.'

Finn did.

'Finn, isn't it?' Mary Brigid greeted him, 'You'll have to do me a sketch of yourself so I can keep a mind of what you look like, I see you so little these days.'

Finn blushed. 'Sorry.'

'I'm only having your leg. What can I do for you?'

Finn handed her the banker's draft.

'It's for my Fianna stuff.'

'Another recruit?'

'Yes.'

'It'll keep you out of trouble, I suppose.' She took the cheque from him. 'I'll tell Mr Colbert you can have what you need.' She opened the bureau, withdrew the accounts ledger and made the entry, 'We must keep things right,' she said as her pen scratched the paper.

While she wrote Finn raked the room with his eyes. On the sideboard was *An Claidheamh Soluis*, an Irish language newspaper. He picked it up and read the headlines with ease, proud of his fluent Gaelic. There were articles on Irish culture, sport, art and politics. Finn opened it to the letters page. Most started with, 'Dear Sir' but some had titles, one of which was, 'Return to Action'.

'Finn, are you listening?'

Finn jerked his head up.

'I said, 'is there anything else or can I get back to my music?''

'Sorry.' Finn glanced at the paper.

'Do you want to take that?'

'Can I?'

'You can. Pat's read it and God knows I had enough of it when he was editor. He used to read me every blessed issue before going to press.'

'Mr Pearse was the editor?'

'Aye, he wasn't born a headmaster,' Mary Brigid laughed, 'Now away with you so I can do something useful.' She swept him from the room, the paper tucked under his arm.

It was cold and raining; Finn wandered through the deserted park to his spot where, sheltered under a Scots Pine, he unfolded the newspaper. The letter, from a Mr O'Connor of

Dublin, was in reply to another. Mr O'Connor was protesting the weakened Third Home Rule Act that was being pushed through Parliament. Finn remembered Mr MacDermott's lecture on the topic. Home Rule was when Ireland would have her own government. This letter, though, said the Third Home Rule Bill offered such limited powers that it was of less value than the ink that would write it out. Mr O'Connor suggested the British government needed to be taught that Ireland would not put up with English oppression. His method: return to action.

Finn tossed the paper aside. It was like reading a detective story to find the last page missing. He fiddled in his coat pocket for the nearly-empty packet of cigarettes left over from the last time he, Charlie and Hal had sneaked out for a smoke. He stroked a match over the pine's coarse bark and touched the flame to the cigarette, letting his thoughts drift with the smoke.

'Finn Devoy, what's this?' Cathleen appeared from behind a tree. 'Smoking? Your Mr Pearse won't be happy.'

Finn scowled.

'Still, I won't tell him. If you're giving me one.'

She sat beside him, tucking her skirts around her knees to keep out the dreich drizzle.

'It's my last.'

'You'll have to share, so.' Cathleen held out her hand, fingers splayed. Finn passed her the cigarette.

She inhaled, blew a cloud of soft white smoke then took up the newspaper and started flapping the pages, reaching the back and closing the paper without pausing.

'What're you reading that for?'

'No reason. What're you doing here today?'

'My da's been sick, a fever, but it's broke now.'

'Oh.' Finn didn't know what to say. He'd only seen her a few times since their tree climb.

'So what have you been up to?' she asked.

'I've joined the Fianna Éireann. At least, I will, tomorrow.'

'Good for you,' she said, taking another draw on the cigarette before returning it. She stood. 'I best be going.'

Finn scrambled to his feet and they faced each other.

'Good luck for tomorrow,' Cathleen said. She lunged forward and there was the warm pressure of her lips on his cheek. Then she was dashing through the trees, leaping fallen branches and ducking low-hanging ones, until she was out of sight.

Twenty-five boys gathered in the gymnasium for the swearing-in ceremony, all in their kilt uniforms. The new recruits gazed enviously at those serving members who swaggered under the brooches and dirks given once the pledge was taken. David Reddin and Mr Colbert were to officiate. The Countess had the final honour of issuing the Fianna knife to each boy once he was sworn in.

Order was called. The pledged volunteers, under Mr Colbert's shoddy conducting and with one boy squeezing a set of Irish bagpipes, sang the Fianna song:

On for freedom Fianna Éireann,
Set we our faces to the dawning day.
That day in our own land, when strength and daring,
Shall end forever more the Saxon's sway.

David took the floor. 'Comrades, before us stand eleven who would join our ranks. I recommend they be accepted. Do I have a second?'

Patrick Healy, the junior hurling team's mousey-haired goalkeeper stepped forward from the company of Fianna members. 'I second, Captain Reddin.'

'Thank you, Corporal Healy.'

Patrick nodded and fell in. A shiver of excitement ran up Finn's back and across his shoulders.

David addressed the new recruits.

'It has been proposed and seconded that you be welcomed into the ranks of the St Enda's battalion of the Fianna Éireann, known as the Red Branch. If any of you have any doubts about joining declare them now.' David paused politely. 'Very well. Raise your right hands. A Fianna boy is; patriotic, reliable, diligent, kind, obedient, cheerful, thrifty, brave, clean, humble, temperate and punctual.'

Eleven trembling voices repeated the words. Then alphabetically the boys were called forward to make their pledge and receive their pin and knife, after which they proudly joined the ranks.

'Do you, Finn Devoy, willingly and of your own choosing, pledge yourself to the Fianna Éireann?'

'I do.'

'Do you accept this brooch, the badge of the Fianna, and all the responsibility it portends?'

'I do.'

'Will you swear the oath here, before witnesses?'

Finn recited the words he had memorised last night.

'I promise to work with all my strength, courage and determination towards the independence of Ireland. This work I vow to continue until Ireland is free from foreign rule. I also hereby undertake never to serve the British Armed Forces.'

David pinned the brooch to Finn's cloak. 'I accept your oath on behalf of the Fianna Éireann of St Enda's. I give you this badge so all who see it know of your purpose.'

He stood back and the Countess stepped up.

'And I give you this blade that with it you may cut Ireland from the ropes that bind her.' Madam Markievicz handed Finn the knife and placed her right hand across her heart; Finn mirrored the gesture. Together they repeated the Fianna Éireann motto.

'Strength in our hands, truth on our tongues and purity in our hearts.'

She shook Finn's hand with a firm grip. 'Welcome to the Red Branch, young man.'

'Please sir, Mr Pearse says can he borrow Finn?'

Mr MacDonagh turned from the blackboard to the first year messenger.

'If he must.'

Blanking the stares of his classmates, Finn followed the boy.

'Did Mr Pearse say why he wants me?'

The lad shook his head and dashed off.

Mr Pearse's office door was ajar; Finn knocked then poked his head round.

'Finn, come in.'

Finn stood in front of the desk.

'Please, sit down, Finn. This morning I received a letter from your father.' From the desk Mr Pearse selected a sheet of paper.

Finn sank into the nearest chair. 'My father?'

'Don't fret. I merely thought you'd be interested in what he says about you,' Mr Pearse continued.

Finn squirmed.

Mr Pearse unfolded the letter. 'Perhaps I should explain. I wrote, telling your father what excellent progress you've made, particularly with the Fianna which I felt would be of interest to him, having a military past himself.'

Finn sat forward. Military past?

Mr Pearse skimmed the page. 'Here, 'I am pleased Finn is making the most of every advantaged afforded him by your establishment. It can only be to his benefit that he has embraced the education and exercise available at St Enda's. I trust he will excel in the Fianna Éireann for it will bring him skills sure to be of use to him later in life, perhaps even resulting in a cause for pride.' After that he talks of other matters, nationhood and so on. I know your father is a busy man with little time for correspondence so on this rare occasion of him writing me a lengthy reply I thought I'd share his personal comments with you.'

Finn gaped at Mr Pearse. His father, who telegraphed him curt commands, wrote, at length, to Mr Pearse. Finn's throbbing chest reminded him to breathe.

'I hope, Finn, there's not embarrassment in this for you?'

'No, sir. Thank you, sir.'

'One more thing, Finn. I have a place in Connemara, a wee holiday cottage built as a retreat, for myself and you boys. Your father indicates that you won't be going home at Easter. I thought perhaps you'd like to accompany me to the cottage. Willie will likely come too and it's chance for you to see Ireland unspoiled and unfettered. It's in Rosmuc, a place of wild beauty; jagged mountains, glassy loughs, rich boglands.

Truly inspiring. You'd do some fine paintings of the scenery there. I could suggest it in my next letter to your father.'

Finn mumbled, 'Thank you, sir,' stepped into the hallway and stared at Íosagán for a full minute before he was steady enough to return to class.

The next few weeks were dominated by Fianna training. Strutting around the grounds in their drill uniform of olive shirt, navy breeches known as 'knicks' and dark green slouch hats, the Red Branch became the precisely tuned unit that was the St Enda's Fianna Éireann. With rifles raised they patrolled, ready to defend their school, leaving Finn no time to further unravel the mystery of his father.

Once they had perfected marching, Mr Colbert set about their other skills. Over three weekends they learnt survival basics. By the end of the third weekend, Finn was so exhausted he could barely tie his shoes, let alone rig up another tent, scratched all over from crawling through brambles and sniffling with a cold caught after marching in the rain. Finn understood now the pain and suffering the handbook mentioned.

But he had to admit, as he sat, sneezing and coughing, over a hot breakfast served by Mary Brigid and eaten at a table, not squatting on damp moss, that it was fun. He'd made the bull's eye three times in a row yesterday and Mr Colbert said he had the promise of an excellent marksman. His aching muscles would ease and the itchy rash, got from tussling with poison ivy, fade. His real concern was that he was no nearer to answering certain nagging questions.

At half-term Mr Colbert announced the Red Branch were to embark on a weeklong expedition in woods a day's march south.

Finn, Hal, Freddie and Charlie began packing.

'This'll be bloody grand,' Hal said, cramming his kit higgledy-piggledy into his haversack.

'Hope it isn't too cold,' Charlie said.

'Think Cúchulainn moaned about the cold?' Hal scoffed.

Charlie chuntered and squeezed an extra jersey into his pack.

'Going on a trip?' Alasteir was in the doorway.

'We're camping with the Fianna,' Finn replied.

'Off to play soldier, how nice. Take extra socks, it's going to be bitter this week, lads.' Alasteir's face twisted into a smirk and he strode out.

'Shite,' Hal muttered.

Charlie said, 'He's a nasty piece of work alright.'

'Who cares?' Freddie said, 'We're off on an adventure.'

Finn dragged his gaze from the empty doorway and threw a glance to Sean's bed. 'Is he coming?'

'Going home,' Charlie replied.

Finn lifted his head. 'Yeah, a grand adventure.'

The Wicklow mountains loomed, purple and regal, as David Reddin led the troop through Dublin and on a winding course past hamlets and farms until they were deep in the countryside, Healy, the steadfast corporal, carrying the standard that proclaimed their proud purpose.

Mr Colbert had wanted to make an impressive sight through town so insisted they wore their dress uniform. Now the wind had picked up and a chill breeze was snaking around Finn's legs, making an endurance test of the kilts.

They'd set off at eight; it was gone noon before David halted the company under the brittle protection of a clump of gorse and instructed them to eat lunch. Finn rubbed his legs and wound the brat, normally worn pinned over the left shoulder, around them. He overheard Patrick suggesting they light fires and Mr Colbert replying that there wasn't time, unless they wanted to pitch their tents in the dark.

By late afternoon the sky was full of rain-soggy clouds. Finn felt himself blown back by angry squalls. The bold battalion that had set out with their heads high, singing the Fianna Éireann song, had been reduced to a ragged column of boys, their heads bowed to the wind and their voices silenced. When the rain broke in thick torrents Mr Colbert ordered the boys into a field. They would camp there and move on in the morning when the weather would surely be better.

Wrestling against the gale to pitch the tents, Finn thought of the Lilliputians trying to pin down a thrashing Gulliver. Every time he managed to secure one corner the tent would rear up, yanking itself free. Finally the tents were pitched but the boys were soaked.

'Remember,' Mr Colbert charged them, 'A Fianna warrior is strong enough to survive a wee storm.'

'It's alright for him,' Charlie hissed, 'He's wearing long trousers.'

The tents were two-man affairs and nine of them clung to the hillside, fluttering and twitching. Finn and Freddie crawled into one, fought their way out of their sopping clothes and dug into their sleeping bags where they lay in darkness, the howling wind shaking the tent.

'Jesus, I'm starving,' Finn said.

'I've chocolate in my pack. Want some?'

'Thanks.'

There was rustling and then the plop of something landing on Finn's sleeping bag. He picked up the bar, broke a chunk off and tossed it back.

'Why did you join the Fianna?' Finn asked as they munched.

'Why did you?'

'For adventure.'

'How's that working out for you, so?'

'Bloody great,' Finn groaned, 'Come on, what about you?'

'Same reason.'

'I don't believe you.'

'Why not?'

'Because you like your adventures between the pages of a book.'

'I fancied a change.'

They chewed so more.

'Freddie, what's fillte go gníomhú*?' Finn put the tormenting phrase into Gaelic as a ruse.

'Where did you hear that?' Freddie's words came slowly, wrestled from him.

---

* return to action

'*An Claidheah Soluis.*'

'What did it say?'

'Not much. Come on, Freddie, I know you know.'

'Why should I know?'

'You always know stuff like that,' Finn said.

'Ask Mr Pearse.' There was more rustling, a snap and the remaining chocolate slapped onto Finn's chest. 'Finish it. I'm going to sleep.'

Freddie rolled over. Finn sucked the last of the chocolate as the storm cried out: return to action, return to…

The next morning the wind had dropped and the clouds vanished. Freddie's sleeping bag was empty; Finn found him hanging their wet kilts to dry. There were three fires burning, tea boiling over one, eggs frying on the second and two boys toasting bread at the third.

'Sure, this is more like it.' Hal rambled over, chomping his toast, and slapped Finn on the back. 'You better get some grub while there's some to be got.'

Hot food made Finn feel human and when Mr Colbert gave the order to break camp he was pleased to get back on the trail.

'Finn, can you do me a wee favour?' David was shoulder to shoulder with him, 'Will you carry the colours? Patrick's hurt his arm.'

'Of course, Captain.' Finn took the flagpole from David.

Mr Colbert blew his whistle, they fell in and stepped out, this time with Finn up front, beside David.

The singing resumed and Finn raised his voice but churning in his mind was last night's bungled conversation with Freddie.

'Captain?'

'Yes, Private.'

'Is your father a doctor?'

'A doctor? No, he's a solicitor. Why do you ask, Finn?'

'You mentioned my father before. It sounded like, well, I thought, maybe you knew him, perhaps because your father was a doctor too.'

'Aye. No, but I've heard of your father, from my father. He's a great man, Finn, doing great things.' David tipped Finn a wink.

The rest of the week was cold but dry. Mr Colbert's campsite was a sheltered glen with a clean stream. There was firewood easily gathered and the troop busied themselves fishing and trapping. They caught three trout, a rabbit and a fat pigeon which supplemented their rations as well as feeding their fantasy of themselves as warriors hiding from the enemy and living well while they were about it.

On day two Mr Colbert marked out a target range. He re-drilled them on assembling, loading and cleaning their rifles before ordering target practice. Finn learnt to correct for a cross wind and after three days he could hit even the forty foot target with dependable accuracy, an encouraging achievement for his week's ordeal.

'Did you have a good time?' Alasteir asked as four ragamuffins barely recognisable as Finn, Freddie, Charlie and Hal trudged into the dorm.

'Aye,' Hal said, 'Finn proved himself star of the show.'

'How so?' Alasteir laid down his newspaper. Finn saw it was *An Claidheah Soluis* but he couldn't tell if it was the one in which he'd ringed the 'Return to Action' letter.

'It was nothing,' he said.

'He's a dead eye with a rifle now,' Hal continued, 'You don't want to get on his bad side.'

'Wouldn't dream of it,' Alasteir sniffed, fluttering out of the dorm.

'What'd you say that for?' Finn demanded, going to Alasteir's bed.

'What?'

'About getting on my bad side. You know he's, well, I don't know, but I feel he's always watching me.' Finn picked up the paper.

'That's called paranoia, so it is,' Freddie said.

'You would know. You know everything. Almost,' Finn retorted as he scanned the newspaper. It wasn't his. 'Anyway, just because I'm paranoid, doesn't mean he's not watching.'

'What's that?' Charlie nodded to the paper.

Finn chucked it to him.

'What's Alasteir doing with this?' Charlie pondered, 'Didn't know he was such a patriot.'

'I don't think he is,' Finn said.

Freddie twirled his finger at his temple, miming crazy; Finn, seeing Sean in the doorway, clutching a suitcase and wearing his coat, rushed to greet him.

'Hallo, Sean. How was your week?'

'Not as exciting as yours, from what I've heard. Bet it was great.'

'Don't reckon I'd call freezing my arse off great,' Charlie grumbled.

'Get away with you, it was a fine time, you softy,' Hal mocked.

Freddie threw his haversack under his bed and left the room with a book in his hand, slamming the door behind him.

Finn had a tricky piece of prep that night and was the last to finish. Upstairs the dorm appeared empty, tidy and ready for inspection. Except the door to his bedside cabinet was open. Maybe Hal or Charlie had been checking for cigarettes; they had taken to going into the grounds for a fly smoke before curfew. A movement drew Finn's eye. He stepped into the room.

'Who's there?'

Alasteir's long neck and greasy blonde head jerked up from Finn's bedside.

'Hope you don't mind but I was looking for another nib.' Alasteir waved his pen.

'I haven't any,' Finn said, 'and you should've asked me.'

'Sorry,' Alasteir said. He bent down. 'I've made a bit of a mess here; I'll tidy it for you.'

Finn rounded his bed and saw the contents of his nightstand on the floor. Face up were two photographs, one showing his mother and father on their wedding day and another with the three of them under the apple tree. The letters his mother had sent littered the parquet. A reply Finn had started but not finished was uppermost.

'These must be your people.' Alasteir picked up the photograph. 'That's your father, is it?'

'Get off.' Finn snatched the picture. 'Leave my things alone.'

'I was going to…'

'I'll do it.'

'Suit yourself.' Alasteir's voice was clipped. He got to his feet, his lanky form still inches taller than Finn despite his recent growth, and about faced.

Finn knelt and started cramming things into his locker. That was when he realised Alasteir was snooping. The photographs had been folded in paper and tucked inside the *Táin* Mary Brigid had given him and he knew he'd put his letter to his mother in an envelop.

Finn was crouching down, peering through railings. He could hear voices, one was his father's.

He was in a hall, dirty yellow light staining his clothes and face. An unfamiliar voice spat words. 'Home Rule…return to action…blow the fuckers…you're not the Michael Devoy I knew… Fremantle…you're a fucking…'

There was a crash then stillness. Finn saw a table, tea things smashed: a gun, cold, black and ready.

Finn was at the bottom of a deep pit. Faces ringed the hole, staring in at him, one was his father's. He reached down, gun in his hand.

Bang. Bang. Bang.

Finn sat up in bed. The bell was clanging.

'How-way, Finn, or you'll miss breakfast,' Hal called.

The dream replayed in his mind; Finn couldn't move.

Finn made a list. Even inked in it wasn't very substantial:

Return to action – Home Rule?

Mr MacDermott

Tom something – the fight

Free Mantle – My father went there
Everybody asks about my father
My father was a great man (David Reddin knows of him)
My father has a military past (Mr Pearse)
My father is proud I've joined the Fianna
David said I would do great things, like my father (what things?) NB – did Mr MacDermott say something similar?
My father is a Fenian (something to do with the Fianna?)

Leaving one line blank Finn added:
Freddie knows something
Freddie said I should ask Mr Pearse
My father and Mr Pearse write to each other (nationhood?)
David knows something
THE GUN
Alasteir!

'Devoy, that does not appear to be a list of the chemical properties of the compounds on the board,' Mr Slattery boomed behind Finn's shoulder.

Finn snapped his exercise book closed.

'Sorry, sir.'

Mr Slattery held out his bony hand.

'It's nothing, sir.'

Mr Slattery gestured again for the book. Finn gave it over. Mr Slattery's eyes, bloodshot behind his wire-rimmed spectacles, skimmed the words.

'Bejesus, nothing, indeed?' He swept the classroom with a glance; all other heads were bent to their books. 'Carry on, lads. Finn, with me!'

Finn cursed as he followed the skeletal chemistry master into the hall.

'What is this?' Mr Slattery asked when the door was closed.

'Nothing, sir.'

'It looks to me like a list of clues.'

Finn could hardly deny it.

'Mother Mary, I think we'd better see Mr Pearse.'

'Please, sir, I'm sorry. I'll stay in over lunch and finish my work.'

Mr Slattery shook his head in a slow left-right arc. 'We need Mr Pearse.'

Mr Pearse was not in his office, nor in the classroom where he taught Irish, literature, law and Latin depending on the hour and the day. Mary Brigid hadn't seen him since breakfast. Mr Willie Pearse suggested he might have gone into Dublin. Mrs Pearse was sure her son was in the Hermitage. Finn traipsed after Mr Slattery, his eyes on the bald spot at the back of the master's skull. With every dead end the expression on Mr Slattery's face became more unyielding and the strands of hair he trained over his patchy scalp more disordered.

They circumnavigated the gardens. Among the vegetable patches they discovered Mr Pearse with Cathleen's father. Mr Murphy was wearing a pair of overalls tucked inside a pair of boots so brown Finn couldn't be sure if that was their colour or a layer of mud. Mr Pearse was in his usual suit plus galoshes. Mr Murphy had a cap pulled low over his eyes. Mr Pearse's hair was ruffling in the breeze.

'Mr Pearse, a word, please?' Mr Slattery gasped.

'We have things decided here, do we, Michael?'

'Aye, Mr Pearse,' the gardener said, leaning on his spade.

Mr Slattery took Mr Pearse aside. Finn stood apart, studying Mr Murphy. He noticed the eyes, buried by folds of leathery skin that told of a life outdoors in Irish weather, were the same light hazel as Cathleen's. Mr Murphy regarded Finn with his own curious eye as he rolled a thin cigarette.

'You'll be Finn Devoy.'

Finn nodded.

Mr Murphy beckoned to him.

'My Cathleen's a good lass,' he said when Finn was closer.

Finn thought of the kiss she'd planted on his cheek.

'Finn,' Mr Slattery called, 'Come with us.'

Finn jog-trotted off, unsure if he'd escaped or been captured.

In the hall Mr Slattery faced Mr Pearse.

'If you'll excuse me, Pat, I must get back to my class.' He attempted to smooth his hair across his crown.

'Thank you, Peter, for bringing this to me.'

Mr Pearse led Finn into his study, pulled two chairs nearer the fireplace, took one and gestured for Finn to take the other. He opened Finn's notebook and scanned the list.

'Do I gather you have been labouring under a mystery?'

Finn pressed his lips together.

'Maybe I can help clear this matter so troubling it interferes with your lessons, to Mr Slattery's grave concern, as he desires to cover periodic table before Easter.'

Finn remained silent.

'Shall I take the liberty of explaining one or two things? Home Rule, for instance?'

'Home Rule means Ireland would have her own government,' Finn chanted.

'That's so. What do you know of previous Home Rule bills?'

Finn shrugged

'Previous bills, raised in the Commons, have been thrown out by the Lords. With this latest there has been a change in our favour; the Lords will not be able to cast aside the third act. If it is accepted by the Commons it will pass.'

'So Ireland will have Home Rule?'

'Hopefully, but this latest bill grants an Irish Parliament strictly limited powers. Some say it's not worth having.'

'What do you think, sir?'

'Any course that helps Ireland to independence is worthy.'

'Including a return to action?'

Mr Pearse weighed the question.

'Perhaps.'

'Does that mean war, sir?'

Mr Pearse's brow creased.

'It means what is says: taking action the like of which has been taken before.'

'What has my father got to do with this?'

'That's not for me to say. I can tell you this, Finn: your father is committed to Irish independence, perhaps more than any Irishman alive today. It is a matter on which we both feel strongly and for which we will both fight, by whatever means we have. For myself, at present, that means my work here at Scoil Éanna,' Mr Pearse rested Finn's list in his lap, 'I think it would be prudent of me to write to your father, suggesting he explain certain things to you.' Mr Pearse got to his feet, 'Until I hear from him concentrate on your studies and your duties with the Fianna.'

'Yes, sir.'

'Freddie, could you do me a favour?'

They were alone in the dorm. Finn had waited two days for the right moment to ask. Hand in his pocket, he crossed his fingers.

'Depends.'

'I caught Alasteir poking through my stuff last week, nosy git. Thought we should teach him to keep out of other's things.'

'What've you planned?'

'A good scare with a couple of the Fianna rifles. They won't be loaded,' Finn added, 'but I need you to help me smuggle them out tomorrow night.'

Freddie shook his head. 'Ask Charlie or Hal.'

'What about helping each other? Isn't that what friends do?' Finn cursed himself for playing on any leftover guilt Freddie might have but there was nothing else for it.

Freddie's trembling lips formed the reply one letter at a time.

'O.K.'

The meeting finished with singing the Fianna Éireann song and restating their pledge before the flag. As the cadets set about tidying away the kit, Freddie engaged David in conversation. 'What shall I say to him?' Freddie had asked. Finn said he didn't give a fig what Freddie and David blethered about as long as it kept David distracted. Finn watched them for a minute, then presented himself with a salute.

'Captain, would you like me to see to the gun cupboard tonight?'

David stopped mid sentence. Finn thought he was going to break off with Freddie but, seeing Finn's panic, Freddie piped up.

'I don't understand, if the Lords can't reject the bill why are people so mithered about it?'

David hesitated then reached for his key ring. 'Aye, thanks Finn. It's because…'

Finn slipped away. In the gun store he checked off the weapons and ammunition with the inventory and stacked things as they should be.

'You're in charge tonight, are you, Finn?' Mr Colbert appeared.

'David asked me to lock up. He's in deep with Freddie, sir.'

'So I see. Well,' Mr Colbert cast an eye over Finn's shoulder, 'you seem to be doing a grand job. Goodnight.'

''Night, sir.'

With Mr Colbert gone Finn closed the cabinet, rattled the key in the hole but made sure it didn't lock. He returned it to David and left.

As he walked through the brisk March air, Finn slipped a hand into his pocket and clutched the pair of small, hard .22 rounds he had lifted from the box and added to the column labelled 'ammunition rounds shot in target practise', being sure to cramp up his writing like Mr Colbert's.

Finn waited out of sight for Freddie and David to appear. They separated at the door. When David's square shoulders had merged into the dark Finn emerged.

'Thought I'd never get away,' Freddie muttered, 'Did you manage?'

'Aye. Come on.'

While Freddie kept guard, Finn climbed in through the window with the broken latch and retrieved two rifles from the gun cupboard, sticking them, butt first, through the window, before climbing out.

Freddie lined the rifles against the wall as Finn dropped to the ground.

'Alright?' Finn asked.

Freddie picked up a rifle, shot back the bolt and peered into the empty breech.

'Told you they wouldn't be loaded,' Finn hissed, his fingers straying again to the two smooth-nosed cylinders in his pocket.

*

Finn listened for the dorm's chorus of snores and snuffles. It was after midnight when he dared move. Across the room Freddie stirred and they sat, mummies awoken in their tomb. They dressed, pulling on warm jumpers and thick socks but not shoes. Finn also grabbed his Fianna knife. Freddie had been for smuggling chloroform from the lab and using it to knock Alasteir unconscious but Finn had argued that moving an anaesthetised body would be impossible so they'd settled on a different tactic. It was part of their Fianna Éireann training: assessing strategies; predicting outcomes.

Finn leant across Alasteir's bed, pressed a hand over his nose and mouth and the blade to Alasteir's scrawny throat. Unable to breathe, Alasteir's eyes opened. Moonlight glinted in them.

'Sssh,' Finn hissed, 'You're going to come with us. Don't make a sound and you won't get hurt.'

Alasteir squirmed; Freddie was sitting on his lower half.

Finn pressed the knife deeper. 'There are two of us and one of you so don't be stupid.'

Alasteir, his eyes bulging, nodded and, still held by Finn, got up. In seconds they had gagged him and bound his wrists. With the knife jabbed between his shoulders, Alasteir was steered downstairs and out the front door.

In silence the trio marched to the clearing where Finn and Freddie had left the guns in some bushes. Pressing Alasteir with his knife, Finn forced him to his knees, his long spindly legs folding like a heron's. Freddie collected the guns and handed one to Finn. Finn pointed it at Alasteir and directed Freddie to remove the gag.

'Why were you going through my things the other day?'

'I…was looking for a nib,' Alasteir stammered.

'Between the pages of my *Táin*?' Finn mocked, 'What were you really looking for?'

'This is ridiculous.' Alasteir tried to get to his feet.

Freddie forced him down again.

'We're too far from the house for anyone to hear you and I'm pointing a gun at your head so you better tell me the truth,' Finn commanded.

'You wouldn't shoot me.'

'Wouldn't I?'

Alasteir shook his head.

Finn whacked Alasteir in the ribs with the butt of the gun. There was a satisfying whump. Alasteir bent forward, moaning.

'Why were you looking at photos of my parents? Why were you reading my letters?'

'Curious,' Alasteir coughed.

'Is that why you were reading *An Claidheah Soluis* too?'

Alasteir shuddered.

'Tell me.' Finn raised the gun and hit Alasteir's stomach again.

Alasteir spat blood onto the grass. A dark dribble of it crawled down his chin.

'I wanted to know what you were telling your father.'

'My father?' Finn's heart throbbed. 'Why?'

'He knows.' Alasteir jerked his head at Freddie. 'Or ask your new pal David or Mr Pearse.'

Freddie avoided Finn's stare.

'You both know. One of you is going to tell me.' Finn took the two rounds from his pocket. With slow purposefulness he opened up the rifle and slotted each bullet into the breech, pressing them down with his thumb until they clicked into place. He pulled the bolt to cock it and took aim. Freddie and Alasteir were no more than six feet away. Alasteir let out a gulping sob.

'Finn, you said they wouldn't be loaded,' Freddie shrieked.

'This one is now. Freddie, I have to know. Tell me so we can get back to bed.' Finn's legs were shaking.

'I can't, I swore.'

'I've a right to know. This is about my father.'

Freddie flushed. Alasteir's eyes darted between them.

'Freddie, please, help me this time,' Finn said cryptically, 'A chairde*, remember?'

---

* friends

Freddie drew a breath. 'Your father's an important man, head of an American organisation called the Clan na Gael. They're Irishmen who want Irish independence.'

'They're murderers,' Alasteir spat.

'What?'

'They run around with bombs and guns, killing innocent people.' As Alasteir spoke his accent morphed, becoming harsh: English. 'Your father tells them what to do. Now he's chief he doesn't have to get his hands dirty, not that a bit of muck bothers him any. It's why he sent you here, so you'd be made into one of them, like he is and his father was. A murdering 'Taig.'

'A what?'

Alasteir whooped a reedy cry. 'You don't even know that? It means Catholic, you…'

Freddie interrupted. 'It's not like that, Finn. Your father's a great man. It isn't his fault the English side with the Orangemen rather than listening to reason.'

'Reason?' Alasteir raged, 'So it's reasonable to murder women and children?'

'He wouldn't!' But a pistol on a table amid broken cups and saucers flashed before Finn.

'Ask him about the Combermere Barracks attack,' Alasteir charged.

Finn glanced at Freddie who shrugged.

'He ordered a bombing, had his Fenian friends plant it in the camp commissary. My mother and sister were inside. Your father slaughtered them as surely as if it was he who lighted the fuse and all from the safety of his New York home. He's a cowardly dog and you're nothing but his runty offspring.'

Finn's grip on the gun had slackened but he stiffened it now.

'Father sent me to St Enda's so I could spy on you,' Alasteir went on.

'You're not Irish?'

'My people are Antrim Protestants, we go by Kane, not Keane. My father's a British cavalry major.'

Finn aimed the gun.

'Go on,' Alasteir taunted, 'Shoot me, be a big man like your daddy.'

Finn rested his finger on the trigger.

'Finn, feck, don't do it. They'll hang you.'

Finn sighted along the barrel.

'Finn, Jesus' sake, this is an execution.' Freddie's voice cracked. 'There'll be no excusing it.'

'Why didn't you tell me?' Finn shouted, 'You knew all along.'

'I didn't, I swear. My cousin told me at Christmas, after he joined the IRB.'

'What's that?'

'Irish Republican Brotherhood. The Clan are their American branch. He went over, met your da. I didn't know 'til he came back, honestly, Finn. He swore me to secrecy.'

'That's why you joined the Fianna.'

'Aye, thought I'd do my bit,' Freddie explained. He lowered his voice, 'Come on, Finn, put the gun down. He's not worth it, so he's not.'

'He's a spy.' Finn steadied the rifle. An easy squeeze would end it.

...Orange boy...Proddie swine...We'll not have any fecking Orangemen around here, Finn-boy...

There'd been no reason for it, if only his father had bothered to explain to him. The gun wilted in his hand. There were better ways to be a hero.

Voices from the Hermitage filled the darkness. Finn swivelled his head. Lamps darted among the trees, racing towards them. Finn turned back, saw Alasteir struggle up and kick Freddie who fell into the bushes and didn't move. Alasteir, head down, charged Finn, barging him off his feet. The gun, Finn's finger feathering the trigger, exploded into the blackness.

Finn opened his eyes. Alasteir was lying on him. Finn thought he'd shot him until Alasteir groaned. The clatter beyond the clearing came on at an urgent pace. Finn shoved Alasteir aside. Freddie's stocking feet were sticking up through the grass. Finn scrambled to him. His eyes were closed and his face, washed with moonlight, blanched and bloodless. Finn put his arms under him. His fingers touched something wet and sticky. When he pulled them back they were daubed with a thick inky liquid.

'What in the name of Mother Mary is going on?'

Finn faced the party of Mr Slattery, Mr Colbert, Mr Plunkett and both Mr Pearses, dressed in their night attire with lanterns raised. Behind Willie Pearse Finn saw Charlie. He must have discovered the empty beds and woke the whole blasted school. Finn cursed under his breath.

'Sir, Freddie's hurt,' he called.

Willie Pearse and Mr Colbert dropped onto their hands and knees.

'Pat, his head's split open. We must get him to the house,' Willie said.

Mr Pearse stood like a statue in the moonlight, one hand on his head, the other holding a lantern aloft, eyes vacant.

'Pat!'

'Aye. Take him. Joe, take Con's place. Con, you and Peter stay with me.'

With a lolling Freddie in his arms, Willie raced towards school, Mr Plunkett dogging him, his dressing gown flapping, a giant bat flying low.

Alasteir, on the grass where Finn had thrown him, let out a theatrical moan. Finn retrieved Freddie's rifle, stepped over Alasteir to pick up his own and handed both to Mr Colbert who took them in grim silence before casting a steely glance to Mr Pearse.

'Finn, what's happened here?' Mr Pearse's voice was hollow.

'Truth on our tongues,' Mr Colbert murmured.

'Alasteir's an English spy.'

Alasteir groaned again.

'Get up, lad, there's nothing matter with you,' Mr Slattery bellowed. He grabbed Alasteir and hauled him up. Alasteir writhed in his grip, a fish on a hook.

'His father sent him to snoop on me because of my father.' Finn fixed his eyes on Mr Pearse whose face was ashen and shadow-scored by the lantern, 'I thought to make him confess.'

'You weren't going to shoot him, were you, Finn?' Mr Pearse words were measured but his voice trembled.

Finn didn't know. 'He was trying to escape. He knocked into me and the gun went off.'

'You took these from the Fianna store?' Mr Colbert accused.

'Yes, sir.'

'You'll face a court-martial for that, Devoy.'

'Con, not now,' Mr Pearse begged, 'Let's go to my office. Peter, for the love of Mary, untie Mr Keane's hands.'

Mr Pearse listened to Finn's story without interjection. Finn made a full, though not entirely frank, confession; he was defending St Enda's and upholding his Fianna pledge. Personal quests were not mentioned. He made it clear Freddie was involved only as a loyal Fianna and breathed easier when Mary Brigid reported that Freddie had come round and, apart from a deep gash and a bad headache, was in fine fettle.

'Is that all, Finn?'

'Yes, sir. I beg your pardon for the trouble I've caused.'

'Well, there's no loss of life, thank the Lord, and you've done the school some service, though not how I'd have wished it done. Nevertheless, I will speak to Mr Keane or Kane, and, assuming he repeats his confession without a gun under his nose, I'll be asking him to leave. I'll telegram his father first thing. And yours.'

'Yes, sir.'

'I expect he will visit.'

Finn raised his head and held his shoulders back.

'There will be the court-martial for taking the guns, too.'

Finn nodded.

'But now 'tis time you were in bed.'

Alasteir was in the hallway with Mr Slattery standing guard. Finn pivoted on his heel and marched off.

The dorm lights were on. Hal and Charlie sat on Alasteir's bed. Alasteir's things littered the ruffled coverlet. Sean was sitting up, rubbing away sleep.

As Finn entered they pounced on him, firing questions.

'What happened? Are you alright? Where's Freddie?'

'How did you get him out there?'

'Did you swipe the guns from the store? Sure, won't you cop it for that?'

'It is true? Alasteir's a spy?'

Sean didn't join in the interrogation but he watched and listened.

Finn dropped onto his own bed and ground grit and exhaustion around his eyeballs.

'Look.' Charlie handed Finn an envelop, bearing a London postal frank. 'He was a spy,' Charlie crowed, skimming the letter, 'It's from his father. Listen, 'Thank you for the information that our friend has joined the Fianna.' He's meaning you, Finn. 'You must be ever watchful. Send me further news when you have it.' Bugger to hell.'

'Alasteir was a spy?' Sean murmured.

'His father's in the British army; he sent him here because his mother...' Finn stopped.

'And our laddie's unmasked the bastard.' Hal slapped Finn's shoulder. 'You're a proper hero.'

'Some bloody hero. Freddie's hurt. They're going to court-martial me over the guns and Mr Pearse is calling in my father.'

'Won't he be proud of you?' Charlie said.

Finn took the knife from the belt of his trousers. It shook in his hands. He tossed it on the bed. The smell of cordite assaulted his nose. He gagged.

'Proud? Oh, aye.'

'What do you mean?' Charlie asked.

Finn told them what he'd learnt and saw the respect on their faces.

'Good thing you were here to spy on the spy,' Charlie said.

'All this time and you never said owt,' Hal mused.

Finn sat on his hands to hide their trembling and didn't correct his friends.

Sean came across to Finn and offered his hand. 'I never did like him. I'm glad you got rid of him.'

Finn caught himself nearly asking whether Sean meant Richard or Alasteir. But only Freddie knew about Richard.

*

By break the next day the school hummed with gossip about the night's adventure. Rumour dallied with truth. Alasteir's father received several promotions, ending up a major general while Finn's father was everything from a patriotic Irish Irelander to a bold Fenian rebel. It was also revealed that Alasteir was four years older than he said, his father lying to ensure he ended up in the same form as Finn. Somehow Mr Pearse kept the story of Combermere from circulating but he couldn't stop the boys from admiring Finn's daring and his reckless actions were heartily congratulated. At some point during morning lessons Alasteir's things were removed from the dorm and the spy vanished, leaving only sensational stories behind. Finn wished he could escape with equal ease.

On Saturday Finn presented himself, in full dress uniform, to the drill hall, at 09:00. Behind an imposing table Mr Colbert, David Reddin and Michael Western, the three senior officers of the St Enda's company, sat waiting for him. Finn was interrogated over misappropriating the guns. Charlie, Hal and Sean were called but having no part in events, added nothing incriminating. Then Freddie was called. His head was wrapped like a swami's but he was recovering. He confirmed Finn had acted to protect the school. He didn't mention Finn loading the rifle. In absence of any evidence it was accepted that the gun had been stowed away loaded.

'The penalty for the charges brought against you, of deception and the unsanctioned deployment of Fianna arms, is dismissal from the Fianna Éireann. Before I pass sentence do you have anything to say, Devoy?' Mr Colbert barked.

The door banged open. Finn turned. Countess Markievicz, dressed in her civvies of tweed skirt and matching jacket, her hat askew, filled the doorway.

'Halt, cease and desist.'

Mr Colbert rose. 'Madam, I…'

'Never mind the bluster, Colbert,' she snapped, tearing into the room, 'I've received an urgent message that there's a court-martial sitting. I command you adjourn proceedings and enlighten me. You may wait outside, young man.' The Countess nodded to Finn.

Pacing up and down in front of the hall, Finn listened to voices a notch too low for him to hear more than the odd cry of, 'nonsense' and, 'poppycock'. After ten minutes the door was flung open by a grinning Countess.

'That's that taken care of, young man,' she said, 'Mr Colbert will inform you of the particulars. Excuse me, I'm late for an appointment.'

She made to sweep past Finn who ducked into her path.

'Madam, please, who was it sent you the message?'

'Your saviour, young man, is Mr Pearse, who thinks most highly of you. As I do myself, having heard of your courageous actions.' She slapped Finn's shoulder, 'Keep up your mettle,' and off she strode.

The Countess had insisted there was no justification for casting one so brave and resourceful from the ranks. Mr Colbert bowed to her judgement and it was decided that Finn's punishment be the withdrawal of his full membership, signalled by the return of his pin and knife, lasting thirty days and his being prohibited from using firearms for sixty days. He would do the battalion's menial duties for the duration of his punishment; scrubbing the gymnasium, preparing rations, blacking boots and pressing kilts, thanking Mr Pearse and the Countess at every stroke.

The reply to Mr Pearse's telegram came the day after the court-martial. His father was expected in Dublin within the week. Finn threw himself into a new painting, spending spare minutes, his hands stained red and green, in the easy company of Willie Pearse who never mentioning 'the incident'. The painting showed the Hermitage from the front with the sun rising behind it. Finn had chosen it because of the significance of the rising sun motif to the Fianna Éireann.

'You know, Finn,' Willie said one afternoon, 'I was wondering if you'd a mind to do something daring with the colour.'

Finn set his brush down. He had been working with a fine badger's hair on the window frames, having already completed the shades of grey brick that made up the building.

'Sir?'

'What do you know of colour symbolism, Finn? For example, green is a deeply symbolic colour. It has overtones of nature, new life, but did you know that it's also the colour of Ireland?'

Finn realised he did know it. Green abounded; their uniforms, the school crest, even the study hall paint scheme.

'You're planning a sunrise,' Willie continued, 'Have you heard the phrase 'Celtic Dawn', Finn?'

'No, sir.'

'It means the rising of all things Irish; music, language, culture, histories and legends. Perhaps you see a significance there to guide your use of colour.'

'Thank you, sir,' Finn said, his attention focused on the white space surrounding his Hermitage.

Willie Pearse drifted away. Finn continued to stare at the painting. Slowly the Celtic Dawn symbolism emerged from darkness, becoming crucial to the painting's message about the rising up of all things Irish. He raised his brush.

By teatime a yellow sun peeped over the corner of the Hermitage, spreading golden orange light. This light faded, not through orange and red to lilac and blue, but to a pale yellow that ran into swathes of white cloud. Gradually the clouds took on a greenish tint, growing brighter and deeper until the heavens were verdant. For the bushes and grasses of the school gardens Finn used the reds, oranges and umbers he had mixed for the sky. Mr Pearse wandered back.

'What do you think, sir?'

'What do you think?' Mr Pearse returned.

Finn squinted at the canvas. 'The foreground's not right.'

'Something in this corner, perhaps?'

'What, sir?'

'I've always had a liking for lilies,' Mr Pearse mused, 'There are some beauties out now. They'd look grand here.' He indicated the empty quarter bottom left. 'If a thing's worth doing, it's worth doing right, Finn.'

It did need something; why not lilies? If they were Mr Pearse's favourites it would be a fair tribute to the master whose creativity had guided his brushes. Finn nodded.

'Righto, I'll away to the flower beds, but don't tell Mary Brigid I robbed her prize blooms,' Willie Pearse joked.

It took Finn three days to paint in the lilies but with the livid green sky, the golden dawn rising, the hard-hewn building in the centre and the fiery foreground cut through with the clean white flowers he was satisfied. Reversing the canvas, he scribbled the title he'd decided on: Green Dawn at St Enda's.

Finn was in Mr Plunkett's French class when his father arrived. Mr Pearse himself collected Finn who solemnly followed him to his office where the door stood ajar revealing his father by the fireside. Mr Pearse coaxed Finn inside. His father faced them.

'Thank you, Pat.'

Mr Pearse bobbed his head. 'Will you take tea?'

'That would be grand.'

Mr Pearse retreated, leaving Finn and his father who, though still tall and dark, seemed shrunken and worn, perhaps from the journey. Finn held himself as on parade, his stomach churning, his mouth dry.

His father extended a hand.

'Good to see you, Finn,' he said as they shook, 'Although I'm sorry to be called here on a matter as grave as that Mr Pearse has recounted.'

'Sorry for any inconvenience, Father.'

'Sit, Finn.'

Finn folded himself into a chair.

'I intend telling you what you want to know but before I do you must accept that once knowing you will not be able to 'unknow'; things will be changed forever for you. Do you understand?' His father studied him with flinty eyes.

Memories of the gun, himself loading and pointing it at Alasteir, caused sweat to ooze across Finn's back. He berated himself. His father was speaking to him like a man. It was upon him to act as one.

'Yes, Father.'

Satisfied with the hardness of Finn's voice, his father settled in his chair.

'You know my father's story of exile, Finn. What you don't know is that he swore to punish the English, making them suffer as he had. This he accomplished by becoming a member of the Fenian Brotherhood, an organisation of displaced Irishmen determined to strike for Ireland's freedom. It was a cause that never left his heart, one he passed to me when I was old enough.'

'How old?'

'Hmm, you're thirteen, are you not?'

'Yes, Father.'

'I'd be a little, not much, older than yourself.'

'So you joined?'

'I did. The Brotherhood became the Clan na Gael. I believe you've heard of them?' Without waiting for Finn's reply his father continued, 'Shortly thereafter a rescue mission was sent by the Clan to Fremantle, Western Australia, where some Fenians had been imprisoned. My father raise the money to fund the rescue but he was frail; I went in his stead. I was sixteen. The mission was a success and I am proud to have been part of it. Today, as Clan president, I head the fight to free Ireland.'

Someone tapped on the door.

His father crossed the room in two strides and flung open the door.

'Pat said you'd take tea.' Mary Brigid set a tray on Mr Pearse's desk. 'If you need anything else, Finn, let me know.'

Finn tried to smile at her.

'Thank you, Miss Pearse.' His father's brusque voice chased Mary Brigid from the room.

With their teacups to hand, his father continued. 'I trust I was not mistaken in keeping this from you until now.'

Finn shuddered at the words.

'But 'tis serious, dangerous work on which I am engaged, though not without its rewards, the greatest of which I hope to live to see. I sent you to St Enda's, Finn, because it's a fine school and Mr Pearse a fine teacher. Here you will become, are becoming, the son I was to my father, one who will carry on my work when I am no longer able.'

But the praise didn't erase Finn's need to hurt his father in return for the silence that had cost so much.

'What about the Combermere Barracks bombing?'

His father was sipping tea. He appraised Finn over the cup, his dark eyes and heavy brows misted by rising vapours.

'In war there are casualties. There've been Irish deaths aplenty at the hands of the British. If we're to convince them of our might and our commitment to the cause we must meet them on equal terms. 'Tis they decree those are terms of violence; we can only respond. Do not think, Finn, that any such action is taken frivolously but that such action must be, and will continue to be, taken is not to be questioned.' His father had set aside his tea to jab a finger while he spoke. Now he leaned back and, resting his elbows on the chair arms, drummed his fingertips together. 'There is something else you should know. While my conscience is clear, there is no doubt the English would see me swinging from the gibbet. My visits to Ireland have to be discrete.' His father stood. 'I return to New York tonight. There is no need to stay longer, is there, Finn? We are straight on all points, are we not?'

Finn put his untasted tea down. His father's words implied things were clear and plain but to Finn they remained hazy.

'Yes, sir. But… I wished you'd told me sooner, Father.'

'Damnit, Finn, no damage has been done. You did the right thing with this Kane boy and there's an end to it.'

'So it's right to kill an enemy?'

'If there's no other recourse.'

'What if later you find out he wasn't the enemy at all?'

His father snorted. 'We don't make mistakes like that, Finn. What do you think we are, a bunch of jackanapes running around taking pot shots?'

The door creaked opened.

'Is all well?' Mr Pearse enquired.

'Fine, thank you, Pat,' Finn's father said, 'We understand each other, so we do, eh Finn?'

Finn scoured the room, Mr Pearse, his father. 'Yes, sir.'

His father addressed Mr Pearse. 'I believe you mentioned taking Finn on a trip at Easter.'

'If that would be agreeable.'

'I think it will, won't it, Finn?'

'Yes, sir,' said Finn to the carpet.

'I continue to put my faith in you and your school, Mr Pearse.'

'Your support is gratefully received, Mr Devoy,' Mr Pearse said and Finn noted the 'misters' and the stiff words masking something.

'Goodbye, Finn.' His father offered a hand once more, 'I expect that nothing said today will reach ears which have no business hearing of it.'

'No, sir,' Finn said, making sure he withdrew his hand first.

'Right, Finn, back to class,' Mr Pearse said cheerfully.

In the hall Finn bumped into Patrick Healy, the Red Branch corporal.

'Sorry I haven't seen you to say it but well done for getting rid of Keane. Pity about the court-martial.'

'Yes.'

'Being a hero doesn't come easy, so?' Patrick winked.

Ahead of Finn lay the dark corridor leading to the classrooms; behind him light poured through the windows. Finn felt the warmth on his back. He went out into it.

Crossing the grass, Patrick's words ricocheted around his head. They thought he'd done a brave thing, revered him for it and, worse, for who his father was. They hadn't seen the hate and grief on Alasteir's face when he'd spoken of Combermere Barracks. His father was a murderer and he'd let Finn, in his ignorance, become one too.

Finn sprinted through the park, dodging twiggy fingers that tried to grab him. He ran until he reached the stone wall bordering the grounds. After three attempts he got a toe-hold and prised himself over the wall. He turned right and began to jog up the hill.

His pace slowed to a dawdle. Thoughts, about Ireland and Britain, his father and the Clan, war with its causalities and heroes, swamped him. By the time he realised he didn't know where he was it was late. He ducked off the farm track he'd been trudging down and into a field where he crawled under a hedgerow. Thorns and rocks prodded him. Too tired to care, Finn slept.

*

A cold dawn broke. Chilled and shaking, Finn scrambled from beneath the hedge and huddled into himself. The sky was stony grey, promising rain.

Finn stumbled over uneven furrows and into the lane. A deep growl and three barks greeted him. He span round to see a border collie with a snarling black face leap for his throat. It knocked him down and as he put a hand up to fend it off fangs sank into his palm. With his free hand Finn struck the dog's nose. It yelped, let go and jumped from his chest.

As he sat forward, Finn saw it running along the lane to a man who walked unhurriedly beside a work-worn horse, leading the beast by a crude rope bridle. Finn got to his feet as the man drew near, the dog trotting at its master's heels.

The man was tall, solid, middle-aged, stoutish, with a firm round face, greying hair but a dark neat moustache. The unmounted mount was a slow-plodding cart horse with mud-spattered fetlocks and a whiskery grey chin. The man halted beside Finn.

'Are you hurt, laddie?' he asked in a voice that betrayed Irish and Scottish tints.

Finn silently nursed his sore hand.

'I beg your pardon on my dog's behalf. He's apt to go off like a cocked rifle at the slightest wee thing.' The man looped the rope reins around a branch protruding from the hedgerow and came over to examine Finn's injury. 'He's laid into you pretty good.' He produced a handkerchief from his pocket and bound Finn's wound. Stepping back, he noticed Finn's uniform. 'Would I be right thinking you're a St Enda's boy?'

Finn bowed his head.

'I'll take it you are, will I? You're a canny way from school. Perhaps I'd best be seeing you make it safely back. I'm James Connolly, by the way.' He extended his hand.

Finn hesitated; accepted the handshake.

'Thank you, Mr Connolly, sir. Finn Devoy.'

'A pleasure to make your acquaintance, Finn, I'm only sorry it's under such circumstances. But fortune favours us somewhat for I am in the rare position of being able to offer you a ride, if you'll be minded to manage it bareback.' Mr

Connolly patted the horse's mottled flank affectionately. 'At the behest of my good friend the Countess I've just this morn rescued this old girl from the knacker's knife so she'll gladly do one last wee job for me by way of thanks.'

'You're a friend of Countess Markievicz?' Finn asked.

'I am, aye. I take it you and she are acquainted?'

'Yes, sir. I'm in the Fianna.'

'I see. Sure, you'll not be the laddie to whose defence Con leapt 'tother day, will you?'

Finn bowed his head.

'Ach, well, that's of no matter now. Up you get.'

Mr Connolly helped Finn mount the horse and they set off for school, the dog running out in front, Mr Connolly leading the horse by her rope bridle and Finn, legs dangling and hands clenching fistfuls of straw-dry mane, jolting around on the horse's bony back. His hand throbbed. He sulked; a daft collie had bested him, so much for following Cúchulainn's example. He dropped his gaze, squeezed his eyes shut and felt a hot trickle on each cheek.

'You look as if you've had a rough night of it, Finn.'

'Yes, sir.'

'Not run away, have you?'

'I don't think so, sir.'

'Mitching, then? Can't say I'd condemn you for that. Sometimes a man needs to be alone with his thoughts.'

'Yes, sir.'

'Tell me, Finn, what troubles you?'

'It's nothing, sir.'

'Come, lad, a problem halved and all that guff,' Mr Connolly coaxed. 'To do with that Fianna business is it, so?'

Finn wondered how much this stranger knew of his problems, was worried about being caught in a lie; afraid of admitting the truth.

'Yes, sir. No, sir. It's my father, sir.'

'The two of you don't get on?' Mr Connolly chuckled, 'Families, eh? Still, these things work themselves right.'

Finn offered no reply. Sensing a stalemate Mr Connolly asked no more questions; Finn settled himself to being joggled along by the horse.

*

As they approached the Hermitage the door swung open revealing Mr Pearse, his arms folded and his face grim.

'That'll be your headmaster, so?' Mr Connolly said, 'I've yet to make the good Patrick Pearse's acquaintance, although I've heard grand things about him. He's looking a might serious this morning. That'll be your doing, Finn?'

'Probably, sir.'

'Not to worry.' Mr Connolly swung Finn down from the mare then struck forward, hand extended, 'Mr Pearse? I've one of your own here, a returning stray. James Connolly, pleased to meet you and have the opportunity of visiting your school after hearing much fine praise for it. If this young man's to go by it's no exaggeration.'

Mr Pearse only blushed and nodded. Undeterred by the diffident welcome Mr Connolly pressed on:

'I'm sorry to report Mr Devoy has suffered at the hands or, more precisely, teeth, of my hound. No need for amputation, though.' Mr Connolly added, 'If it's not too great a liberty, Mr Pearse, I recommend least said, soonest mended.'

Mr Pearse glanced from Mr Connolly to Finn and back again.

'I'm grateful for your advice,' the headmaster murmured, adding with greater ease, 'Finn, ask Mary Brigid to look at your hand, please.'

Finn slipped inside, leaving an ebullient Mr Connolly struggling to engage the reserved Mr Pearse in conversation.

After Mary Brigid had made a fuss of him, she directed Finn to rest until lunch. Alone in the dorm, Finn's eyes were drawn to Alasteir's vacated bed, a visceral reminder of his father's legacy.

He lay down. His hand pulsed with a dull ache. He closed his eyes and let it become a drumming in his ears, lulling him into a doze where he dreamed a hundred hounds charged at him, snarling and slavering. He cut them down only to realise they were whimpering puppies that bled and died at his feet.

Dear Mother,
We are arrived safely in Rosmuc. The train journey to Galway took nearly three hours and would have been terribly dull if not for Mr Pearse and Mr Willie's company as the countryside we went through was flat and featureless. Only when we changed at Maam Cross did I start to see the rock-strewn mountains and shimmering loughs Mr Pearse had promised.

A pony and trap took us the last few miles to Gort Mór, the hamlet where Mr Pearse's cottage sits overlooking Lough Aroolagh. I wish you could see it, Mother. It really is the most beautiful spot though with a certain bleakness to it; I'm not sure I'd be so happy to visit in winter.

A mile from the cottage Mr Pearse sent the trap on ahead and, while we strolled along the lane, he pointed to the Twelve Pins and declared them the finest mountains on earth but I suspect this is only because he has not seen the Colorado Rockies.

Finn set his pen on the grass and glanced across the lough. Polished grey clouds had turned the water into a sheet of burnished silver. Later he would swim in it, as he had last night, feeling the coolness like silk against his skin. Behind him, a short stretch up the hill sat the whitewashed cottage, its walls brilliant against the rich green land, its thatched roof glowing golden even on this dull day. He recalled their arrival, picturing the childish grin on his headmaster's face when they rounded the bend and first saw the cottage, a solitary dwelling punctuating the barren hillside, isolated like a hermit's den. On seeing it Mr Pearse had halted, clapped his hands, murmured 'baile*' and fairly trotted the rest of the way. Finn had never seen such pure joy and felt as if he'd intruded on an intimate moment, one he couldn't betray. He picked up his pen:

The cottage is very comfortable with two good sized bedrooms plus one under the thatch, which is mine, and a generous living room with a grand hearth, the rising heat from which makes my room wonderfully warm. There is also a large

---

* home

pantry at the back of the cottage and an even larger outbuilding that stores turf for the fire, bicycles, tools and the like.

Today we are resting after our journey but tomorrow we plan to cycle into the Connemara countryside. Mr Pearse has promised to show me the sights and Mr Willie says he knows some wonderful spots for sketching. I will do one for you and send it next time I write.

Evenings feel colder out here than in Dublin, although it is spring, but we were quite cosy around the fire last night and Mr Pearse cooked up a grand meal. Tonight Mr Willie and I take our turn. We have a plentiful supply of cabbages so if I can remember your recipe I may offer to make sauerkraut.

Finn paused, reread his work and knew it was, finally, the kind of letter his mother wanted: one that told of his adventures. Emboldened, he continued:

Sorry I didn't have time to write before we left Dublin but Mr Pearse was eager to get out of the city so I wasn't able to tell you my news but you can have it now – I won last term's art prize for my painting 'Green Dawn at St Enda's' and Mr Pearse left instructions for it to be hung in the entrance hall. Although I am not in a hurry for my holiday to end, I look forward to being greeted by my own painting when we return to school! Perhaps you might be able to visit next term and see it yourself. Plus, Mr Pearse is planning a week long school fete in June; it's sure to be a spectacular so if you are thinking of coming that would be a good time.
Well, Mother, that's all for now. I'll write soon,
Your ever loving son,
Finn

Behind him the grass rustled. Finn turned to see Mr Pearse coming down the path from the cottage.

'I thought to find you here,' he said, smiling. He dropped down beside Finn. 'Magnificent, isn't it?'

'Yes, sir,' Finn said, noting again the glee in his headmaster's expression.

'Near to the gate of Heaven,' Mr Pearse added, gazing out over the mountains, losing himself in their craggy peaks. 'For this land would I gladly sacrifice myself.'

Overhead two swifts screed. A shiver rippled through Finn as the birds' harsh calls underscored Mr Pearse's solemn declaration. Then sunlight pierced the clouds, throwing a glittering path across the lough and onto the bank where Finn and Mr Pearse sat.

'To be sure, Finn, I'm a gloomy old gus at times. You must keep me cheerful these holidays,' Mr Pearse laughed, 'Come, we'll take a baaz around the lough.'

Trinity Term 1913

Mr Colbert addressed them at the first Fianna meeting of term. 'You have shown yourselves to be courageous, honest and true; the things expected of a Fianna. Some of you have gone beyond that. Those exceeding expectations will be promoted from the ranks. First Captain Reddin will address you.'

David took his place out front. The weather was warmer than July though it was only April. They were on the lawn behind the gymnasium instead of inside it. A trickle of sweat ran down Finn's spine and he cursed the order to assemble in their kilt uniform with brat and jersey, not the cooler knicks they wore for drilling.

'Hallo and welcome back.' David pushed a lock of damp hair from his forehead. 'By now you'll have heard of the plans for the fete which will include music, dancing, pageants and displays. Mr Pearse has informed me he'd like us to play a major role, both drilling and enacting scenes from the Ulster Cycle as we are named the Red Branch after those stories. For this we'll practise armed combat with weapons, like those used by Cúchulainn, which we'll make ourselves. I propose beginning at once. Does anybody second?'

'I do.' Michael Western stepped forward and saluted.

'Anybody object?'

No one did. Finn, Hal, Freddie and Charlie exchanged grins.

'Grand. Mr Colbert?'

'Thanks, David. Righto, boys,' Mr Colbert pulled out a piece of paper and ceremoniously unfolded it, 'Without further ado: to the rank of corporal the following are promoted; Fredrick Blackwell, Henry O'Hanlon, Sean O'Malley, James Benson and Charles Barrett. Come forward for your stripes.'

Feeling the sting of this final punishment for the disgrace he had brought on the Fianna, Finn watched his friends collect their stripes. He forced a smile and added his applause.

'And to the rank of sergeant, for services beyond the call of duty to St Enda's, Finn Devoy.'

Still brooding, Finn missed Mr Colbert calling his name.

'Wakey-wakey, Devoy, you're a sergeant now,' David teased.

Hal shoved him forward. Mr Colbert pressed the stripes into his left hand while pumping his right. He leaned into Finn and said in a low voice:

'Countess Markievicz sends her apologies for not being here to present you with your stripes. Sure, it's on her recommendation you're getting them. She asked me to tell you she thinks you a fine Fianna warrior, Finn and I accede to her splendid judgement. Don't let us down,' he smiled and added, 'again.'

'No, sir.'

That night the dorm was full of cursing as five boys unanimously useless with needle and thread set about sowing on their new stripes.

'I knew you'd get sergeant,' Charlie said.

'Doesn't he deserve it, though?' Hal said.

'Aye,' Sean spoke up, 'You do, Finn, well done.'

'Thanks, Sean,' Finn replied, glad they were on friendly terms, 'and well done you for corporal, all of you. It's great, isn't it?'

'Aye,' Freddie said, 'now we'll be able to boss around the privates.'

'We'll keep those wee 'uns in line,' Hal said.

'Reckon I'll get them to polish my boots,' Charlie replied.

'Maybe we should see if they're any cop at sowing,' Freddie joked as he stabbed his thumb.

'No,' Finn said, 'We should do this ourselves. There.' He held up his handiwork.

'It's crooked,' Charlie declared.

'Is not.'

'Is so. It's as crooked as a mule's hind leg.'

'Looks alright,' Hal said, casting an eye to his own woeful needlepoint.

'You need specs,' Charlie teased, 'Lend him yours, Freddie.'

'Let's see yours then,' Finn challenged.

'Haven't finished yet,' Charlie protested.

'Let me know when you have,' Finn said, 'I'm ready for a laugh.'

He folded his uniform and sat with his copy of the *Táin.*

'Don't you read anything else?' Freddie asked.

'I'm just swotting up on Cúchulainn's weapons.' Finn settled into his pillows and his pages:

Cúchulainn was trained in arms by Scáthach. She taught him to use a shield rim to deflect his opponent's blows; to hurl a javelin, hitting any target, no matter how far; to leap on a lance-point in mid flight and to slay with his sword all who would come between Cúchulainn and victory. She showed Cúchulainn how to ride a chariot balanced on one leg while defending himself when attacked on four sides and she trained him in unarmed combat until he could strike his enemies with the force of a blade. Finally she taught him to wield the most deadly of weapons: the gae bolga. When his training was complete Cúchulainn was a true Ulster warrior.

For the next two months Finn lost himself in daydreams; he, Charlie, Freddie and Hal rode into battle and cut down the enemy to stand triumphant, four lone champions of the Ulster Cycle. He endured lines or extra prep as punishment for the pages of doodles showing shields, spears and swords instead of chemical formulas, algebraic equations or French verbs. Finn didn't care. No longer would the *Táin* stories be words on a page; they would come to life, Cúchulainn included.

'Mr Slattery, may I borrow Finn?' Mr Pearse was hovering in the doorway of the chem. lab.

'Certainly, Mr Pearse. Perhaps while you are conversing with Mr Devoy you might remind him of the usefulness of his studies. I fear he may suffer in next week's examination as I am not planning to include questions regarding the weaponry of the boys of Eamhain Macha,' Mr Slattery replied.

Finn followed Mr Pearse towards his office and stopped, head hung, by the door. Instead of turning in, however, Mr Pearse proceeded to the entrance.

'It's a fine day, Finn. I've a mind to baaz around the gardens. Will you be agreeable to joining me?'

'Yes, sir.'

They meandered among the flowerbeds, sunny with daffodils, and down the gravel path that cut towards the main road. Mr Pearse sauntered. Finn trotted alongside.

'So you are keenly involved in preparations for the pageant?'

'Yes, sir.' Finn readied himself for a scolding.

'Grand. I have the script for Cúchulainn's boyhood deeds about completed and know the Red Branch can be relied upon to provide weapons and props. My dear brother is engaging some of his fine artists on costume design. Still, I am anxious that we show the best of St Enda's. Especially as I am charging people for their tickets.' Mr Pearse shot Finn a sidelong glance.

Finn was puzzled. This rambling speech seemed a strange way of getting to the fact that he had been distracted in lessons.

'However, there remains the matter of casting the play. The right boys, and girls, for I'm borrowing a few young ladies from St Ita's, must be set in the right roles. Do you have any thoughts on this, Finn?'

'Only that you're right, sir. It's important.'

'Aye, Finn. That is why I have decided that you should take the part of Cúchulainn.'

'Me?'

'Surely, Finn. You'll make the part your own because you have much about you of Cúchulainn, Ireland's greatest warrior,' Mr Pearse concluded.

Finn knew what Mr Pearse said was true but not in the way his headmaster meant. Having done with Mrs Hutton's juvenile verse telling of the *Táin*, Finn had sought out others and, with the improvement of his Gaelic, had read four different versions. In some Cúchulainn was ruthlessly devious and ardently violent.

He mumbled his thanks.

'Would that be you accepting?'

'I suppose so, sir.'

'Grand, Finn.' Mr Pearse directed his steps back to the school. 'Of course I understand Cúchulainn had not to concern himself with chemistry; it wasn't then understood as a science. But if it had been he would have applied himself to it as he did his other undertakings.'

'Yes, sir.'

The Red Branch claimed an outbuilding as their weapons workshop. Seconded by Hal, Finn commanded seven privates in crafting battle axes, swords, shields and lances. He designed each weapon and oversaw production. Their early attempts were crudely hacked chunks of wood. Then the blacksmith volunteered his services, showing them the rudiments of welding and riveting, bringing pieces forged at his smithy; the weapons became menacing. Only Cúchulainn's gae bolga remained a problem. Finn was surveying with frustration the latest attempt at fashioning a weapon good enough for this great warrior when the stable door swung open announcing Mr Colbert and the horseman who rescued Finn from the hound last term. They made for Finn's workstation.

'Good day, Finn,' Mr Connolly said, 'Mr Colbert has offered me a tour of the works. Would you look at this beauty?' He picked up an axe. The stout handle had been precisely carved and the head, supplied by the smith, proved the perfect balance. 'You could chop down a good many of the enemy with this.'

'Thank you, sir.'

'Mother Mary, is this a gae bolga?'

Finn flushed as Mr Connolly swooped on the unsatisfactory item. 'It's not finished, sir.'

'How are those swords coming, Finn?' Mr Colbert asked, taking the gae bolga from Mr Connolly.

'There's been a delay casting the hilts,' Finn admitted.

'I heard O'Connell sliced off his finger,' Mr Colbert replied.

'Not off so much, sir, as open. Well, maybe he took the very top off.'

'He'll survive,' Mr Colbert chuckled.

'Humph! A good many of Dublin's factory owners could learn from you, Finn, if it's only the one accident you've had,' Mr Connolly interjected, 'I've men, Mr Colbert, who long to work in an environment such as this. You wouldn't believe the conditions some of my members endure.'

'Your members, sir?' Finn asked.

'Mr Connolly is the secretary of the Irish Transport and General Workers Union,' Mr Colbert explained.

'Do you know about workers' unions, Finn?' Mr Connolly asked.

'No, sir.'

'There are employers, a deal too many, who view the working man as fodder, to be chewed up and, pardon me, defecated when his usefulness is spent. I've members, Finn, working seventeen hours a day. So tired they are it's hardly surprising they fall asleep at their machines, ending up maimed. And does the owner help the man who, because of his callous greed, cannot work? Bejesus he does not! He throws him out to starve and takes in the next able man.'

'But sir, why do the men work at such dangerous jobs?'

'Dublin's a poor city for the working man. Everything here not ruled by the Crown is ruled by the half-crown, eh?' Mr Connolly nudged Mr Colbert, 'If one man refuses a job there's another ten desperate to take it.'

'Still, there might be something done about that, if Mr Connolly has any sway.' Mr Colbert patted Mr Connolly's shoulder.

'What do you hope to do, sir?' Finn said, encouraged by the grown-up way Mr Connolly talked to him.

'Unionisation. Where there are many there is power. We can refuse to work, as you suggest, but not one or two: all of us. That's a strike, Finn. If working men strike together owners will bend to our demands. They forget they need us to grind the grist if they want flour to sell,' Mr Connolly replied, 'Well, I best be heading to see Mr Pearse. Thanks for your time.' He extended his hand to Mr Colbert. 'And, you, Finn.' And Finn was also offered the hand of Mr James Connolly, secretary of the ITGWU.

'Who was that?' Hal came up.

'Mr Connolly, the union man. Have you figured out how we're going to attach the straps to the shields yet?'

With Mr Pearse's blessing they worked late every night on preparations for the fete, which would soon be upon them.

When they began Finn had felt confident they would be ready but things had not gone smoothly. Along with O'Connell, two other boys had hurt themselves using their hammers for a mock duel. With his squad down two progress was slow. David had borrowed four lads from Finn's workforce to help with the chariots, leaving Finn, Hal and the injured O'Connell to limp on. Freddie tried to help but he was rubbish at manual tasks. Sean chipped in whenever he could be spared from his workstation. Finn was grateful; Sean was a skilled craftsman. And still Finn couldn't fathom how to make a glorious gae bolga.

Rehearsals for the pageant scenes were equally trying. Mr Pearse had an exacting idea of how each line should be performed and was anxious to show both his lads and his script in ideal light.

Plus there was the Fianna drill to perfect. Their display would be a central part of the fete. Every manoeuvre, turn, step and salute had to be honed. As a sergeant Finn was expected to ready his own platoon with frequent practise.

The work was never ending yet the end approached and Finn was so exhausted that even dreaming of himself as Cúchulainn was too great an effort.

'Still working on that gae bolga?' Mr Connolly asked, peering over Finn's shoulder on his second visit to the workshop.

Finn's brow creased. 'Yes, sir.'

'What you're needing is a mechanism, perhaps a spring loaded trigger. Is there no one who could make such a thing?'

'Michael Murphy, our groundskeeper,' Mr Colbert broke in, 'The devil I didn't think of him sooner.'

'Please, sir, I'd like to do this myself.'

'Your determination is noted, Devoy, but there's no sense overburdening yourself,' Mr Colbert said, 'Sean, run for Mr Murphy.'

Sean shot Finn a sympathetic glance before trotting off. Mr Colbert and Mr Connolly moved away. Finn sulked. If only he'd thought of a spring loaded trigger.

He was still brooding when Cathleen's father appeared at his workbench.

'Mr Colbert says you're having a time of it making something.'

Finn pointed to the gae bolga.

Mr Murphy took up the weapon. 'Reckon I can sort you a thing.' He produced a measuring tape from one pocket, a tattered notepad from the other, took a pencil from behind his ear and scribbled the measurements.

'What do you think, Mr Murphy?' Mr Colbert asked.

''Twill be no trouble, sir. Ready in a couple of days.'

'Excellent,' Mr Colbert proclaimed and walked off leaving Finn with Mr Murphy.

'Right show you're looking to put on, isn't it?' Mr Murphy stowed his notepad and left.

With a scant fortnight before the pageant Finn stayed behind oiling the mechanism for the gae bolga, to be used in his final Cúchulainn scene, 'Combat with Ferdia'.

'Finished, Finn?' Mr Colbert asked.

'I think so, sir.' Finn gathered up his tools.

'I'll give you a hand.'

Mr Colbert clattered around, moving finished weapons to the store cupboard before coming to hover at Finn's elbow.

'You're showing devotion to duty tonight, so you are.'

'Yes, sir.'

'And every night for a good while since.'

'There's been a lot to do, sir.' Finn crossed to the bench where the gae bolga lay. It was no weapon for mercifully dispatching the enemy. Appearing like any other javelin, a wooden shaft topped by a pointed head, at the base of the head were six further blades (Cúchulainn's had thirty) longer, thinner, barbed and with serrated edges. The hair-trigger Mr Murphy had devised using a pin-and-lock movement was slick and smooth. When pulled, the weapon gave a solid clunk and the barbs fired out from the shaft into a fan. Once impaled the only way to remove the barbed javelin was to cut away the flesh in the area pierced by the gae bolga. Finn shuddered.

Mr Colbert edged closer. 'You like things to be right, Finn.'

Finn waited for Mr Colbert to go on.

'I'm thinking of the night you exposed Keane as a scoundrel. That was because you wanted things to be right, wasn't it?'

'I suppose, sir.'

'It's good to know there are boys like you, Finn, passionate about right and wrong.'

Finn glanced up. Mr Colbert was studying him. Finn had grown enough to be taller than Mr Colbert but Mr Colbert towered over him now.

'Aye, Finn, there are others like you, who want things putting right. I consider myself one. And there's much to be done, too much for one man. But by working together we accomplish the hardest tasks.'

Finn knew the conversation was no longer about pageant preparations.

'Such as, sir?'

'Well, what Mr Connolly was talking of, helping the working man. Of course, the greatest task is the freeing of Ireland.' Mr Colbert added, 'Would you agree with me, Finn?'

'Yes, sir.'

'Sure, then you're of the same mind as a wee organisation I'm member of. We call ourselves the Irish Republican Brotherhood. A fellow like yourself ought to join us.'

The IRB! 'Aren't I too young, sir?'

'Given my recommendation and your eagerness, to say nothing of the eminence of your family connections, I'm sure you'd be welcomed. David's a member.'

Although buried amongst Mr Colbert's encouragements, Finn noted the reference to his father. It wasn't Finn Devoy that would be joining the IRB but Michael Devoy's son.

'If you think I should, sir.'

'Good man, Finn.' Mr Colbert patted his arm. 'But you mustn't tell anyone, not even your pals. We're a securely guarded secret.'

More secrets and lies. Finn sighed and nodded.

'I'll propose you a week on Thursday. We meet at City Hall. Don't worry about a pass out; I'll arrange that.' Mr Colbert made for the door.

Finn had no choice but to follow him.

Finally everything was ready for the fete; props, drills and displays, costumes and the *Táin* scenes. Finn had been fitted with an impressive Cúchulainn outfit of belted tunic embroidered with Celtic symbols, flowing brat fastened by a brooch, winged helmet and shoes with bindings that snaked up his legs. He would carry a hurley and shield with a sword on his belt. The gae bolga was to make a dramatic entrance in the final scene when he had to kill Ferdia.

Mr Pearse, expecting fine June weather, proposed performing in the Hermitage grounds using the undergrowth, streams, follies and bridges as readymade scenery and, despite merciless rain, on the Thursday before fete week all were assembled outside for dress rehearsals. Finn was annoyed; he had already perfected his three scenes (the slaying of Culann's hound, Cúchulainn's defence of the ford and the combat of Ferdia and Cúchulainn), knew every thrust and parry of the drill the Red Branch were to perform and the running order for each of the six days of the fete, including musical interludes, dances and addresses by Mr Pearse, Countess Markievicz and W. B. Yeats. He stood getting soaked, only half listening to the directions Mr Pearse called out from beneath his ample umbrella.

'How goes it, Pat?'

The boys held their warrior poses as Mr Pearse lapsed in his directorial duties to speak to Mr Colbert.

'It'll be a grand spectacle, Con.' Mr Pearse's voice sounded sunny, despite having spent two hours in a deluge, instructing bedraggled boys who longed for toasted crumpets, hot tea and dry socks.

'Do you not think it's a bit wet to have the lads out, Pat? Sure, they know their parts by now, don't you, lads?' Mr Colbert raised his voice over the wind; got back a loud chorus of 'yes, sir'. 'It wouldn't do if your star turns came down with fever before the call curtain.'

Finn watched the idea ticking round in Mr Pearse's brain.

'Aye, Con, you've a point there, so you do.'

Finn sagged out of his bold Cúchulainn stance.

'We'll have a final run through tomorrow, boys,' Mr Pearse added.

The others trudged off the mud-churned lawn, leaving Finn juggling his shield, sword and gae bolga, trying not to cut himself on the fiendish barbs.

'Pat, I've a meeting this evening, Fianna business. As you've finished rehearsals would you mind if I borrowed Finn? I need someone for the minutes and David's busy swatting for Trinity.'

Finn dropped all three weapons with a clatter and stood among the jumbled armoury, waiting for Mr Pearse to challenge the lie.

'Aye, Con, I'm sure Finn'll be happy to help.'

City Hall was rammed with men calling welcome to each other over Finn's head as Mr Colbert guided him amongst them. Some stopped to greet Mr Colbert and be introduced to Finn who noted their curious gazes; they looked on him but saw his father. Finn's membership would be a blood tie connecting the Clan and IRB.

The meeting was called to order. The format was similar to Fianna meetings. First they repeated their pledge, then the agenda was read and the first item tabled: the induction of new members.

That night there were three plus Finn, called to the front. They were informed that IRB meetings were conducted 'in camera', behind closed doors, and had to swear to keep secret IRB affairs. A promise, Finn realised, that his father had broken. Next they recited the IRB oath to serve Ireland and her causes. Lastly they were taught a handshake by which they could identify brothers-in-arms and presented with an IRB pin.

Finn was the last of the four to be pledged. The presiding officer, a bulky man called Dennis McCullough, propelled Finn forward.

'I'm sure there'll be some of you wondering about taking one so young among ourselves,' Mr McCullough boomed, 'And there'll be others who know why 'tis right this young lad should join. To those in doubts I'll say this: welcome Finn Devoy, son of Michael Devoy whose name had better be known to you all, so it had.'

They stared at Finn darkly. Finn stared back. A hot wave of cheering crashed through and around him.

'Where'd you get to last night?' Charlie asked as they dressed for breakfast.

'I was on Fianna business with Mr Colbert. David was busy.' Finn ducked his gaze.

'What business?'

'None of yours.'

'Just wondering.'

'Don't.' Finn snatched his tie and marched from the dorm.

In the dining hall Finn gobbled breakfast and left before the bell. He was already in the classroom, head down, when the others filed in.

It was Greek mythology with Mr Plunkett. Finn couldn't concentrate; every time he looked up his eyes found Charlie's boring into him. The midmorning bell rang at last.

'Not you, Devoy,' Mr Plunkett called without glancing up from his marking.

Finn stood by his desk. When the class had emptied Mr Plunkett came over, his long black master's robes flowing behind him in magnificent swirls.

'Having trouble applying yourself this morning, Devoy?'

'Sorry, sir.'

'Tired, Devoy?'

Finn said nothing.

'What would it be keeping you up late last night, I wonder?'

'I was with Mr Colbert, sir,' Finn replied, eyes on the floor.

'Aha! Yesterday was Thursday, was it not?'

'Yes, sir?'

'The first of the month?'

'Sir?'

'Thus Mr Colbert was attending to business always attended to by him on the first Thursday of each month.'

Finn clenched his jaw.

'Leading me to certain conclusions.' Mr Plunkett sucked in a breath, held it then spat it. Finn looked up. The master's eyes glinted behind his pince-nez. 'Welcome to the IRB.' He seized Finn's hand and helped him fumble through the secret shake. 'Now that's a surprise for you.' Mr Plunkett, still gripping Finn's hand, leaned in. 'I seconded you.' He slapped Finn's shoulder then stepped aside.

Finn moved towards the door.

'Wait! I have more to say and 'tis of great importance to fellows like us.' Mr Plunkett removed his pince-nez. 'If one has secrets one must act at all times as though one's life is an open book from which any may read.'

Finn frowned.

'For if no one thinks you have secrets, they won't seek to make you talk, just as the man who needs to hide does so best in plain sight!' Mr Plunkett replaced his pince-nez.

'May I go, sir?'

'You may.'

Finn scuttled from the room. Outside Charlie and Hal were waiting for him. Hal munched on an apple.

'Where's Freddie?'

'Library. What was that?' Charlie asked.

Inspired by his master's advice Finn said, 'Mr Plunkett was giving me a ticking-off for day-dreaming.'

The matter of fact tone and scowl worked. Mr Plunkett was right; if you were convincing, others would be convinced. But that didn't ease Finn's guilt.

Each evening, Monday to Friday, 7.30-10pm pupils, staff, special guests and audience were drowned under grand Irish rains that cursed St Enda's gala fete. Each day the school steamed with drying costumes and convulsed with sneezing, shivering boys. A feverish Finn lambasted the weather for ruining Mr Pearse's showcase event and prayed that Saturday would be sunny and the finale, at least, a success.

*

Finn sprang out of bed and over to the window. The day was overcast but dry. He sighed, dressed and was on his way while Hal, Charlie, Freddie and Sean were rubbing sleep from their eyes.

The dining room was bustling. Finn helped himself to porridge and tea. He was reaching for the honey when a grinning David Reddin sat next to him.

'Morning.'

Finn mumbled a 'hallo'.

'Heard you got the full treatment last Thursday,' David said in a low voice.

Finn nodded.

'Lucky your father being who he is. I had to wait 'til I was sixteen.'

'Aye, lucky.'

'Mastered the handshake?'

Finn shook his head. David glanced around. No one was watching so he stuck his hand out. Finn took it and tried to remember the steps. David laughed as he botched it.

'It's thumb over first, like this.'

He was still demonstrating when Mary Brigid appeared.

'What's that, a new game?' She nodded at their hands.

Finn snatched his away. 'Nothing, miss.'

'Really?'

She lingered, a tense smile on her face; Finn said nothing more. Mary Brigid tutted and left.

'Bugger,' David muttered, 'Still, even if she saw it won't mean a deal to her. But they're hot on secrecy; watch yourself, Finn.' He snatched a piece of toast, 'See you later.'

Finn finished his breakfast and wandered to the performance area. Five boys were drowning under a deadweight of canvas trying to erect the marquee Mr Pearse had hired yesterday in a pre-emptive strike against another downpour. At irregular intervals instructions were bandied:

'Lift your end up.'

'It's up.'

'Not high enough. I can't get the fecking pole under it.'

'That's as far as it's bleeding going.'

'You're useless.'

'It's you, you eejit.'

Finn was enjoying the show until he spotted Mr Colbert and Mr Pearse. Mr Pearse beckoned to him.

'Ah, Finn, didn't I think you'd come to help us,' the headmaster said.

'What can I do, sir?'

'Con?'

'Mass your battalion; assemble the Fianna mess tent. We can store the props in it and it'll be shelter for the performers.' Mr Colbert cast an eye to the gathering clouds.

Mr Pearse faced Finn, 'We're starting at two-thirty; I'd like the performers ready for two. I've a few words to say before we begin.'

Finn dashed off, found Hal and Sean already working under Michael Western's orders. He pitched in and Charlie soon joined them. When Freddie arrived he made himself useful reciting mathematical formulas for calculating the most robust construction of a collapsible structure.

From breakfast 'til elevenses boys fetched and carried, industrious as ants.

By half past eleven the tent was full of props, costumes and instruments for the performance.

From twelve until quarter to Mr Colbert re-drilled the Fianna in their display.

At one o'clock the saturated sky began to drip-drip on them. They retreated to the school.

One twenty-five, as Finn shivered into his mug, the sodden clouds tore wide open.

'Sure, it'll be a bloody joy standing in that for seven hours,' Hal muttered.

'It's only a shower,' Freddie said.

A white flash lit up the soggy gardens. Thunder boomed.

'Feck it is.'

Mr Pearse entered the dining room in a dripping ulster, 'Can those of you involved in the *Táin* tableaux make haste with your lunches.'

Finn chewed his bread and butter to a pulp and rinsed his mouth with lukewarm tea. He and Sean, who was playing Laeg, the charioteer, pushed themselves up from the table.

'Good luck, Cúchulainn,' Charlie teased.

Finn whirled back, fist raised. Sean put himself between them.

'Mind you keep out of our road, or I'll run yous down with my chariot,' he joked, 'How-way, Finn.'

They strode off together, Finn muttering oaths.

The short dash to the mess tent was enough to soak them. Cheerlessly, Finn donned Cúchulainn's cloak, fitted the sword into its sheath and sat the helmet on his head.

'Now is it Finn Devoy I'd be calling you or the Hound of Cullan?'

Finn whirled round. Cathleen stood dressed in a long robe, her sandalled feet peeping from beneath a ragged hem. She too wore a hooded cloak and a helmet, hers minus the wings.

'You may address me as Queen Medb.' She laughed at Finn's confusion. 'Now kneel before me, unworthy dog.'

'What are you doing here?'

'Taking my place as Queen of Connacht,' she said, switching to Gaelic.

'Cad é*?'

'Nora Cafferty's got the chicken pox so here I am. This'll be the gae bolga, so? A pretty time this gave my da.' She twirled the javelin in her hands. 'Let's see how it works.' She presented it to Finn who flicked the trigger. Six barbs fired out with a clang. 'I'd not like to be caught on the end of that, so I wouldn't,' she said.

Finn reset the weapon and laid it down.

'It's a pity we've no lines together,' Cathleen continued, 'I wish Mr Pearse was doing 'The Last Battle'. We'd've got a kiss then.' She winked and pinched Finn's arm. 'Haven't got any cigarettes, have you?'

'Charlie might,' Finn said, trying to make his voice sound normal.

'Get us one before we go out and make fools of ourselves.'

The other players were filling the tent, dressing and arming. Cathleen slipped away amongst the St Ita's girls as Mr Pearse entered, clapped his hands and welcomed them.

---

* what?

Cathleen caught Finn's eye. Finn blinked and ducked her gaze. He hoped he wasn't blushing; Sean was next to him.

On the other side of the canvas the audience gathered. They sat under shelters thrown together from tarpaulins and spare tent poles. A few of the men stood holding umbrellas and getting their trousers wet. All shivered, grim-faced. The photographer, called in to capture the glorious St Enda's pageant, wiped his lens with a soggy handkerchief and adjusted the camera's cover so it protected his backside.

In his opening speech Mr Pearse challenged the audience to not let fickle Mother Nature ruin a grand spectacle of Irishness and joked that the tickets were non-refundable. Then he introduced the school's GAA members who demonstrated their prowess with hurleys, sliotars and footballs. This was followed by the first Cúchulainn scene.

As they emerged from the tent into icy sheets of rain, Finn wished Cúchulainn had fought the hound in sou'ester, galoshes and overcoat. He had to battle his hood, which kept blowing over his eyes, while fending off Cullan's hound, played by a first year in a woolly suit with a stuffed-stocking tail that hung limply over his backend as the newspaper padding soaked up a gallon of rain. Finn mused that if Cúchulainn's hound was half such a sorry whelp his defeat of it was nothing to crow about. But everyone remembered their cues and lines and, chased by the rain, they were cheered from the field.

Next came Countess Markievicz's rousing speech, rudely cut short by wind approaching gale force. She bowed out to the pipe band who marched and played, their waterlogged kilts clinging to their legs as they sloshed through puddles. Mr Pearse, determined to complete the programme before the storm drowned the audience, rushed into the next *Táin* pageant. Finn and Sean drove their chariot onto the field at a slug's pace, the pony, yanked from her dry warm stable, a reluctant performer. On the battlefield Cúchulainn and Laeg faced the single combatants sent by Medb from her safe place in Cuailnge to Cúchulainn at Delga. Cúchulainn cut them down, first having Laeg make him a false beard because Nadcranntail, the upstart, refused to fight a beardless boy.

Cúchulainn killed him, leaving Medb fretting over who could defeat this fearsome boy warrior.

Finn and Sean climbed aboard the chariot to ride off, victorious. The pony, sensing her work was done, fairly cantered for her cosy stable. The chariot bogged down in the mud. The pony continued to pull. The chariot lurched, threatening to dump Finn and Sean. They leapt down. The pony pulled harder and the flimsy axel cracked under the strain. The pony shot off at a gallop, abandoning Finn, Sean and the chariot.

'Feck! What'll we do?'

'Bow,' Finn hissed. They bent low twice and dashed for cover, tittering.

Following a refreshments break the performance recommenced with a poetry reading by Mr Yeats followed by Irish dancing and a quartet of folk singers.

Finn and the other players huddled in the wind-whipped tent, the faint refrain of, 'the wearing of the green,' scudding on the breeze. Charlie, in his dress uniform, poked his ginger head through the flap.

'Don't stand there, you're letting in the draught,' Finn snapped.

Charlie came inside. 'How you doing?'

'Great.' Finn rolled his eyes. 'Have you any cigarettes?'

'Aye. Want one?'

Cathleen was with the other shivering St Ita's girls. Finn waved her over. 'Still want that cigarette?' he whispered and she nodded. They made for the fluttering tent flap, passing Sean. Finn stopped.

'We're nipping out for a smoke. Want to join us?'

Sean's face showed surprise then he smiled. 'Aye, alright.'

The two of them went after Charlie and Cathleen. The rain had eased to a drizzle but whoops of air snatched at his, Sean's and Cathleen's cloaks and Charlie's kilt as they hurried round the back of the tent. Finn saw Charlie frowning when he realised Sean had tagged along and he deliberately offered his cigarettes last to Sean who said a polite thank-you. Finn shrugged it off in the struggle to light his cigarette, which took five matches, him turning his back to the wind, putting up his hood and using the tent as a windbreak. When it was glowing he passed it to Cathleen, Sean and Charlie to light theirs from it.

'So you're Finn's girlfriend,' Charlie blurted.

'I'm a girl and I'm his friend,' Cathleen said, 'so if that makes me his girlfriend will it make you his boyfriend?'

Charlie's face turned the same shade as his hair. Finn and Sean smirked.

'Cathleen,' he said, 'Charlie, a boy who's my friend, and Sean, my faithful charioteer.'

She offered her hand to a still red-faced Charlie, who took it as though it was a leper's. Sean smiled and saluted her.

'Are we any good?' Cathleen asked Charlie.

'Fine,' Charlie mumbled.

'Should think so too, all that rehearsing,' Finn added.

'Bloody right,' Sean said.

The first year hound, complete with soggy dog suit, rounded the tent. 'Yous are on!'

'Bugger,' Finn said.

They dropped their cigarettes and chased after the bedraggled dog, Charlie heading back to the Fianna Éireann and Sean inside the shelter of the tent while Cathleen and Finn went to face the audience.

The last scene was of Medb persuading Ferdia to fight Cúchulainn, his foster brother. Mr Pearse had scripted it to emphasise their brotherly bond and Cúchulainn's unwillingness to kill his kin, hoping to move the audience to tears by the interplay between Finn and James Benson, as Ferdia, while wicked Queen Medb, who was to blame for Ferdia's death because she tricked him into challenging Cúchulainn by offering her daughter, Finnabair, in reward for slaying the boy-warrior, was sure to draw boos and jeers. Despite Cúchulainn's pleas, Ferdia refuses to abandon the duel and they fight with a variety of weapons, ceasing at night to be returned to strength by herbs, potions and fortifying food and drink which they share as brothers should. Finn thought Mr Pearse had cleverly shown Cúchulainn's compassion, not something found in every version of the cycle, while not undermining his courage and warrior skill.

Finn took his place on the bank of the shallow stream that ran through the park and which was now the ford where they would do battle. Ferdia faced him. It wasn't Benson.

'What's going on?' Finn hissed to Freddie, who stood, his tunic on backwards, his brat pinned at the right instead of left shoulder and wearing his school shoes instead of sandals and leg bindings.

'Last minute sub,' Freddie replied, 'Jimmy went arse over elbow on the wet grass.'

'Do you know what you're doing?'

'Mr Pearse gave me a look at the script and haven't I read the *Táin* as much as you?' Freddie said.

Finn knew that was why Mr Pearse had picked him; no one could beat Freddie at memorisation and Finn knew he'd have the lines right. He was less certain of Freddie's ability to dual like a warrior, even in sham.

During their frantic whisperings Mr Pearse had concluded his introduction. They faced off. Freddie began:

'You are welcomed, Cúchulainn.'

'It is I who welcome you, brother Ferdia, for 'tis you who comes to me. Pray, why have you come?'

'My queen sends me as the challenger who will slay you and win for myself the loveliest of prizes.'

'You are wrong, brother. With heavy heart I say this: you will win nothing today. Haven't I laid down all who challenged me?'

'Only because none who challenged you knew you as that chicken-hearted boy who polished my sword.'

'In our training we were as one heart's blood. But that trembling boy am I no longer and my sword will slash not softly. You shall fall by a hero's hand.'

Finn leaped into the stream. Freddie copied, slipped and Finn had to grab him to stop him falling. Then with the clattering of their wooden swords, they began to dual, Freddie stabbing erratically, Finn doing his best to block the audience's view of Freddie's stumblings while keeping himself out of range of the wilder parries.

They bungled through three rounds of combat, first with swords, then shields and darts and, lastly, spears. Between each battle they laid down, one either side of the stream, on sopping-wet grass to recite Mr Pearse's dialogue. On the eve of what would be their fourth and final combat Finn had the first line:

'Ferdia, how I lament your coming for 'tis to your doom are you sent.'

'Cúchulainn, my brother that was and is, you are wise and true, a warrior and a hero. Do not sorrow for me. Everyone must come to the earth that is his last bed.' Freddie intoned each word with excessive emphasis. Finn wanted to laugh, despite the chill on his backside.

'There is no man born for whom I would do thee harm. Let us set aside our combat.'

'I cannot. To do so would shame me.' Freddie swept a woeful hand to his eyes and shrieked 'shame me'.

Finn smothered the titter tickling his throat. 'My heart is a knot of blood at the thought of our fight on the morrow.'

'The morrow will bring for you victory and heroship. No one will think you at fault. Now sleep, my brother.'

The dialogue done, they feigned sleep for the count of five then stood, yawned and waded into the stream for the final battle. Finn attempted to surreptitiously peel his sodden tunic from his legs while adopting an aggressive stance. Their spears click-clacked. Freddie lunged at Finn to deal him the scene's pivotal death blow, missed, slipped and splashed into the water. An uninjured Finn clapped his hands to his chest and also fell, as scripted, calling Laeg to bring his gae bolga to end their combat.

Nothing happened. Finn shouted again.

'Friend Laeg. Bring my gae bolga to me that I may end this woe.'

Nothing.

'Laeg.' Finn screeched the word and Sean scrambled from the tent, slid over the slick grass and skidded down the bank, yelling as he came:

'Beware the bae golga.' But the switching of two consonants went unnoticed amid bigger mishaps.

Freddie, his pride and backside bruised, slithered to his feet. Finn did the same only to promptly lance him with the death spear. Freddie had to fall again, this time deliberately. Finn knelt beside the wounded Ferdia and clutch him to his bosom as Freddie proceeded to his melodramatic death, coughing more than Finn thought was likely for someone with a gae bolga stuck in them. When he had gasped his last, Finn uttered the final words of the scene:

'It was all play, all sport, until Ferdia came to the ford. Now he is dead and I alive. Bravery is battle-madness.' With Cúchulainn's last words Finn dropped his chin to his chest and held the pose. The photographer's flash bathed them in lightning whiteness.

Someone yelled, 'Fire, fire. The tent's blazing.'

Finn threw a dying Freddie from his embraced and leapt up. The costume tent was spilling black smoke into the grey sky. Through the flap a trail of sooty actors from the *Táin Bó Cuailgne* fled, coughing more than Freddie in his death throes. Back-lighting them, yellow and orange flames licked the canvas. Sean crept over.

Freddie scrambled up. 'Jesus, how's that happened?'

Finn and Sean exchanged shamefaced looks.

'Having a fly smoke, were you?' Freddie asked.

Finn nodded.

'It's not so fly now,' Freddie remarked as men with buckets ran to dowse the flames.

'Hadn't we better help?' Sean said.

Finn sighed. 'Guess so.'

Willie Pearse shepherded the audience to the school where the Pearse women served tea while a squad of staff and boys attacked the fire. It took an hour to extinguish it; the flames especially enjoying the tarred guy ropes. When they'd succeeded, and drenched themselves, masters and boys joined the Dublin gentry for much needed fortification, sending Mary Brigid scurrying about the school in a quest for dry towels. Finn didn't see the point; they were going to have to go back out and get soaked again for the day's last rites. Mr Pearse could only wander about, hands on his head and horror on his face, struck mute by the day's unscripted tragedies.

At eight-thirty, an hour behind schedule, the Fianna Éireann drilled their weapons, fired the salute and marched to the drum and the pipe against the backdrop of a charred and smouldering tent. The parade done Mr Pearse closed the fete with praise for valiant spirits not quashed by rain, wind or fire. Honoured guests were transported to town, a brass band and the Red Branch in escort. They were cheered through the streets and Mr Colbert, heading the column, his face smeared with soot, doffed his cap while the boys marched, their chests puffed and their rifles high on their shoulders: all except Finn. For Cúchulainn never got his chariot stuck in the mud or had to fight Bookie Blackwell and he definitely never set a fire with a carelessly tossed cigarette. The whole thing, in coming off the pages of his books, had become ridiculous. He scuffed along, head bowed.

After supper Finn slipped out. He mooched through the wreckage, kicking burnt flaps of canvas; soggy material slapped back and forth. He kicked with greater vehemence.

'That'll do no good.'

Cathleen was at his side.

'You're still here?'

'I'm staying at my da's tonight,' she paused and Finn could feel her eyes on his face but didn't meet them. 'We certainly gave them a show,' she added.

'Suppose so.'

'I've not seen much of you.'

'I've been busy with this.' Finn gestured at the scorched tent.

'And other things too?'

'I guess, studying and stuff.'

'That's not what I've heard.' Her eyes were glassy; Finn couldn't tell if she was bluffing.

'What've you heard?'

'That you've been busy unmasking spies.'

'One spy.'

'That you've found out your da's a big man in this wee town.'

'Who told you?'

'And where was it you were heading on Thursday night?'

Finn stiffened. 'Nowhere.'

'My da saw you leaving with one of the masters.'

'It was Fianna business.'

'Was it?' She inched closer. 'I heard you were off joining the IRB.'

'What?'

'One of the maids at St Ita's is sweet on an IRB man. He told her. They love gossip, maids.'

Finn grabbed her arms. 'You mustn't say a word.'

'Not even to my da?'

Finn shook her. 'Especially not to him. He might let it slip to Mr…' Finn stopped. His grip on Cathleen slackened and she wriggled free.

'Let slip to who, Mr Pearse? Sure, doesn't he know?'

'You'll get me into bother.'

Cathleen held her breath, puffing her cheeks out. Finn grabbed her again and shook her. She blew a hot jet of air in his face.

'I was practising,' she said, 'not saying anything. It's hard, you know.' She pulled away from him. 'Of course I won't say anything, Finn, I'm not an eejit, but what've you to get mixed up with that mad lot for? You're not even Irish.'

'My father…'

'Is American. Oh, I know, he's in this secret society so he'd have you be member of something the like over here. I'm glad my da's not so barmy.'

She turned to go but Finn caught her arm again.

'Cathleen.'

'I promised, didn't I?'

Finn lunged at her, kissed her pursed lips then let go. He ran all the way back to school.

That night five boys lay in their dorm, stuffing their mouths with pillows to muffle the laughter that threatened to wake the school.

'That daft dog suit, I thought he'd rip the tail clean off.'

'No, when your hood kept blowing over your eyes.'

'What about when the bleeding pony ran off?'

'And we stood there bowing like eejits.'

'What 'bout you? Enough ham for a whole pig.'

'No worse than, 'beware the bae gogla!''

'Aye, and Finn going down when you'd missed him by a good six inches.'

'Sure, it was you throwing Freddie like a hot potato.'

'I don't know, I like the look on your face best, when you saw the bloody tent blazing,' Charlie cackled.

'Stop it,' Finn pleaded, forcing more goose down into his mouth.

They laughed until they were as helpless as newborns. Finn wallowed in the merriment; it made things right again.

Michaelmas Term 1913

It felt like Finn had been away from St Enda's for ever when he rode towards school, Mary Brigid driving, as he had for the first time two years ago. He'd spent hot summer days in New York's congested metropolis and was relieved to be back in Dublin: home.

'You're quiet,' Mary Brigid said after they had covered half the distance in silence, 'Did you have a good holiday?'

'Yes, thank you.'

'What did you get up to?'

'Not much.'

'My, you are chatty, aren't you?' She flicked her whip across the pony's back, a thing Finn had never known her do. He stopped himself from berating her but it was an effort.

He was fourteen now, taller, stronger, feeling a man's weight on his broadening shoulders. At home he'd been allowed to read the volumes in his father's study that detailed Ireland's struggles. When his father entertained men who were, Finn was sure, Clan members, he had been paraded and introduced with the words, 'This is my son. He's a St Enda's boy, so he is.' Finn felt sure his father also told his cronies of his sergeant's stripes and IRB membership.

Mary Brigid yanked the reins, halting the trap by the steps. The block grey building was as he'd left it two months ago but Finn was not.

Another week of the holidays remained but his father, securing a cheap passage, had sent him back early. Finn gazed around the empty dorm, wondering what this year would bring.

His possessions stowed, Finn poked his nose into the other dorms, said a few hallos and wandering off again. Downstairs the classrooms were in their end-of-term order. Only the art room showed signs of use, an easel by the window, a tray of paints abandoned nearby. Finn went to inspect the canvas. To his surprise he saw himself, or rather himself as Cúchulainn with Freddie as Ferdia, lying slain in his arms in the ford, the water reddened, the sky behind them on fire. Finn was grinning at the memory when Mr Willie Pearse entered.

'Finn, nice to have you back early. Perhaps we'll get in some painting before term begins.' He shook Finn's hand.

'Yes, sir. I've hardly done any this summer.'

'What're you making of this effort of mine? I've taken a few licences but I think it's a fair likeness of yourself. I hope you've no objections.'

'No, sir. It's grand.'

'Glad you like it,' Willie Pearse seated himself at the easel, 'Are you going to keep me company?'

'I think I'll go for a walk if that's alright, sir.'

Mr Pearse smiled. 'If you've a mind to take in the west gate you might be graced with company your own age.'

Finn blushed at the subtle reference to Cathleen.

On his way Finn paused to study his 'Green Dawn' painting and vowed he would spend the rest of the week working on something magnificent that could take its place. He was considering what when the door of Mr Pearse's study opened a crack.

'It has to be done, I know, Pat, and I'm not a man to shirk duty. But it's the men I'm feared for. They'll have to be prepared to go the whole way.'

'Things will be hard for the workers but you've the right of it.'

With that the door opened wider but the two men, Mr Pearse and Mr Connolly, stayed inside and Finn heard the rest before he realised he was eavesdropping.

'Murphy'll not take it lying down, not if it's to interfere with the profits of his precious trams or the Imperial. Still, there's nothing else for it. Larkin has told the men to come out on the twenty-sixth.'

'We'll support you, James. Things will be fine.'

'We'll see. Praise God we have the backing of people like yourself and the excellent Madam Markievicz. Her strength is a wonder to me.' Mr Connolly stepped through the door. 'Finn Devoy, you're keen to be at your studies.' He shook Finn's hand. 'Good summer?'

'Yes, sir,' Finn said, 'You, sir?'

'Aye, but busy. There's much that's been done and more in the making. Be seeing you, Pat.' Mr Connolly doffed his cap to Mr Pearse and dashed from the hall.

'Finn, wonderful to see you back safe and well,' Mr Pearse said in Gaelic.

Finn wondered if this was a quick refresher or a way of diverting his thoughts from anything he might have overheard. He replied promptly in the Irish that was fluent on his tongue after two years of practise.

'Thank you, sir. The crossing was quick and it's nice to have some time before term starts. I was talking with Mr Pearse about starting another painting while I've the studio to myself.'

Mr Pearse switched to English. 'We always have room for more of your work. Excuse me.'

Mr Pearse closed the door with a determined click.

Finn found Cathleen in the grounds with an armful of lavender.

She dropped the bundle when she saw Finn and ran to him, pecking him on both cheeks before he could stop her.

'It's good to see you,' she said in rapid Gaelic, 'I've been thinking of you all summer. Finn, I'm sorry if we parted on bad terms. I want us to be friends.'

Finn wasn't sure how they'd parted. He remembered kissing her. Seeing her bright eyes and pink lips he wanted to kiss her again.

'Of course we're friends. Anyway, I'll not cross you, Queen Medb.' He made a gallant bow.

She giggled. 'Let's sit. What news from America?' Taking his arm, she pulled him under the shade of their chestnut.

Settled beneath the spreading boughs in the flickering sun, Cathleen produced some cigarettes from her pinafore pocket.

'I borrowed these from my da.' She passed them to Finn.

At the mention of her father Finn recalled what he'd overheard.

'Cathleen, do you know a Mr Murphy?'

She laughed. 'Aye, my daddy.'

'No, another one, a businessman. I think he must run the trams and something called the Imperial.'

'You mean the Imperial Hotel? Wouldn't I love to be well acquainted with the owner of a grand place like that. But I'm not, worse luck. Why?'

'It's just something Mr Connolly was telling Mr Pearse.'

'Who's Mr Connolly?'

'A union man,' Finn said it in English because he wasn't sure of the Irish.

'Union?'

'It's for workers' rights.'

'Oh, them. My da says all they do is lose men jobs, not get them better ones.'

'Forget it.'

Cathleen shrugged and settled herself against the tree. A worry itched Finn.

'You didn't say anything, did you?'

She squinted at him. 'About what?'

Finn trailed his fingers through the grass until they found a smooth pebble. He skimmed it as far as he could.

'About… the IRB.'

She snorted and closed her eyes. 'What are you doing on Tuesday?'

'Nothing.'

'Want to go to the horse show with me?'

Tuesday, 26th August was hot. Sweat pricked Finn's back as he and Cathleen walked into the city for the annual horse show.

On the city fringes they caught the tram to the showground and spent a pleasant afternoon admiring the beasts and inspecting the gigs which were far more solidly built than the one that had almost been the undoing of Finn's Cúchulainn. They laughed about that day, especially the fire which had become school folklore, drank sour lemonade and munched tart apples. Finn spent more of his allowance than his father would have approved of on a wooden horse Cathleen fell in love with and when they'd seen enough they set off home.

The tram was crowded with people returning from the fair. Finn and Cathleen stood bumping into each other as it stuttered through the city. Finn had his back to the driver and was trying to maintain some merry banter with Cathleen when the tram stopped yet again. He braced himself for it to move on but nothing happened. He turned and saw the driver getting off.

'Where's he going?' Finn grumbled, impatient to be back in the Hermitage's cool shady grounds.

The passengers craned their necks; the driver walked around the side of the tram. A sensible fellow suggested there must be something wrong and the driver was checking. It didn't look like it to Finn as the driver threw down his cap, squatted on the curb and proceeded to roll a cigarette.

Someone called, 'That one's stopped too. What's happening?'

'I'll find out,' said a red-faced, fat-bellied man. He pushed by Finn, jumped from the tram and approached the driver.

Through the grimy window Finn saw him point at the tram and speak. The driver took another drag on his cigarette, glanced up and replied, the words puffed out in a grey cloud. The fat man stabbed the air with his finger, waving his arms like a windmill. Finn caught the words, 'can't do this'. The driver shrugged. The man gave up and reboarded the tram.

'It's a strike,' he said.

Chuntering, the passengers fought their way off the tram. Most glared at the driver. One man spat at his feet but he continued to smoke calmly.

'What are we going to do?' Cathleen asked.

'Walk.'

She sighed. 'We'd best be off then.'

'In a minute.' Finn went to the driver. 'Excuse me.'

The driver raised his head.

'Are you one of Mr Connolly's men?'

'Aye, his and Mr Larkin's.'

'This is their strike?'

'Aye and by Christ it better work,' the driver said.

'I'm sure Mr Connolly knows what he's doing,' Finn replied.

'Know him, do you?'

'Yes.'

'Well, yous can tell him from me that if it don't there's gonna be more trouble for us than him and I hope he's right in his mind about it.' The driver nodded his head in a terminal way. Finn wanted to defend Mr Connolly but Cathleen tugged his sleeve.

As they rounded the last bend in the drive Finn saw both Mr Pearses on the school steps like men on a ship's prow, watching for land. On seeing Finn and Cathleen, Willie Pearse pointed and leaned in to Mr Pearse.

'Are you in trouble?'

'Don't see why,' Finn said although his heart beat harder.

Cathleen stopped. 'I best head to my da.'

Finn stopped too. 'I suppose so.'

'Thanks for this.' She raised the wooden horse.

'You're welcome.'

She moved off. Finn drew a breath and strode forwards.

'Finn,' Mr Pearse said, 'I was starting to worry.'

'Sorry, sir.'

Mr Pearse's pale eyes rested on him. 'You've had trouble getting back, have you?'

'There's a strike on the trams, sir.'

'I see. That's all, is it?'

'Yes, sir.'

'Very well. You best hurry if you want tea.'

The dining room was quiet; fewer than a dozen boys had arrived so far and most were first years who sat glumly picking at their food.

Finn occupied his usual table and set about the trembling red glob in his bowl, Mary Brigid's homesickness remedy. He hacked at it and slurped up spoonfuls of strawberry wobble. It slipped down his throat untasted.

It wasn't much, a man getting off a tram, refusing to drive it. A dozen cross people having to find another way to lug their shopping home. But when Finn pictured Mr Connolly and the way he decried the plight of Irish workers, Finn knew it was the beginning of something big.

For four days tension simmered under the heat that clung to Dublin as the Indian summer continued. At the Hermitage

Finn was cut off and pounced on any newspapers he chanced upon, to no helpful end. Mr Murphy, owner of the trams and the Imperial, also owned the three principle dailies; anything printed in them Finn learnt to mistrust. His mind kept returning to Mr Connolly's speech on the rights of workers. He longed to be involved. Everything he'd done so far was playing at it. Out there people were really doing it: fighting for what they believed in.

'They're not doing anything, so they're not,' Hal said on Saturday as Finn finished another rant about the strike and his wish for action or at least news. Sean had been back since the day after the strike with Hal and Freddie arriving yesterday and the four of them sat together, chewing the fat along with their teas. 'They're standing around waving placards. There's no war on, Finn, so settle, will you?'

'I don't know about there not being a war,' Freddie replied, 'They might not be shooting each other but there are other ways of fighting.'

Hal stuffed a wedge of Mrs Pearse's fruit cake into his mouth. 'Such as?'

Freddie pushed his spectacles up his nose. 'The political way.'

'What's that?'

'Sanctions.'

Sean joined in. 'Sanctions?'

'Aye, that's why Murphy's locked the men out. As punishment for striking he'll keep them out, even when they want to work because they need the money,' Freddie explained.

'But he'll have to let them back,' Finn said, 'Who'll drive his trams?'

'Scabs,' Sean spat, 'My da's always on about them, stealing folks' jobs.'

'What?'

'People who aren't in the union; they'll take the work. Then Murphy'll have his businesses running again and the strike'll be pointless,' Freddie added.

'So that's it.' Finn sagged in his seat. 'They can't win.'

'It depends on nerve. We'll have to see what Larkin and Connolly do next,' Freddie said, 'They may have a great plan.'

It was like a backwards version of the *Táin,* Finn thought, instead of Cúchulainn single-handed as the champion of the people he was the villain, his power deployed in trampling the masses. It wasn't fair.

The air in the dorm that night was as thick as cotton wool. Finn flung open a window. The sound of a horse clopping up the drive drifted in. He leaned out. Mr Connolly was riding towards the school.

'Who's that?' Hal mumbled from his bed.

'No one.' Finn pulled his head inside and went to his own bed. He blew out the lamp and lay down.

After a few minutes, despite the oppressive heat, Finn heard Hal's snoring. He listened hard for Freddie and Sean's quieter breathing and, when he was sure they were sleeping, crept from his bed.

The entrance hall was deserted. Finn slipped across it, inched back the oak door that secured the front of the building and went around the outside. There was only one ground floor window showing a light. It was open. He stepped back and saw Mr Pearse at his desk with Mr Connolly pacing in front of him in jerky strides. Finn moved under the window and squatted down in the flower bed.

'...I'm worried, Pat, that it's going to come to nothing.'

'James, you must stand your ground. Be patient. Have faith.'

'But what'll become of the men if Murphy gets the strike-breakers in?' Mr Connolly's voice was strained.

'There's a rally tomorrow?'

'Aye.'

'Perhaps that'll be the turning point. If many mass Murphy may admit the futility of his position.'

'Do you think that's likely?'

'Anything's possible. Larkin will speak?'

'He will, though against my wishes. He's too hot for this town now.'

'He must be there for the men he's leading.'

'But what use is it if he lands himself in gaol?'

'I'm nothing so newfangled as a socialist and I'll not advise you on your own business but I will say this: fear not the baton of leadership falling to you. What time do you expect Larkin? I'll try to be in attendance.'

'The Countess is bringing him to Sackville Street at ten. She's been sheltering him at Leinster Road, at no small risk to her own position. Your support, and hers, are a great comfort.'

'Sure, mustn't we support each other in our causes? For seeming separate, they are, I think, one and the same.'

Next morning Finn didn't get up. When Hal asked why he proclaimed a headache. Sean offered to fetch Mary Brigid. Freddie said nothing. They left and a short time later Mary Brigid appeared. She felt his forehead, declared there was no fever and offered him something for the pain and the chance to miss morning mass. Finn declined the first but accepted the second. She closed the curtains and withdrew.

Finn lay in the red morning darkness for a few minutes. Then he leapt from his bed and arranged a bundle of blankets under the quilt before throwing on his Fianna uniform of kilt, brat and slouch hat. Recalling Mr Plunkett's words, 'the man who seeks to hide does so best in plain sight,' Finn put his hand on the doorknob, yanked the door open and strode down the stairs and out, unchallenged.

He continued to stride along the drive, through the grounds and was at the gate when Cathleen and her father emerged from the groundskeeper's house. She spotted Finn, smiled and waved. Finn returned the wave but kept going as though he was in a hurry. Helpfully, her father pulled on Cathleen's hand, dragging her towards the school where they were heading for chapel.

The last obstacle overcome, Finn's heart lightened and he ran down the road towards Dublin.

The crowds gathered in Dublin's main thoroughfare were hundreds deep and swelling when Finn joined the throng. Swept along on the tide of people moving, as one, down

Sackville Street to the General Post Office, Finn wormed his way through, under and round bodies, catching glimpses as he went of the three Romanesque statues perched atop the GPO. He envied their view of the rally.

Using sharpened elbows and chanting, 'Excuse me, pardon me,' Finn made it to the heart of the throbbing crowd, which had massed under the balcony of the Imperial Hotel where two men, Mr Connolly and another with a bushy moustache and medals pinned to his breast, waited.

Finn balanced on tiptoes and craned his neck. He spotted the Countess, standing on the running board of her motorcar, which was parked in front of the hotel. Her expression was grim and her right hand clutched a stout walking stick Finn had never known her to carry before. She was scanning the crowd. Finn followed her gaze and saw, flanking the assembly on all sides, men in Dublin Metropolitan Police uniforms, their bell shaped helmets pulled over their eyes. Each clutched a baton and stood, readied for action.

Mr Connolly stepped forward, armed with a strange conical shaped object. Only when he raised it to his mouth, addressing the crowd in an artificially loud voice, did Finn realise it must be a bullhorn.

'My warmest thanks to you for supporting our cause: your cause. Many of you have made sacrifices in recent days but only through such sacrifice can we achieve the change we fight for. And this is a fight, be in no doubt. Look about you.' Heads obliged. 'You will see the DMP gathered, intent on denying us our right to rally. But we will not be denied. Nor will we be steered from our purpose. We will fight; for reforms, for dignity and for the freedom of the working man and woman.'

People clapped, stamped their feet and whistled. Finn noticed Madam Markievicz adjust her stance and raise the walking stick so she held it across her chest. Mr Connolly held up his hand for silence.

'But fear not for there is a guide to lead us along this dark road we travel. A man who will stand and fight, as will I and as will Captain White, alongside you. Mr James Larkin.'

There was another upsurge of applause as a clean shaven man in a faded brown suit emerged onto the balcony. He took the megaphone from Mr Connolly, opened his mouth and the crowd pitched forwards; Finn was knocked off his feet and as he struggled up a high, shrill note cleaved the air, the heat and the crowd.

DMP men surged forwards, tearing apart the throng, raining blows on shrieking protestors who shielded themselves, struck back where they could, ran and fell when they couldn't. Mr Connolly called to the crowd as police stampeded into the Imperial. The Countess leapt from her motor, lashing out with her cane, becoming lost in the scrum. Mr Larkin and Captain White vanished from the balcony.

Tossed about in the mob, Finn glanced around desperately. A woman lay on the ground nearby, her dress hitched to her knees revealing her red petticoat, a torn stocking and blood gushing from her leg. She wore only one shoe. Beside her two constables knocked a young man down every time he tried to stand. Red fountained from the man's nose as a constable's baton smashed into it; the man bent forward and spat something hard and white from his mouth. Recoiling, Finn saw another man floundering towards the prostrate woman. Someone struck him from the side; he was shoved back and devoured by the mob.

A solid whack landed on Finn's shoulders, knocking the breath from his lungs. Another blow caught his legs, buckling his knees, and he crumpled. Cowering, Finn raised his arms over his head, as madness raged round. A third blow struck his right forearm; Finn heard the crack, coming from inside him, closer and louder than any other noise. Pain surged along his arm and across his chest, making him gasp and retch. He tried to shake the blackness from his eyes; his Fianna knife was at his belt and he reached for it awkwardly with his left hand, fumbling for the hilt.

'Leave him, he's only a laddie.'

Through the flickering chaos, Finn saw one of the men who had been next to him in the crowd standing with an arm outstretched to the constable readied with raised baton. The man's face was grizzled with hard labour and harder drinking.

He was small and thin, threadbare strands of hair crossed the dome of his head; his suit was patched and his shoes scuffed at the toes. Everything about him was faded, dim and poor, except his eyes. The reddened whites and watery irises flamed as he stood to protect Finn.

Finn staggered to his feet, legs trembling, and abandoned attempts to unsheathe his knife so he could nurse his right arm to his chest. The constable, his baton overhead, his eyes filled with bloodlust and darting from Finn to the man and back, took stock. His face contorted into a snarl, teeth gnashing wild and rabid. The old man stayed solid, a statue posed, arm out, hand up and open, shoulders squared, eyes fierce. For a moment the constable and the old man were caught in each other's gaze then the constable sprang forward, pummelling the old man until he fell, the end of the baton becoming drenched in red.

Drops like rain showered Finn's face.

The old man kicked at the constable, his foot catching empty air. Finn tucked his useless right arm inside his shirt and groped again for the knife, this time catching the hilt in his palm. The constable struck the old man's leg; it bent on itself, the white tip of sheered bone tearing through the thin trouser. The old man screamed, an animal cry of agony and terror. The howl crushed Finn, a paralysing weight on his chest, powerful jaws strangling his throat. Fear and panic and madness throttled life from him, trapping him in a death-grip he'd no hope of escaping. The old man clutched his leg and tried to roll away but the constable put his boot on the man's shattered bone, keeping him from moving, making him roar with renewed pain. Then he leaned forward and whacked the old man's head, once, twice, too many times for Finn to count. The skull split, spilling grey stuff that churned to red as the constable kept up his volley of blows. The old man stopped shrieking; his silence was a pressure wave against Finn's eardrums.

A blast of heat, an opened furnace door, rushed over Finn. Everywhere arms and legs thrashed, heads ducked, fingers snatched and feet danced. It became a game of dodge-tag. Finn ran, darting and weaving, leaping from the opponent's clutching fingers. Finding himself free, as though a rope had snapped, he dashed for the safety of an alley and crouched down, his broken arm hugged to his chest, the knife still sheathed. Pain rippled through his body in violent shivers. He panted and stared at the churned mess in Sackville Street; it began to blur and fall away from him.

Finn bobbed up and down. A wave repeatedly caught and dropped him. Each time he rose up there was relief; each time he sank pain surfaced. He prayed he would drown.

'Wakey-wakey, young man.'

Finn obeyed the commanding voice and saw Madam Markievicz, a purple bruise on her cheek and a blood-crusted gash above her eye.

'Up you get,' she ordered, gripping Finn's shoulders and hauling him to his feet.

Finn blinked straining eyes. He was in her motorcar. Trees jigged on one side of him. On the other the Hermitage's windows winked, stretched and yawned. The Countess bustled him from the car.

'Sorry if you were a bit jolted there,' she said, 'but it seemed best to get you from harm's way at top speed, with that arm of yours.'

Finn's arm, held across his chest by a silk scarf tied at his neck, hurt. He peeked behind the sling and saw the skin mottled purple and black. Bile rushed up from his stomach and out in a hot jet. The Countess stepped neatly aside, laughing.

'Your first battlefield injury, young man, a mere broken arm. Nothing to such a fine boy.' She strode up the steps and banged on the door. Finn leant against the motor, his breathing jagged and his head light enough to float away. Acid had filled his mouth and was dribbling down his chin.

'Finn, whatever've you done to yourself?'

Mrs Pearse's stern grey eyes scanned him.

'A minor accident,' Madam Markievicz winked at Finn, 'Schoolboy shenanigans.'

'And your eye?' Mrs Pearse enquired, her tone unsympathetic.

'Hunting accident. So it appears we've both been in the wars today, haven't we, young man?' the Countess continued, 'But while mine is a mere scratch I suggest a doctor be called post-haste for that arm.'

The Countess and Mrs Pearse glared at each other. Finn, fearing more conflict, groaned theatrically and Mrs Pearse abandoned her wordless dispute with Madam to help a shaky Finn into the family living room.

She sat him on the sofa and took Finn's arm in her mother's hands, touching and pressing. Finn watched with curiosity. His arm no longer felt like his.

'Does it hurt much?'

Finn said, 'I can't feel it at all.'

Mrs Pearse frowned. 'Stay here.'

Finn rested the arm in his lap. It couldn't be that bad; it didn't hurt as much as his sprained ankle. He tried wriggling his fingers but they wouldn't move.

Mrs Pearse was gone several minutes. She returned with Mr Slattery and Finn overheard them as they entered.

'...but said he couldn't come. There's been a to-do in town and he's rushed off his feet.'

'You're sure about the arm?'

'Aye, we'll have to do it ourselves.' There was urgency in Mrs Pearse's Irish.

The moment they saw Finn looking to them, they smiled toothily.

'Finn, you've been in the wars, I'm hearing,' Mr Slattery said in a jolly voice.

'It's nothing,' Finn said.

'I'll judge.' Mr Slattery examined Finn's arm, prodding the flesh rigorously and resting his fingers on Finn's pulse point.

'What's the matter, sir?'

'Finn, you've broken your arm. Jesus knows how. The doctor will be able to set it but he's busy and normally that'd not matter but you've managed to bend it so's you're not getting blood to these fingers. That's why it's numb.'

'Oh.'

'You're not to worry, Finn. I've a deal of knowledge on human anatomy and Mrs Pearse has attended her share of fractures. All we need do is straighten this and get the blood flowing.'

While Mr Slattery explained Mrs Pearse produced a bottle filled with clear brown liquid, a drop of which she poured into a tea cup and brought to Finn.

'God forgive me but I think it's better with than without,' she said, 'Now drink it down quick.'

Finn took the cup. The smoky smell identified the contents as whiskey. With the paper-thin porcelain between his lips, Finn tipped the liquid into his mouth. It scorched a tract down his throat. Mrs Pearse took the cup and Mr Slattery propped a woozy Finn against plump cushions. Finn mused on what a funny story this was; the first time he'd been drunk his headmaster's mother had supplied the liquor.

There was an almighty tug. Finn yelped, sure his arm had been ripped from his body. Pain surged in heavy waves.

'There, Finn, that's the worst over,' Mr Slattery said, 'perhaps you might give him another wee dram, Mrs Pearse, he's gone pale.'

Warmth gushed into his arm and Finn watched his greyed fingers flush pink.

'Aye, but in a brew, I think.'

Finn closed his eyes. If she ever brought the tea he didn't know.

He stood alone in the ford. The armies of Connacht swarmed over a distant hill, coming to overwhelm him and capture his position. The wind tossed their warrior cries to him. He took up his gae bolga. He would litter the land with the blood and gore of their rent bodies. He tightened his grip on the handle of his death spear and fixed his eyes on the approaching mob. A black sea of men poured into the valley but he feared not; he was Cúchulainn, victorious in all his skirmishes. The black mass charged toward him, men running into fire and death. He saw they wore not the tunics of Queen Medb's household. Their helmets bore no wings. They carried not spears but batons. Their breasts glittered with His Majesty's crest. He knew the battle was lost; he was Finn Devoy, victorious in nothing. He looked to that which he clutched so fearsomely, his hope of salvation, and saw it was his own severed arm.

Finn awoke soaked in sweat. A candle flickered on the nightstand. His right arm was heavy, sealed in plaster from fingers to elbow. Mrs Pearse was at his bedside. She set down her sowing and smiled.

'It's fine now, Finn. The doctor's seen to everything. If you feel a little strange don't fret, it's just the ether. Is there anything you want?'

'Thirsty,' Finn croaked.

She fetched a pitcher of water, a glass and Mr Pearse.

'Don't keep him long, Pat.' She closed the door on her way out.

Mr Pearse took her chair and handed Finn the glass which he cradled in his lap, eyes fixed on it.

'How are you, Finn?' Mr Pearse said in his softest lilt.

'Fine, sir.'

'Sorry I wasn't here to help you,' Mr Pearse continued, 'I was in town. I'm wondering where it was you were to be getting yourself a broken arm? Madam Markievicz was strangely reticent about the precise details of her coming to bring you home. Were you in town too?'

Knowing Mr Pearse was watching him, Finn said, 'Yes, sir.'

'Do you remember what happened?'

'Yes, sir.'

Mr Pearse rested his hands on the bedspread.

'I'm proud, Finn, that a St Enda's boy would concern himself with the troubles of our country.'

Tears scalded Finn's eyes. 'I didn't help him, sir.'

'Finn?'

'There was a man, sir. He saved me from the DMP. I thought to get my knife but I was afraid.' Tears dropped from his eyelashes. 'I think he might've been killed, sir.'

'Finn, this isn't your fault. I understand you feel you should have done more but you were hurt and rightly scared.'

'Sir…'

'Finn, listen to me. It's a terrible thing you've witnessed and lucky you're here and whole. That man saved you because he wanted to, without expecting anything from you. But you must learn prudence, Finn. A dead hero is but a memory; a living one is a force for change.'

Finn's guilt throbbed worse than his arm.

'We'll say no more about any of this, if you please.'

Finn rubbed a sleeve over his face. He'd been back at school so short a time and already there was trouble. If he was a real hero he would have saved that man.

Term trundled on. For eight weeks Finn couldn't join Hal, Charlie and Sean on the hurling pitch. On parade with the Fianna he couldn't shoulder his rifle. The pencil sketches for his Cúchulainn masterpiece were thrust to the back of a drawer. His grades suffered; at first it hurt to write, later he couldn't make himself care. He wouldn't tell Hal, Charlie and Freddie how he'd broken his arm and his silence made them pull away from him. Instead of trying to fix things Finn spent his time in the school chapel, where he was left alone, shamming that he'd found God.

News of the strike was his only interest and it was hard to come by. Expecting their IRB membership to grant them inside information, Finn asked Mr Plunkett and Mr Colbert often. They reported what they read in the papers, those not owned by Murphy: there was some unrest following the riots in Sackville Street; the muttered view was that the DMP had been heavy handed; three men were killed and more injured. After a few days the papers talked of other things and the day dubbed Bloody Sunday was pushed aside by everyone except Finn.

'The workers are still out, there's no talk of an end,' Mr Colbert repeated.

'But, sir, can't we do something?'

'We?' Mr Colbert snapped.

Finn swallowed the three letters that were ripe on his tongue.

'This is a matter for the unions. It's not for others to get involved,' Mr Colbert barked.

'Sir, about the strike.'

'It's the same as yesterday, Finn,' Mr Plunkett sighed.

'Isn't there anything we can do to help, sir? You know, the...?'

'A man must choose his battles, Finn. Sure, we can't fight in every one.'

Finn hung around Mr Pearse's office, hoping to bump into Mr Connolly. But Mr Connolly didn't visit. Finn hung around the Fianna hut in case the Countess attended a meeting. But she didn't. Finn sulked. He was out of the hurling team, couldn't paint or drill his platoon, his friends weren't talking to him, his arm hurt and three men were dead. All for nothing.

The cast came off on a blustery autumn day. Fallen leaves pulped to sludgy brown mulch under the trap wheels, making the rear skitter as Mary Brigid drove Finn home from the hospital, his arm flaky, greyed and cold.

'Now that thing's off I hope you'll stop moping.'

Finn pouted.

'I know it's been a miserable time for you but that's done with. You can get back to normal,' she encouraged.

'The doctor said I wasn't to play any sports for the rest of term.'

'Aye, well, there's other things you can do. Willie was telling me you've plans for a new painting; you can get that underway.'

'There's no point.'

Mary Brigid yanked the reins. The mare struggled to a slippery halt.

'Now see here, Finn Devoy, I've had enough of this, so I have. You've been wandering around with a face like a rotten potato ever since you broke your arm but it's mended now so there's to be no more self-pity. Pull yourself together.'

'It's nothing to do with my arm,' Finn snapped.

'Then what it is about?'

'I don't have to tell you. You're not one of the masters.'

'I thought I was your friend,' Mary Brigid said, 'but if not, fine. Wallow away. What do I care if you've cut yourself off from your friends and the things you care about and you're in danger of failing this term and being sent home in disgrace?' Mary Brigid whipped the reins and the mare trotted on.

Finn faced into the wind and held his eyelids open until they stung and watered. He wished the tears were real.

They were at the Hermitage before guilt wrestled an apology from him.

'I'm sorry, Mary Brigid. You are my friend. Well, you were.'

'Still am.' Her voice was sad. 'Don't take on the problems of the world, Finn. There's time enough for that when you're grown up.' She laid a hand on his. 'Be about you, play your games. Leave other things to us adults.'

Normally they spent half-term together at school but this time Hal, Freddie and Charlie went home. To get away from him, Finn thought as he sat alone by the open dorm room window, his bedspread around his shoulders, smoking and thinking. As icy air wormed its way under the blanket Finn analysed his problem. He'd done nothing at the moment when something had to be done to save that man. Ever since fear had grown on him, crippling him.

The next day Finn went to the Fianna Éireann stores. Although technically still a sergeant his behaviour hadn't warranted the rank all term; he was determined to re-earn his stripes. He started with whitewashing the gym walls, moved on to cleaning the rifles then got busy patching up some tents. By missing lunch he was finished when Mr Colbert came in at three o'clock.

''Tis a fine job you're doing, Sergeant Devoy.'

'Thought it was about time I did something useful for the brigade, sir.'

'Sure, it's grand having you fully fit,' Mr Colbert continued, 'It's been a troublesome time. Still, all behind you now.'

Mr Colbert was hovering. Finn busied his hands winding a guy rope.

'If you're feeling up to it, perhaps you might accompany me to a meeting on Thursday night.' Mr Colbert's voice dropped to a whisper.

'If you think I should, sir.'

'I know you've been mithered over goings-on lately. Sure, if you didn't set me thinking,' Mr Colbert continued.

Finn stopped looping the thick twine. 'Sorry, sir, if I spoke out of turn.'

'It's me should be apologising. Sometimes we're too caught up in the big picture to see crucial details. I've raised the matter with our brothers and it's agreed that anything concerning the rights of Irish men and women is a matter demanding our involvement.'

'And the meeting, sir?'

'Just a wee gathering to see if we can't rally more support.' Mr Colbert patted Finn's shoulder then, checking behind him, led a fumbling Finn through the IRB handshake.

The meeting was held at Wynne's Hotel. Finn accompanied Mr Colbert and Mr Plunkett who, as usual, was resplendent in a flamboyant outfit with overly tall top hat, gold brocade waistcoat, jangling bracelets and a purple-lined cloak that billowed behind him. As their threesome strode through Dublin Finn expected Mr Plunkett to take flight.

Dennis McCullough, IRB commander who had taken Finn's oath, greeted them in the lobby and they exchanged the handshake.

'Good to see you again, Devoy. How's your da?'

'Well, thank you, sir,' Finn guessed.

'This is a fair do tonight,' Mr McCullough said to Mr Colbert and Mr Plunkett, 'We hope to have satisfaction on the issue of numbers but, given the attendees, we'll keep a low profile.' He cast a withering stare at Mr Plunkett. 'I see you came dressed for such an eventuality, Mary.'

Mr Plunkett smiled his small knowing smile. 'I assume you want people to see us, just not to know our allegiance, Dinny.'

Mr McCullough coughed. 'Quite. Better remove that, Devoy.' He pointed to the IRB pin Finn had attached to his lapel.

'Undercover,' Mr Plunkett hissed as Mr McCullough's broad shoulders led the way.

The conference room was packed; Finn recognised a handful of faces from his induction and Mr Larkin. Head down, eyes averted, Finn followed Mr Colbert and Mr Plunkett as they circulated. He watched each greeting, learning the IRB men from the others. They made their way to the far side where a tallish man with an angular face and high cheek bones, stood. His fair hair was swept back from a high forehead; his sunken eyes and drawn features gave him a skeletal appearance. He inspected them through small round spectacles, his thin lips pulled into a tight line. He pressed his hand to Mr Colbert then Mr Plunkett and Finn saw he wasn't IRB.

'Good to see you, Con, Joe,' he said, 'Who will this young fellow be?'

'Eoin, this is Finn Devoy. Finn, Professor MacNeill, vice-president of the Gaelic League.'

'Go mbeannaigh Dia dhuit*, a dhuine uasail♣,' Finn said.

Professor MacNeill smiled. 'I detect a hint of America in your otherwise charming Irish. Not related to Dr Michael Devoy, are you?'

'He's my father, sir.'

'Well, 'tis a pleasure, indeed. Your father is a great supporter of my humble organisation. It's gratifying to know those abroad have not forgotten their Irish roots.'

'Yes, sir,' Finn said, realising the promise of money was why Professor MacNeill was so delighted to meet a schoolboy.

Mr Colbert said, 'I felt the chance for Finn to make the acquaintance of so many great Irishmen was too good to pass up.'

'Certainly,' Professor MacNeill replied, withdrawing his hand. 'Perhaps we can talk later.' He nodded his head and they turned to see a small man with a stoop limping to the large table set in the room's centre.

---

* Pleased to meet you

♣ sir

Finn gasped, quickly masking it with a gargled cough.

Mr Colbert slapped his back and whispered in his ear, 'Sean MacDermott, a fellow brother.'

Since Finn had last seen Mr MacDermott in Liverpool his health had not improved. He remained slight, his complexion waxen, his left arm dragging at his side. He leaned on his stick as Finn remembered him doing two years ago.

'Was it Sean invited you?' Mr Plunkett asked Professor MacNeill.

'It was and I couldn't refuse, so much he's done for the League and the GAA. I believe his hand is also in with Griffin,' Professor MacNeill replied.

Mr MacDermott hailed the room in Irish before switching to English.

'Gentlemen, be seated, if you can, for we are oversubscribed by backsides and undersubscribed by chairs.' Chuckles flittered around the room. 'I'm sure you'll excuse me claiming one myself.' With a murmur of ascent Mr MacDermott seated himself at the head of the table.

Finn shuffled forward as Mr Colbert, Mr Plunkett and Professor MacNeill took seats. Finn stood behind them. When most of the men were sitting Mr MacDermott cleared his throat with a dry cough.

'Our agenda tonight is the founding of a National Volunteer Movement.' His voice was clear and steady. 'Our cousins to the north have, for some time, had at their disposal the Ulster Volunteer Force. Latterly they have armed themselves and declared their intent to resist Home Rule by force. My proposal is the formation of a parallel nationalist organisation, the purpose of which would be to defend the Home Rule bill against armed resistance from Unionists.'

There were exclamations of consensus.

'I suggest, gentlemen, we vote, on the understanding that details are finalised later,' Mr MacDermott continued when his audience had regained their sobriety.

Professor MacNeill spoke. 'Won't the formation of a volunteer force be seen as an act of aggression?'

'Do we view the formation of the Ulster Volunteers as an act of aggression?' Mr MacDermott challenged.

'By Christ, I do.'

The assertion came from a man whose face was scored with lines. His domed forehead was exposed by retreating hair while a bushy moustache covered his mouth and spectacles perched on his nose. He looked to Finn like a battle-hardened veteran.

'Ah, Tom, grand to see you,' Mr MacDermott said, 'Please give us your views.'

'With pleasure.' The veteran pushed back his chair and stood, chest out, head up. 'The UVF have declared their plans for war if Home Rule is introduced. Their founding is an act of hostility to those who would welcome Home Rule. But let us not forget that the UVF represent the minority. By our tolerance of their resistance and failure to counter it with our own force we send a dangerous message: that we, the majority, will lie down to die at their command. Sure, I've no such bloody intention. 'Tis our duty to raise a nationalist force. My only regret is that we've been so tardy about it.'

Cheers of support flexed around the room, intoxicating the air.

'What do we suppose the British will do while we're arming ourselves? Perhaps Mr Clarke would lecture on that,' Professor MacNeill sneered.

Mr Clarke glared at him; the professor examined his fingernails.

'Nothing,' he answered, 'For they've done a deal of nothing against the UVF. The precedent's been set.'

'Indeed, Tom,' Mr MacDermott said, 'I understand your concerns, truly, Eoin, but we must protect our interests. If we believe Home Rule is the way to Irish independence we must defend it. As for the British, surely they'll consider it our constitutional obligation to see bills past by Parliament are enforced.'

The room swayed.

'We should declare, with a written constitution, that any national volunteer force will rise in arms as a last resort and by the unanimous consent of all members of its council,' Professor MacNeill said, 'and if you wish the support of the

Gaelic League I'm afraid I shall insist on being on that council.'

'Sure if you aren't already,' Mr MacDermott replied without hesitation.

'Very well.'

'Then we vote?'

'We vote,' Professor MacNeill affirmed.

'Those in favour of a National Volunteer Movement?'

Finn watched hands rise.

'Against?' No one moved.

'Mr Devoy, you abstain?' Mr MacDermott fixed his dark eyes on Finn.

'I didn't think you expected me to vote, sir.'

'Do you understand what we're voting for?' Mr MacDermott asked.

'For a volunteer force like the one in the north.' Finn tried to keep his voice from cracking.

'What would your feeling be on the matter?'

Finn had thought he was here as a curiosity, to be inspected. Now he was being called upon to speak, to act. His legs trembled.

'To any who don't know, our young friend is the son of Michael Devoy, that great Irish expatriate, supporter of all our causes, generous benefactor to our organisations and dear friend to many,' Mr MacDermott proclaimed, 'Apologies, gentlemen, for my digression. Perhaps, Finn, you might think how your father would vote.'

Finn's blood drained away; he was here to cast his father's ballot on behalf of the Clan na Gael and, though only a token gesture, to cast his own too. His 'yes' would mean all the major organisations had agreed to the volunteer force: the IRB; the Gaelic League and GAA; Sinn Fein; the ITGWU and, with Finn's vote; St Enda's and the Clan.

'I think,' his voice sounded hollow in the grand room, 'we should have our own force. We're as important as the others.'

'Maith thú*!' Mr Clarke got to his feet again and clapped hard.

---

* well done

'Tom, let the lad finish,' Mr MacDermott said, 'So you vote in favour, Finn?'

'I do, sir.'

The room, giddy from passing the nationalist cup, cheered. Mr MacDermott called for a break.

Finn huddled between Mr Plunkett and Mr Colbert as tea circulated and cigarettes were lit. Longing for a smoke, he wasn't listening properly as both masters congratulated him on how he'd carried himself. Finn cursed them for not warning him about the vote. Then Mr MacDermott limped through the parting crowd.

'Finn, William that was.' He offered his hand. 'Sorry to be so formal.'

'That's alright,' Finn said, 'Nice to see you, sir.'

'I didn't realise you were acquainted,' Mr Plunkett exclaimed.

'We are although it's many a day since we met,' Mr MacDermott replied, 'How goes the Count, Joe?'

'The old man's well enough.'

'And Con, good to see you again,' Mr MacDermott said.

'Grand to have you back in the fold,' Mr Colbert replied.

'Well, Finn, fáilte♣,' Mr MacDermott said and, lowering his voice, 'Sorry it wasn't me that inducted you. I've been away these past few months. Now I'm returned we'll surely meet often. Send my regards to your father.'

The trio retreated to school, leaving Professor MacNeill and Mr MacDermott debating the volunteer force constitution. Mary Brigid was on the front steps as they approached.

Catching sight of her, Mr Colbert said, 'Think I'll check the Fianna store.' He veered off, as Finn and Mr Plunkett mounted the steps.

'Joe, where've you been? You've missed tea.'

'In town on some minor matter,' Mr Plunkett replied, 'where I happened to chance upon this fellow. Don't fret, Mary Brigid, we took tea in town.'

Mary Brigid frowned. 'Was that Con with you?'

♣ welcome

'It was. The three of us dined together and merry it was, eh, Finn?'

'Yes, sir.'

'Finn, you should mind the rules. You've to tell someone when you go to town. Perhaps, Joe, you'll have the sense to see students home promptly if you find them roaming Dublin.' Mary Brigid span on her heel.

'She's a canny one,' Mr Plunkett mused, 'Excuse me, Finn.'

Alone on the steps, Finn knew he needed allies. The meeting at Wynne's had shown him how much that mattered. Secrets and lies were no good to him; he needed his friends.

Tomorrow, the twenty-fifth of November, in the grounds of the Rotunda Hospital, the rally, held for the purpose of recruiting men to the new Irish Volunteer Movement, would take place. Finn, Charlie, Hal, Freddie and Sean were busy with boot black and brass polish.

'That'll do,' Hal grunted, pushing a strand of dark hair out of eyes that gleamed brighter than either his boots or buttons.

'That's rubbish,' Charlie scoffed. He dropped his own boot, snatched Hal's and scrubbed the leather hard enough to wear a hole through it then held the boot at arm's length. 'You've got to give it welly.'

'Or get some eejit to do it for you,' Hal laughed.

Charlie hoiked the boot across the room, Hal ducked, and the boot plummeted onto Freddie's bed, in the middle of the page of Latin verbs he was memorising while polishing his own boots with absent-minded strokes.

'Look what yous've done.' He held up the book, revealing a black smudge and a rip.

Sean hid a grin.

'Give over, it's only Latin. You know it backwards anyway,' Hal snapped.

Finn smiled at his friends: his comrades. He couldn't help thinking of them in those terms now, even Sean. When he'd resolved to tell them about Bloody Sunday and the IRB he'd agonised over including Sean. He was glad he had; Sean was first to accept, support and forgive. Finn was surprised they believed him but they did, relieved to know at last why Finn had been so distant all term. Mr MacDonagh had read them *Henry V* and Finn thought of the king's speech to his troops, 'We few, we happy few, we band of brothers.' It was apt. 'Us ourselves against the bloody lot,' Charlie had decreed. Finn agreed and thought of Cúchulainn. If one could defeat armies then five could win untold victories.

'What is it Colbert wants us to do today?' Hal asked.

'Hand out recruitment forms and keep order,' Finn said. Mr Colbert had asked the Red Branch to marshal at the rally to help things go smoothly. Lately the master had been heaping responsibility onto Finn. Finn had doubts, despite the second lieutenant's badge on his lapel. He thought the promotion premature but Mr Colbert, overjoyed with Finn's performance at Wynne's, had said it brought Cúchulainn to mind, when he too, but a boy, took his place in the world of men. Finn didn't want to hear that; Cúchulainn was a true hero.

'Should be grand,' Charlie said, 'as long as it doesn't rain.'

'Still think rain's our biggest problem?' Hal asked as they halted outside the Rotunda gardens next morning. An immense crowd had assembled on the immaculate lawns. Finn glanced to David, relieved he'd stayed on as brigade commander despite being at Trinity now.

'Quite a turnout, Devoy.'

'Yes, Captain,' Finn gulped.

'I'll go right; you left and we'll have this covered.'

David took up position in front of his squad and called drill commands; Finn, a beat behind, did likewise. Forty boys in green took to the gardens, losing themselves among the shrubbery as they battled to pass around enrolment forms and direct men to the correct queues.

They hadn't been on the field long when a hand bell drew their attention to the hospital's rear steps where six men had congregated. Finn, recognising Mr MacDermott and Professor MacNeill, whispered their names to Charlie who passed them on.

Professor MacNeill was handed a loud hailer. His voice, crackling and hollow, echoed out.

'A plan has been deliberately adopted by one of the great English political parties to make the menace of armed violence the determining factor in the future of relations between this country and Great Britain.'

Cheers drowned out the rest of the speech, clearly signalling Professor MacNeill had convinced them of the legitimacy of a volunteer force. Finn wondered who had convinced him.

It was a chilly day straddling autumn and winter; the sky was clear and the sun dazzling. Finn elbowed and jostled through the undergrowth of willing men desperate to sign up, organising them into queues. By lunchtime his tunic was soaked with sweat.

Charlie bumped up alongside Finn. 'Aren't we due a break?'

'We could have a few minutes,' Finn puffed.

Edging their way around the perimeter, they found and took possession of a doorway. Charlie produced a pack of cigarettes from under his kilt.

'Looks like this Volunteers thing's gonna be big. What do you reckon Mr Pearse thinks to it?' he said.

Finn shrugged.

'I'm sure Mr Pearse thinks it's grand if what I've heard of him is true.'

Finn and Charlie jumped from their slump against the door, dropping their half smoked cigarettes. Finn recognised the veteran who had spoken at Wynne's and automatically saluted, jabbing Charlie in the ribs when he didn't do the same.

'Steady lads, at ease,' the old soldier replied. He studied their faces and pointed at Finn. 'You were at Wynne's. We weren't introduced. I'm Tom Clarke.'

'Pleased to meet you, Mr Clarke,' Finn said, 'I'm…'

'I know, lad. Your father and I are well acquainted, though it's many a year since we met but sure, we've been through it together.'

Impulsively, Finn stuck out his hand and, when Mr Clarke took it, gave him the IRB shake, his most fluent so far. Mr Clarke returned it perfectly then faced Charlie but Finn shook his head.

'This is Corporal Barrett of the Fianna Éireann, Red Branch and a good friend of mine,' he explained.

'Aye, my wife's always saying you need to know who your friends are and by God she's right in that and many other things too,' Mr Clarke replied as he transformed his outstretched hand into a salute, 'You lads've some work on today.'

'Yes, sir,' Charlie said, recovering from Finn's handshake shenanigans.

'I seem to have interrupted your break. Perhaps you men would care for one of these.' Mr Clarke pulled a packet of Players from his pocket and offered them to Finn. When Finn hesitated he smiled. 'I own the tobacconists down there.' He gestured towards Parnell Street. 'Call in any time, I'll tell Katty to look out for you. Marching men need their comforts.'

'Thank you, sir,' Finn said and took a cigarette.

'Keep them,' Mr Clarke replied when Charlie, having taken one, attempted to return the pack. 'It's chilly today. Bet your legs're feeling the pinch.' Mr Clarke nodded at their kilts, 'This is the best thing for an Irish winter.' From his other pocket he took a small flask which he passed to Finn. Finn drank a sip and offered it to Charlie who did the same, grimacing at the whiskey's burn. 'That's the fella,' Mr Clarke said when he had swallowed his share and repocketed the flask. 'Well, I best get back. Remember me to your da, Finn.' Mr Clarke disappeared into the crowd.

Charlie stared at the cigarettes. 'Is he one of those IRB men?'

'Yes, though I wasn't sure 'til now.'

'Queer lot, aren't they?'

'Thanks.'

'I didn't mean…'

'I know. Come on.'

By the following week it was known that three thousand men had joined the Irish Volunteers at the Rotunda rally. While others rejoiced, Finn had to conceal his disappointment. Imagining legions of soldiers off the pages of the *Táin*, he didn't think three thousand enough. But he kept to his vow of action, throwing himself into his studies, the hurling team and the painting he'd planned at the end of the summer.

Wednesday nights became 'art night'. After dinner Finn went to the studio and, sometimes with Willie Pearse for company, worked on his canvas. Using his Cúchulainn sketches, one a close up of the warrior and the other a long view showing the armies of Ailill and Medb charging the boy warrior, the painting progressed. It was a massive canvas, four foot by three and Mr Pearse had set aside a corner of the studio where the painting remained in full view because there was no other option for its storage. At first Finn disliked this; his mates could see when he messed up. But, as the painting advanced, he became proud of the sight of it.

The Wednesday after the recruitment drive Finn was bent over his work, a crick in his neck and his eyes stinging from keeping them fixed on the tiny figures he was painting to swell the ranks of the advancing armies. Mr Pearse had implored Finn to content himself with creating an impression of a massing army with vague brush strokes but Finn couldn't do that. Each soldier counted so each would be painted, however long it took. Glad Willie Pearse wasn't there, persuading him to take shortcuts, Finn pressed on.

He'd done one hill's worth of soldiers when a shadow fell across his work.

'That's a terrible job you've given yourself there, Finn,' Mr Connolly said.

'Yes, sir. But I'd rather not do it in half-measures.'

'Good for you, lad,' Mr Connolly patted Finn's shoulder, 'Have you a minute?'

Finn laid his brush down.

'My apologies for not coming sooner, Finn. If I'd realised you were there, at the...that terrible Sunday in August, I'd have come at once. Dear Constance, she should have told me but her loyalty to her Fianna boys knows no bounds and she thought it best to say nothing. Only now, in light of recent developments, did she think to let me in on it.'

'Please, sir, you don't...'

'I do, Finn.' Mr Connolly rubbed his forehead. 'I've come to tell you we've formed a defence force, the Irish Citizen

Army. Those in it will protect men on picket lines in the future. I hope that'll put your mind at rest.'

'Yes, sir. What about the strike, sir?'

Mr Connolly twirled his trilby in his hands. 'We're running into the gale. Well, I'll let you to your labours.' He turned and was gone, leaving Finn with the understanding that that particular battle was lost.

Mr Pearse called an extra-ordinary assembly on the last day of term. Finn sat at the back with Freddie, Hal, Sean and Charlie, as their senior status stipulated. The hall rustled with whispered questions.

When Mr Pearse took the stage Finn realised how little he had seen of his headmaster that term. His suit was baggy, the collar gaping around his neck. His hair sat further back on his forehead. The corners of his eyes were crowded with wrinkles and he appeared to be squinting as if his sight was failing. His face was pale. He seemed to have faded, to be fading still, right before them. One day he would vanish completely and no one would recall what he looked like.

'Dia dhuit ar maidin*, boys.'

'Dia dhuit ar maidin, sir,' chorused the seventy-strong school.

'A thousand pardons for calling you here so abruptly.' Mr Pearse's hand fluttered to his brow as if brushing away a fly, then settled at his side again. 'I have an announcement that affects you, the life blood of my humble school.'

Finn and Freddie exchanged glances. Freddie's brows were raised, his green eyes, as they met Finn's blue ones, glinted behind his spectacles.

'When you return hence I will not be here to greet you. I travel to America in service of the two loves of my life: St Enda's and Ireland. I hope to return before the end of term but wish to prepare you for the eventuality that I may not.'

The hall gasped.

---

* good morning

'While I am abroad, my brother will undertake the role of acting headmaster. You will look upon him as you would me and I shall hear nothing but praiseworthy reports from him.'

As Mr Pearse spoke Willie stood from his seat on the stage, bowed to the school and sat again.

'I wish you a peaceful holiday and remind you that you have done St Enda's proud this term; I expect nothing less in the new year. Nollaig Shona♣.'

The pause between Mr Pearse's parting words and the repeated cries of, 'Nollaig Shona,' and, 'Merry Christmas,' was too long for comfort but Mr Pearse merely smiled and nodded before departing with clipped steps.

'What the bloody…?' Hal burst out.

'Dunno, but he's making it clear he doesn't want to be asked.' Freddie gestured to the door that swung with the force of Mr Pearse's exit.

'I'm going to find out,' Finn said.

'You're not going to ask him?' Charlie cried.

'No. But I am going to find out.'

Finn appraised his masterpiece. Sunlight blazed above a wild and barren landscape. In the distance, emerging from beneath the horizon and pouring over the moor, were the individually painted soldiers of the attacking armies. Bottom left, close to and in glorious detail, was Cúchulainn, holding aloft his gae bolga, the wind blowing his hair and the swirling torrent of the ford snaking his legs. As the last of night's darkness faded the hero stood bathed in gold, readied for a victory that was his for the taking.

'It's a grand work.' Willie Pearse rested a hand on Finn's shoulder.

'Thanks, sir.'

'We'll have a formal unveiling next term. Before he leaves, I'll speak to Pat about where he'd like it hanging.'

'Why is Mr Pearse going to America?'

'The school needs funds and there's support for our enterprise among Irish exiles,' Mr Pearse explained.

♣ Merry Christmas

'And that's going to take all term, sir?'

'Mr Plunkett?'

The master was attacking a pile of finals, slashing ticks and crosses, tutting to himself.

'Aye, Finn?'

'Have you a minute, sir?'

'I do.'

Finn pulled up a chair and sat. Mr Plunkett removed his pince-nez.

'Spit it out, Devoy, afore it chokes you, so.'

'Why is Mr Pearse going to America?'

'In service of St Enda's and Ireland.'

'With respect, sir,' Finn replied, his mouth dry, 'I'm old enough to join the IRB, vote at their meetings and help with recruiting Volunteers. I'm old enough to be part of all this.' Finn waved his hands though 'all this' was nowhere to be seen. 'Aren't I old enough to be told the truth? Sir.'

Mr Plunkett blinked once then chuckled.

'Perhaps, as you feel so strongly, you would prefer to ask Mr Pearse. It's not my place to tell you another's business.'

Finn opened his mouth to protest. Mr Plunkett held aloft his hand.

'However, I suppose I could point out a few pertinent facts and allow you to reach certain conclusions. Where would you guess Mr Colbert is tonight, Finn?'

'Mr Colbert?'

'What is today, Finn?'

'Thursday.'

'And where does Mr Colbert go on Thursdays, and I, if not for this marking?' He laid a hand upon the papers. 'And you, on occasions. Mayhap tonight there's another accompanying Mr Colbert.'

'Mr Pearse? He's at the, he's with, they've gone to…'

Mr Plunkett winked. 'The baptism before the American expedition. Now, Finn, I've this marking to finish.' With the replacing of his pince-nez Mr Plunkett made it plain he would say no more.

The dorm was in its usual end of term chaos. Trunks, their lids thrown open and their stomachs stuffed with clothes and books, formed an obstacle course. Finn hesitated in the doorway, scouting for a way through. Hal and Freddie were by their beds, packing. Freddie spotted him first.

'Finn, what's up?'

Finn shook off his trance. 'I don't know.' He glanced around the room. 'Where's Charlie?'

'Hunting for his coat,' Sean said.

'Right.' Finn lurched across the room, fumbled in his bedside cabinet and found the remains of the packet of Players Mr Clarke had given him. 'I'm going for a smoke. When Charlie gets back can you all join me?'

'Aye,' Hal said, 'Usual place?'

Finn nodded and made his way downstairs.

'Where're you going?' Mary Brigid called to him.

Finn stuffed the Players into his pocket.

'Nowhere.'

'You go there an awful lot these days. Meeting anyone? Con? Joe?' She crossed the entrance hall, opened the door and leaned out.

Her shoulders relaxed at the sight of the empty lawn.

'I just fancied a walk. It's not past lights out.'

She closed the door and came to Finn. 'Why is Pat off to America?'

'For the school.'

'Don't lie, Finn.' Her words were hot against his cheek.

Finn pressed his lips together, avoiding her gaze.

'Perhaps I'll ask Con or Joe, shall I?'

Finn shuffled.

'What is it they've you mixed up in?' She grabbed his arm. 'I'm feared for you and for Pat. Tell me, Finn, or I'll learn of it some other way.'

'Mary Brigid.' Finn looked at her. 'You mustn't.'

'Mustn't I?' She threw his arm to him and stalked off.

Snow had fallen that week and the lawn in front of the Hermitage was a pie-bald tapestry of white and green. Finn's feet crumped and squelched as he headed for the trees. He squatted under his chestnut on a patch of drier ground in the lee of the trunk. With shaking fingers he lit a cigarette and held it like a wand, tracing smoky letters in the air: I-R-B.

Mr Pearse was going to America to meet with his father.

The Clan na Gael and the IRB were working on some scheme for the independence of Ireland.

Four figures emerged and clustered around him. Finn shared out cigarettes and told them what he had deduced.

'Are you sure?' Charlie asked.

'It's the only thing that makes sense.'

'I agree,' Freddie replied.

'Are you going to ask your father about it?' Sean asked.

'No,' Finn said, 'I'd rather not have him know I know. Anyway, we don't really know anything.'

'But what's the IRB want with Pearse?' Hal demanded, 'He's a teacher.'

'Maybe that's the point,' Finn said.

'How?' Sean asked.

'No one would suspect him of being involved in a revolution,' Charlie guessed.

'No.' Finn shook his head. 'Because people will listen to him, believe in what he says. If he was a soldier it'd be too incendiary. Instead he's an educated man who'll make rational whatever the IRB are planning. I think the IRB need him because he can get people to follow him.'

'Who the feck'll do that?' Hal asked.

'Us.'

Hilary Term 1914

Finn stood on deck, scanning the Atlantic. He flipped up the collar of his new winter coat, snuggling into the scarf his mother had knitted him. With aching teeth he pulled on another of the caramels from his Christmas stocking as he searched the horizon for a liner like his travelling in the opposite direction, carrying Mr Pearse, buried in his own winter coat and on course for his American mission.

Christmas had been the usual presents, carols, a tree, mince pies and turkey. More unusual was how his father had thrown himself into the festivities with artificial cheer, saying nothing about St Enda's other than asking after Finn's studies. It was as if the Clan, the IRB, the whole Irish question, had vanished under the snow that blanketed New York.

Finn had attempted to raise the topic with his father. It was the first week of the holidays and Finn was helping hang the outside garlands. His father perched on the ladder; Finn passed him nails as he hammered holly above the lintel.

'Have you heard, Father, of the new Irish Volunteer Movement, formed to defend Home Rule from the Ulster Volunteers who plan to resist its introduction by force?'

His father missed the nail; the hammer rebounded off the brickwork. He cursed then mumbled:

'The right to bear arms, all countries should have such a constitution as ours.'

Finn pressed on. 'Our Fianna brigade helped at the recruitment drive.'

'Glad to see you're doing more than prancing around with wooden swords.'

Finn brushed off the verbal slap.

'I was there when it was decided to establish the Volunteers. I voted in favour.'

His father smacked his thumb. 'Bejesus!' He wedged the injured hand under his armpit and climbed down the ladder.

'I met Professor MacNeill too,' Finn added, 'He said to pass on his thanks for your support of the Gaelic League.'

'We have a duty to offer assistance when we can,' his father grunted, 'Fetch some ice for this thumb.'

Finn didn't move. His father glowered at him.

'I'd charge you to remember why I sent you to St Enda's, boy. Your efforts are best devoted to your studies. Ice, Finn, hurry up!'

His father's unwillingness to discuss it confirmed that whatever was happening was too big, in his father's view, for a fourteen year old boy. His father could try shutting Finn out of the business that he, not Finn, had started but once he was at school he would be in the midst of it, through the Fianna and the IRB. His father couldn't do anything about that. Finn walked to the prow, leaned over the undulating waves and watched for Ireland's rising from the sea.

Morning bell was ringing. Finn sat up. Instead of rapid jangling notes, the bell tolled a steady 'dong, dong, dong'.

Finn reached for his uniform; the fabric felt alien. When he inspected it he saw not the green and grey of everyday but black, both blazer and trousers. The bell continued clanging. Alone in the dorm, he donned the black clothes and rushed downstairs.

At the bottom a line of boys, dressed alike in black, filed past him. Finn tried to break through but found his hands were a ghost's, transparent and powerless. He opened his mouth to speak but no sound emerged.

Finn was in the hall. The same line of boys paraded by him with the same stately ritual. They formed ranks, facing the stage, its rich green curtains drawn, and continued to march on the spot. Where were the masters? Mr Pearse? His friends?

The curtains drew aside, revealing a coffin. Willie Pearse took the stage to address the lads, who marched monotonously in place. Finn became aware of a tightening around his throat. He put his hands to it. His fingers touched thick rope.

Finn was on the stage, balancing on a stool, the noose around his neck tighter than before. The coffin was in front of him. The lid was up. Mr Pearse lay inside it, his face waxen, his arms folded across his chest. An IRB pin was attached to his lapel.

Finn felt a jerk as the stool was kicked from under him. He jigged the hangman's dance.

In the hall the ranks of boys continued to march and get nowhere.

'It was a dream. What're you getting mithered for?'

Finn shuddered again at the memory. He and Cathleen were sitting under the chestnut. It was the first day when frost had not covered the ground.

'But it was horrible.'

They were talking in Gaelic, as they usually did, and sharing a cigarette. It was a sunny Saturday afternoon. Cathleen was visiting her father, who, because of the thaw, had gone to dig the gardens, leaving her free to sneak off with Finn. Without intending to he'd told Cathleen of the dream he'd had a week ago but which lingered vividly, especially the frozen death pallor on Mr Pearse's face.

'I keep thinking it means something.'

'Don't be daft. You're missing your precious Mr Pearse, that's all.' Cathleen kissed Finn on the nose. 'Poor laddie, did your headmaster leave you alone?'

'It's not funny, Cathleen. I've got a bad feeling.'

'What did you have for lunch?'

'Not that kind of a feeling,' Finn snapped.

'What about this kind of feeling?' Cathleen pressed her lips to his. Her mouth was warm, smoky from the cigarette and sweet from the last of Finn's caramels. He kissed her back and slipped his arm around her waist. She cuddled up to him and he felt a tingling inside. The troubling dream faded.

'At ease. Dismissed,' Finn barked.

His platoon dropped arms and relaxed in their ranks.

'You've them well drilled,' Mr Colbert praised.

Only a few weeks into term, Finn was pleased with how his squad were performing. 'Thank you, sir.'

'Won't Mr Pearse be impressed when he returns?'

'Do you know when he'll be back, sir?'

'I don't, Finn.'

Mr Colbert moved away. David Reddin sidled over.

'Was Colbert telling you about the meeting tomorrow?'

'What meeting?'

'Must've slipped his mind,' David mumbled and punched his hands into his pockets as he walked off.

Finn waited until Mr Colbert was alone, about to lock up.

'There's an IRB meeting tomorrow, sir?'

'Who told you?'

'David mentioned it, sir.'

'Oh. Aye, there is, Finn.'

Finn waited for instructions.

'I think it's best if you concentrate on your studies this term, Finn. After all, you are here to learn,' Mr Colbert muttered.

'But, sir…'

'Curfew soon, Devoy. Up to school with you.'

Mr Colbert slammed the door before scarpering through the grounds to the Hermitage, not checking Finn was doing as told.

Finn frowned. Then he remembered hanging the garlands, his father hitting his thumb. His bloody father had told Colbert to lay off the IRB stuff. It wasn't fair. Finn kicked out and the toe of his boot struck a rock. He plucked it up, hurled it at the drill hall and listened with satisfaction as it shattered a window.

'That's a good thing,' Cathleen said when Finn told her of his being kept from the IRB. He hadn't dared tell his pals yet.

'How so?'

'Because, you eejit, we can spend more time together.' She ducked under his arm as they walked through the Hermitage's park.

Finn pulled away from her. 'Don't you see what it means?'

'What, Finn Devoy, does it mean?' she said, music in her words.

'They don't want me for whatever it is they've planned.'

'Or they've the sense to keep you out of it.'

Finn quickened his pace.

Cathleen said, 'They're dafter than bairns with their silly handshakes and coded messages.'

'No.' Finn snapped the word.

She dog-trotted up and tugged his arm.

'Finn, stad*.' She pulled him back. 'Don't worry about it.'

'You don't understand,' Finn stormed, 'They're going to fight.'

'What the devil for?'

'Home Rule. Irish Independence.'

Cathleen burst out laughing. 'They're even madder than I took them for. How many of them are there?'

'Enough,' Finn said, not knowing if this was true.

Cathleen laughed again. 'Sure, I hope that's so but you listen to me, Finn, they've let you out of it and you stay out. Do you want to get yourself killed? Because I couldn't stand that.' She pouted at him and Finn wasn't sure he could stand it either. But it was his duty to defend Ireland.

St Enda's without Mr Pearse was adrift in the doldrums and Finn was reduced to the tedious routine life of a St Enda's boy. With no revolutionary developments his pals had stopped asking about the IRB, which was as well because it stayed off-limits to Finn. The only advantage to this was that Mary Brigid stopped stalking him, hoping to catch him going 'nowhere'.

'Finn Devoy, I do believe you're miffed not to be the centre of attention this term,' Cathleen crowed as Finn finished another lengthy moan.

'Am not.'

'Are too. I would've thought you'd be glad of a quiet time,' Cathleen added.

Finn folded his arms and tucked his chin to his chest, hiding the flush that ran along his neck.

'Leave it be,' she advised.

'What're we up to today?' Hal asked.

It was Saturday afternoon, slack time.

'Why don't we wander into town?' Finn suggested.

---

* stop

'I'll have to pass,' Sean sighed, 'I've to get this essay done.'

The four lads set out.

'How's Cathleen?' Charlie asked when they were on the road to Dublin.

'Fine, I suppose.'

'Not had a lovers' tiff have you?' Hal teased.

'What?'

'Come on. Yous are like a married couple,' Hal went on.

'Are not.'

'Oh, Cathleen, you're so beautiful. Give me a kiss,' Charlie mocked.

'It's not like that,' Finn growled. Three faces grinned at him.

'How is it, then?' Hal asked, 'Better than just kissing, eh?'

'Piss off!' But Finn was glad they thought kissing was the reason he was spending so much time with Cathleen.

'Don't be touchy, Finn,' Freddie said, 'We're pulling your leg. Good man yourself.'

Finn trained his eyes on the shop fronts as they turned into Parnell Street, ignoring the pantomime of elbowing, nudging and winking playing out behind him. He was searching for Tom Clarke's tobacconists.

The tiny shop was sandwiched between a public house and a hardware suppliers. Finn noted the sign 'T. S. Ó'Cléiriś. Tobacconist & Stationer.' then crossed the threshold. As his eyes adjusted to the dim light filtering through smog-stained windows, he saw, standing behind the counter, the pale face and slim figure of a youngish woman. Her hair was loosely pulled back, her dress plain and practical while rimless glasses framed calm steady eyes. She smiled at them.

'What're we doing here?' Hal hissed.

'Cigarettes,' Finn replied.

'Good morning, boys. What can I do for you?'

'Are you Mrs Clarke?' Finn enquired.

'I am. It is my husband you're wanting?'

'Yes, please, ma'am.'

She studied Finn. 'Would you be Michael Devoy's wee boy, by chance?'

'I...'

'Tom said he'd met with you. I bet your father's proud of you.'

Finn scowled.

'But you've more important things to do than chat with me. You're on a mission, if I'm not mistaken,' Mrs Clarke declared, 'I'll fetch Tom.'

She slipped through a door and returned with Mr Clarke, his glasses perched on his nose and his hair curling around his protruding ears. He took Finn through the IRB shake that he hadn't used for months. The others watched, amused and curious.

'Finn, grand to see you.'

'Dia dhuit*, Mr Clarke,' Finn replied, 'We were passing; hope you don't mind?'

'Not at all. You've made acquaintance with my better half, I gather.'

'We're now known to each other,' Mrs Clarke answered, 'Finn, you'll find a welcome here any time. Shall I put the kettle on while you boys have a natter?'

'Ah, Katty, you're too good to me. But, sure I can manage if you'll hold court.'

'Don't I always?' Mrs Clarke said with a wry smile.

Mr Clarke led them into the back room where he hung a blackened kettle over the fire and took five mugs off a shelf. The kettle began to whistle. Mr Clarke served each a brew as they perched themselves on the boxes that filled the cubby-hole.

'Well, Finn, 'tis grand to see you,' the veteran repeated.

'And you, sir.'

'Do the introductions, so.'

Finn introduced Hal, Freddie and reminded Mr Clarke of his meeting with Charlie.

Mr Clarke turned the conversation to school, asking what they studied and whether or not they played hurling and Gaelic football. He asked some of his questions in Irish, Finn wondered if he was testing them, but he seemed nonplussed, despite Hal's stilted pronunciation. Then the tea was drunk

---

* hello

and Mr Clarke said he must complete his stock-take. They passed through the shop, nodding their goodbyes to Mrs Clarke. She caught Finn's eye and seemed to signal to him. As the others headed onto the street, Finn hung back and heard Mrs Clarke say:

'Didn't you give the boys some cigarettes, Tom?'

'To hell, I'm loosing my mind, so I am, Katty. Just a minute, Finn.'

Finn tugged Hal's jacket. 'Wait for me.'

He ducked back inside; Mr Clarke was rummaging under the counter. Mrs Clarke stood by her husband.

'I had a feeling you didn't get all you came for, Finn,' she said, her eyes piercing him.

'A-ha.' Mr Clarke offered Finn two packs of crumpled Woodbines. 'They're a bit crushed but they'll smoke alright.'

'Never mind the cigarettes, Tom,' Mrs Clarke said, 'Finn has other business with you, don't you?'

'I, well, it's just that,' Finn mumbled, glancing between Mrs Clarke and her husband. He couldn't understand how this woman he'd met only moments before could see his purpose so plainly.

'You can speak freely in front of Katty, Finn. We've no secrets from each other,' Mr Clarke reassured.

'It's the IRB, sir,' Finn blurted the words.

'What about it?' Mr Clarke asked.

'The meetings, sir. I'm not allowed to go.'

'Is that so?'

'My father thinks I should concentrate on my studies.'

'Isn't that the thing?' Mr Clarke stroked his moustache. 'Happen you're not of his mind on the matter?'

'No, sir.' Finn gulped.

The veteran leaned against the counter. Mrs Clarke stood motionless, her composure undisturbed.

'It's not fair,' Finn exclaimed, 'First my father wants me in the IRB then he keeps me from going. I know it's because of who he is that they took me.'

'And who would that be, Finn?'

'Head of the Clan na Gael.'

''Twas he told you that?'

'Yes, sir.'

Mr Clarke rubbed his thumb and forefinger through his moustache.

'What mind have you on this, Katty?'

'I see nothing to be gained from keeping a lad as bright as Finn in the dark,' she replied.

Mr Clarke nodded. 'Do you know why Mr Pearse has gone to America, Finn?'

'To meet the Clan. They're planning something,' Finn said, 'And I don't see why I should be left out of it.'

Mr Clarke clapped his hands. 'Maith thú*, you're right. There's a plan afoot. It might come to nothing yet. We're playing a waiting game and while we're waiting it doesn't do to have too many in the know. I'm not saying I think that should apply to yourself but that's what's happened I think.'

Finn started to protest.

'Tom, can you not do something to influence the situation?' Mrs Clarke prompted.

'Aye, perhaps.' Mr Clarke patted Finn's shoulder and steered him to the exit. 'Leave it with me, so. And don't you let on to Mr Pearse I gave you those. I've heard he's none too keen on smoking.'

From the doorway Finn mouthed a 'thank you' to Mrs Clarke who bowed her elegant head.

The interminable term was almost at an end. Exams were taken and results posted. With nothing distracting him, Finn's studies had gained; As in literature, Irish history and Gaelic, Bs in mathematics, biology and geography plus a special commendation for his epic masterpiece. The painting, called 'The Armies Encounter Cúchulainn', hung in the main hall, at Mr Pearse's suggestion, and Finn was pleased to see it as they filed in daily for prayers, lectures and exams.

Soon boys would begin their mass exodus, emptying the school for Easter. Finn was again to be among those that remained but this time by choice. His planned vacation of reading, drawing, studying and strolling around Dublin with

---

* well done

Cathleen seemed infinitely better than being at home with his father.

They were in biology. Mr Slattery had been dissecting a pig's lung and was passing the bronchial tubes among them when a first year entered. Mr Slattery held up two bloodied hands.

'Donovan, what is it? Can't you see we've our hands full.' He snatched the severed lung and flapped it in Donovan's whitening face.

'Sorry, sir. It's Mr Pearse, sir. He's sent me to say, sir, will you please, sir, take your boys to the hall at once. Sir.'

'Very well. Dismissed.' Mr Slattery waved the lung at Donovan who fled, hand clamped to his mouth. 'To the hall, men.'

Finn raised his eyebrows at Freddie who shrugged. They filed from the lab to merge with the boys streaming from other classrooms. Charlie slipped from his line to join Finn and Freddie.

'What's up?'

'We're about to find out,' Freddie said as they headed into the hall.

Inside Finn could sense the school awakening. He leaned across to Charlie.

'He's back.'

Charlie was forming the word 'who' when the younger Mr Pearse mounted the stage.

'Dia dhuit ar maidin*, boys,' he called and Finn knew from Willie's grin that he was right. 'I'm sorry to drag you from your lessons but I've a special guest I felt you'd want to welcome.'

The curtain stage-left rustled and Patrick Pearse emerged. There was colour in his cheeks and light in his eyes. Finn wondered what that meant for his Easter now.

Finn kept to himself the first few days of the vacation. Several times he crossed paths with Mr Pearse and it appeared the headmaster wanted a word. Finn contrived to be on an

---

* good morning

urgent errand. But he knew he wouldn't be able to dodge Mr Pearse indefinitely. Complicating the situation was Mary Brigid. Whenever Finn saw Mr Pearse, her lithe shadow lurked nearby.

It was gone ten. Curfew abandoned, Finn stayed up, reading one of his versions of the *Táin*. This one detailed the string of relationships Cúchulainn had with the women of the *Táin*; Emer, Aife and Uathach upon whom Cúchulainn was said to have, 'forced himself with violence until she succumbed to let his sword be rested between her breasts.' Finn was pretty certain that 'sword' was metaphorical.

A light knock on the dorm door broke his concentration.

Mr Pearse's head poked through the gap. 'May I enter?'

Finn nodded. Mr Pearse wandered around as if inspecting the room. Completing a circuit, he halted at Finn's bed.

'You keep a tidy dorm, Finn.'

'Thank you, sir.'

Mr Pearse glanced to the ceiling, to the floor, the window, Finn's bed. His eyes fell on Finn's book, facedown on the coverlet.

'May I?' The headmaster reached for it. '*An Táin*,' he said, switching to Irish, 'A fine work although not my preferred version.' He skimmed the page Finn had been reading, that of the rape of Uathach. Finn's face burnt. The headmaster read in stern silence, coughed once and laid the book where he found it. 'I thought we might have a wee chat, Finn.'

Finn sat up straighter. Mr Pearse seated himself on the end of the bed.

'I've learnt of late that you and I have a few acquaintances in common.'

Finn avoided incriminating himself.

'Professor Eoin MacNeill,' Mr Pearse murmured, 'speaks highly of your Gaelic.'

Finn allowed himself a nod.

'I think you are also acquainted with Mr and Mrs Clarke and Mr MacDermott?'

Finn kept silent.

'I too have recently gained their confidence,' Mr Pearse added.

Finn fantasised about giving Mr Pearse the secret IRB handshake; he contented himself with asking, 'Did you see my father in America?'

'I did.'

'Did he speak of me?'

'We spoke a good deal of you. He thinks you a fine lad and I agree. You excel at your studies and are thrilling on the hurling field, a sight I'm sorry to have missed this term. I'm thankful for your willingness to participate in all our endeavours here.' The 'all' was heavy. Mr Pearse regarded him shyly.

'Perhaps, sir, we'll have occasion to meet outside of school?'

Mr Pearse smiled. 'I think we will and I'll be glad to know another person there. We can support each other.'

'Yes, sir.'

'I'll leave you to your reading. Óiche mhaith dhuit*.'

'Óiche mhaith dhuit.'

Mr Pearse crossed the room. Before the door closed, Finn heard Mr Pearse greet someone on the landing. Finn knew of only one person who would skulk around the draughty corridor while he and Mr Pearse were sequestered together.

---

* good night

Trinity Term 1914

The Irish Theatre on Hardwicke Street was ideal for the performance of Mr Pearse's play *The Master* run, as it was, by Mr MacDonagh and Mr Plunkett. The play was unlike Mr Pearse's other writings; Finn recognised the innocent Iollan Beag as a reincarnation of Íosagán but the play's conflict was different. Finn felt some key to understanding Mr Pearse lay in the drama.

He surveyed the stage. On it were two arches; the left led to a mystical countryside landscape dominated by a forest and a sunlit hill. The hill was a painted backdrop with sunshine provided by a spotlight. The forest was half a dozen conifers cut from plywood and painted by Cathleen's father and the Fianna Éireann boys. The result suggested a sparse woodland. Through the right arch lay a monk's humble cell. The backdrop had been spackled grey and the cell furnished with a table, chair and wooden plank bed. The trick was ensuring the sunlight-spotlight didn't spill into the monk's cell which was to be dark and have a 'contemplative' atmosphere.

After a term spent memorising lines, sowing costumes, painting scenery and a hundred dress rehearsals, tomorrow was opening night. A three night run was scheduled with an additional matinee on the Saturday; every performance was fully booked already. Mr Pearse was even more anxious about this than the fete. Finn hoped this show would not end in fire.

Finn was playing Daire, a Celtic king befitting the pages of the Ulster Cycle. Willie Pearse was Ciaran, a monk and master at a Christian boys' school. Iollann Beag, the archetypal 'wholesome laddie', fell to Donovan, a petrified first year who fluffed his lines in terror. Mr Plunkett had the role of the Archangel Michael and delighted in the costume of silver wings, golden cloak, purple tunic and Irish warrior helmet. A handful of boys were required for the classroom scenes and four more would operate the lights and curtain. Three others had the nerve-wracking job of hoisting Mr Plunkett on a pulley above the stage. Mr Slattery had provided a smoke bomb to herald the Archangel's arrival. It was operated, via a coil of wire, from the wings. Finn had tripped over it twice and was sure that his Daire would fall, not to a wrathful Christian deity, but to the trailing fuse.

Although it was a triumph that Ireland's elite would be attending, Finn wished it wasn't so; they would expect their two shillings' worth. The list of attendees Mr Pearse had reeled off included Countess Markievicz, W. B. Yeats, Mr Connolly and Mr Larkin, Mr MacDermott, Professor MacNeill, Mr Clarke and Sir Roger Casement.

'Daire, you have come to pay me a wee visit. Shall we have a rousing debate over your god or mine?' Willie Pearse swished across the stage in his monk's robes.

Finn laughed at the pair they made, he dressed as a regal warrior-monarch with Willie as the impoverished holy man.

'I'm thinking we'll put on a grand show,' Willie continued.

'I hope so, sir.'

'You wouldn't be suffering from nerves, would you?'

Finn was about to deny this.

'Because I am. Praise Mary, I don't forget a single word or Pat'll be after my hide.'

'Aye, sir.'

'Want to run a few lines?'

'Yes, please.'

They took position in Ciaran's cell, Daire lounging on the chair and Ciaran standing erect.

'From page fifteen?' Willie suggested.

Finn's was the opening line. He readied himself for the onslaught of dialogue.

Daire: You have come into my country preaching to my people new things, incredible things, things you dare not believe yourself. I will not have this lie preached to men. If your religion be true, you must give me a sign of its truth.

Ciaran: It is true, it is true!

Daire: Give me a sign. Nay, show me that you yourself believe. Call upon your God to reveal Himself. I do not trust these skulking gods.

Ciaran: Who am I to ask that great Mystery to unveil Its face? Who are you that a miracle should be wrought for you?

Daire: This is not an answer. So priests ever defend their mysteries. I will not be put off as one would put off a child that asks questions. Lo, here I bare my sword against God; lo, here I lift up my shield. Let one of his great captains come down to answer the challenge!

Ciaran: This the bragging of a fool.

Daire: Nor does that answer me. Ciaran, you are in my power. My young men surround this house. Yours are at an ale-feast.

Ciaran: O wise and far-seeing King! You have planned all well.

Daire: There is a watcher at every door of your house. There is a tracker on every path of the forest. The wild boar crouches in his lair for fear of the men that fill this wood. Three rings of champions ring round the tent in which your pupils feast. Your God had need to show Himself a God!

Ciaran: Nay, slay me, Daire. I will bear testimony with my life.

Daire: What will that prove? Men die for false things, for ridiculous things, for evil things. What vile cause has not its heroes? Though you were to die here with joy and laughter you would not prove your cause…

'Ar dóigh♦!' Finn and Willie broke their poses as Mr Pearse clapped. 'Finn, you make more of my dialogue than I hoped for.' Mr Pearse patted his shoulder.

'And I, a dheartháir♣?' Willie asked, pouting.

'Fabulous, as always, Willie, a stór♥,' Mr Pearse replied, throwing his arms around his brother's neck.

At curtain fall Finn posed arm in arm with Willie, Mr Plunkett and the shaking Donovan. They bowed to the audience who stood in ovation. As the curtain was lowered the cast congratulated each other. Finn had not tripped on Mr Slattery's wire. The four boys working the hoist had not

---

♦ Excellent

♣ brother

♥ darling/my dear

dropped Mr Plunkett. Not once had any of them, including Donovan, staggered over the dialogue.

'Is that it?' Finn hissed to Willie.

'It is,' the master replied, 'Until tomorrow.'

Mr MacDonagh had laid on sticky buns and triangle sandwiches. Finn longed to slope outside with a cigarette but as the show's star his presence was demanded.

'Here he is. Once my Cúchulainn, now my Daire. Finn, join us.' The proud playwright was beckoning. Alongside Mr Pearse were the twin pillars of Mr MacDermott and Professor MacNeill.

'A magnificent performance, Finn,' Mr MacDermott said.

'Agreed,' Professor MacNeill added, 'I was intrigued by the conflict between the Gaelic warrior and the Christian pacifist. A relevant dilemma, given current affairs.'

'I thought you'd identify with that ideological impasse, Eoin,' Mr Pearse said, 'One I've ponder much myself.'

'A thorny problem,' Mr MacDermott agreed, 'Let's hope when it comes time we know which way to turn.'

'To our consciences, surely,' Professor MacNeill sniffed.

Finn rested his head against his cherished chestnut and closed his eyes, concentrating on the chirping of goldfinches, the dried grass that tickled his bare legs, the smell of clover and the condensed heat on his arm where it touched Cathleen's as she sat, as still as he, in the comfort of the summer's evening.

'What time is it?' she sighed.

Finn squinted at the sun.

'Around eight.'

'When have you to be back?'

'Not for another hour,' Finn lied. He wouldn't see Cathleen for two long months. She was leaving tomorrow to spend the summer with her aunt in Cork. Her uncle had fallen ill and Cathleen's help was needed. Finn cursed the sickly uncle, who languished on his deathbed, forcing Cathleen's departure.

She sighed again and laced her fingers through his. 'I'm sorry I'm going, you know.'

'Yeah.' The words of reassurance he wanted to offer her refused to come.

'It's my duty.'

Dualgas*: something you owed your country, your leaders and followers, your god. Not some uncle that couldn't make up his mind to live or die.

'You'll be gone yourself in a few days. And you'll be too busy at home to think of me.'

Finn sat up. 'That's not true, Cathleen. I'll do nothing but think of you.'

'And I you,' she replied, 'When I'm scrubbing floors, cleaning dishes and peeling spuds.'

'Great.'

'It'll soon pass.'

Finn said, 'I wish you could come with me, see New York.'

'Tell me what it's like, so I can picture you there.'

Finn called to mind the city.

'It's got buildings that reach up into the sky, towering so high the streets below are always in their shadow.'

'I'm not sure I'd like that. Don't you have any fields?'

'There's Central Park.'

'What's that like?'

'Like this, but massive. You can stand in the middle of it and hear nothing but the birds singing and the bees buzzing. There are trees to climb, rolling lawns and beds filled with every-colour flowers.'

'That's where I'll put you when I think of you,' Cathleen said.

'Where am I to put you?'

'On the top of a windswept cliff, a churning sea crashing on the rocks below, looking towards America, my lost love in my eyes.'

'That's...where did you learn that?'

Cathleen laughed. 'I made it up.'

'Oh...Well, as long as you don't throw yourself off,' Finn teased, trying to turn the solemn moment inside out.

'I won't as long as I know you're coming back.'

Cathleen fell quiet. Finn tried to study her without her catching him. He wanted to memorise every curve of her

---

* Duty

body, every shade in her hair, so he could carry them with him all summer. He drifted into a daydream.

'I saw Mary Brigid the other day.'

Finn jolted back to reality. 'Where?'

'At St Ita's.'

'Did you talk to her?'

'Of course.'

'What did she want?' His words were sharp.

'She was asking about you.'

'Asking what?'

'How you are.'

'You didn't tell her anything?'

'What would I have to tell her?'

Finn forced himself to breathe. 'Nothing. Just don't. You promised, remember?'

'This is to do with your IRB shenanigans, is it?'

Finn lit another cigarette and offered it to Cathleen. She ignored it.

'What's to do, Finn?'

'Forget it. Let's not row, not tonight.' He waved the cigarette at her again. Cathleen eyed him for a moment then took the peace pipe and said no more.

They settled against the trunk, Cathleen nestled against Finn, his arm around her shoulders. The orange sun was sinking fast. Shadows crawled towards them.

'What time is it now?'

'Late,' Finn said.

'We'll have to be going.'

'Yeah.'

Finn pulled his arm free. It tingled as blood rushed into trapped fingertips. He got to his feet and helped Cathleen up. She brushed her skirt and smoothed her hair.

'How do I look?'

The last ray was on her. It streaked through her hair, sparkling gold and bronze, dazzling Finn. Her hazel eyes blazed with light. Finn traced her delicate features with a fingertip; the tiny nose with its slightly upturned tip, the narrow chin, the high cheekbones. She was a picture he could never paint. He pulled her towards him, putting his soul into one last kiss. She kissed him back, moving her body tight against his. Finn wrapped his arms around her. He fought against a feeling he wanted and feared. Cathleen pulled away first.

'That's enough of that, Finn Devoy,' she said. She skipped off through the trees. Finn followed as soon as he had recovered enough to walk.

Freddie was alone in the dorm when Finn returned. He dropped down on his bed. Freddie glanced up from his book. Finn picked a volume from his own nightstand, flicked the pages for a moment, tossed it aside. Freddie kept his nose buried in his. Finn paced the room.

'Have you ever had a strange feeling?'

Freddie sighed and shut his book.

'What kind of feeling?'

'Sort of, I don't know, just strange.'

Freddie laughed. 'You'll have to be giving me more to go on.'

Finn shrugged.

'Been saying goodbye to Cathleen, haven't you?'

'Yeah.'

'And that was when you had this strange feeling that's keeping me from reading?'

Finn blushed.

'Maybes you should ask your father.'

'Why?'

'He's a doctor, isn't he?'

'So?'

'So I bet he can tell you a deal more about human biology than me.'

'Do you think something's wrong?'

'Not unless you consider being love-sick an illness,' Freddie teased.

Finn flopped onto his bed.

Freddie raked through his locker and produced a thin pamphlet. 'Get your nose in this.' He flicked it across to Finn.

The pamphlet was 'A medical practitioner's guide to human development and reproduction' by the Reverend Doctor

Jonathan Simpkins. Finn opened it at random to see a diagram of male reproductive organs, not dissimilar to those they had studied in biology, except these were human not bovine.

He was kissing Cathleen. A strange tingle was burning through his body, starting in the groin and radiating out. She pulled back from him, her red lips forming an 'O' then splitting into a grin. She skipped away, her skirts swinging round her knees, her boots kicking up as she darted off. He chased her, watching the ripple of hair as it bounced against her back and danced over her eyes when she turned to see if he was gaining on her. Finn reached out, felt her soft flesh squeezed in his grip and twisted her round to face him. He kissed her again, pressing into her, feeling her so close to him. A wave crashed over him, drenching him in blissful release.

Finn woke up. His pyjama bottoms were wet and sticky. For a few minutes he couldn't bring himself to move. There was a bubble of pleasure floating around his body. He didn't want it to burst and didn't get up for clean clothes until the feeling had faded. When he got back into bed he closed his eyes and conjured the image of Cathleen's rippling hair as she flitted through the trees, just beyond reach.

August 5 1914

The New York Times

ENGLAND DECLARES WAR ON GERMANY; BRITISH SHIP SUNK; FRENCH SHIPS DEFEAT GERMAN; BELGIUM ATTACKED; 17,000,000 MEN ENGAGED IN GREAT WAR OF EIGHT NATIONS; GREAT ENGLISH AND GERMAN NAVIES ABOUT TO GRAPPLE

Finn stared at them until the words merged into a senseless mass. There was war between Britain and Germany. He tore off the front page and tucked it in his pocket. What he had told Cathleen of Central Park was true; around him life hummed peacefully. People strolled with dogs, prams, children. Two kites fluttered in the heat haze that had settled on New York. Opposite a man sat, his bowler hat beside him, his lunch in his lap. Finn longed to wave the newsprint under his moustache. 'Look! War's been declared.'

His mother was quiet at dinner; the day's news made her meatloaf unpalatable. His father ate seconds, downed three glasses of wine and took brandy in his study, the good cognac, not the cheap firewater.

Finn and his mother adjourned to the sitting room. She attended her sowing. Finn jabbered, trying to entertain her, and ended up recounting *The Master* line by line. Her mood lightened, she even chuckled when he confided his fears that Mr Plunkett would plummet to the stage.

At nine his father appeared wearing his hat.

'I've to go out.'

'It's late, Michael, must you?'

'For Jesus' sake, yes, otherwise I wouldn't.'

'It is a patient?' But his father was already gone.

'I'm sure it is a patient,' Finn said.

'I'm sure it's not,' his mother remarked. Finn heard the fury in her voice and decided it was time he went to bed.

Finn sat at his desk with his artist's pad. He had started a series of drawings of New York for Cathleen. Working by candlelight, he began shading the large sycamore he had sketched in Central Park that afternoon. His mother appeared in the doorway, told him not to work too late, wished him goodnight and retired.

He was nearly finished when the front door slammed. Finn snuffed the candle and listened to his father stumbling around downstairs. Another door banged; Finn flinched. A third then a fourth were hurled shut. His father's boots thumped up the stairs. Finn followed the sound as it passed his door, paused and moved on. Down the hall there was a creak, a bang and the muffled voices of his parents rose from the silence, followed by the shattering of glass and a shriek. Finn, fingers fumbling, relit his candle. It shook as he crooked his hand around the flame and carried it across the room. He listened, ear to the wood panel.

A second crash, heavier than the first, rang out. Finn flew into the hall, slithering across the polished floor. The door to his parents' room was wide open. He slid to a halt, his candle throwing a pathetic circle of wavering yellow into the room, onto the floor and over his parents. His mother was on her back. Finn saw the whiteness of her naked legs, one either side of his father who was on his knees between them, back arched, hand raised to strike. Finn dropped his candlestick. Hot wax spattered the floor and ignited, flames running like spilled milk. Finn fled.

He climbed the apple tree and, shielded by the mass of green, tucked himself up. Lights flew from window to window. A sash was raised. Ashy clouds plumed across the midnight sky. The backdoor opened. A gruff baritone barked his name. Finn stayed in his tree all night, his mother's naked legs haunting him.

The dawn sky smouldered. Exhausted, aching and cold, Finn trudged across the garden, dew soaking his socks.

His mother was seated at his desk, yesterday's sycamore sketch in her hands. Her face was white with powder. Beneath it bruises throbbed. She came to him and draped a blanket round his shoulders.

'You must be cold.'

Finn wanted to throw himself into her arms and tell her he was sorry but she turned from him to trace the outline of the sycamore with her forefinger before he could speak.

'You have real talent, Finn. You mustn't waste it,' she said, 'I'm sorry things have been,' she gave a hollow half-laugh, 'difficult. I've been worrying, needlessly I'm sure, about you going back to school with this war on.'

'Ireland's not in the war,' Finn said, 'I don't suppose they'll be rushing to help the English.'

'I don't suppose they will,' his mother echoed, 'Finn, you will be careful, won't you?'

'I'm sure Germany won't invade Ireland, Mother.'

She smiled but her eyes were filling with tears. 'That's not what I'm afraid of, Finn.' She brushed a hand through his fair hair, removing a twig. 'Look at you. You're so grown up. All those adventures you've been having, they're making quite the man of you.' She twirled the apple sprig, 'Your father was right about that.'

Finn almost gagged. 'Mother, I…'

She put her finger to his lips. 'Remember, Finn, you are not your father.' She patted his shoulder and left.

Finn snatched the sycamore sketch and ripped it to shreds.

Michaelmas Term 1914

Four figures fanned out across the street, plotting a course for the Gaelic League building.

Finn wished he could fly above them, to better view the spectacle. On the right was Mr Plunkett, dressed as for the opera in silk-lined cape and bracelets. At his side strode the more compact form of Mr Colbert in a neat grey suit. Next to Mr Colbert marched Mr Pearse, resplendent in a frock coat and top hat, befitting the formality of the occasion. Finn had donned his Fianna uniform because it seemed his only suitable outfit for their evening rendezvous.

Finn had scarcely unpacked when Mr Pearse informed him there was an important IRB meeting. He was scheduled to speak and could he impose upon Finn to be there, for moral support? The outbreak of war had quickened the pulse of every Irishman with the result that Finn walked alongside his masters to a meeting that should have been no place for a fifteen year old.

Mr MacDermott directed them to an office bearing the nameplate, 'Sean T. O'Kelly'. The room was small and crowded. Finn recognised people from the Wynne's meeting, including Professor MacNeill and Tom Clarke. He positioned himself off to the side while men greeted each other with covert IRB handshakes. A dense heat saturated the room, the densely packed bodies stoking a furnace already warmed by sunlight on grimy windowpanes.

'Shall we begin?' Mr MacDermott shut the door and limped to the oval table that half-filled the poky office; men sat where they could. 'War has been declared, gentlemen. In Parliament last week Lloyd George made the following declaration, which I will read to you as it pertains to our position,' he produced a sheet of paper and read, ' 'This is the story of two little nations. The world owes much to little nations. The greatest art in the world was the work of little nations...The heroic deeds that thrill humanity through generations were the deeds of little nations fighting for their freedom. Yes, and the salvation of mankind came through a little nation.' Gentlemen, is the right honourable Lloyd George talking of anyone but we Irish?'

A cheer of agreement filled the room. Mr MacDermott continued:

'Furthermore he says, 'If we had stood by when two little nations were being crushed and broken by the brutal hands of barbarism, our shame would have rung down the everlasting ages.' Where, gentlemen, is our shame, if not in allowing ourselves to be crushed and broken by British barbarism?' The question stood alone for a moment. 'Pat, I believe you've an address for us.'

At the invitation Mr Pearse rose, his top hat cradled in the crook of his arm. All eyes fixed on him; Finn was reminded of school assemblies.

'Go raibh maith agat*, Sean. It is with pride that I stand before such fine Irish company. I consider it an honour to be permitted to say a few words. On this hot eve, I shall strive to keep them few.'

There was an appreciative chuckle. Finn ran a finger round inside his collar, bringing it up dripping with sweat.

'A European war has brought about a crisis which may contain, as yet hidden within, the moment for which the generations have been waiting. It remains to be seen whether, if that moment reveals itself, we shall have the sight to see and the courage to do; or whether it shall be written of this generation, alone, of all the generations of Ireland, that it had none among it who dared to make the ultimate sacrifice.' As he spoke, Mr Pearse's eyes glowed, his face flushed and he stabbed the air. The words, exploding from him, embedded themselves in the hearts of his audience. His speech concluded, he sat abruptly.

'What say you to that?' Mr MacDermott challenged.

'The Lord has given us the opportunity we've been wanting this long time,' Mr Clarke said.

A murmur rippled around the room as men recovered their senses.

---

* thank you

'Haven't we missed one chance already, during the Boer War? But not this time, bejesus,' Mr Colbert added.

''Tis truly our shame if we're the first generation for over a century to not rise in arms against our oppressors,' another concluded.

'Agreed, Sean,' Mr MacDermott replied, nodding to the office's namesake.

'And you're right to mark us with it,' Mr Plunkett declared.

Professor MacNeill interrupted. 'Can we clarify our intentions?'

'To rise against the English, expel them from Ireland and regain sovereignty of our country!' Mr MacDermott spoke with a boyish grin, as if it was a game for playing and winning.

'A fine plan.'

'Aye, grand.'

'Pray tell, with what are we equipped for defeating the mightiest military power in Europe?' Professor MacNeill sneered.

'The courage of Irishmen too long shackled,' Mr Pearse said.

'A powerful weapon,' Mr Clarke agreed.

'Not a matter-of-fact one, though,' Professor MacNeill muttered.

'We've the Irish Volunteers. They have been training a good while.'

'Arms?'

'We've the means to obtain guns and ammunition.'

'From whence?'

'The Continent.'

'Germany?'

'The enemy of our enemy is our friend,' Mr MacDermott intoned.

'What have we by way of numbers in the Volunteers?' This new speaker, a fresh-faced young man, was only a few feet from Finn. If not for his luxuriant moustache it would have been hard to believe he was anything more than a lad. Finn suspected he'd grown the moustache for that very reason.

'In excess of five thousand, Eamonn,' Mr O'Kelly replied.

'And we'll recruit more before we act,' Mr MacDermott said, 'Sure, no one is proposing we strike tonight.' He raised an eyebrow and a few men chuckled.

'What about the Fianna?' Finn was surprised to hear his own voice.

'An excellent point, Mr Devoy. Con, would you have thoughts on that?' Mr MacDermott asked.

'We could call on those of age.'

'There's the Citizen Army,' Mr Plunkett offered, 'We might be able to come to agreement with Connolly. I believe he is chief-of-staff since Larkin's departure.'

'You are acquainted with him, Pat, could you moot the idea?' Mr MacDermott asked.

'Indeed.'

'Given the scope of our endeavour it should be clear our purpose tonight is not to finalise arrangements, merely to agree the direction of our efforts. I propose a vote,' Mr MacDermott said.

'Seconded,' Mr Clarke offered.

'In that case, indicate aye or nay to an armed uprising.' Mr MacDermott circulated ballot papers.

Finn worried the white square in his hands.

'You may abstain if you prefer,' Mr Pearse whispered to him.

'It's not that, sir. I didn't bring a pencil.'

Mr Pearse, having written, offered Finn his.

Without hesitation Finn wrote 'aye' on his square.

The papers were collected, the votes counted aloud. Only one fell to the 'nays'. Finn thought he knew who had cast it but the decision to rise with arms was carried by a sizeable majority.

Returning after lights out, it felt strange not to be sneaking in. Finn and Mr Pearse strode into the entrance hall. The headmaster faced him.

'That was a good night's work, Finn.'

'Yes, sir.'

'You should away to bed. I've a few things to attend.' Mr Pearse reached for the handle of his office door; before he got a hand to it, it sprang open and Mary Brigid leapt out, a trembling candle in her hand.

'Mary Brigid, in ainm Dé*, you frightened me.'

'That'll be your guilty conscience, Pat.'

Mr Pearse, who had been clutching his chest in jest of fright, dropped his arm and straightened his back. 'What are you doing up at this hour?'

'Nay, Pat, it's you that'll tell me what it is you're about and with Finn, too.' She soaked Finn in candle-light.

Mr Pearse smoothed his hair. 'We were taking a…'

'Mother Mary, give me strength,' Mary Brigid muttered. Lifting her voice to them, she said, 'You'll tell me no lies tonight, Pat. Truth on our tongues, or does that not apply to yourself?'

Mr Pearse glanced at Finn. Mary Brigid glared at them both.

'I think she knows, sir,' Finn whispered.

'Aye, Pat, I do. I know Con and Joe have your students mixed up in things they've no business with, things you're now mixed up in. I know whatever you were doing in America it wasn't for St Enda's. And I know whatever you're doing it'll come to no good end.' Her voice rose to a shriek.

'Can freeing Ireland be no good end?'

'Pat, catch yourself on! Do you believe you'll achieve such a fantasy?'

'Aye.' Mr Pearse folded his arms.

'How when better men have failed these seven hundred years?' She raised her hands in despair.

'By any means necessary.'

'Words, Pat, that's all you've got.'

'Soon we'll have the deeds to match.'

Mary Brigid shook from her auburn curls to her lace-up boots, glass vibrating beyond pitch. Finn thought she would shatter, braced himself for the blast and watched, horror-struck, as she slapped her brother stiff-palmed across the face with a sharp clap. She raised her hand again but Mr Pearse caught her wrist. She writhed as though she would rather pull

---

* for goodness sake

her arm off than have her brother holding it. They struggled against each other and the candle fell. Finn charged in, stamped out the flames and stony moonlight dowsed them.

'Mary Brigid, sir, please.' Finn plucked Mr Pearse's sleeve.

'See, Pat, what you're doing,' Mary Brigid cried, freeing her hand, 'Getting boys doing men's work and doing it yourself when you've no call.' She gave a savage shriek.

Light flickered down the hall. Footsteps trotted along the parquet floor.

Mrs Pearse appeared, fully dressed, her hair in its hard bun beneath her widow's cap. 'What in the Lord's name is going on?' She stood between her two children as she must have during their childhood spats. Two answers crashed into each other.

'Nothing, Mother.'

'Pat's going to war.' Mary Brigid pressed her fist to her mouth to catch the sob wrung from her.

Mrs Pearse noticed Finn. 'To bed.'

Finn darted for the stairs.

The dorm was in darkness. Finn closed the door and pressed his ear to it.

'Finn?' Charlie hissed.

'Sssh.'

'What's going on?'

Finn slammed his hand against the frame. 'Jesus, shut up, will you!' But there was nothing to hear.

The chaos had woken the others. Sean lit a lamp; Freddie put on his glasses.

'What's up, Finn?' Hal asked.

Finn told them.

'What'll happen now MB knows?' Charlie asked.

'Don't see what she's getting mithered for,' Hal grumbled, 'So he's joined the IRB, so what?'

'There's something else, isn't there?' Freddie said.

'The plan!' Charlie exclaimed, 'Tell us.'

Finn was going to, despite his IRB oath, but Mary Brigid's scream had taken his words and left hers in his mouth: Pat's going to war…

'I will, I swear, but not yet.'

'If you can tell us later you can tell us now,' Hal declared.

'I've said, I'll tell you, but not tonight so don't bloody ask me.'

'But I don't see…' Charlie began.

'No, you don't,' Sean interrupted, 'Leave Finn be. Sure, I trust him, he'll tell us when he can.'

Finn flashed Sean a smile. 'I will,' he said as Charlie put out the light, 'I promise.'

Trinity Term 1915

Mr Pearse had chosen the Hermitage's sweeping drive as backdrop. From a suitable distance on the lawn the photographer positioned his camera, the lens trained on St Enda's; building, boys and masters. Finn thought, as he lined up with his friends, that the school appeared to have been turned inside out.

Mr Pearse arranged them in order of seniority with masters at the ends of every row. Mr Plunkett was ahead of Finn with Mr Colbert and Mr MacDonagh on the other side; Mr Slattery, when he arrived, would take his place next to Finn. The Pearse family were in front, on chairs amongst the first years, complicating the composition.

'Would've been less bother if they'd got you to paint us,' Hal grumbled. Breakfast had been curtailed to accommodate the photographer's schedule.

'Why does he want a picture?' Charlie demanded.

'It's proof,' Freddie replied.

'Of what?'

'All this.'

'Suppose, don't see why it matters, though.'

Finn had an idea. Ever since the vote, months ago, for an armed rising, Mr Pearse had been preoccupied and distant. The school remained part of his world but it was no longer the heart of it; a greater adventure loomed. Yet while Mr Pearse entrenched himself in this greater course, the weeks had rolled into months, the months into terms and the terms to this day, the last of another St Enda's year.

'Right, boys, big smiles,' the photographer called, 'Hold still.'

Finn grimaced. Stay still, do nothing, smile and pretend you're happy about it; that had become the frustrating order of his existence. Before the photographer could complete the exposure Mr Plunkett exploded into a coughing fit. It was five minutes before he stopped, apologising all round. Finn noted the pallor on his face. He'd missed most of last term, offering no excuse for his absence and, although he had taught them this term, it had been with half a mind to the job.

'Ready now?' the photographer asked.

The camera blinked. The flash popped. The boys and masters of St Enda's in the year 1915 were immortalised forever.

'Right boys, off you go.'

Finn tugged on Mr Slattery's sleeve, the blue-white glare of the flashbulb blooming wherever he looked.

'Sir, can I have a word?'

'The lab in five minutes, Devoy.'

Finn strolled around the chem. lab, trailing fingers over the equipment. He paused at the chemicals' cupboard and scanned the bottles.

'Ahoy!'

Finn whirled around. Mr Slattery advanced and perched on a desk. 'Fire away, Devoy.'

'The camera flash, sir, what makes it explode?'

'Planning a career in photography, Devoy?' Mr Slattery grinned.

Finn jingled some loose change in his pocket. 'Just curious, sir. How do you get an explosion like that?'

'A paltry flash-bang! If you were interested in bigger booms we could discuss this further.' Mr Slattery winked at him.

'Sir?'

'Let's talk next term, when we've time for such a fascinating topic. Who's to say what might come of it?'

Finn sloped for the door, confused.

'You might spend your summer on something useful, Devoy.'

Finn span around to see a textbook hurtling towards him. He ducked; it skimmed his head and clattered to the floor. He retrieved it. *Practical Chemistry: a guide to chemical formulas, compounds and their application for use.*

'I recommend chapter five.'

Finn ruffled the pages. 'Chapter five: explosions, explosives and pyrotechnics.'

'Thank you, sir.' He tucked the book under his arm. 'See you next term.'

'Indeed you will, Devoy,' Mr Slattery said and there was another wink.

The dorm was pandemonium.

'You'd think we'd have the knack by now,' Charlie said, cramming clothes higgledy-piggledy into his case.

Finn put the chemistry tome in his locker and sat enjoying the farce.

'It's bad luck you not going home,' Sean said.

'I've stayed before, it's alright.'

'A couple of weeks at Easter's different to the whole summer,' Charlie said.

'You can thank German U boats for that.'

'Sure you won't come to mine?' Freddie asked.

'I'm fine,' Finn said.

Normally they'd be laughing, cheering that school was finished and the lazy summer stretching before them but the packing continued in silence. Maybe it was the anti-climax, harder for coming after the year's dramatic start. Finn had been sure then that by now they'd be heroes and Ireland would be free. The others didn't even bother asking about the IRB now and the vote for an armed rising seemed a waste of ballots. Finn unclenched the fist he hadn't realised he'd made and saw four red crescents in his palm.

He sighed and slipped his hand under his pillow, retrieving a small box. Inside was a silver locket, the front decorated with a Celtic knot. Finn plucked it from the velvet interior and slid his thumbnail in the groove that split the two halves. It popped open and Finn inspected the intertwined F&C he'd paid extra for the jeweller to engrave.

'Haven't you given her that fecking thing yet? What good is it under your pillow? You'll not get anything for it there, Finn.'

Finn coiled the chain and settled the locket inside its case.

'Bloody hell, Hal.'

'Well, Jesus, what's the point of spending your money on it, so?'

'Never mind,' Finn snapped the box closed, 'I've something to tell you.'

'You're swapping it for a ring?' Charlie dug his elbow into Hal's ribs.

'No. Look, stop, the lot of you, I want to tell you something before you go.'

Freddie studied Finn, eyebrows raised.

'There's going to be a war.'

'Not seen the papers lately, have you?' Charlie snorted.

'I mean one here, in Ireland. For independence.'

'How the bejesus do you know that?' Hal scoffed.

'I was at the meeting, when the IRB voted. We voted,' Finn corrected, 'You won't remember. It was back in September.'

'The feck I don't,' Charlie proclaimed, 'I'll lay wager it was night Mary Brigid slapped Mr Pearse.'

Finn nodded.

'Sure, I remember that,' Freddie said.

'I remember her screaming. Nearly gave me a bloody heart attack,' Hal said.

'A war,' Sean whistled.

'I don't know why they've not set to it yet and I didn't want to say anything until it was certain. But I'm sure it is now.'

'Why?' Freddie asked.

'The photograph.' Finn shrugged, 'It feels like the end of something.'

'And the start of something else?' Charlie prompted.

'I hope so,' Finn replied.

He tried to justify telling them: he'd done it because he wanted them to be prepared; because he wanted them to know it would happen; because, by telling them, he could maybe make it happen. Finn reached into his pocket and let his fingers stroke the leather box. He hoped Mr MacDermott would understand.

Cathleen was waiting by the gate. She wore a die-straight skirt that stopped above her ankles and boots, high heeled, pointed and shiny. The matching jacket, a short bolero-thing, was fastened with one button at her waist. Poking from the cuffs and at the neck were the frills of a white blouse. The whole thing was crowned by a tiny cocked-hat with a feather in the band. When he was close she twirled.

'What do you think?'

'It is you?'

She slapped his arm. 'You said you were taking me somewhere smart so I raked through my ma's old clothes. Will I do?'

Finn said, 'You're a proper lady.'

'You're not bad, yourself.' Cathleen waved a hand at him. Willie Pearse had given Finn an old suit which Mary Brigid had adjusted. 'We're both fit for service,' she added, 'Only another year of school then off into the world.'

'Let's not think about that today.' Finn took her gloved hand and they strolled through the gates and toward Dublin.

They entered St Stephen's Green, passing under Traitor's Gate, and wandered among the colourful patchwork of flowerbeds, drifting along trailing paths that led nowhere. They sheltered from the midday sun under the bandstand then moved to the duck pond, teasing the birds by putting their hands in their pockets as though for bread. Cathleen laughed and Finn let the sound soak through him, sweet and warm like chocolate.

At four o'clock he steered her to the park gates.

'Haven't you walked me far enough?'

'That's why I'm taking you for a sit down.'

Across the road the magnificent Shelbourne Hotel arose. Six rows of windows, each framed by intricate scrolls and arches, punctuated the red brick. The entrance was a portico of four creamy pillars topped with wrought iron and stained glass and crowned by a balcony with balustrades shaped like Grecian urns. At the door a porter in green and gold livery bobbed his head to arriving guests.

'Come on.' Finn pulled Cathleen's arm.

'We're not going in there!'

'We are.'

The faintest trace of a smirk betrayed the porter's private views as he let Cathleen and Finn into the hotel's lobby resplendent with marble and crystal.

In the dining room, at tables cloaked in crisp white linen and gleaming with silver tea services, granddames in grander hats sipped and nibbled.

'Stop staring,' Finn hissed when they were seated at a table overlooking the Green.

'I can't help it. Whatever're you doing bringing me to a place like this, Finn Devoy?'

'Showing you I know how to treat a lady.'

'Why, have you hopes of getting yourself one?'

The waiter returned and set out the tea pot, two miniature cups and saucers, two side plates and a large platter of fancies, sandwiches and scones. He bowed low and backed away, leaving Cathleen to pour while Finn grinned at her.

'I'm glad I'm providing you with such amusement,' she said after she had slopped tea on the pristine linen.

Finn said, 'I'm just thinking I'll have to bring you again, so you can practise.'

She pinched his arm, deftly changing the movement into lifting a piece of cake when she saw herself watched by two matrons at the next table.

'You wee shite.'

'This'll change your tune.' Finn withdrew the box from his borrowed britches and set it on the table. With one finger he pushed it towards her.

Warming to her role, Cathleen dabbed the corners of her mouth on a napkin and picked up the box. She flipped the lid, her eyes widened and a pink flush bloomed on her cheeks.

'Finn, it's a beauty. But I can't take it, it's too much.'

'It's no good to anyone else.' Finn opened the locket and showed her the engraving.

'Why, Finn Devoy?'

'Because I,' it was Finn's turn to blush, 'wanted to give you something nice. Because I like you.' Cross with himself for not saying 'love', he couldn't meet Cathleen's eyes.

She was quiet a moment. Then Finn felt her hand on his, her fingers lifting the locket from his grip.

'Go raibh maith agat*,' she whispered. When he raised his eyes Cathleen was fastening the clasp around her neck. 'Me too,' she added.

Finn said goodbye to his pals as they rode off with Mary Brigid for the station. The poor pony had been busy all day ferrying students to the docks or the station. Now the school was an empty shell and, as Finn stood out front, he could scarcely believe only that morning the place had been noisy with the chatter of boys taking their places for the photograph. Freddie was right; it was proof St Enda's lived and breathed. Finn decided he would see about getting a copy. It would be a nice memento to show his grandchildren.

Finn went inside. A yellow strip cut across the darkening hallway; the door to Mr Pearse's study was ajar. Finn was almost out of earshot when the telephone in Mr Pearse's office jangled. Curious, Finn stopped.

'Yes, I'll take the call… Michael? How are you?… No, I hadn't heard… Have you no hope of him rallying?... Sure, his loss will be keenly felt… Very well. Goodnight.'

The caller was his father. Finn tracked back to the headmaster's door, knocked and entered to find Mr Pearse replacing the telephone receiver on the unit sat atop the bureau.

'Finn, what a coincidence, I've this minute had your father call.'

'I heard.' Finn nodded towards the door which remained open.

'Ah, well, as you're here.' Mr Pearse waved at the empty chair in front of his desk. 'Your father rang with some sad news.' Seeing alarm on Finn's face Mr Pearse hurried on, 'A fellow Fenian, perhaps second only in greatness to your father, is not well, not well at all. His death, when it comes, will be a tragedy for Ireland.'

'Yes, sir,' Finn mumbled, 'Did my father give you any message for me, sir?'

---

* thank you

'Finn, forgive me. Certainly, he wished you a pleasant summer and sent his and your mother's lamentations that they wouldn't see you.'

The lie made Finn want to laugh. Mr Pearse rubbed his temples.

'Finn, I've a sudden, urgent longing for the sanctuary of things wholly Gaelic. Would you care to accompany me to Rosmuc?'

'I would, sir.'

At last the train dropped them at Maam Cross. Mr Pearse had arranged for the trap to meet them. The driver, who, with his wife's help, minded the cottage during Mr Pearse's absence, had brought with him two of the bicycles normally stored in the outbuilding. He unloaded them and took the luggage.

'I thought we'd cycle to Gort Mór,' Mr Pearse explained, 'To best enjoy every minute in this wonderful land.' He swept the scenery with an arm.

Finn nodded, they mounted the bicycles and rode off.

It had been two years since Finn was last at Rosmuc but, as they crested the final knoll, the view was as Finn remembered.

Mr Pearse halted. 'Sure St Enda's is hermitage by name but here is my true haven, nature's cloister, where I may contemplate even the most severely barbed problems to satisfactory conclusion.'

The cottage nestled in its hillside dell, the thatch of its roof a buttery yellow in the sunlight, its whitewashed walls bright against the surrounding green, the lough below it sparkling with cool promise. Guarding the Connemara wilderness, the Twelve Pins watched darkly, their ragged faces turned to Mr Pearse as though welcoming him home to his west coast landscape of Irish heroes.

As Finn studied the scene, Mr Pearse beside him glowing with innocent joy, it poured off the pages of the *Táin* in vivid colour.

The next day they established a routine they followed all week. In the mornings Mr Pearse cooked porridge which, while not matching his mother's, was edible. This they ate outside, the bowls cradled in their laps, watching the wind ruffle the lough. The days they spent roaming the countryside, lunching on soda bread, hunks of cheese and apples carried in a rucksack Mr Pearse found in the store-house. As they hiked Mr Pearse talked of his childhood with Willie, how they created imaginary worlds populated by the things boys dream of; warrior heroes featured frequently. Every story was bright and shiny, as though from yesterday. He even revealed the leather rucksack was the one he and Willie had used for their picnics as lads, the 'PWF' scored in messy lines on the flap standing for Pat and Willie Forever.

In the afternoons they would return to the cottage, Finn to swim in the lough while Mr Pearse sat on the bank, the book in his lap read from only sporadically. Afterwards they would cook supper, coddle being a favourite. That done they sat outside while daylight lasted. When the sun had disappeared they would retreat indoors, Mr Pearse kindling the fire while Finn lit lamps. Under the glow of these they read or wrote: Finn, letters; Mr Pearse, poetry. By day four Finn had finished the chemistry book and was eager for some practical experiments when term started.

Some nights Finn sketched too, at first drawing Cathleen but it turned out a poor likeness. Better were views of the Connemara scenery but after a while one hill became much like another. His eyes roamed the cottage for a subject and fell on the man opposite, bent over his papers, his forehead wrinkled, his eyes darting. Finn had known Mr Pearse for four years but his headmaster remained a mystery. How could one man be so many things? The pages of Finn's sketchbook began filling with silvery-grey Mr Pearses. Finn hoped one would answer the question he couldn't ask the flesh and blood man.

One day, as they picked their way over boggy ground, watched from afar by suspicious sheep, Finn felt the weight of this question keenly.

'Do you know what I feared when I was a lad, Finn?'

'No, sir.'

'That the day would come when I was no longer a lad.'

Finn was startled by the statement.

'I don't suppose that makes a deal of sense to you but I felt it was marvellous being a boy, having the whole world ahead of one. I think that still; 'tis the reason for St Enda's. With you boys in my life, your eyes so wide, your dreams so fresh and pure, I feel I've kept a piece of my own boyhood alive.'

'But, sir,' Finn protested, 'When you're an adult you can do what you want.'

Mr Pearse clutched his sides and fell to his knees, his eyes streaming, as laughter shook his body.

'Sir?'

'Forgive me, Finn,' Mr Pearse gasped, the words punctuated by chuckles, 'I don't mean to startle you.' With supreme effort he gained the uppermost; the laughter died to a titter. He wiped his eyes, got to his feet and draped an arm around Finn's shoulder. 'Indeed, 'tis no laughing matter. I merely wish what you say were true. Perhaps if it were 'twould compensate for growing up. Mark this, Finn.' A solemn expression clouded his face. 'Stay a lad as long as you can.'

They walked on. Mr Pearse waxed lyrical about boyhood, turning to myth and literature. Cúchulainn and Íosagán became his examples but Finn heard places where his or his headmaster's names would better suit the lecture.

When they arrived at the cottage Mr Pearse said, 'Don't think too hard on what I say, Finn. Mine are but the philosophical ramblings of a romantic Gael. Are you going for a swim?'

Finn was hot and longing for the silky lough waters to soothe him.

'Yes, sir.'

Mr Pearse smiled and took his seat on the bank.

For five days they enjoyed the freedom of their mountainside sanctuary.

On the sixth morning, as they breakfasted, a messenger boy, red-faced and puffing, peddled up the track. He jumped from his bicycle, saluted, and handed Mr Pearse a telegram. Finn watched his headmaster scan the card, noting a twitch in his left eye, as though a sudden pain stabbed through his head.

'Wait, please. I must reply.' Mr Pearse dashed into the cottage, emerged a moment later and pressed an envelope and some coins into the boy's hand.

The boy free-wheeled down the hill. Finn stirred his porridge. Mr Pearse gazed out to the Pins.

'The dreaded tragedy has struck,' he intoned, 'O'Donovan Rossa is dead and I called upon by our friend Mr Clarke to orate at his graveside. But I must await further advice to know best how far I may go in what I say.'

They hugged the cottage hillside that day, Mr Pearse straining his eyes towards Maam Cross, watching for the word. At teatime it came.

'Any reply, sir?' the lad asked.

'No, thank you,' Mr Pearse murmured, fishing in his pocket for a tuppenny tip. As the messenger slid down the track Mr Pearse held the telegram to Finn. 'See my orders,' he said, grinning, 'Apparently sometimes grown ups do get to do what they want.'

The telegram, signed 'T. Clarke', read, 'Make it as hot as hell!'

That night a gale rattled the cottage windows and tested the door. Mr Pearse worked feverishly, his nib scratching the pages of an exercise book. Finn chewed his pencil, stealing glances at Mr Pearse who was doubled over papers dog-eared with thumbing. Finn's latest sketch wasn't any better than his previous half-dozen Mr Pearses.

He turned to a clean page and, with fluid strokes, swept down cheeks, forehead and chin. He let the pencil fly, drawing from memory and imagination. The face filled with features both familiar and strange; eyes, brows, nose, lips. Finn focused on one part at a time, not allowing himself to view the whole, fearful the spell guiding his lines would be broken. A shadow under the nose, flecks of light in the irises: his pencil took command; smiling lips, an arch to the brows, fullness in the cheeks. Finn put his pencil down. His eyes wandered over the lines and shadows. He saw Patrick Pearse aged fourteen or fifteen, returning his stare.

Who are you?

You should know, you drew me.

I drew you so you'd be able to tell me.

I can't tell you what I don't know.

Are you him?

I used to be.

Is he you?

Only in his dreams… awake, he's you.

Finn speared his pencil into the paper. The point snapped. He slapped the sketchpad closed. The cottage's normally ample living room seemed cramped; Finn felt the power of the man opposite threaten to overwhelm him. He went to the fireplace with his pocket knife and scraped slivers of wood from the pencil's shattered tip. When he turned back Mr Pearse was gazing at him.

'I broke my pencil.'

'I see.'

Finn sat, pulled the pad towards him and poised his sharpened pencil over a fresh page. Mr Pearse stared. Confused, annoyed, Finn glanced up. He caught Mr Pearse's eye and could not break the contact; Mr Pearse was peering into the corners of his mind.

'Are you having trouble tonight?' Mr Pearse reached for the drawing.

'No!' Finn clutched his book. 'No, thank you, sir. It's not important.'

'Finn, everything you do is important.'

For ten seconds Finn didn't draw breath as Mr Pearse's hand remained outstretched, coaxing, tempting.

'Well, if I can't help you, perhaps you'll help me.' The master dropped his arm. 'May I read this to you for a second opinion?' Mr Pearse shuffled his papers.

The sketchpad pressed to his chest, Finn nodded.

Mr Pearse cleared his throat. 'O'Donovan Rossa was the man that to the masses of his countrymen then and since stood most starkly and plainly for the Fenian idea. For Rossa would not only have Ireland free but he would have Ireland Gaelic. And here we have the secret of Rossa's magic. He was of the Gael. He might have said, 'If I die it shall be from the love I bear the Gael'…'

Finn's sweating palms dampened the edges of his pad as Mr Pearse's elegy caught fire, becoming a rebel's speech.

'... We pledge to Ireland our love and we pledge to English rule in Ireland our hate. This is a place of peace but I hold it a Christian thing, as O'Donovan Rossa held it, to hate evil, to hate untruth, to hate oppression and, hating them, to strive to overthrow them.' Mr Pearse leapt to his feet. 'Life springs from death and from the graves of patriot men and women. The Rulers of this Realm think that they have pacified Ireland.' He crumpled the pages in his fist. 'They think that they have foreseen everything but the fools, the fools, the fools! They have left us our Fenian dead, and while Ireland holds these graves, Ireland unfree shall never be at peace.' At the word 'peace', he unclenched his hand, dropped the pages and sank into his chair.

Finn sat paralysed. The peaceable man who'd taught him patiently, who penned stories of innocent children, who prized Christian compassion, had been overpowered by a hate so painful he had lost himself to it. It was a terrifying answer to Finn's question.

'Well, Finn?' Mild Mr Pearse had resurfaced.

Finn murmured, 'Very moving, sir.'

'You felt yourself moved by my words?'

The fire hissed angrily.

'Will it be soon, sir?'

'Finn?'

'The rising, sir?'

'One hopes,' Mr Pearse replied.

In his bed beneath the thatch the day's events swirled around Finn. Íosagán, pure, golden and holy, and Cúchulainn, bloodthirsty, barbaric and merciless, fought each other for Mr Pearse's soul. In the last moments before sunrise Finn saw Mr Pearse torn in two, Íosagán claiming one half and Cúchulainn the other.

Finn got up. In the living room his sketchpad lay on the table. He tore out the drawing of young Patrick Pearse, kindled the fire and threw it into the flames.

'You've lit the fire, I see.'

Mr Pearse hovered at Finn's elbow, peering into the hearth. The last corner of his drawing still fought the flames. They watched until the paper was ash.

'Are we ready now to turn to the road before us, Finn, and the deeds we must do?'

The great Fenian Jeremiah O'Donovan Rossa had lain in state in City Hall, returned at last to his homeland after thirty-five years in exile. Today, August 1st, he was making his final journey: to Glasnevin Cemetery.

Alone in the dorm Finn adjusted his slouch hat in the mirror above the washstand. Mr Pearse had asked Finn to accompany him to the funeral, saying he had need of a friendly face among the stern mourning crowd to support him during his oration at this momentous public event. As he regarded his reflection in the glass Finn wished Rossa had died in term time so his friends were present to support him.

'Are you ready, Finn?' Mr Pearse had slipped into the room.

Finn was startled by the sight of his headmaster in the dress uniform of the Irish Volunteers; cap pinched under his arm, buttons gleaming, sword sheathed at his waist. Involuntarily, Finn saluted. Mr Pearse blushed, raised his hand to return but didn't, instead fumbling in his tunic pocket, producing a slip of paper.

'You'll need this.'

It read 'O'Donovan Rossa Funeral Committee – Pass to Graveside'.

'We're expecting a sizable turnout,' Mr Pearse explained.

The cortege moved with stately solemnity, flowers cascading from the carriage which was pulled by four black mares and driven by the undertaker, his top hat leading, like company colours, the procession, thousands strong, who marched to Glasnevin. Finn walked alongside Mr Pearse. Flanking them were companies of Volunteers and the Citizen Army. Ahead, Mr Clarke strode out, his head raised in defiant respect. Beside him his wife matched his pace. Finn wondered if such an august funeral one day awaited his father.

They reached the cemetery. Finn presented the pass and was ushered in, the throng tightening around him. Mr Pearse steered Finn toward the graveside platform from which he was to give his speech.

'If you can manage it I'd be grateful to you for staying in my eyeline,' he whispered.

'Yes, sir,' Finn said, feeling Mr Pearse squeeze his shoulder then let go.

He watched, queasy and dry-mouthed, as Mr Pearse mounted the platform. Finn was afraid of the words he knew were coming, words that would enflame hearts and rend souls, not because of the enraged patriotism they would foster but because, once said, the man on the platform would no longer be Patrick Pearse, headmaster of St Enda's; he would be that other strange, warmongering creature Finn had glimpsed at Rosmuc: the Mr Pearse that Ireland required.

Mr Pearse cleared his throat and began.

Michaelmas Term 1915

Finn checked the clock on his nightstand. It showed a minute past nine; three long hours to go. The clock didn't want him to reach sixteen at all.

'Finn?' Mary Brigid poked her head through the doorway. 'Are you alright up here, alone?'

'Fine,' Finn lied, 'I'll turn in soon.'

'Aye, you're getting too old for stopping up late,' she teased.

Finn was about to reply with a jibe when a shadow materialised on the landing.

'Excuse me, a dheirfiúir bhig*.'

'Pat, if you're after giving me a proper fright you've a good job to pride yourself on there.'

'I was after a word with Finn.' Mr Pearse looked between them, drumming his fingers on the doorframe, his brow creased. 'I'll come back.'

Mary Brigid called after him, 'It's alright, Pat. Goodnight, Finn.'

Mr Pearse took her place inside, shutting the door, but said nothing. Finn was about to speak when Mr Pearse nodded as if a decision was now reached.

'Join me in the hall in five minutes. Wear a coat, it's nippy out.' And he was gone again.

Finn shoved his feet into boots and grabbed his coat. Wrestling the buttons as he clumped downstairs, Finn was in the hall before Mr Pearse, who emerged from his office, fastening his own coat and with a leather satchel under his arm.

'Shall we, Finn?'

Intrigued, Finn shadowed Mr Pearse as he crossed the school grounds. They passed through the gates and up the road heading away from town. After less than a mile Mr Pearse stopped at a small, squat cottage with a slate roof. The walls had been whitewashed, but not recently; the windows either side of the door were grimy, one showing a light; the

---

* little sister

green front door needed repainting. Mr Pearse pushed on the handle and the door swung on well-oiled hinges. He stepped over the threshold. Finn followed.

They were in a narrow passageway with two doors to the right, one on the left and one at the end. From behind the left hand door came the sound of a hacking cough. Tutting, Mr Pearse entered the room.

'Tom, if you'd not smoke so there'd be a chance of poor Joe not choking to death,' he said as he draped his coat over a chair.

Hovering in the hall, Finn peered inside. A threadbare sofa was pushed against the far wall. Two alcoves flanked the chimneybreast, one housing a glass-fronted cabinet and the other a bookcase populated by a few spine-cracked volumes. The grate was empty. In the centre of the room was a plain table and half a dozen chairs remarkably like those in the classrooms as St Enda's. The tabletop was covered with vast sheets of paper, maps or diagrams Finn deduced.

Mr Clarke leant on the mantelpiece, a cigarette between his fingers, his glasses perched on his nose. Mr Plunkett sat by the open window, coughing and fanning himself. Mr MacDermott, Mr MacDonagh and another, younger, man were seated at the table. His youthful face with its luxurious moustache helped Finn recognise him.

Mr Pearse sat at the table. 'Close the door, Finn, there's a draught.'

Finn shuffled into the room.

'I believe you all know Finn,' Mr Pearse murmured.

'Good to see you again, lad.'

Mr Clarke came forward and Finn carefully shook out the IRB gesture before nodding shyly at his teachers and Mr MacDermott whose unwavering eyes unsettled him further. Ducking the stare, Finn regarded the baby-faced stranger.

'Sure, you've not been introduced,' Mr Clarke said, 'Finn Devoy, Eamonn Ceannt; Eamonn, this is Michael's laddie.'

The young man got up and extended his hand.

''I hope you'll forgive me bringing Finn tonight without your leave.' Mr Pearse addressed the papers spread before him, not the men about him.

'That's alright, Pat,' Mr MacDermott replied, 'Have a seat, Finn.' He indicated a chair and Finn slouched into it. 'I'm sure you've wondered what we've been doing this while.'

Finn fought down a surge of excitement. 'Yes, sir.'

'We, Finn, are the IRB Supreme Military Council,' Mr MacDermott announced, 'Our purpose is the planning and leading of an armed rising in Ireland to establish an independent Irish Republic and busy it's kept us these past months. Joe?'

Mr Plunkett closed the window and sat opposite Finn. He wiped sweat from his brow and rasped his throat clear of phlegm.

'Aye, busy.'

Mr Clarke took the chair next to Finn. 'Come along, Joe,' he prompted.

Mr Plunkett opened his mouth.

Mr MacDermott held up a hand. 'What you learn here, Finn, must be kept to yourself.'

Finn glanced around the table. Mr Pearse continued to stare at the plans. Mr Plunkett mopped his forehead again. Mr Ceannt leaned back in his chair. Mr Clarke puffed his cigarette and Mr MacDonagh's eyes flitted to the ceiling. Mr Pearse pushed the plans away and met Finn's gaze. Finn nodded his reply.

Mr Plunkett began by explaining his absence two terms ago. He had been abroad, meeting German officials who pledged their support to an Irish rising. They would provide men, arms and artillery. Sir Roger Casement was finalising the details. With this additional military might plans were moving apace. Mr Plunkett's speech gave way to several coughing fits, somewhat marring the astounding information.

'You see, Finn, we've not been idle,' Mr Pearse said.

Mr Clarke banged his fist on the table; the papers leapt up nervously.

Mr MacDermott chuckled. 'Steady, Tom. No, Finn, as you realise, we are engaged on forming a battle plan. Do you have anything to ask?'

'Yes, sir. When?'

Mr MacDermott shared a quick look with Mr Pearse who nodded.

'Easter next.'

There was a decisiveness in the words that made Finn shiver.

The Council meeting commenced; Finn sat quietly, worrying over why Mr Pearse had brought him. Was it because of his father? Or what passed between them at Rosmuc? Was his imminent birthday a coincidence? Fretful, he picked up only snippets of information: they would occupy key positions in Dublin; the GPO would be Rising headquarters; they'd have a German U-boat at Kingstown and call out the Irish Volunteers. He didn't notice the hours passing.

'Gents, time grows upon us,' Mr MacDonagh said, examining his pocket watch.

'And we've still the most crucial decision to make,' Mr MacDermott added, 'Now our plans are so nearly complete we must settle on someone, an individual whose discretion, silence and capability we can rely upon. This person shall be entrusted with custodianship of our plans.'

'Is that necessary, Sean?' Mr Ceannt asked.

'Indeed, Eamonn, for if we six are arrested there must be someone able to pass our plans along the chain of command. This must be a person unlikely to be suspected or arrested but someone in whom we can have full confidence,' Mr MacDermott explained.

'Have you someone in mind, Sean?' Mr Clarke asked.

'I do: your own dear wife.'

'Katty? But…'

'Now, Tom, I'll have no false modesty on that good lady's part,' Mr MacDermott interrupted, 'There can be none who've ever met her would doubt her suitability for this role. I see Finn agrees.'

Finn, now aware that he had been nodding, stopped as all around the table stared at him. Recalling his only meeting with Mrs Clarke, Finn was surer of that than of anything else deliberated so far.

'I know the responsibility is great and the risk not inconsiderable so if you would prefer her kept from it I will think again but with your agreement I should propose her,' Mr MacDermott concluded.

'Sure, she'll not be kept out of it, whatever my wishes,' Mr Clarke snorted, 'And she'd skin me if she thought I'd prevented her from being of service to us. If you're certain, Sean?'

'I am. Will somebody second?'

'Seconded,' Mr Pearse said. He raised his eyes to Finn. 'I, too, have had the honour of meeting Mrs Clarke and I could not think of a better guardian than she.'

There was an unnecessary, unanimous vote in favour and the motion carried with Mr Clarke muttering, 'Well, won't she be surprised when I tell her.' Mr MacDermott drew Finn aside and asked him to pass the news of Mrs Clarke's role to his father, coded in an innocent letter home.

'I want to be prepared for all eventualities,' he explained, 'If the need should arise your father must know who to contact and he will approve our choice, I'm sure.'

The clock chimed midnight; the Supreme Military Council began tidying their papers.

Mr Pearse whispered to Finn, 'Go maire tú an lá*.'

'Thank you, sir.'

''Tis your birthday, Finn?' Mr MacDermott demanded.

Finn nodded.

'Sure, we must raise a glass.' He went to the cabinet, gathered a bottle and half a dozen glasses and began pouring whiskey.

Mr Pearse covered his glass with his palm. 'Not for me, Sean. I think we should be going, Finn.' Mr Pearse rose.

'Jesus, Pat, sit down,' Mr Clarke ordered, 'The lad's sixteen, old enough to join us in battle. 'Tis a poor show if he can't also join us in a dram. Sláinte agus saol agaibh♣!' He downed his drink in one swig before banging the glass on the table.

Finn was quick enough to catch Mr MacDermott grinning as Mr Pease slunk down into his seat. Mr Clarke seized the

---

* many happy returns

♣ health and long life to you

bottle and poured himself another measure before filling Finn's glass and Mr Pearse's. Then, getting to his feet, Mr Clarke said:

'A toast: to Finn Devoy.'

They stood and repeated the cry. Mr Pearse barely touched the glass to his lips but there was a hard light in his eyes.

'And to the rebellion,' he shouted, 'And a free Ireland hereafter.' With that he drained his glass.

'Finn, come quick.' Mary Brigid sprang into the art room, rebellious strands of auburn hair escaping her bun. Her collar was undone and there was a brown smear on her cheek. Finn leapt up.

'What is it?'

'Just come.' She dashed from the room.

Finn followed as she darted to the dining room. When she stopped at the bottom of the stairs he crashed into her.

'Mary Brigid, what's wrong?' he gasped, sniffing the air for smoke and trying to guess the origin of the brown smear.

She stepped aside.

The basement was a colour explosion. Paper chains were draped from the beams, balloons hung from light fixtures and clustered around a table, wearing colourful hats, were both Mr Pearses, Mrs and Miss Pearse, Mr Colbert, Mr MacDonagh, Mr Plunkett, Mr Slattery, Finn's four friends, Cathleen and her father plus two dazed second years, who, returned to school early, found themselves thrown into the melee.

Mr Pearse stepped forward. 'Hip, hip, hurray; hip, hip, hurray.' Everyone repeated the cheer.

Mary Brigid pressed a glass of lemonade into Finn's hand.

'You've something on your face.' Finn pointed.

She rubbed the smear onto her hand, sniffed it, laughed and licked it.

'Mother's always saying what a slapdash baker I am.'

Finn found himself besieged. People pumped his arm, kissed his cheek and slapped his back.

'Forgive me, Finn, I couldn't resist a wee party.' Mr Pearse flashed a grin.

Finn let himself be steered to the table where a large chocolate cake with sixteen candles blazed and dribbled icing.

'What are you lot doing here?'

'Mr Pearse wrote saying if he promised cake would we come back early for your party,' Charlie explained.

'Thanks.' He punched Charlie's arm on one side, Sean's on the other and reached across the table to Freddie and Hal.

'Nay bother,' Hal replied, 'Now are you gonna cut that?'

Finn picked up the knife.

'Make a wish, Finn,' Cathleen said. She was sitting further down, her father at her side. Mr Murphy was in his Sunday best, tugging on his collar.

Finn drew the cake towards him. Last night danced through the flames. He took a deep breath and blew.

There were cards and gifts: candy and a Bible sent by his mother, her love written on the flyleaf; a new, illustrated copy of *An Táin* from Cathleen. Mary Brigid handed him a small box.

'From us Pearses; it was Pat's idea.'

The box contained a silver medallion engraved with the image of a saint.

'It's St Colmcille,' Mary Brigid added, 'From the dorm you were in your first year here.'

Finn remembered but when he flipped the disk over and read the saint's motto, 'If I die it shall be from an excess of love for the Gael', he knew the real reason Mr Pearse had suggested this gift. He fastened it around his neck.

They sang and played games until Mr Pearse declared it time to clear away.

'Not yet, Pat,' Mary Brigid begged, 'Give us one of your stories.'

'No one wants to hear me,' Mr Pearse chuckled.

'Finn, tell him,' Mary Brigid pouted.

'Please, sir.'

Mr Pearse smiled. 'For you, so, Finn. Perhaps you'd like to hear more of *The Wandering Hawk*?'

Mr Pearse slipped away to fetch the manuscript amid a volley of cheers. Since publishing the first episode a few months ago Killgallon, a bold Fenian rebel otherwise know as

'The Wandering Hawk', had become a sensation. Everyone wanted to know what The Hawk and his two helpers would get up to next; the story was especially popular because it was set at St Fintan's, which bore St Enda's an uncanny resemblance, and because The Hawk's allies were two courageous schoolboys.

Mr Pearse returned and settled himself by the fireplace. 'When last we saw our adventurers, Young Clery and John Dwyer had hastened on a midnight mission over the moors to pass a message from The Wandering Hawk to his men. We shall see now how they are received by the Fenians:

"Clery spoke the message in clear straightforward sentences. He told of the Wandering Hawk's midnight visit, of the message we were to give the tin whistler and of the tin whistler's arrest. The men made no comment.

'When the tin whistler was arrested we thought the best thing to do was to come on with the message ourselves,' said Clery as he finished up.

'Ye did well,' said the man we understood to be the captain. 'I wouldn't doubt ye. If the Hawk was your masther I'll wager ye're thrue.'

The other man appeared to raise some objection.

'I'll stake my life on the truth o' this,' said the captain. Then, turning to us, he asked: 'Do you know who the Hawk is?'

'We do.'

'Do ye know what his work is?'

'We do.'

'Did ye ever take an oath from him?'

'Never. We didn't know who he was until the day the police came to arrest him. We only saw him once since, – that was when he gave us this message.'

'Will ye take an oath from me?' said the captain.

'I will,' said Clery without hesitation.

'I will,' said I in the same breath.

The captain and the other man took off their hats. Clery and I took off our caps. In the silence and dark of the night we took the Fenian oath. When we had repeated the words after the captain, he gripped each of us by the hand.

'Ye may come with me now,' said he, putting on his hat again.

We followed him into the Priest's Cave. About two dozen men were gathered there, seated on stones or on logs of wood on the ground. I recognised one or two of the faces, but the majority were strange to me. They seemed to be mountainy men, and were for the most part young, tall and dark, with that suggestion of wildness which the mountainy men always have in the glint of their eyes and the carriage of their heads and the make of their clothes. But I liked their looks and felt honoured in being their comrade. As we entered, inquiring glances were thrown on us.

'These are friends, boys,' said the captain, 'They have brought a message from the Hawk.'

He sat down at the table and stated briefly the gist of the message we had brought. When he had finished he said: 'We have only got an hour. I want five volunteers for Inishglasogue. I'll make the sixth myself. Who can steer a boat to the Eagle's Nest?'

The men looked at one another. The very name was unfamiliar to them. We were obviously the only two in the present company who could know where the Eagle's Nest was. Clery and I glanced at each other.

'We'll steer you to the Eagle's Nest,' said Clery.

The captain hesitated a little.

''Tis dangerous work for gossoons,' he said.

'We're in for it now,' said Clery with that smile of his which disarmed opposition.

The captain glanced round the circle. No one had any suggestion to offer.

With sudden decision the captain said: 'In God's name, be it so.'

The five men promptly rose. The captain and young Clery and I rose at the same moment. And we followed him out of the Priest's Cave and down the dark hillside."

Mr Pearse peered over his pages, 'Now, lads, I knocked this up this morning and it's a little rough, but it should give you an idea where I'm taking my young Fenian adventurers next.' He folded the pages and hid them in his pocket.

'Sir, you can't stop there, so you can't,' Hal moaned.

Mr Pearse displayed his empty hands.

'It's grand, Pat.' Mary Brigid clapped her brother; the room followed.

Mr Pearse smiled at his audience, catching Finn's eye as he did; Finn was certain last night's expedition had inspired this recent Wandering Hawk exploit.

Hal interrupted Finn's thoughts. 'What're you doing now, birthday boy?'

Cathleen was alone at the foot of the stairs, wearing her ridiculous party hat; Mr Murphy had left after the cake was cut.

'I better walk Cathleen home.'

Charlie opened his mouth but Sean dug his elbow in Charlie's side. 'We'll sort our stuff and meet you later, in the grounds?'

The evening sun was warm as Finn and Cathleen crossed the lawn.

She tucked her arm through his. 'Have you enjoyed your birthday?'

'Yes. Thanks for coming and for the book. You shouldn't have spent your money.'

'Ah, I'll soon be earning plenty.'

Finn halted.

'I'm not going back to St Ita's. I'm for the Rotunda Hospital.'

'The Roto?'

'I've a place there to learn nursing.'

'Nursing?'

'The one certain thing is that folks always get sick. Plus, they're wanting us badly just now. I might even go to France.'

They had reached the shade of the trees whose leaves were already bronzing. Finn yanked his arm away.

'You can't.'

'Why not?'

'Go to France? To help the English? Just so's they can keep us down?'

'What 'us' Finn? You keep forgetting: you're not Irish!' Cathleen's face was white. 'What right have you, telling me what to do? English, Irish, what's it matter? A sick man's a sick man but you'd kick him while he was down, unless he could plead mercy in Gaelic.' Her words were angry, rapid and English. Finn couldn't remember the last time he heard her speak Irish.

'Is Éireannach mé*, m'athair♣...' he said defiantly.

'...Is a bloody American,' Cathleen raged, 'because his daddy fled there, when things here got tough. Don't speak as if you're Ireland's redeemer. Haven't I lived here my whole life? My da and his and his, stayed on this God forsaken isle and suffered for it. It's no business of yours who I help; English, Irish, from the moon for what it matters.' She shook from head to foot.

'But,' Finn pressed in Gaelic, 'that's the fault of the English; they cause the suffering. That's why we've got to fight them.'

'Fight?' She grabbed him.

He pulled free.

'Tell me or I'll never speak to you again,' Cathleen shrieked.

'I didn't mean it like that.'

'Don't fecking lie to me.'

For five seconds neither of them spoke. Cathleen stood rigid, her fists clenched, her face twisted.

'Fine, I'll be off, will I?' She started stalking away through the trees.

Finn called after her. 'There's to be an armed rising. To throw out the British. At Easter.'

Cathleen stopped, revolved slowly, her movements mechanical, and raised a hand to her throat. Her voice came from far away. 'You eejits! You'll all be killed.' Her fingers looped the chain beneath her blouse, dragging it free, the

---

* I am Irish

♣ my father

locket swinging. She tugged. The chain snapped. She dropped it to the ground and ran.

Finn was frozen, watching the last glimpse of her red party hat vanish, a flame going out. Numbly, he fished the chain and locket from the fallen leaves, punched it into his pocket and set off towards school.

Four figures intercepted him on the lawn.

'That was quick,' Hal said, 'Didn't she have another wee present for you, your Cathleen?'

'She's not 'my Cathleen'.'

'Sorry! Just seeing how we can hardly get yous two apart without a crowbar.'

'I'm going for a smoke.' Finn stomped across the stream, far from the spot of his row with Cathleen. When he stopped there he was surprised to find he wasn't alone.

'Thought maybe you could use some company,' Freddie said.

'And one of these.' Charlie held a packet of cigarettes.

'Thanks.' Finn took one and sank to the ground.

'Budge up.' Hal squeezed in next to him and offered a light.

'Grand party. MB makes a great chocolate cake,' Sean said.

'Aye,' Hal agreed.

Freddie sprawled on the grass. 'What did yous make of that bit of *The Wandering Hawk*?'

'It's hot, alright,' Charlie said, 'Wonder how he'll end it.'

'In victory for the Fenians, how else?' Hal crowed.

'Which of them's The Hawk, I mean, the masters here?' Sean asked.

'Colbert?' Charlie suggested, 'Or Plunkett?'

Freddie said, 'I think Pearse made him up.'

'It's himself,' Finn said.

'But isn't he Old Snuffy, St Fintan's president?' Charlie asked.

'Maybe to us,' Finn replied, 'But in his own head he's Kilgallon, The Hawk. Maybe in real life too. Or if not yet, soon.'

'What d'ya mean?' Hal asked.

Finn had already blown his oath with Cathleen; he might as well tell them. 'You have to swear, on pain of death, that you won't tell anyone.'

'What's up?' Charlie asked.

'Swear first.'

'Alright, I swear, on pain of death, blah, blah. Come on.'

Finn shook his head. 'Properly.'

'Alright, I won't say a word.' Charlie held up a hand.

'I swear, so I do.'

'Aye, me too.'

'I hereby swear myself to secrecy forevermore.'

Finn steadied himself. 'There's a Supreme Military Council of IRB members. Mr Pearse's on it. They're getting ready for war with Britain.'

'He's never!'

'What?'

'For sure?'

'Bollocks!'

'It's true,' Finn said, 'Mr Plunkett and Mr MacDonagh are on it too.'

'Are you?' Freddie's eyes narrowed.

'Not really. Mr Pearse took me along last night, to a meeting.'

'So that's been going on this whole time?' Freddie asked.

'Aye.'

'When?' Hal demanded.

Finn hesitated.

'Don't tell us if you shouldn't,' Sean said.

'But do if you can,' Charlie added.

Finn grinned. 'I can but what if you got taken by the enemy? Tortured? You might crack.'

'Freddie would,' Hal teased.

'I bloody wouldn't!'

'Alright,' Finn laughed, 'But it goes no further.'

'Let's do a blood oath,' Charlie suggested.

He produced his penknife and slashed a shallow cut on the palm of his left hand then he offered Finn the knife. Finn did the same and passed the knife on. When each had a red smear on his palm they took turns taking Finn's hand and giving him their bloody vow that they would die before they talked. St Colmcille was no longer alone in his readiness to lay down his life for Ireland.

'It's Easter.'

The boys gathered in the gymnasium. As lieutenant, Finn stood before his platoon. There were two other platoons and two other lieutenants; Hal and Patrick Healy, the steady lad who had been a corporal when Finn first joined, had been promoted last term. Sean and Charlie had their sergeant's stripes; Freddie had a special commission in logistics and orienteering.

Mr Colbert and Countess Markievicz entered, both in their dress uniforms. Finn about faced and saluted. The Countess winked at him.

'At ease, lads,' Mr Colbert said.

The ranks relaxed.

'There's good news and bad,' Mr Colbert began, 'We've some new recruits.' He indicated a huddle of eager first years. 'But we've to say farewell to one of our own.'

Mr Colbert gestured to the door and Finn saw David Reddin, who had captained the Red Branch as long as Finn had been a member. Though David left for Trinity the year before last he had continued his captaincy. Now he entered not in the kilt and jersey of the Fianna but in the trousers, blouse and slouch hat of the Irish Volunteers.

'David has pledged to the Volunteers full time.'

David came forward; Finn noticed the three-striped mark of a sergeant on his shoulder.

'This leaves us a vacancy to fill, not easy after David's outstanding leadership.' Mr Colbert paused. 'Finn?'

Thinking he was being given a task, Finn saluted. 'Yes, sir?'

'Have you a mind to do it?'

'Do what, sir?'

Mr Colbert half chuckled-half tutted.

The Countess spoke. 'Captain the brigade, young man.'

'Me, Madam?'

'To whom else would I entrust my most important company of Fianna warriors, Finn?' she replied,

'Aye, sure,' Mr Colbert added with a wink.

'Yes, Madam. Of course. Thank you,' Finn looked to Mr Colbert, 'Thank you, sir.'

Madam Markievicz carried out the swearing in herself and declared Finn, Captain Devoy.

Next morning Mr Pearse opened his first assembly of the term with stirring words.

'At St Enda's we purpose to serve Ireland with all our fealty and our strength. It is right and proper that we purpose thus for aren't there two occasions spoken of in ancient Irish story upon which Irish boys marched to the rescue of their country when it was sore beset? Once when Cúchulainn and the boy-troop of Ulster held the frontier until the Ulster heroes rose, and again when the boys of Ireland kept the foreign invaders in check until Finn had rallied the Fianna. It may be that when men come to write the history of the freeing of Ireland they shall record that the boys of St Enda's stood thence in the battle gap.

Here we believe, as Irish boys whose hearts have not been corrupted by foreign influence must, that our country ought to be free. I hold it true that there is, in our great country, a brotherhood of young Irishmen strong of limb, pure in tongue and heart, chivalrous, who are ready to spend themselves in service of their country. And so in the coming year, which is likely to be momentous in the history of our country, I address myself to you, the boys of Ireland, my boys, and invite you to act valiantly in knightly service for your country.'

As the school applauded Hal leant over. 'He's mad keen on this Rising business, i'n't he?' he muttered in Finn's ear.

Finn choked on a laugh, disguising it as a cough. Charlie unhelpfully thumped him on the back.

Mr Pearse signalled for quiet. 'To make my point I ask you to note one amongst you who is all those things Ireland hopes for in her boys: Finn Devoy.'

'You're on!' Charlie grabbed Finn's wrist and dragged him up into an arm-raised glory pose.

The whole school span around to glimpse their own boy-hero.

'For Christ's sake, get off,' Finn hissed, shoving Charlie.

'Finn, as we already look to you for strength and inspiration, I should like to propose you for head boy,' Mr Pearse continued, 'Unless you've any objections?'

Finn wished the ground would swallow him. 'No, sir.'

'Splendid. Any other boy from the upper fifth also wishing to stand should pass his name to me by teatime today. Voting in a fortnight. Thank you, Finn.'

Finn dropped into his seat, certain that, come election day, his would be the only name. When they were dismissed he skulked behind Hal's broad back.

A hand slapped Finn's shoulder. 'Devoy, a word.' Mr Slattery drew Finn off to a niche in the corridor. 'A favour,' he barked, 'Some bodies.'

Nervous laughter bubbled in Finn's gut. 'Bodies, sir? Dead or alive?'

'Alive. Best for our purposes.'

'Our purposes?'

'The matter we discussed last term. You read the book I leant you?'

'I did, sir.'

'Righto. We'll need, say five, aside from yourself. Work commences immediately.'

'What work, sir?'

'Bomb making, of course.' Mr Slattery blinked twice. 'Choose your men and assemble in the basement after dinner.'

'We're gonna do what?' Charlie asked.

'Make bombs.' Finn tried adopting the casual tone Mr Slattery had used but his voice slid up. 'For the Rising.'

'We're not even supposed to know about it,' Freddie said.

'Slattery'll let on it's for the Volunteers.'

Freddie removed his glasses and rubbed the bridge of his nose. 'What if the Military Council find out we know?'

'They won't unless you tell them. Anyway, you're in the Fianna so by default you're Volunteers, maybes even honorary IRB members,' Finn bluffed.

'Do you think we should join properly?' Sean asked.

Finn saw a flicker on Charlie's face and remembered he was half English.

'Maybe later, this is more important.'

'Who else you gonna ask?' Hal said.

'Patrick Healy. He's been in the Fianna a while, I reckon we can trust him.'

The others exchanged glances.

'Wouldn't we be able to manage without him?' Charlie asked.

'Mr Slattery said six.'

'Aye, but…'

'Look, it's Patrick I'm asking.'

Hal muttered, 'Bollocks,' and pushed his hand through his hair. The others fidgeted but said nothing.

Captain's word was final.

In the basement Mr Slattery had set up an improvised lab with chalkboard and work benches. Six boys, still in their school uniforms, perched on the benches; Mr Slattery hadn't thought of chairs. There was, though, an impressive array of test tubes, beakers, Bunsen burners, tongs, goggles, aprons and gauntlets.

'Ahoy, gentlemen. Explosives.' Mr Slattery wrote the word on the board. 'First, the basics.' He went to write but turned back immediately. 'Incidentally, if anyone were to ask, you are considering majoring in chemistry at Trinity so I'm giving you a head start.' He winked. 'Righto. High explosives and low explosives.' He added the phrases to the board, forming two columns. Underneath he scrawled the words detonation and deflagration. 'Who'll tell us what these terms mean?'

Freddie's hand shot in the air. With a grin, Finn did likewise.

'Mr Devoy.'

'Deflagration is basically burning, what combustible materials of low explosive properties do. Detonation is what high explosives do, a supersonic reaction, pushing forward a wave of energy.'

'Where did you learn that, I wonder?' Mr Slattery smirked. 'As Mr Devoy explained we've two options.' He waved a bony hand over the blackboard. 'To which I'll add two terms I'm sure need no explanation.' He wrote 'gunpowder' in the low explosives column and 'dynamite' in the high explosives one.

Sean whistled. 'Are we really going to make dynamite, sir?'

'Possibly,' Mr Slattery said, 'but I think we'd best start with gunpowder.'

Mr Slattery spent the rest of the evening detailing the process of dissolving mercury filings in nitric acid and adding ethanol to make mercury fulminate, the primary explosive. This he promised they'd manufacture at the next meeting.

The following Wednesday they made five blasting caps, containing mercury fulminate, for sparking the gunpowder. All ignited efficiently when lit with a match via a lengthy fuse. Over the next two weeks they proceed to make their first batch of gunpowder.

It was election day, time to say 'aye' or 'nay' to Finn Devoy as head boy. A belligerent Finn marked his ballot paper 'nay'.

After tea Mr Pearse sent for him.

'I have tallied this morning's poll and will make the announcement during prep but I thought to inform you first.'

'Thank you, sir.'

'The vote was as I wished; a majority for you as head boy. It was, in fact, almost unanimous.' Mr Pearse scrutinised Finn with those light grey eyes that were capable of seeing through walls and lies alike.

Finn became fascinated with the patterned rug beneath his feet. It was green, red and gold. Flowers and leaves scrolled together.

'Tell me, Finn, have you enemies here?'

'I don't think so, sir.'

'Hmm. I wonder then, who was the one boy who voted 'nay'?'

Finn's legs wobbled.

Mr Pearse rested his fist on the leather writing pad and relaxed his grip. Finn raised his eyes. The green and gold head boy pin sat in Mr Pearse's palm.

'This is yours, if you want it.'

His heart beating, Finn stared at the pin.

Mr Pearse rose from his chair and came to Finn's side, the pin in his cupped hand. Finn swivelled his eyes, following it.

'You have my confidence and the school's, to say nothing of Mr Colbert and the Fianna. You have only to convince yourself.'

'The Fianna's different, sir; I've worked up to that.'

'There's not another lad in St Enda's today I would have as head boy this year.' The last two words were heavily stressed. 'I'll respect your decision but remember, Finn: all can follow; few can lead.'

'And you think I can, sir?'

'I do.'

Of all the roles cast upon him this was surely the least onerous. Why was he resisting? Perhaps to see if he could. He straightened his spine and took the pin.

Mr Pearse said, 'Sure, 'tis a splendid job I have here with boys like yourself.'

That night, with the head boy badge fastened to his lapel, Finn and the rest of the squad completed their first batch of gunpowder. It fizzed sluggishly.

'We may require some small modification but in essence we are there, gentlemen.'

'How'll we use it, sir?' Patrick asked.

'I've been pondering that. I propose designing a hand held device, one for throwing thus.' He lobbed an invisible something overhead. 'It may well be the case, men, that the Volunteers will need portable ammunition that is effective at close range.' Mr Slattery met Finn's eye before continuing, 'Who knows what the UVF may do if Home Rule is proclaimed.'

'A grenade, eh, sir?' Hal asked.

'Precisely. For which I have procured these.' Mr Slattery picked two empty tins from the workbench. One was labelled 'peaches'. 'By removing the top and bottom,' Mr Slattery held the tin side-on and squinted through it, 'filling it with projectiles and covering the ends with something that may be blown out after a sufficient build up of pressure we might be right.'

'The projectiles, sir?' Charlie asked.

'Scrap metal?' Mr Slattery mused.

'The blacksmith might give us some.'

'Excellent idea, Devoy. I'll leave that to you.'

Finn rolled his eyes at Charlie who mouthed, 'I'll come with you.'

'To work, gentlemen,' Mr Slattery barked.

'Work, sir?' Sean asked.

'Aye, what to stop up the ends with, how to attach the primary charges, etcetera. Thinking caps on, men.'

A fortnight later they occupied the woods behind the school armed with the finished grenades, a collection of misshapen tins, their scrap iron contents rattling and their puckered mouths trailing fuse wire. Finn balanced one in his palm as their feet crunched over the frosty grass. It had a menacing weight.

'Righto, gentlemen.' Mr Slattery halted the party in a clearing.

Hal and Sean began unpacking the grenades, dividing them into two piles; gunpowder and dynamite, for they had persuaded the master to try both. Finn added his to the gunpowder pile. Mr Slattery satisfied himself that the tins had been correctly sorted by checking for the daub of red paint used to identify the dynamite grenades.

'Much too unstable to not know it's dynamite you've got hold of. I remain unconvinced as to its usefulness.' Mr Slattery held up a red-spotted tin. 'Perhaps we best stick with the gunpowder.'

'But, sir,' Sean protested, 'We've made it now.'

'Aye, all that effort on nitro-whatsit for nothing, that's terrible, sir,' Hal grumbled.

'Don't you want to know if it works, sir?' Finn added.

'Damnit, you make a good point, Devoy. But we'll start with the gunpowder ones.'

They paced out the clearing; Mr Slattery set up a target and selected a sturdy gorse bush for protection.

'Behind the shelter, gentlemen. I'll throw the first. We'll see what we have ourselves.'

They crowded behind the bush. From his pocket Mr Slattery took a cigarette lighter, flicked back the lid and stroked his thumb down the wheel which span up, igniting the wick. The small flame writhed. Mr Slattery selected a grenade from the gunpowder pile and kissed the flame to the fuse. A starburst of white light sprinted towards the blasting cap. Mr Slattery arched his arm and let the grenade fly. Finn followed its trajectory. It peaked and began a wild, spinning fall, as if sensing its own impending doom. One brief moment of ultimate freedom then…

'Get down, Devoy.' Mr Slattery yanked Finn's blazer.

The noise of the blast shook Finn's teeth loose. For a moment the lads were paralysed by it then they jumped up as suddenly as they had dropped down.

A cloud of smoke hung in the air. The clearing smelled burnt.

Mr Slattery grinned. 'Let's see what she's done, so.'

They found fragments of shrapnel imbedded in the ground and up tree trunks but most of it was fused to the inside of the tin.

'No too bad,' Mr Slattery said, 'Record the findings, Blackwell.'

Freddie produced a notebook.

'Finn?' Mr Slattery held out his lighter and another tin.

Finn took them and did as Mr Slattery had; light, throw, duck. There was a satisfying bang and a sound like heavy rain falling on dried leaves. Finn felt something strike his head. Charlie shouted, 'Ow,' and Freddie, crouched next to Finn, flinched and fell into him as hot metal peppered the ground.

'Perhaps too much black powder in that one,' Mr Slattery mused, 'Take a note, Blackwell.'

Freddie, still inspecting himself for injuries, fumbled for his notebook. Finn pressed his hand to his head; singed hair crackled in his fingers.

They took turns throwing the gunpowder grenades until one remained. Ready to drop down, the others watched eagerly; this would be it: a real killer. Sean sparked the fuse, hurled the tin, dashed for cover and all seven, fingers pressed to ears and eyes screwed shut, waited. And waited.

Mr Slattery inched his head above the leafy parapet.

'We seem to have a damp squib, gentlemen.'

'What do we do, sir?' Patrick asked.

Sean stood. 'It's mine. I'll check it.'

'Sean, wait…' But Sean was already hunting among the trees.

The bomb squad listened to the rustles of a feral cat, as Sean dug around for the dud.

'Found it!'

A bright flash and a deafening bang ripped through the clearing.

Finn opened his eyes; sparks of light pin-pricked his vision. He blinked them away and peered through swirling smoke, the blast echoing in his ears. He staggered to his feet; the ground heaved. He yelled Sean's name but couldn't hear his own voice. He lurched ahead, plunging into the smoke. His eyes stung and sooty fumes choked him. He gagged and coughed, blindly stumbling forwards, shoving through thick grey air that scattered and reformed around him. His foot nudged something soft. He fell to his knees and patted around, feeling the scratchy wool of a school jersey. He felt his way along until his fingers touched something wet and sticky. He lifted his hands to his face. The fog shrank back, showing smears of red. Finn's mouth opened; he strained his throat, shouting words he couldn't hear. He started running, the world a green-brown blur.

A hand grabbed him. Mr Murphy, his face pock-marked by specs of flashing light, was shaking him and speaking. Finn pointed to his ears and shook his head. Mr Murphy boxed him, a sharp blow to either ear. Finn felt a pop and sound flooded in.

'Whoa, lad. What's to do?'

'There's been an accident. We need a doctor.' Finn felt wetness on his face. He rubbed his cheeks.

'What's this?' Mr Murphy snatched Finn's hands. 'Blood?'

'Please, over there.' Finn gestured.

Mr Murphy shouted, 'Cathleen.'

She appeared, saw Finn and stopped, saw the blood and ran to him.

'I'm away for help.' Her father set off at a gallop.

'Finn, what's happened? Are you hurt?'

His throat was too tight for speech. He pointed and ran for the clearing.

The smoke had thinned. Freddie, Hal, Patrick and Charlie formed a standing circle, as though enacting a pagan rite. Mr Slattery was in their midst, holding something, eyes fixed on it. His head moved slowly, side to side. At the sound of footsteps he lifted his gaze, dropped it on Finn and held aloft the remains of a tin can streaked blood red.

'It was dynamite,' he said in a flat voice.

Finn pushed through the ring, dragging Cathleen with him.

She stumbled. 'Jesus Christ.' Crossed herself.

Sean lay on the grass like a starfish. The fingers of his left hand were opened, as if to wave. His right arm was ripped and ragged at the wrist. A sliver of creamy bone protruded from the stump.

'Finn, come away.' Cathleen tugged his sleeve.

Finn shrugged her off, sweeping the ground with his eyes, searching for Sean's hand.

'Finn. Please.' Cathleen plucked his sleeve again.

Finn tore himself from Cathleen's grip and crashed through the undergrowth, trampling bushes, stumbling and panting until, exhausted, he fell to his knees, sobbing.

Someone dragged him up and clamped him in a tight embrace. Finn gulped back tears.

'Anois*, anois.' Willie Pearse smiled down gently.

Finn let himself be led away.

---

* there

Willie took Finn into the family room, sat him on the sofa, fetched whiskey and gave it to him.

Mrs Pearse entered. 'Goodness, Willie, whatever's going on?'

'A wee accident, Ma.' He shepherded her out.

There, there.

Finn drank the whiskey, squeezing the glass in his hand.

Anois, anois.

Red stained his hand.

There, there.

The hand that had gripped Sean's, made them friends.

Anois, anois.

The hand that had carried a grenade and placed it on a pile.

There, there.

Another hand, torn off and thrown to the wind.

Anois, anois.

Two warriors, two brothers, each claiming the prize.

There, there.

The red hand of Ulster.

Finn's grip tightened. The glass broke.

Mr Pearse came in one door; Willie back through the other. They met in the middle. Mr Pearse's face was white.

'Pat, have you…?'

He brushed Willie aside. 'Finn, there you are. I was worried.'

'Pat, the..'

'I know, a dheartháir*. I must speak with Finn.'

'Now?'

Finn bent his head; on the rug shattered glass glittered. A drop of red splashed from a jagged cut on his palm. Finn made a fist. Before his eyes, the fist divided, multiplied, became two, four, many.

'Aye. Finn, come with me.'

Finn dragged a sleeve over his wet face.

'It's alright,' he said to Willie, 'I'm fine.'

Willie opened his mouth but Mr Pearse hurried Finn from the room.

---

* brother

The bomb squad had assembled in Mr Pearse's office. Mr Slattery was there and Mr Colbert.

'A dreadful thing has happened,' Mr Pearse began, 'You are all brave beyond imagining, your efforts tell as much, and upon that bravery I must, with heavy heart, now call.'

The Dublin Metropolitan Police were coming. They were to say they had been working at a science project that had tragically resulted in the loss of a promising student.

Finn knew the lie was Mr Pearse's way of protecting them and the Rising.

Mr Colbert dismissed them to the dining room where Mary Brigid and Mrs Pearse plied them with sweet, whiskey-laced tea. When Mary Brigid brought Finn his her eyes flashed the same angry terror Finn had seen the night she'd slapped Mr Pearse after catching them returning from the IRB meeting.

Finn was beside Mr Pearse's desk, studying the hem of his Fianna kilt, trying to ignore the sniffles of Sean's mother, his father's racking cough. Mr Pearse was speaking. Sean had died serving Ireland. As nationalists, this was meant to comfort them.

'Would it be a trouble if we had a word with Finn, Mr Pearse?'

'It wouldn't, would it, Finn?'

'No, sir.'

A floorboard creaked. The headmaster slipped from the room.

'You're Michael Devoy's boy?'

'Yes, sir.'

'You and Sean were friends?'

Finn faced Mr O'Malley. Eyes, hooded and raw, stared back.

'Yes, sir.'

'It's a grand thing you're doing here.'

A single sob popped like a balloon behind Sean's father. Mr O'Malley flinched but pressed on.

'I've a feeling what's happened's hit you boys hard.'

Finn nodded.

'Maybes you're not of a mind to go on with the work.' Mr O'Malley rustled in his pocket. 'I've something to show you, a letter Sean sent last week. He says, 'There's a few of us from the Fianna doing something important for Ireland. I'm not to tell you what but it's a grand thing, one I'm proud to do. Don't I think myself lucky to be in on it with my friends, playing my part for Ireland's freedom?' Mr O'Malley held the paper for Finn to see, as if he must know its truth. 'Sean would be wanting you lads to carry on for him. Will you, Finn?'

The next day Mr Slattery called an extra-ordinary meeting of the bomb squad. They drifted to the basement where Mr Slattery, along with Misters Pearse, Plunkett and MacDermott awaited them.

'Righto, men, be seated,' Mr Slattery directed.

Exchanging nervous glances, they sat facing the adults. Finn had told the others about Sean's letter, his father's request, and they agreed to carry on. He'd also filled Patrick in on why they were really making bombs. He hadn't been expecting a confrontation with Mr MacDermott. Now the IRB commander was eyeballing his friends. Finn fingered the change in his pocket.

'Hallo, Finn,' Mr MacDermott said, 'Boys, I'm Sean MacDermott, a friend of Mr Pearse's. I hoped to avoid the action I'm about to take but recent events compel me to…' he glanced to Mr Pearse who kept his eyes stubbornly forwards, '…take you into my confidence.'

Finn stood to attention. 'They know about the Rising, sir. I know I was forbidden from speaking of it, but they're all in the Fianna so I thought it'd be alright. Plus, they're my friends, I trust them; it wasn't fair to involve them under a pretence.'

Mr MacDermott shot Mr Pearse an acidic glare. Mr Pearse, ignoring it, stepped over to Finn.

'You were right in your disclosure, Finn.'

'Suppose it saves me a deal of explaining,' Mr MacDermott muttered, switching his glare to Finn. Finn met it resolutely; Mr MacDermott blinked first. 'Fair play to you, Finn.' He swept the rest of them with his serious eyes. 'If Finn trusts you happen I can do the same, with one condition:

you must lay your hands upon the Bible and swear, as St Enda's boys and Fianna soldiers, to tell no one what you know.'

Mr Plunkett proffered a Bible. Having ruined his last oath, Finn stepped forward and renewed his promise. Freddie, Hal and Patrick followed. Charlie hesitated. Finn tensed.

'No one should pledge himself if he harbours doubt,' Mr Pearse said.

Charlie squirmed. 'Sorry, sir. I was just wondering, is this alright, I mean, because, well, I'm half English.' He burbled the words.

'As am I,' Mr Pearse said quietly, 'but what you are matters far less than what you aspire to.'

Charlie laid his hand on the Bible. Finn relaxed.

Their oaths sworn Mr MacDermott began explaining the importance of their work.

'It's alright, sir,' Finn interrupted, 'We've already decided to carry on. Sean would've wanted us to.'

'Mo mhacaomh*,' Mr Pearse murmured.

'Right, men, to work,' Mr Slattery commanded.

When Finn and the others emerged from the basement the sky had been blackened by a winter's night.

'I'm fecking starving,' Hal moaned.

'It'll be dinner soon,' Patrick said as they made their way to the dorms, 'I'll just have time to move my stuff in with yous.'

It had been decided it would be easiest if the squad bunked together.

'We'll help,' Charlie offered.

They rounded the corner. Cathleen drifted from the shadows.

'What're you doing here?' Finn asked.

'Looking for you,' she replied, 'Will you walk with me?'

Finn left his friends and headed outside with Cathleen where they set off on a circuit around the Hermitage.

---

* my boy/lad (literally) but also a term used to refer to Cúchulainn and one used by Pearse for his ideal of an heroic yet scholarly young Christian/Celtic warrior

'How are you?' she asked.

'Alright, I suppose. You?'

'I keep seeing him lying there.'

'Yeah.'

'And thinking how glad I am it wasn't you. Isn't that awful?'

Finn didn't think it was.

'At least that's an end to it.'

Finn didn't correct her.

'It is an end to it, isn't it?'

'No.'

Cathleen halted abruptly. 'You're still after fighting?'

'And you're still after going to France?'

'To help people, aye.'

'And what we're doing's not a help?' Finn knew they were talking, as much as walking, in circles.

'It's madness. For Christ's sake, yous are making a war for yourselves.'

Finn started to walk again. 'Because we have to.'

She chased after him. 'No you don't.'

'If we don't they win and Sean died for nothing.'

'And when the British crush you it'll still be for nothing.'

'Thanks for having such faith in us.'

They'd arrived at the front of the building. Mr Murphy hovered in the drive, his cap low over his eyes. 'Cathleen, we've to go.'

'It's for you I'm doing this,' Finn said.

'Shite it is! It's for yourself. So you can be a bloody hero. But a dead man's no hero of mine.'

The next six weeks were spent perfecting the dynamite grenades and going into full-scale production.

When he wasn't in the gloomy basement Finn was drilling the Fianna Éireann. All thirty members were now tolerably accurate with the small bore rifles they carried. In addition, they refreshed their survival skills and every other weekend joined up with David Reddin's Irish Volunteer company so the two troops could fight each other in mock battles.

When he wasn't being Captain Devoy, head boy, bomb maker or student, Mr Pearse took Finn to the Supreme

Military Council meetings. On the occasions Finn was too busy to go he'd watch Mr Pearse head along the road, slouched in his overcoat, dragging his feet, unsure which of them was more disappointed.

As much as Finn was eager to visit the safe house, home of the being known as the Easter Rising, it could be an uncomfortable place. The problem was a mathematical one, three against three if a vote was called; Finn kept out of the way, making tea, bringing up coal or visiting the privy. It wasn't confusion or doubt making his mouth dry, the room cold or his bladder full; it was dread of having to vote against Mr Pearse. But there were only so many times he could contrive to be in the jacks so Finn studied the maps, listened to the plans, asked questions and made absolutely sure before he cast his vote.

His life was full and, as much as Finn regretted it, there was no time for art. He saw Willie Pearse only as they flashed past each other in school. Willie wasn't on the Military Council, although he'd joined the IRB, and Mr Pearse made clear that Finn's silence applied to Willie as to anyone else outside the safe house. Finn thought the reason for keeping Willie ignorant ridiculous; Mr Pearse claimed Willie was too much the artist to be burdened with military stratagems. He said it before disappearing into his office to pen the latest instalment of *The Wandering Hawk*.

Three weeks before term's end Finn's father ordered him home for the holidays, the risks of crossing the Atlantic outweighed by the need to pass plans for the Rising to the Clan. Locked in Mr Pearse's office, Finn was at the Rising's mercy, studying the papers, memorising details which changed with frustrating frequency.

Snow prevented Fianna Éireann exercises the last weekend of term. Finn, Freddie, Hal, Charlie and Patrick took their hurleys onto the field behind the school, swooping up and down, lobbing passes, jeering and cheering.

The back door opened. Mary Brigid, a shawl around her shoulders but her head bare, crumped through the snow, carrying a tray. Finn dropped the sliotar.

'I thought you'd like something warming,' she called, waving to them. They flung their hurleys down, thanked her as she handed round mugs of cocoa and took to jawing and swigging. Mary Brigid lingered by Finn.

'You seem tired.'

'I'm fine.'

'You've that same look about you.'

'What look?'

'The one Pat has so often these days. Joe and Con, too, even Willie. Would you know the cause of that look, Finn?' She held his gaze.

Finn's stomach lurched. Hot chocolate bubbled uneasily. He swallowed.

'If there was anything I could say to stop him, you'd tell me, wouldn't you?'

Finn dropped his eyes. 'There isn't.'

'That's what Mother said,' she sighed, 'How's Cathleen these days?'

His stomach gurgled again. Two rows and not wanting to make it three, Finn had been avoiding Cathleen.

'I hear she's impressing them at the Roto,' Mary Brigid added.

Acidy chocolate filled Finn's mouth.

'You'd do well to think on those that care for you.' Mary Brigid snatched Finn's half-empty mug, span, stirring up a flurry of snow, and tramped away.

Hal came over, wiping a chocolate moustache from his lip.

'That was grand.'

'Yeah.' Finn stared after Mary Brigid's shrinking shape. 'Come on, I'll kick your arses, four on one.' He grabbed his hurley, dashed across the snowy ground and belted the sliotar into the improvised goal.

Finn beat them as Cúchulainn would have and rewarded himself a very un-Cúchulainn-like hot bath. Then he searched out Mary Brigid.

She was in the family room, her fingers trailing her harp strings. Mrs Pearse was also there, sowing to hand.

'Finn, everything well?' she asked.

'Yes, thank you, Mrs Pearse, I was, well, I'm packing and...'

'Have you lost something?'

Mary Brigid twanged a string hard enough to snap it. 'I'll go, Mother.' She came to the door, closed it and started for the stairs. 'What's missing?'

'Nothing.' Finn dragged her into an empty classroom.

'What're you doing?'

'I'm sorry, Mary Brigid, if you're sore with me but we have to do this.'

'He's got you well versed, my dear brother. When's it to be?'

'I can't tell you, Mary Brigid, please.'

'I know anyway. It's Easter I've got until, to make you see sense.' Her lips quivered. Her eyes glistened. She didn't cry.

Finn frowned. 'Why'd you ask if you know?'

'I wanted to see if you were man enough to tell me, because Pat isn't.'

She'd played a mean trick on him; he clenched his fists.

'Finn, you shouldn't be involved in this. Cathleen's right, it's madness.'

'Did she tell you?'

'Does it matter? Help me, Finn. Tell me how I can stop him. Save him.' Her eyes grew wide and dark.

'You can't.'

Hilary Term 1916

Finn's father called him to the study.

'Are you packed?'

'Nearly, sir.'

'Ready for the off?'

'Yes, sir.'

'I'm not talking of school, you understand?'

'Yes, sir.'

His father stroked his beard. A fortnight ago there had been a glimmer of pride when Finn revealed his involvement with the Rising, how much he was trusted. Now, standing before his father in the gloaming light of a winter's evening, his palms sweaty, Finn felt the weight of it on him.

His father put an envelope on the desk.

'Open it.'

Three documents tumbled to the mahogany surface; an American passport, a British passport and a set of German identity papers. Finn fingered all three and waited for an explanation.

'I am preparing you for every eventuality. If the Rising succeeds you are to exchange the British passport for an Irish one, become a full Irish citizen. If the Axis powers invade you're to use the German papers; they're in your mother's name.' His father thrummed his fingers on the desk. 'The American passport is for general travel, a requirement of the Federal Government for the duration of the war. Plus,' he paused, 'if things should go against us it will guarantee your safety.'

'My safety, sir?'

'Don't be foolish, Finn. What do you suppose the British will do to those who rise against them in an open act of treason and fail to defeat them?'

Finn's throat closed around the word, 'fail'.

'Boy, they'll be hanged. If arrested present your American passport and demand deportation. They will not dare imprison, much less execute, an American citizen.'

His father gathered the documents and pressed them on Finn. The American passport burnt his hand as he pocketed it. With a nod his father reached for the safe behind his desk, span the dial and the door sprang open. From inside he withdrew a bulky item wrapped in an oily cloth and presented it to Finn.

'I expect you to be capable of handling this.'

Finn unwound the cloth, revealing a revolver. 'We have rifles in the Fianna, sir.'

'Pah, bee-bee guns. What are they, .22s? Here.' His father seized the gun, showed Finn how to load, cock it and put on the safety catch. He plonked a box on the desk. 'Ammunition. Enough, I trust, for your purposes.'

The gun trembled in Finn's hand.

'You'd better finish your packing.'

Finn about faced.

'Finn.'

'Sir?'

'Ádh mór ort*, a mhic♣.'

His mother travelled with him to the docks.

'Can you expect much excitement this term?'

A helpful porter saved Finn from answering, checking his ticket and marking up his trunk. Finished, he tipped his cap and retreated. Finn's mother tried again.

'I understand we'll not see you at Easter.'

'No, Mother.'

'Take good care of yourself, won't you?' She hugged him tightly; Finn couldn't breathe.

'Please don't worry, Mother. I can take care of myself.'

She stroked his hair. 'Your babies are always your babies. You'll understand that one day, Finn.' She stretched up and kissed his forehead, 'Be safe, my darling, be happy.'

'I'll write, as always,' Finn promised, 'and see you in July.'

She summoned a tiny smile. 'God willing.'

*

---

* Good luck

♣ son (affectionate term)

On the first day of term Mr Pearse spoke of how, at the knee of his great aunt, he first heard the inspiring tales of ancient Irish heroes. He made no reference to more modern conflicts.

'Do yous believe that?' Hal cried as they headed to the gymnasium for their first Fianna meeting. 'He didn't say a bloody thing about the Rising.'

'Don't you think that's deliberate?' Freddie said.

'Suppose. Still, he could've said something, in code like. For us.'

'What did your father say?' Charlie asked Finn.

'Not much but he gave me something.'

'What?'

'Show you later.'

Mr Colbert's opening address was less guarded. He ended by quoting the final verse of the Fianna Éireann song, 'O boys of na Fianna, advance o'er the nation/ Let every home greet you with joy and delight/ May God give you courage, to love Him and Ireland/ And when the day dawns, give you courage to fight.'

'And that day is fast approaching,' the master proclaimed.

Donald MacCabe, a quiet boy whose timidity had landed him the role of company piper, raised a hand. Mr Colbert signalled permission to speak.

'What do you mean, sir?'

'Just what I say,' Mr Colbert barked, 'That the day is coming when Ireland will fight her oppressors.'

Donald's lip trembled. He dropped his gaze to the floor. But he'd already invoked the wrath of the great Con.

'What do you think this is, MacCabe, the fecking boy scouts?' Mr Colbert bellowed, 'We that pledge to the Fianna are not here for jolly japes in the woods, rubbing sticks together and tying knots.'

Finn recalled the weekends when they'd done those very things but he wouldn't have reminded Mr Colbert of them for all the peat in Ireland.

'We are here for what, Devoy?'

'To serve Ireland, sir.'

'Thank you, Captain. Did you hear that, MacCabe? Did you all hear that?' Mr Colbert shouted. Forgetting they were on parade, they bobbed their heads.

'A Fianna boy is, what? The oath, now!'

Twenty-five voices recited, 'A Fianna is patriotic, reliable...'

Before they could finish Mr Colbert interjected. 'Patriotic! The first and most important of our tenets. And this,' he grabbed a corner of the flag that was, as usual, pinned to the wall, grasping it with such force he nearly pulled it loose, 'What's this on the flag? Will one of you eejits remind us?'

Freddie stepped forward.

'Blackwell.'

'A pike, sir, like those used in the 1798 rising.'

'Praise God some of you know your history.'

Finn scowled. 'Sir, beg pardon, but I think we all…'

Mr Colbert rampaged on. 'And like the men of '98 we'll fight to free ourselves from tyrannous rule.'

'Didn't they lose in '98?' Hal hissed.

'Lose!' roared Mr Colbert, 'Sure, they did not or we'd not be here. Lose! A villainous English propaganda. Thrice to the school and back. Fall out.'

It was raining outside; they were in their dress uniform; it was three quarters of a mile from gym to school. Nobody moved, not believing the order to run 5 miles in the rain, in their kilts.

'Five times, so! Fall out before I make it ten!'

Finn bolted for the door, his company falling in behind him. They ran like the devil was after them.

'I don't know what's worse,' Hal grumbled when they were cosy in the dorm, their kilts steaming by the fire, 'Colbert with his arse on fire or Pearse a damp squib.'

'Never mind that,' Charlie said, 'What did your father give you?'

All four gathered round Finn's bed. He rummaged inside his trunk until his fingers touched the cold metal of the revolver.

'Ready?' He whipped out the gun, training it on them.

'Jesus,' Hal whopped.

'Your da's mad,' Patrick declared, grinning.

'Is it real?' Charlie asked.

Freddie recoiled. 'Is it loaded?'

Finn answered one at a time. 'Aye, he's mad, yes, and no. Not yet.'

'And you're gonna use it?' Freddie asked.

'I am.'

'To kill people?'

'That's the idea.'

The air blew cold despite the fire. Finn replaced the gun; the others drifted to their beds.

'It's real, now, isn't it?' Charlie whispered.

A bang woke Finn. He fumbled for a match; weak light flicked about the room, showing nothing out of place. He heard another bang and a scuffing, something heavy being dragged. The match burnt down.

'Shite.' Finn tossed the hot splinter from him and lit another. The glow illuminated a sleepy Charlie rubbing his eyes.

'What's up?' he asked through a yawn.

'I heard something. Shhh.'

They strained their ears.

'I can't...' Charlie began but an alarming clatter cut him off.

Finn went to the window, opened it wide and ducked into the bluely cold January air. It snatched his breath and watered his eyes.

'It's freezing.' Charlie joined Finn at the window, squeezing in next to him. The effect was of some weird, two-headed, four-armed creature that didn't get along with itself.

'Move over.'

'I was here first.'

'You're on my foot.'

'I'll be on more than your bloody foot in a minute. Shhh!'

An oblong of light dropped onto the frost-sparkled grass. Finn and Charlie stopped jostling and gripped one another. Disjointed phrases floated up. Still clutching each other, they leaned further through the window.

'Kidnap...'

'Bejesus!'

'...no choice...reckless...ruin...'

'Madness...'

'IRB orders.'

Into view came the outline of three men clumped together with a fourth trailing behind. The middle man of the trio was slumped between the others, either unconscious or having difficulty walking.

'Have they got him tied up?' Charlie asked and Finn noticed the middle man's hands were twisted behind his back. 'Who is it?'

Finn recognised the stocky figure and receding line of smoothed-back hair.

'It's Mr Connolly, the union man.'

'What're they...? And who's that? Hell, it's Pearse.' Charlie pointed to the fourth man.

'And that's Mr Clarke.' Finn gestured towards the man on the left of Mr Connolly's drooping figure.

They watched as the prone Mr Connolly was half dragged, half carried along the drive. A clip-clop and a rolling crunch signalled the arrival of a cart. Mr Plunkett occupied the driver's seat, his spectral face illuminated by light from the doorway. With a struggle the three men, Plunkett, Clarke and the other, who Finn suspected to be Mr Ceannt, wrestled Mr Connolly onto the trap. Then all three climbed aboard, Mr Plunkett snapped the whip and the horse trotted away. Throughout Mr Pearse stood, arms folded, head bowed, taking no part in what appeared suspiciously like the kidnap of Mr James Connolly. The trap shrank in the darkness; Mr Pearse turned towards the building.

'Quick!' Finn snatched Charlie from the window and they tumbled to the floor.

'Did he see us?' Charlie gasped.

'Dunno.'

Light splashed out suddenly. Hal held his cigarette lighter aloft and smirked at Finn and Charlie who were tangled together on the floor.

'What's this, lads?'

Finn thrashed free, charged over to Freddie's bed, then Patrick's.

'You're never gonna believe what we've seen.'

The next day Mr Pearse's office door remained locked; enquiries about him received the reply, 'He's away on business.' Mr Plunkett was also absent, his excuse of ill health made plausible by the wracking cough, deathly pale skin and scarecrow's fit suit that had been so noticeable lately. St Enda's, minus two teachers, struggled to cover the classes. After lunch the boys were herded into the main hall for a lecture.

They had taken their seats and Willie the stage when the door slammed, revealing Countess Markievicz, dressed for riding, her whip in her left hand, her hair windblown.

'Why's she here?' Patrick asked.

'Not for the lecture, that's for sure,' Finn replied as the Countess strode towards the stage, her tall frame dwarfing the seated audience.

She raised her whip to Willie. 'Where are you bastards keeping him?'

There was a nervous titter.

'Please, Madam Markievicz,' Willie protested, his eyes roving the hall.

Mr Colbert rose from his seat.

'Stay where you are, Colbert, or I'll shoot.' The Countess raised her right arm, brandishing her gun, the revolver Finn had seen her handle so confidently during many Fianna drill sessions. She levelled it at Mr Colbert. 'This is loaded and you know I'm a dead-eye shot with it. Now,' she swung on Willie Pearse who rubbed trembling fingers through his curls, 'tell me where you sons of bitches have James Connolly.' She trained the gun on Willie.

'I assure you, Madam Markievicz, I have no idea...' Willie's voice was a squeak.

'Don't lie.' She scanned the hall. 'Where's your dear brother?'

'Pat's away today.'

'Indeed! Pray, tell, what is it takes him from his precious school?'

Unseen, Mr Colbert inched closer to the Countess. Mr MacDonagh got to his feet.

'He had business to attend.'

'The business of holding an innocent man captive.'

'Please, Countess,' Willie pleaded, 'I know nothing of this. As for my brother's business, you'll have to ask him.'

'I will, indeed!' She span again on Mr Colbert who had crept near. 'Don't be stupid, Con,' she sneered, switching her aim to Mr Colbert, waving the gun at the assembled school as she did. 'I've no care for you today if you've a part in this.' She started backing out. 'You can tell your brother that unless he releases James at once I'll have the Citizen Army free him by force.'

'She'll have to find him first,' Charlie muttered.

'Bet I could tell her where,' Finn whispered, keeping his head down to avoid the searching gaze of Constance Markievicz.

Her gun sweeping the scene, the Countess reached the door, stepped through it backwards, closed it and the hall listened as her riding boots rapped off down the parquet flooring. Finn pictured her mounting her horse and riding like the devil's wife. He longed to cheer her.

A clamour arose. Willie sank to a chair, mopping his brow with a trembling hanky. Mr Colbert dashed to the front and bellowed to the sea of students. The uproar fell and, in pin-drop silence, he proclaimed lessons were ended for the day but before he could dismiss them Mr MacDonagh whispered into his ear. Mr Colbert's eyes widened and his mouth gaped but he nodded at Mr MacDonagh.

'With the exception of Devoy, you are dismissed. Don't be late to prep.'

'What's going on?' Charlie asked Finn as chairs scraped and feet stamped.

'Think I'm getting an errand.'

Boys ebbed from the hall. Mr MacDonagh led Finn out of range of Mr Colbert and Mr Slattery who were huddled around a shaking Willie Pearse.

'Do you know where you might find Mr Pearse just now?'

'I've an idea, sir.'

'Then perhaps you'd away and tell him what's happened.'

Finn sprinted to the safe house and brayed on the door. There were scuffling sounds behind it.

'Who's that there?'

'Finn Devoy. Mr MacDonagh sent me with an urgent message.'

The door opened and Mr Ceannt ushered Finn through but kept him in the hallway.

'Shouldn't you be in lessons?'

'Countess Markievicz came to the Hermitage.'

'The Countess?'

'Yes. Into our assembly. With her gun.'

The sitting room door was flung wide. A tieless Mr Pearse, his collar unfastened and his hair sticking up in tuffs, seized Finn's arm.

'Is everyone alright? Willie?'

'Yes, sir.' Finn felt the grip on his forearm relax. 'She left, but… she said unless you release Mr Connolly she'd send the Citizen Army.'

Mr Pearse slumped against the doorframe, a chuckle on his lips. 'A most courageous and resolute woman.'

'Never mind that, Pat. What'll we do?' Mr Ceannt snapped.

'Tea, Finn?' Mr Pearse headed for the kitchen. 'You'd best show Finn into the front, Eamonn,' he called over his shoulder.

Eamonn Ceannt eyeballed Finn a moment then allowed him into the parlour. Strapped to a chair, his hands bound, a handkerchief gagging him, was Mr Connolly. A purple bruise stained his cheek and an angry welt shimmered at his temple but he lifted his head to Finn and winked. Mr MacDermott was also there, reclining on the flattened sofa, smoking a cigarette.

'You bring news, Finn?' he asked.

Finn repeated the tale. At mention of Madam Markievicz Mr Connolly grunted through his gag. Mr Ceannt growled but

Mr MacDermott merely dragged on his cigarette. Mr Pearse returned with tea and poured five cups.

'Drink, James?'

Mr Connolly nodded.

'Finn, would you help Mr Connolly?'

Finn tussled with the knots, untying a hand and removing the gag.

'Thank you, Finn,' Mr Connolly said, accepting his tea from Mr Pearse. He raised the cup, 'To Countess Markievicz. Good old Constance. You'd be advised to tread carefully, Pat.'

'Aye.' Mr Pearse sat at the table. 'Come, Finn, take a cup. Does Madam Markievicz know where we have James?'

'Not yet, sir.'

'Then we have time.' Mr MacDermott got up.

'Time for what?' Mr Ceannt demanded.

'To hold council.' Mr MacDermott wandered out, teacup in hand. Mr Pearse and Mr Ceannt followed.

'How's yourself, Finn? School?' Mr Connolly asked.

'More exciting than usual,' Finn grinned.

'I suppose she caused a fair stir, dear Constance?'

'Yes, sir. But then she usually does. A few of the younger lads might've thought she'd start shooting.'

'But sure, you knew better, Finn. Constance is bold but wise with it. I half suspected she would pay you a visit but perhaps she thought the direct approach best, hoping not to embroil you in a conflict of loyalties,' Mr Connolly mused.

'Will she really command your men to free you?'

'I doubt that'll prove necessary. She could, of course. She is in charge now I'm incapacitated.'

Mr Connolly sipped his tea. Finn twirled his cup.

'I saw them take you last night, sir. I didn't know what to do.'

'Who would, Finn? Sure, don't fret on it.'

'But why have they, sir?'

'I understand there's a rising planned?'

Finn started to nod but stopped himself.

'I had a mind for something similar myself, calling out the Citizen Army. I believe the IRB want to wait until Easter. I thought next month would suit.'

'Wouldn't it be better to strike together, sir?'

'There's sense in that,' Mr Connolly mused, 'I've only myself to blame; idle chatter has caused alarm where none was intended. I'm sure all will be well.' He drank again. The door reopened. 'We'll see about it now.'

Finn moved aside as Mr MacDermott and Mr Pearse sat at the table. Mr Ceannt remained standing, his back to the door.

'James, wouldn't I love for us to work together, united as we are in the name of a free Ireland,' Mr MacDermott began.

'A free socialist republican Ireland,' Mr Connolly interrupted.

'Indeed,' Mr MacDermott agreed, 'And to that end I propose we co-opt you onto the IRB Supreme Military Council. In return we ask for two assurances: first, that you'll commit your Citizen Army to fight alongside the Irish Volunteers; second, that you'll take no action unless sanctioned by this Council. That means no serving the stew before we've finished seasoning it,' Mr MacDermott chuckled.

'You're agreed?' Mr Connolly glanced at Mr Ceannt.

'We are,' Mr MacDermott replied, 'I've telephoned the school and got assent from Joe and Tom MacDonagh. Unfortunately I can't reach Tom Clarke so I'll have to remand you here until we get his word, which is sure to be in favour.'

'Then I accept.' Mr Connolly held his hand to Mr MacDermott.

Mr MacDermott shook it vigorously. 'Welcome, James, to the Supreme Military Council in charge of planning the Dublin Easter Rising.'

A week later, the new accord between James Connolly and the IRB having put the Rising on firmer ground, the school was lunching when Mary Brigid shouted:

'Look, Mother, police.'

Finn saw, through the high-set windows of the lower ground floor dining room, four black DMP-issue boots.

'Where's Pat?' Miss Margaret asked.

'He's in town, and Willie.' Her mother ladled soup as she spoke.

'What'll we do, Ma?' Mary Brigid asked.

'Open the door, lass.' Mrs Pearse banged down the pot, slopping soup.

Finn got up. 'I'll go, Mrs Pearse.'

'Go raibh maith agat*, Finn.' She swiped a cloth over the soup puddle.

Finn opened the door to two constables, their bell-shaped helmets covering their eyes, their mouths puckered beneath identical bushy moustaches. They looked at Finn, at each other and back at Finn.

'Is Mr Pearse at home?'

'No, sir.'

'Mr Patrick Pearse? He's not at home, is he not?'

'No, sir.'

'What about Mr William Pearse?'

'Nor him, sir.'

'Who is at home?'

'Would you like the names of all the boys, sir?'

'Look, laddie, don't get smart. What's your name?'

'Finn Devoy.' Finn watched him write it down. 'No 'o',' he corrected.

The constable jabbed his pencil against his notepad; the point splintered.

'Away and fetch me a teacher, lad,' he snarled.

'Right away, sir,' Finn said, shutting the door on them.

Mr Slattery was not in the lab. Mr MacDonagh was not in his classroom. Mr Colbert was probably in the gymnasium; Finn doubted he'd get away with making the peelers wait while he ran out there. He climbed the stairs and knocked on the door to the tiny attic room, once his own cell, which Mr Plunkett used when he needed rest.

A faint voice croaked, 'Enter.'

As his eyes adjusted to the dim interior, Finn made out a wooden chair with a jug on it, a tea chest and the narrow bed he'd once slept in. The air was so fuggy with camphor it stung his eyes. Mr Plunkett was lying, fully dressed, his arms folded across his chest, his face waxen.

'Finn, is something the matter?'

---

* thank you

'Sorry, sir, but there are two policemen looking for Mr Pearse and I can't find any of the other masters…'

Mr Plunkett struggled to his feet, steadying himself against the wall. 'Would you pour me some water, Finn?' He pointed to a glass by the bed; Finn filled it from the jug. Mr Plunkett drank, wincing with every swallow, unhooked his master's robe from the door, swung it around his shoulders and followed Finn downstairs.

Seeing the closed front door, he tutted. 'You didn't, Finn? Leave them outside?' Grinning, he shook his head. 'You'll get us hanged afore we've done anything to deserve it.'

Finn lingered long enough to see Mr Plunkett take the rozzers into Mr Pearse's office and hear Mr Slattery's name. The rest of luncheon was spent in wild speculation. Finn couldn't finish his pudding.

Mr Slattery had disappeared.

'I think we should ask him,' Finn whispered.

'Ask who what?' Charlie whispered back.

They were in prep; Mr Colbert patrolled the hall. Finn kept an eye on the master, two rows ahead.

'Pearse, about Slattery.'

'We who?'

'The bomb squad.'

Charlie rolled his eyes. Finn scowled.

'Fine.' Charlie sighed and murmured the plan to Hal.

In covert whispers it was agreed. Finn concentrated on the grandfather clock in the corner. When it chimed the hour he headed straight for Mr Pearse's office.

'Now?' Charlie grabbed his arm.

'Before we lose our nerve.' Finn dragged Charlie on, leaving the others to follow.

Finn halted at the door.

'Hurry up,' Hal chuntered, 'It's nearly suppertime.'

Finn knocked.

Mr Pearse called, 'Just a moment.' The door inched back; the headmaster peered out. 'Finn. Lads,' he smiled, 'Come in but excuse the mess.'

The usually tidy study was a shambles. On either side of the fireplace crates stamped 'D. W. & M., Hamburg' were stacked high. On one of the armchairs a box spewed dozens of armbands marked, 'Irish Volunteers'. Papers covered the desk and the hearth rug. Those on the desk were diagrams and maps while those by the fire were cramped with Mr Pearse's handwriting. There were several balled up wads in the vicinity of the bin.

Mr Pearse kneaded bloodshot eyes and sank into his chair.

'Sorry to disturb you, sir,' Finn said, ' but we've something to ask.'

'Certainly, Finn.'

'It's Mr Slattery, sir; is he in trouble?'

Mr Pearse massaged his brow.

'Perhaps.'

'Is it anything to do with Sean, sir? The accident…'

'Oh…No, Finn. Thank goodness,' he sighed, 'Mr Slattery has been arrested on the charge of possessing explosive material.'

Finn felt air rush into his lungs and heard the gasp echoed around him.

'I hope we may soon secure bail but come what may, Mr Slattery will have to stand trial.'

'What's the punishment, sir, if he's convicted?' Freddie asked.

'I believe it's ten years hard labour.' Mr Pearse rubbed his brow again. Finn wondered how he had any skin left on it.

'Do you think he will be found guilty, sir?' Charlie pressed.

'I fear he may.'

Supper was abandoned, even Hal admitting he couldn't eat in the face of such a calamity. They strolled the grounds, chewing it over. What if Mr Slattery told of what he knew about the Rising for a lesser sentence? Uneasy thoughts plagued Finn, in particular, his American passport. It was a shameful key that would open the cell door should he ever find himself captured.

*

Mr Pearse, determined nothing would interfere with their preparations, supervised the final batch of grenades then arranged for their storage at the safe house. He brought the trap to the Hermitage late one night and the bomb squad loaded the boxes. Then, seeing there was room, Mr Pearse directed the boys into his office to collect the crates flanking the fireside which they added to the cargo.

'What are these, sir?' Charlie asked as he and Finn slid the last into place.

'Guns,' Mr Pearse answered.

'For the Rising, sir?' Hal said.

'It was thought but, no. They are antiquated; far too dangerous. The ammunition explodes on impact and is outlawed in modern warfare. I plan to rid us of them.'

'Sir…' Patrick began but Mr Pearse had already mounted the trap, lashed the whip and ridden off.

'He's mad,' Hal raged, 'Getting rid of guns.'

'He can't go against the rules of engagement. It's not fair.' Freddie replied.

'Bollocks to that,' Hal said, 'Since when's war fair?'

The bomb-lab was cleared from the subbasement. On Shrove Tuesday a printing press was installed, to the distraction of Mr MacDonagh's class, by two tradesmen wearing greasy leather aprons. The history lesson was halted, the strange contraption identified as it passed the window then the order given to complete their compositions on Emmet's 1803 insurrection.

On Ash Wednesday, after a plain supper, Mr Pearse called on the dorm.

'I've a new job for you, boys,' he said.

'Yes, sir,' Finn said, 'Come on, lads.'

They trailed Mr Pearse to the basement where they were permitted to examine the printing press. He showed them how to set the type, block everything, ink the rollers, smear the gooey black liquid across the reversed letters, lay the paper and use the weight to produce pages of hard crisp words. Their first efforts were smudged and scruffy.

'You'll improve,' he enthused.

'What are we printing?' Patrick asked.

'Pamphlets. I plan a series. There are mad ideas circulating.' Mr Pearse gesticulated, indicating the whole world was insane and they alone rational. 'The authorities suppress truth to feed their own murder machine. It is prohibited now to say anything against recruiting Irishmen for war in France. No printer dare undertake such a commission so I propose to undertake it myself.'

Loyal to his word, on Friday evening Mr Pearse returned to the dorm, bid them leave their studies, not a loss as concentrating was impossible, and accompany him to the basement. There he handed them five copies of his first pamphlet: *Honesty*. It stated the duty of Irishmen was to stay at home, in defence of their country, which was not England but Ireland.

'What do you think, lads?'

'It's grand, sir,' Hal said, having barely skimmed the dense pages of Irish. Even had it been in English Finn doubted Hal would have got on any better with the wordy rhetoric.

'Finn?' Mr Pearse probed.

'Yes, sir, but,' Finn summoned his courage, 'It's awfully direct.'

'You're worried the authorities will suspect our up-coming adventure? But we need people to fight with us. I think the risk justified.'

So, working throughout Friday evening and Saturday, copies were printed, as many as they could. On Sunday, as the Red Branch paraded through Dublin, they distributed the pamphlets to the crowds, who delighted in seeing fine Irish boys marching so smartly, their rifles shouldered, their kilts swishing. The Red Branch returned to St Enda's without a single pamphlet, instigating a regular print-and-deliver routine.

Mr Pearse was clever; every few weeks he changed the title, typeface and masthead, leaving the authorities imagining a host of underground presses producing rebellious publications. If the Fianna were stopped it was no difficult thing to say they were carrying out orders the origin of which would prove impossible to discover. They were only stopped once, however, by a DMP outside the GPO. Luckily a scuffle over the road caught his attention and the Red Branch offloaded that week's issue to the crowd who gathered to watch two drunks knocking shite out of each other.

Early one Monday an ambulance arrived at the Hermitage. Finn watched from the top floor washrooms as Mr Plunkett was stretchered into the back.

The following Sunday Mr Colbert outlined the route for the Fianna Éireann parade, as much a fait accompli on the Sabbath now as church. The Rotunda hospital was their final calling point, so they might show support for the hospitalised Mr Plunkett. Over breakfast Finn thought, guiltily, not of the poorly master but of Cathleen; he'd not spoken to her all term.

'What's up with that?' Hal spluttered, pointing a licked-clean spoon to Finn's untouched bowl.

'Have it.'

'Ta.' Hal grabbed the bowl.

Freddie scrutinised Finn. 'Cathleen's at the Roto these days, isn't she?'

'So what?'

'What happened between you two?' Charlie asked.

'Nothing.'

'Huh! One minute we can't keep you apart and the next you won't have her name said,' Charlie grumbled.

Finn pushed away from the table. 'I'm going for a smoke.'

The damp air cooled his rage. He cursed himself for snapping at Charlie. If only he knew whether or not things with Cathleen were as bad as he feared.

'Finn Devoy, how long've you been smoking? And you head boy!'

Mary Brigid jumped out before Finn, hands on hips, mouth puckered. Finn dropped his cigarette and started stammering an excuse.

'Don't give me any blarney; I'm not here to tell you off.'

'Why are you here, then? To have another row with me?'

'Would there be any point if I did?' she asked.

'No.'

'That's what I thought.' Mary Brigid shrugged. 'I know there's no turning Pat from his cause, not that I won't keep trying, with him that is. But I'd rather you and I were friends again.'

'We'll be fine, you know.' Finn squeezed her arm.

'Sure,' she said with a slight smile, 'Let's not talk of it.'

'Alright.'

They had a moment of not talking. Finn fiddled with his lighter.

Mary Brigid said, 'I saw you leave breakfast, is there something on your mind, Cathleen, perhaps?'

'Have you seen her?'

'She was working yesterday, when Pat and I visited Joe. He's not so well.'

Finn fixed her with his eyes.

'Sorry. Aye, Cathleen, she doing well, really taken to nursing.'

'Did she ask about me?'

'What if she did?'

Finn blushed.

'What if she didn't?'

He looked away.

'It's as well she did. My advice is make it up with her. The two of you shouldn't be fighting each other. Not now.'

South of the Liffey the Red Branch met David Reddin's company of Irish Volunteer as they had the last three Sundays. It encouraged Finn seeing David's cheeky wink as they saluted each other and fell in between the columns of folk lining their route to the Roto. Finn made sure most got Mr Pearse's latest pamphlet.

At the hospital both companies halted and, on Finn's and David's synchronised command, presented arms to the nurses, doctors and patients gathered on the soggy grass. Then MacCabe, the quiet third year piper, played the Fianna anthem and the Red Branch sang while those Volunteers who'd never been in the Fianna fidgeted. Then David, a lieutenant now, and Finn ordered their troops at ease as nurses brought tea.

Under the guise of distributing his remaining leaflets, Finn moved among the crowd.

'I thought you'd be here.' Cathleen came at Finn from the side; he scarcely recognise her in her uniform of blue dress and white apron.

'Dia dhuit*, Cathleen,' he said, his voice gruffer than he intended.

'What have you there?' She snatched a pamphlet, scanned the front and tucked it into her pocket. 'And how's yourself?'

'Alright. You?'

'Busy but enjoying it. I've no regrets of leaving St Ita's.'

'How's Mr Plunkett?'

'Not well, eager to leave, though. There's talk of an operation but what good it'll do I've no idea,' she replied.

'That's bad.'

'It is.'

'Well.'

'Aye, well. I best get back.' She made no move to go.

'Are you planning to visit your da soon?'

'I wasn't but I'll come and see you, if you like.'

Her eyes locked on Finn's. He grabbed the chance.

'Tonight?'

'Alright.'

Cathleen had changed into a long dark skirt that clung to her legs, making her walk with dainty steps, and a winter coat with a fur collar that Finn guessed was a hand-me-down. She looked much more the grown up than the last time he'd seen her in that daft party hat. But it wasn't just her clothes; it was the lines on her face.

As he walked through the trees to her, Finn put his hand into his jacket pocket and felt the locket cold against his palm. He'd had the chain repaired in the hope that Cathleen would take it, and him, back. Seeing her waiting for him, he felt the weight of their fights and the pain of her absence.

'Hello, Finn.'

'Dia dhuit*, Cathleen.'

---

* hello

'Too cold for kilts, is it?' she asked with the hint of a smile.

'A bit,' Finn replied, switching to English. He flipped up his collar. 'Are you warm enough?'

'I am.'

Finn took out some cigarettes.

'Would you like one?' He offer the pack to Cathleen.

She helped herself and permitted Finn to light it for her.

'Shall we walk?'

'If you like.'

They wound in and out of the trees, going nowhere and coming back on themselves. Cathleen didn't take his arm and Finn was shy of offering it.

'Is the work hard?'

'Long hours, aye. Matron's strict, works us like a Tartar, but that's because there's so much to be done. I like it, though, helping someone who's been sick for an age get on their feet. Makes me feel I'm good for something.'

'You always were.'

'To you, you mean?' she teased, her smile growing.

'I was thinking of your da, but, yes, to me as well,' Finn replied, returning her grin.

'So what've you been up to?' That momentary glimmer of the old Cathleen slid beneath the surface of the new, grown up one.

'Nothing much, studying.'

'I heard one of your master's got caught carrying bombs.'

'How did you…?'

'It was in the *Evening Herald*.'

'Oh.'

'Are you involved?'

'Am I in gaol?'

'I'm worried for you.' Cathleen stopped walking.

Finn bit his tongue, would have bitten right through it if it was the only way to prevent another row.

'I read that pamphlet,' she said, 'Was it Mr Pearse wrote it?'

'Yes.'

'He certainly has a lot to say for himself.'

'There's a lot to be said.'

'So I'm learning. What about Home Rule? Mr Redmond says…'

'Redmond's more of a fool than we are if he thinks the English will resurrect that after the war.'

'Fool or no, he'll be alive.' Cathleen's eyes flashed darkly in the moonlight.

Finn lost himself; his arguments flew from him. He pulled her to him and kissed her, hard, on the mouth, then more gently. At first she struggled, then yielded, kissing him back. He moved his mouth away from hers, afraid of losing so much he wouldn't find himself again, and settled for holding her to him and burying his face into her neck, breathing in the smell of lavender and camphor. He held on tightly.

'Finn, it's snowing.'

Thick grey clouds had moved over the moon and were showering them with feathery flakes.

'We'll have to go,' she said.

'Not yet.'

'I'm not staying out here,' she replied.

'I know a place. Come on.'

Finn led Cathleen to the west gate. A hot flush of shame swept him as they sneaked past the cottage there; Finn pictured Mr Murphy by his fire.

'Where're we going, Finn?'

Without answering, he ploughed up the road to the safe house. There were no lights showing but to be certain he knocked hard.

'Whose is this?'

'Mr Pearse's.'

'Will he be home at this hour?' she replied, brushing white flakes from her sleeves.

'Let's hope not. This way.'

Finn made a track through the snow around to the rear. Instructing Cathleen to wait, he jumped the wall into the yard and unlatched the gate. Then he opened the back door using the key kept on the ledge above.

'Finn, what are you doing, breaking in?'

'I'm not breaking, am I?' he said, 'Anyway, I'm here all the time, with Mr Pearse. He won't mind.'

He guided Cathleen through the kitchen to the parlour. Making sure the curtains met from rail to hem he lit a lamp and kindled the fire.

'What are these?' Cathleen peered at the latest plans, spread on the table.

'Nothing.' Finn took a sheaf of paper from her hand, placed it facedown and steered her to the sofa. 'Would you like tea?'

'Are you sure we'll not get into bother?'

'Yes.'

He made the tea only to find the milk had soured.

'I hope you don't mind.' He indicated the black liquid.

'That's alright.'

'Wait!' Finn put the tray on the table, opened the china cabinet and fished inside until his fingers touched the glass neck. Silently, he praised Mr Clarke's readiness. When Cathleen saw what he had unearthed her eyes widened in protest. 'Just a drop, to warm us up,' Finn insisted, splashing whiskey into their tea cups. He handed her one, took the other and sat on the sofa beside her. Hot tea and whiskey burnt the inside of his mouth, scorching all the way to his gut.

'Why did you come tonight?'

'You asked me.'

'If it's to try changing my mind please don't; I don't want another row.'

'Nor do I. And I know you well enough, Finn Devoy, to know there's no changing your mind if you're set for a thing.'

Finn sipped his tea. 'Are you away to France soon? Is that why?'

'I'm not going to France.' She spoke quietly. 'I've changed my mind.'

'Why?'

Grimacing, she swallowed a mouthful of tea. 'There's something your Mr Pearse and I agree on. I'll not lend my efforts to the war. Fixing up poor lads to send them to their deaths; I might as well shoot them myself. Anyway, it's not nurses they're needing but undertakers.' She shuddered.

'Cathleen?'

'We had a one at the Roto. Seventeen, he was, blinded by gas and riddled with bullets. We patched him up. They were after sending him back before his stitches were out.' Now she smiled. 'But when they came for him, he'd gone.'

'He died?'

Cathleen giggled. 'He did not. It was the strangest thing, though; one minute he was there and, next, he'd vanished. And wasn't it the damnedest but didn't we find him after they'd left.'

'You hid him from the British Army? Jesus, Cathleen!'

'We did, aye. Not just him. He was the first though.'

'If you're caught helping deserters they'll throw you in gaol.'

'And I'll have you for company if they catch on to what yous are up to. It's still Easter, is it?'

Finn nodded.

'Then I'd best stick around. If it's people to help I'm after there'll be plenty here come Holy Week.'

Finn gaped at her.

'I still think it's bloody crazy but it'll happen whatever I think so I might as well throw in my hat,' she added.

'What's happened, Cathleen?'

'Why should anything have happened?'

'You wouldn't play a different tune so easily if it hadn't.'

'Shows what you know.' Cathleen unpinned her hat. 'Here.'

Finn clenched his hands into balls. 'I'll only take it if you tell me the truth.'

Cathleen twirled the hat. 'My da's been talking, about our family. My great grandfather was thrown off his land. They were left with nothing, had to flog themselves half to death to keep alive. During the blight they scavenged like crows. Granddaddy got himself thrown in gaol during the land wars where he stayed 'til he rotted. It's the same story with my ma's family; it's the same story everywhere. Now Da says it's time to fight. And he's right. I wish he wasn't but he is.' Tears sparkled in her eyes but Cathleen's voice was strong and her lips fired out each word. 'I won't have the two of you going into it without me.'

Finn lifted the felt brim and sat the hat on her head before taking her hands in his.

'You're not going into anything. More tea?'

Finn made a second pot which they drank with a double measure of whiskey. Warmed through they stripped off their coats and hats and said nothing further about the Rising. Cathleen let Finn put his arm around her shoulders, then kiss her. Her fingers stroked his cheek, wandered down his neck and lifted his chain. She reversed the St Colmcille medallion and mutter the inscription on the back in Irish. 'If I die it shall be from an excess love of the Gael.' When she let go the silver was hot against his skin. He kissed her deeper. Suddenly he was lying down with her, their bodies pressed together, his fingers undoing the buttons on her blouse.

'Finn?'

'Hmm?' He kissed her neck.

'You mustn't die.'

'Not even if it's from an excess love of you?'

'Definitely not for that. Promise me.' She held his face in her hands. 'Geall dom*?'

'Geallaim♥.'

Her eyes became glassy. She closed them, nodded and said nothing more. Finn held onto her, kissing, caressing. It was like falling from a great height; equal parts joy and terror. A hot explosion came from deep inside him, cooling slowly and pleasantly. Afterwards they stayed on the sofa, locked together.

When Finn awoke he thought he must have had a nightmare and his mother had got in beside him to soothe him to sleep; her hair was tickling his cheek. Then the woman next to him turned and he saw the fair skin, dappled with freckles, and last night was returned to him in a warm rush.

A grey dawn crept into the room. Trying not to disturb Cathleen, Finn got up, straightened his clothes and stirred the

---

* promise me

♥ I promise you

fire but there was only ash in the grate. He settled for a fresh pot of warming tea.

When he brought it Cathleen was pinning her hair at the tiny looking-glass by the door.

'Tea.'

'Thank you.'

'No whiskey this time, eh?'

'Better not.' She sat at the table to drink it.

Finn retrieved his jacket, dug into the pocket and withdrew the necklace. With the locket trapped in his fist, he held his hand to Cathleen. She raised an eyebrow but put her palm out.

Finn dropped the locket into her hand. 'I'm sorry it's not a ring. Maybe when this is over?'

'Maybe.' Cathleen prised it opened and gazed at their intertwined initials. 'Have you a pair of scissors?'

'Scissors?'

'I want a lock of your hair.'

'Oh.'

Scissors found and hair snipped, Cathleen curled the blonde ringlet in the locket, snapped it shut and fastened it around her throat.

'What'll you tell them at the hospital, about last night?'

'I'll say I was at my da's.'

'Won't they check?'

'Probably not.' She smiled. 'What about you?'

'The lads'll have covered up for me.'

They left the way they entered, Finn leap-frogging the wall after putting the gate on the latch. Hand in hand they strolled towards school.

'Would you like me to see you back to the Roto?'

'Because that wouldn't set tongues wagging, would it?' Cathleen teased.

They drew to a standstill out of sight of the gate cottage. Finn encircled her waist with his arms.

'I meant what I said last night, Finn. You're not to die.'

'And I meant it too, about you not getting involved.'

'I won't if you won't.'

Finn knew the promised he'd made her was an impossible one. 'I've got to do this, Cathleen. Your father's right; there's no stopping it.'

'Even now?'

'Especially now.'

She wriggled from his embrace. 'Maybes we shouldn't see each other, until it's over, at least.'

'Cathleen?'

She stretched up, brushed his cheek with a kiss and turned away. Finn grabbed her back.

'Tá mé i ngrá leat*.'

Her smile was sad, sorry. 'I love you too but now's not the time for that. Will you do me one favour, though? Come to me if you need help?'

In answer he kissed her furiously.

By the end of that week Mr Plunkett was back at the Hermitage. Sweating, coughing and making light of his sufferings, he taught only the examination classes. Finn thought on what Cathleen had said about his prognosis. Seeing the master reinforced Finn's belief: the Rising was keeping him alive.

Routine fogged them. The basement pamphleteering continued. Fianna parades continued, always accompanied by David Reddin's Irish Volunteers. Lessons continued, although they had become a perfunctory affair; Finn and his friends would have preferred target practice to trigonometry. Meetings at the safe house continued; Finn went frequently. In their free time the lads lobbed a sliotar around. They read when sleep refused to come, dozing off during prep and getting an ear-bashing from Mr Colbert, despite the master knowing the cause of their sleepless nights. Occasionally Finn would creep into the art studio. He did little more than doodle, smearing displeasing lines with his finger as his mind roamed.

---

* I love you

One such evening in early March Finn was about to scrap his efforts when Willie Pearse, who was moulding a clump of clay into the elegant form of Íosagán, stopped him.

'I thought you, like me, found art a solace, Finn.'

'When I can do it right,' Finn grumbled.

'May I?' Willie took the unfinished sketch. "Tis Cathleen.'

'Don't know how you can tell, it's such a poor likeness.'

'Hmm, one or two wee tweaks.' Willie made the changes with Finn's own pencil. 'Is that more to your liking?'

It was much improved. 'Thanks, sir.'

'When I'm working from memory I put pad and pencil by my bedside, think of what it is I'm after drawing as I fall asleep and wake with the image clear in my head. I dash it off and finish later.'

'I'll try it.'

Willie laid his hand over Finn's. 'You've not to let fear of a thing keep you from accomplishing those goals that matter to you.'

Finn didn't think he was talking about art anymore.

They were heading to the safe house, Finn, Mr MacDonagh and Mr Plunkett. The March wind gusted and Finn feared it would blow the fragile Mr Plunkett skyward; he was relieved when they arrived and were admitted by Mr Ceannt.

'Where's Pat?' Mr Ceannt asked as they removed their hats.

'He's taking a telephone call, said to start without him,' Mr MacDonagh replied.

They entered the parlour. Although Finn had been there numerous times since his night with Cathleen he still blushed at sight of the sofa. Tonight he hoped the heat from the fire would explain the colour on his cheeks.

Seated around the table were the other members of the council: Mr Clarke, Mr MacDermott and Mr Connolly. They had been joined by two others. Countess Markievicz, wearing her Citizen Army uniform, sat, ramrod-straight, back to the hearth, revolver holstered at her waist. Mr Connolly was to her left. On her right sat Mr Colbert. The three were studying a large-scale map similar to ones Finn had seen there before. He recognised the Liffey's serpentine form winding through

Dublin. New to this map were arrows drawn in red and green, emanating from the suburbs and converging on Xs marked in Dublin's centre. Finn saw one indicating the GPO, another the Shelbourne and a third Dublin Castle.

'So we're agreed on this route?' Mr Connolly asked.

'We are,' Mr Colbert confirmed.

'How'll we cordon off the centre?' the Countess enquired.

Mr MacDermott spoke. 'The Volunteers will take care of that and I've assurances that there'll be no interference from the DMP.'

'Then it's settled.' The Countess took a cigarette holder, tipped it with a cigarette and accepted a light from Mr Connolly. 'Splendid to have you with us, young man,' she said, nodding to a curious and confused Finn who hugged the doorframe.

'Perhaps you'd like a look,' Mr Connolly suggested, spinning the map round.

In the top corner, previously hidden by Mr Connolly's hefty hand, was written, 'St Patrick's Day Display'. Finn frowned.

'You're a might befuddled. Have you minded something amiss?' Mr Connolly probed.

'I'm just not sure what this is, sir.'

'These, Finn,' Mr MacDermott tapped the paper, 'are plans for our St Pat's day celebration, marking the occasion with a gallant display, the efforts of the Volunteers, Citizen Army and Fianna Éireann. We're going to take the city, in jest, of course. Dubliners will see how well their young men,' the Countess coughed; Mr MacDermott smiled, 'and women acquit themselves when wearing the uniform of free Irelanders.'

Mr Colbert explained; companies of Volunteers, Fianna and the Citizen Army would march on the city from every bearing, to meet at the GPO where, taking the salute, would be Professor MacNeill for the Volunteers, Mr Connolly for the Citizen Army and a gentleman Finn hadn't heard of, Mr Bulmer Hobson, co-founder of the Fianna movement, when it first began in the north.

Finn said he was sure the Red Branch would be excited to learn of the display.

'Who's for tea?' Mr MacDermott suggested.

Tom Clarke spoke. 'My turn. Finn, would you lend a hand?'

Mr Clarke boiled the kettle. Finn measured spoons of tea and reached out cups and saucers.

'Don't be blinded by that blether,' Mr Clarke said, 'A smart laddie like you can see what's what here.'

Finn didn't hide his grin. 'If it was a play I'd think this was the dress rehearsal.'

'You'd be right.'

'How much do the Countess and Mr Colbert know, about the Rising?'

Mr Clarke's eyes, sparkling behind his spectacles, met Finn's. 'Enough. They'll ask no hard questions, though.' He placed the full-to-the-brim teapot on the tray.

While they'd been in the kitchen Mr Pearse had arrived in the front room still wearing his hat and coat, his face flushed; he was pouring forth a torrent of greetings, apologies and assertions. Seeing Finn he marshalled his gibberings.

'Finn, excellent news.'

'Will you not sit, Pat?'

Mr Pearse waved away the chair. 'Mr Slattery has been acquitted.' The words set off a barrage of exclamations.

'Bejesus, how'd the old dog manage that?'

'Sweet Mary, 'tis a blessing.'

'I was certain he'd be doing time.'

'Wasn't the evidence against him conclusive?'

''Twas downright damning.'

'On what grounds?'

'A favourable jury.'

It was Mr Pearse who said this last.

'You think, Pat?'

'The outcome was a forethought, caught as he was, but the jury refused to convict, I gather to the outrage of some.'

'Fucking Orangemen!' Mr Clarke spat into the fire; it sizzled.

Mr Pearse clicked his tongue.

'If you please, gentlemen and lady,' Mr MacDermott tipped his head to the Countess, 'a toast to the freeing of a patriot and the awakening of our countrymen to the shame of being ruled by London or Belfast.'

As Mr MacDermott spoke Mr Clarke and Mr Ceannt passed round measures of whiskey, even pressing one into Mr Pearse's hand.

Mr MacDermott raised his glass. 'To Peter Slattery, a free man. And to Ireland, soon to be a free country. Sláinte*!'

On St Patrick's day thick crowds clotted behind rope barriers. Small children clambered on fathers' shoulders or weaved through grown up legs. Women threw flowers, laying a multi-colour carpet for the marching battalions. Men waved homemade flags, emblazoned with harps and shamrocks. Even Mother Nature came out dressed in her richest gold and finest blue.

Finn led his company through the throngs. Freddie, their standard-bearer, walked between him and the ranks, the drill hall flag attached to a pole resting against his shoulder. At the rear Donald MacCabe piped and young Donovan carried a drum on which he'd been taught to sound a steady beat. In sharp formation they paraded to Trinity College where they were met by David Reddin's Volunteers. With an unsoldierly grin he saluted Finn; Finn returned. The Volunteers, most wearing their Sabbath suits adorned with IV armbands, fell in alongside the uniformed Red Branch, and on they marched.

As they came into the city Finn and David found themselves in a scrum of companies waiting to cross O'Connell Bridge and enter Sackville Street. Finn ordered his troop at ease while they waited their turn. Cheers and whistles fanfared them up to Nelson's Pillar where a platform had been erected for the dignitaries. Professor MacNeill, regaled in his Volunteer chief-of-staff uniform, was his usual stern self. Mr Connolly, in the livery of the Citizen Army, saluted in the proper fashion but winked when he spotted Finn. The third man, dressed in a long loose coat and broad-brimmed hat that

---

* cheers

were vaguely military, Finn guessed to be Mr Hobson. He waved to the passing platoons.

It had been decided to stage mock attacks on strategic points so, the salute given, Finn led his lads to Liberty Hall, home of the Citizen Army and their target. The two storey building occupied a whole block. Strung up, stretching the length of the red brick front, was a banner declaring, 'We serve neither King nor Kaiser but Ireland!' Finn ordered his lads into position and, command by command, they completed the drill; aim, fire, reload, aim, fire. During the manoeuvres Finn studied his troop. He hoped they would be as sure with their guns when it was real.

Countess Markievicz came out; Finn saluted.

'You boys are a fine example of Ireland's youth,' she proclaimed, returning the salute. Then she sprang down the steps to Finn. 'Keep your mettle up, young man,' she said with a wink.

'So's that what it'll be like?' Charlie asked. 'The Rising?'

They'd enjoyed a hearty meal then snuck into the woods for a smoke.

'Finn?' Hal squinted at him through one eye.

Saliva pooled in his mouth as four faces fixed on him. Finn swallowed. 'I guess.'

'But?' Charlie asked.

Finn remembered the day they'd gathered round his bed staring at the revolver his father had given him. 'But it'll be for real,' he said, the words jarring more than he'd intended, 'If you get shot you won't be laughing about it afterwards.' He dragged on his cigarette and flicked the end away. 'If some bugger's likely to shoot you, you've got to get him first.'

'That'll be hard,' Patrick said, picking a loose thread on his sleeve.

'Get away. You just do like in target practise: aim straight and pull the bloody trigger,' Hal sneered.

Patrick snapped the stray thread. 'And kill someone.'

'What's that gonna be like?' Charlie muttered.

Finn caught Freddie staring at him. 'Fucking horrible,' he replied.

Hal snorted. 'Nah, not when it's the enemy.'

'Even then,' Finn said.

Charlie plucked at some grass. 'What makes you the expert?'

Finn looked to Freddie again, who nodded his head a fraction. He took a breath. 'You remember Richard MacDonnall?'

'That git,' Hal snarled.

'It was me,' Finn said, 'I...killed him.'

'What?'

'You're fecking joking?'

'Really, Finn?'

Confronted by the stares of his friends Finn shuddered. How could he tell them of all the fears he'd felt then, fears that had made him kill Richard as he strode from the field of battle? Now their commanding officer, readying to lead them into a much more dangerous fight Finn knew he couldn't.

'We were scrapping. He had me beat, was gonna kill me if I didn't stand up to him. Next thing he was down: dead.' That wasn't the truth of it but he couldn't bring himself, or them, any closer to it.

Freddie spoke up. 'We understand. You had to, Finn. You'd no choice. He started it.'

Finn reached for another cigarette. 'I'm telling you so's you'll understand, even when there's no choice, how hard it is, afterward. You've to live with it the rest of your life. Don't be part of this if you can't go through with it.' He leaned against his tree. 'It's war for Christ's sake.'

'Aye, it is,' Hal said, 'But I'm with you, so I am.'

'And me,' Freddie said, 'Hindsight's blind.' He took off his glasses and polished them on his shirt.

'It's horrible that happened to you, Finn,' Patrick said, 'but it doesn't change things now.'

Hal said, 'Course not. MacDonnall had it coming to him.'

Had he? Finn wondered.

'And so do the British,' Hal added.

Finn nodded. Of that he was certain.

Charlie stayed quiet. Finn stared at his cigarette until he felt the heat of its burning tip in his eyes. On the edge of his vision he saw Charlie getting to his feet. Blood pumped through Finn's ears. A hand came into view. Finn looked up.

'Come on.' Charlie wiggled his fingers.

Finn took hold and found himself yanked into a bear hug.

'Christ, Finn, if we'd known, we wouldn't've let you go through that on your own.'

'Thanks, Charlie.' Finn wriggled free and swept the four faces. 'Now, are you sure about this? It's not just the killing.'

'We know,' Freddie murmured.

Charlie grinned at Finn. 'What's that line in the *Táin*, of Cúchulainn's? About living a day and dying a hero? Come on, Finn, you're our expert on the great macaomh*.'

Finn quoted it:

'I care not though I live but one day and one night if only my name and deeds live after me.'

'Yeah,' Charlie repeated, ' 'I care not though I live but one day and one night if only my name and deeds live after me.' Brilliant.'

Freddie got up and stood with Finn.

'I care not though I live but one day and one night if only my name and deeds live after me.'

Patrick did the same. Hal watched lazily then followed him up.

'Ah, shite,' he said, 'sure, it's better to go out with a bang.'

The Easter vacation was two hours old when Finn set his lads to work. In a downstair classroom they pushed aside desks, stacked stools and dragged in half a dozen easy chairs, transforming the space into a common room for the Fianna boys who were staying for the holidays: for the Rising. At the end-of-term Red Branch meeting Mr Colbert had informed the brigade there was to be a mobilisation during the holiday and invited boys in the upper forms to stay with a view to taking part once they knew the details. This had caused an outcry among the younger lads but it was the decree of Mr Pearse that only senior boys stay. So, grumbling and cursing,

---

* used here to refer specifically to Cúchulainn

the others had gone home, leaving a dozen boys for whom the common room was being readied.

Finn manhandled a hefty wingback into the centre of the room and flopped into it.

'You look knackered,' Hal scoffed.

'Aye, you do,' Patrick added.

'Never mind that.' Finn called Charlie and Freddie over. 'I've thought of something else we should do.'

'What?' Freddie asked.

'Swear you lot into the IRB. If you want to that is.'

Their answer was a unanimous 'yes'.

Finn knocked on Mr Pearse's office door and entered when the familiar voice called out.

'Finn, how strange, I was about to come for you. There's something I've been writing that I'd like your view on.'

Finn nodded. 'But first, sir, I've a favour to ask.'

'Aye?'

'I've four more for the IRB, if you'll have them.'

Mr Pearse leaned back in his chair and kneaded his brow, trying to rub out the lines that creased his forehead.

'Your friends from the Fianna?'

'Yes, sir.'

'You're sure this is what they want?'

'Yes, sir.'

'Very well. Bring them to the safe house tonight.'

Mr Pearse's eyes met Finn's. There were dark shadows under them but the light in them was brighter than Finn had ever seen it.

'We're so close, Finn,' he said. His hands clenched at empty air.

'I know, sir.'

'You have no doubts about joining us?'

'None, sir.'

'The dangers may be greater than we anticipate. I wouldn't want you being unclear on that.'

'I'm not, sir.'

'I expect nothing, Finn, from you, or any member of the Fianna Éireann or St Enda's, head boy or no.'

'Sir, I...'

Mr Pearse interrupted. 'For one reason only, do I permit those of you who wish to, to join us. The freedom we will win for Ireland belongs to you lads. This thing I do that others shake their heads at, 'tis for you I do it and I feel it fair you be granted a part in your own destiny.'

Mr Pearse pushed across a parchment. A crisp new phrase emblazoned the top: Poblacht Na H Éireann - the Republic of Ireland.

'If everyone accepts this document as doing justice to our endeavours I may impose upon you to print me some copies.'

'Yes, sir.' Finn began reading:

'The Provisional Government of the Irish Republic to the People of Ireland. Irishmen and Irishwomen: In the name of God and the dead generations from which she receives her old tradition of nationhood, Ireland, through us, summons her children to her flag and strikes for her freedom…'

That night Charlie, Freddie, Hal and Patrick were sworn into the IRB by Mr MacDermott. Charlie jingled the loose change in his pocket. Freddie cleaned his spectacles three times. Hal filled the room, bumping around it. Patrick kept his eyes on the floor. Finn, seeing how strange it was for them, realised how at home he felt there.

'Fáilte*, lads,' Mr MacDermott said as each council member shook hands with the newest recruits. 'It's grand to have you and a pity that I must ask you to leave but we've a few matters to discuss that are,' he cleared his throat and glanced at Finn, 'classified.'

Finn made for the door, his new comrades following.

'Actually, Finn, if you could stay,' Mr Plunkett said from the sofa where he reclined under a blanket.

Finn showed his pals to the door.

'What's up with Plunkett?' Charlie hissed.

'Guess I'm gonna find out.' Finn gave them the IRB handshake and they left.

Back in the parlour Mr Plunkett had struggled upright. His face was blanched with pain and his efforts threw him into a

---

* welcome

coughing fit. While he recovered, Mr Pearse passed around copies of the proclamation he'd shown Finn.

'It's grand, Pat,' Mr Clarke said.

'Who's to sign it?' Mr Ceannt indicated the bottom where it read, 'signed on behalf of the Provisional Government,' and a space waited.

'You, Pat,' Mr Clarke offered, 'They're your words.'

'But inspired by all of you,' Mr Pearse replied.

'We should each sign it,' Mr Connolly said, 'We are jointly the Military Council and, hence, the Provisional Government. We share the honour and the responsibility.'

'Agreed,' Mr MacDermott said, 'But there's another consideration.' He drew an empty teacup towards him and twisted it round. Then he raised his eyes and there was such fire in them Finn felt the heat on his face. 'Let no man put his name to this that is not prepared to die for Ireland.'

'We're all prepared for that,' Mr Clarke snapped, 'Else we'd not be readying ourselves for war.'

'To die fighting, sure. But are you prepared to swing by the neck?' Mr MacDermott demanded, 'For if we fail those who put their names to their deeds will pay the price.'

'Aye, Sean, we will,' Mr Clarke said, 'And I've already made a decent down payment, fifteen years worth.'

''Tis true, Tom,' Mr MacDonagh said. He rose from his seat, 'And for that reason the honour of being the first signatory should be yours.'

'Nay, lad,' Mr Clarke said, 'I'm not wanting honours.'

'If you don't sign first I'll not sign at all,' Mr MacDonagh insisted, 'It's your courage, enthusiasm and example that's led us young scrats to where we are today.' He laid the parchment before Mr Clarke.

Mr Clarke sighed. 'You praise me too highly, Thomas; I'll not rebuff you.' He took the proffered pen and glanced at Mr MacDermott. 'We're together on this, Sean,' he said. He signed his name and pushed the paper to Mr MacDermott who, with a violent swirl, scrawled his name next, using, Finn noted, the Irish spelling: Mac Diarmada.

Finn watched as the seven signed, pledging their lives. Mr Plunkett was the last, dragging himself from the sofa.

'And that'll have to do me for a few days,' he said as he dropped into a chair. Seeing Finn he continued, 'Aye, Finn, I'm to have a little surgery. Hopefully it'll get me through to Easter.'

'Are you sure you'll be well enough to join us?' Mr Pearse asked.

'Even if I'm not, bejesus, I'll be there,' Mr Plunkett declared, 'And if I die on the operating table I demand you take my corpse to GPO and make the Rising my wake!' He laughed. No one joined him. He puffed his cheeks and slapped the table. 'Don't worry. Finn,' he reached out his hand and Finn found it cold and clammy against his, 'remember my advice: if you're needing to hide, do it in plain sight. No one ever looks there.'

Spy Wednesday 19 April

At breakfast a dozen boys sat dotted around the dining room. What a change from Finn's first weeks at school when the chatter and clatter of boys eating and talking loaded the air. Finn was about to sit at his usual place when he spotted Donald MacCabe, the quiet piper, alone and tiny on a vast table. Diverting his course, Finn sat next to him.

'What're you doing here, Donald?'

Donald jumped, spilling his tea. 'I'm staying.'

'But I thought you were…'

'I'm in the upper fifth,' Donald replied, scowling at Finn.

'That's right,' Finn said, remembering, 'You got moved up last year.'

Donald nodded.

'So you shouldn't be here,' Finn said in a lower voice.

Donald blinked twice. 'Are you going to tell?'

'Donald, if Mr Colbert or Mr Pearse realise…'

'They won't unless you tell.'

'What about your folks? Won't they wonder where you are?'

Donald shook his head. 'There's only my auntie. Actually she's my great auntie. She's half batty, won't even miss me.'

Finn stirred his porridge. 'But…'

'My folks are dead; my wee sister too.'

'Oh. Sorry,' Finn mumbled. He spooned up some porridge, felt a gagging in his throat and slopped it back into the bowl.

'That's why I'm staying.'

Finn pushed his porridge away and met Donald's gaze.

Donald spoke steadily, dry-eyed and calm. 'My da came out in '13, for Mr Larkin. Lost his job because of it, thought they'd have to take me out of school and maybes lose the house. Then the war started and he joined up for the money. He was shot before that first Christmas. Then Bella took a fever and died; my ma's heart broke; she cried herself to death.' Donald's jaw flexed, 'It's for them I'm staying.' He glared at Finn. 'You've got to let me stay.'

'Alright, Donald. Hell,' he grinned, 'I'd be an eejit to send anyone home when we've so few.' He offered Donald his hand; the soft skin was broken by calluses from the pipes.

'Thanks.' Donald squeezed hard on Finn's hand.

Mr Colbert's boots rapped the flagstone floor.

'Assemble in fifteen minutes,' he barked and stamped out.

Wind rattled the drill hall windows and blew through chinks in the masonry. Finn was glad they weren't in their kilts.

Mr Colbert entered, marched over and saluted them. 'At ease, men. I'll be brief. You've been members of the Fianna Éireann for several years. You are also old enough to act as your consciences determine. I remind you that, upon entering the Fianna, you swore to work for Ireland's independence. The moment for you to do so has come. If there are any who would shy from that duty I ask you to turn in your badge and leave.'

No one moved.

'Grand.' Mr Colbert mopped his brow; his hand shook. 'To business, so. On Easter Sunday there is to be an armed Rising in Dublin and across Ireland. We will march from the school at ten o'clock to positions in the city centre. Full service equipment is to be worn, eight hours rations carried, full arms and ammunition. Rifle inspection and the issue of live ammunition on Saturday at 0900 hours. Captain Devoy, detail two members to take account of how many rounds we have.'

'Yes, sir.'

'You are to tell no one of this. You may write a letter to your parents which can be deposited with Mrs Pearse and, if necessary, sent home on your behalf.' Mr Colbert let his eyes rest on each of them, checking they understood the implication of his order. 'During exercises each of you has proved yourself an excellent soldier. I have no doubts that each of you will prove yourselves excellent soldiers in battle also. By God's grace and our own hands Ireland will be free.'

It was early afternoon before Finn felt the Red Branch had done what they could and sent the lads to write their letters. Having no desire to pen a mawkish note to his father and knowing he couldn't send his mother such he called on Willie Pearse.

The studio door was open; Finn saw Willie bending over his desk, pen in hand. Finn cleared his throat. Willie raised his head and beckoned to him.

'Have a look, Finn. It's not my usual line but I think it's a tolerable attempt.'

On the desk were two pieces of paper, both headed with the Dublin Castle crest. One was a short memorandum with a signature proclaiming 'General Friend'. The other was a longer typed text with the same signature. At Willie's elbow was a piece of tracing paper onto which were scrawled two dozen copies of the signature.

'Is it a good likeness?' Willie asked.

Finn compared the real and forged signatures closely.

'Yes, sir.'

'Grand!'

'What is it, though?'

'A ruse.'

Finn skimmed the letter to which Willie Pearse had added the counterfeit moniker. In military jargon it outlined a plan to swoop on key members of the Irish National movement, including those in the Gaelic League and Sinn Fein. The date for this strike was the first of May.

'I don't understand, sir.'

'Sure, it's so clever, Finn, I nearly didn't myself. Pat and Sean concocted it,' Willie explained, 'I've the humble task of making it appear genuine.'

'So it's not true, about the arrests?'

'Not a bit.'

'But, sir, won't this General Friend tell everyone it's fake?'

'He may, but he won't be believed, at least, not by the person at whom this is aimed,' Willie grinned, 'I think you've made the acquaintance of Professor MacNeill.'

Willie explained that when Professor MacNeill learnt of these plans, supposedly by the British at Dublin Castle, to arrest Nationalists, he would be forced to acknowledge that Home Rule, and the Irish Volunteers, were under threat. That being accepted the professor would agree to the Rising he didn't yet know about, a vital point because he was chief-of-staff of the Volunteers and his command required to send the troops into battle. Once in action they would be controlled by the IRB but to ensure the smoothest possible start to the Rising MacNeill's assistance was crucial.

'I need someone to deliver this to the *Dublin Evening Mail*,' Willie said, placing the letter into an envelope.

'I'll take it myself.'

'If it's not a trouble to you?'

'No trouble to me, sir,' Finn said.

Finn handed the forged Castle letter to a junior journalist, claiming he'd been given the mysterious envelope by a stranger, along with a shilling for delivering it. The journalist scoured the letter and charged inside the newspaper headquarters, leaving Finn picturing the letter falling into and out of various interested hands until it landed on Professor MacNeill's desk.

Around midnight, with the letter flapping through his dreams, Finn got up. He would nip out for a cigarette and walk about until he was tired. He was on the last stair when the telephone in Mr Pearse's office rang. Finn slunk back up as Willie Pearse dashed down the hall. He was gone barely a minute, racing to the Pearse family room; Finn heard him shouting.

'I'm away after Pat, Mother. That was Eoin MacNeill.'

Willie reappeared, coat half on and cap in hand. He caught sight of Finn on the stairs and winked.

Holy Thursday 20 April

There was hardly room for a flee circus in the safe house's pokey parlour. The IRB Military Council, minus Mr Plunkett, had gathered along with Countess Markievicz, Mr Colbert and another dozen men. Finn caught a few names; Michael Collins, Sean Heuston, Eamon de Valera, Michael Mallin and Ned Daly, Mrs Clarke's younger brother whose quiet composure, like his sister's, impressed Finn more than the bluster of the others. Finn might have taken in more if he'd had breakfast but Mr Pearse had hurried him out before daybreak; the dawn meeting had been scheduled so those commanding troops during the Rising could gather unobserved.

As he gazed around the room, Finn met curious eyes. He shifted his weight to his other foot and abandoned attempts to attach names to faces; mustering his attention, he reminded himself he was a commander too, of sorts, with a right to be there.

'The Aud has sailed, and Casement too, on the U19. Both should arrive in Tralee Bay any day.'

'Have we arranged to land the arms on board the Aud?

'The Kerry lads have it in hand.'

'What does Germany send us?'

'Twenty thousand rifles, a million rounds of ammunition, ten machine guns.'

'Troops?'

'Casement sails with the Irish soldiers captured on the Western Front who have allied themselves with our cause. I don't have numbers.'

'How's Joe?'

'Hopes to be home tomorrow.'

'And he'll join us?'

'His heart is set on it.'

'The schedule for Sunday?'

'We converge on the city separately,' Mr Connolly said, 'As on the seventeenth.'

'To mark the Rising's commencement?'

'We take the GPO at noon, raise the flag and, Pat, will it please you to read the proclamation?'

Mr Pearse nodded at Mr MacDermott's request.

'There's also a wee display planned at Phoenix Park Magazine Fort,' Mr Clarke chuckled.

'We strike in unison?'

'Aye. You know your positions. Move in directly the Rising commences, fortify and be ready to defend.'

'Any questions?'

Mr Pearse interrupted the silence. 'I'd remind you to take the utmost care to protect the lives and property of our citizens.'

'An important point, Pat. There will be casualties, that's unavoidable, but 'tis our duty to keep them to a minimum,' Mr MacDermott added.

'I think we know what we're to do,' Mr Pearse concluded, 'So I suggest we are about our business, gentlemen. The business of freeing Ireland. Éire go bráth*!'

It was past lights-out but lights-out was for boys; they were men now: soldiers, so Finn, Hal, Charlie, Freddie and Patrick were lazing in the Red Branch HQ/St Enda's common room. Freddie was flicking through a book. The others were playing cards. Finn had a terrible hand and was about to jack in for the night.

The front bell clanged. Freddie dropped his book. The bell clanged again. Finn chucked his cards down. It was late for a visitor. The bell clanged a third time.

'Who's that?' Patrick asked.

Finn got up. 'Let's see.'

The five of them paused in the darkness of the hallway, staring at the door. The bell jangled incessantly and there was no sign of anyone coming to answer it.

'Shite to it.' Hal yanked the door open.

A hatless Professor MacNeill, clothes rumpled, face red, hand clutching the bell-pull, saw Hal and stopped mid-pull.

'Who are you?' he demanded.

---

* Ireland forever

'Me?' Hal snorted, not knowing Professor MacNeill from a wandering tinker, 'You're knocking at my door in the middle of the night so I reckon you should be telling me who you are.'

Charlie sniggered but Finn suspected Professor MacNeill's arrival wouldn't be funny for long.

The professor straightened his hat, tightened his tie and buttoned his jacket. Eyes blazing on Hal, he ran out of holes with a button carried over. Dismissing the stray fastener, he spluttered forth a torrent of Irish.

'I am Professor MacNeill, president of the Gaelic League and chief-of-staff for the Irish Volunteers. I demand you take me to Mr Pearse immediately.'

Hal was unimpressed and immovable. 'Mr Pearse isn't here.'

'Not here!' MacNeill exploded into English, no doubt to Hal's relief, Finn mused. 'You're lying, boy. I insist on seeing him.'

'If he was here, sure, he'd have answered the door himself,' Hal barked.

'This is an outrage. If he thinks he can deceive me then disappear like a phantom he's mistaken. Tell me where he is.'

'How would I know?' Hal drawled.

MacNeill's bottom lip twitched. A vein on his forehead pulsated. Fearing spontaneous combustion, Finn stepped forward.

'Professor MacNeill, sir.' He shoved Hal aside. 'I'll give Mr Pearse a message, if you like.'

'A message?!' MacNeill spat as though Finn had suggested he dance a jig naked on the lawn. 'I don't want to leave a blasted message. You know where he is, Devoy, take me to him.'

Finn bristled at MacNeill's use of his surname.

'I can't, sir.'

'Don't be insolent, Devoy. I find out, in the middle of the night, that orders have been issued to every Volunteer brigade to mobilise for a rising on Easter Sunday. Orders given on the say-so of Patrick fucking Pearse, who has no authority whatever to command my Volunteers. This...' MacNeill waved a crumpled sheet of paper; Finn made out the Dublin Castle crest and Willie Pearse's carefully forged signature. '…is a blatant treachery. That he thinks he can dupe me, raise an army and march on Dublin is ludicrous. He'll get everyone killed, including himself, which would be no loss. But I'll not have him leading my men to their deaths. There'll be no loss of life for which I'm responsible. The calling out of a half-armed force is insanity. If you want a message for your Mr Pearse, Devoy, you can tell him I'll be doing everything in my power to prevent this Rising, up to, and possibly including, ringing Dublin Castle myself!' MacNeill threw the letter at Finn, pivoted on his heel, flew down the steps and vanished into the blackness.

Freddie picked up the paper and began to read.

'Jesus Christ,' Hal yelped, 'if he goes charging off to the Castle it'll ruin everything.'

'He wouldn't, surely?' Charlie said.

'What's this?' Freddie rustled the letter.

Finn explained.

'And MacNeill's realised it was a sham. No wonder he's pissed off.'

'What now?' Patrick asked.

'I'll run to the safe house. Hopefully there'll be somebody I can report too,' Finn said, 'They'll have to deal with it.'

Good Friday 21 April

Finn lay on his bed, watching the black sky morph through indigo and navy to royal then pale blue as the dawn sun painted from an indecisive pallet. He had found Mr Pearse and repeated MacNeill's tirade. The Council agreed they'd have to prevent MacNeill spoiling the Rising and had made plans to call on him early. Mr MacDermott had mooted holding him captive until Sunday if he refused to let the orders stand. Finn balled his hands into fists. He should have stopped MacNeill last night. He dressed and searched out the revolver that had lurked in his trunk all term. Tucking it into his belt, he went to find Mr Pearse.

In the kitchen Mary Brigid was loading a tray with breakfast things, including the large, plain Pearse brothers' teacups, both chipped on their red-ringed rims.

'Finn, you're up early.'

'Has Mr Pearse left?'

'No, I'm making him tea before he dashes off. He won't say where to.' Mary Brigid narrowed her eyes.

'Oh.'

'Here, you might as well take this.' She held the tray to Finn.

Finn backed into the family room, tray heavy in his arms. Mr Pearse was tying his tie at the mirror above the sideboard. Seeing Finn, he started but mustered a smile.

'Mary Brigid's making use of you.' He finished with the tie, took the tray and filled the two huge teacups, one of which, to his surprise, Finn was sipping from a moment later. 'Is there something aside from you bringing me this excellent tea?'

'Yes, sir. Professor MacNeill.'

Mr Pearse smiled over his king-sized cup. 'What else could you do but that which you did?'

'My father, sir.'

Mr Pearse raised his eyebrows. 'What have you in mind?'

'Perhaps we should telephone him. If he could explain about the Clan's support I don't think Professor MacNeill'd go against that.'

Mr Pearse pondered the suggestion. 'A grand idea, Finn. Come.'

They left their tea cooling and went to Mr Pearse's office. He put the call through and, while they waited to be connected, cautioned Finn.

'It's not impossible that people other than ourselves are on the line. You best be the one to speak to your father, there can be nothing suspicious in that, but guard what you say. Ah, here we go.' He handed Finn the receiver.

His father's voice crackled down the line. 'Hello?'

'Hello, Father.'

'Finn? By Christ, what's going on?'

Finn wasn't sure if his father was annoyed or concerned.

'I'm sorry to disturb you but I've a problem.' He paused, casting around for a way of surreptitiously explaining; on the bookcase sat a copy of the photograph of himself carried by his victorious hurling team.

'Finn?'

'There's a fellow here, Father, who's on the hurling team but only plays occasionally. He's found out we've a big match this Sunday and we need him to play but he's refusing. He thinks we'd be best off cancelling and if we don't he says he'll talk to the opposition and get it put off that way instead.'

'Do I know this chap?'

'Yes, his name's…' Finn looked to Mr Pearse who mouthed the professor's Christian name. 'Eoin. I know he respects you so I thought you might be able to get him onside for Sunday, for the big game.' There was a silence; Finn wondered if they'd been disconnected.

'This is what you do, Finn, you tell Eoin about the international co-operation, from east and west, that helped organise this game. Let him know it's my wish it goes ahead.' There was an echo on the line; Finn heard the orders twice. 'If he's any doubts I'll speak to him myself. Remind him of the hurling fans who'll be a mite cross if he cancels. I don't think he wants to upset anyone handy with a Tipperary rifle.'

'Thank you, Father.'

'I'll await news of a glorious victory, eh? Goodbye.'

The line clicked dead. Finn returned the receive to the cradle and repeated his father's side of the conversation. Mr Pearse saw no alternative but to take Finn with him to MacNeill's house so he could personally pass on the words of the president of the Clan na Gael.

'That's a crisis successfully avoided,' said Mr MacDermott as the foursome of Mr Pearse, Mr MacDonagh, himself and Finn left MacNeill's house and headed for St Enda's.

'But I fear not the only one we may have to face,' Mr Pearse replied.

'Nay, Pat, with MacNeill on board we're safe,' Mr MacDonagh reasoned.

'What about Bulmer Hobson? Who else but the secretary of the Volunteers could have turned MacNeill against us? We must find him.'

'Pat may have a point,' Mr MacDermott agreed.

'Finn, did Professor MacNeill mention it was Mr Hobson who alerted him to the orders for the Rising?' Mr MacDonagh asked.

'No, sir.'

'Not to worry,' Mr Pearse said, 'We'll investigate and take whatever action is necessary.'

Over a belated breakfast Finn reported the morning's events to his friends. At eleven o'clock he summoned the Red Branch and confirmed the Rising was to take place in two days so they should check their kit and weapons and ready themselves for that longed-for moment when Ireland would rise up, shake off her shackles and become a free nation.

After speaking so extravagantly to his company Finn felt a flush of embarrassment. It was his first undirected act of leadership to his Fianna company; the second was already pressing him. As the common room cleared he grabbed Hal, claiming a problem with his rifle.

'When's it jamming?' Hal raised the gun to his eye.

Finn, one last glance at the closing door, took the gun from him.

'It's not. There's something else. I'm afraid it's an order.'

'Aye?'

'On Sunday,' Finn swallowed, 'if I'm injured, or killed, you're in charge of the company.'

'Me? Patrick's been in the Fianna longer, he outranks me.'

'I don't give a fuck about ranks; it's you I trust to make hard decisions in the heat of it.' Finn removed the gun he had been carrying since a strange impulse made him take it as he dressed that morning. 'Let me show you how to load this.'

'Jesus, steady on, Finn.'

Finn snapped, 'We've got to be prepared. It's easy, look.' He went through the motions of loading, cocking and emptying the gun. 'If anything happens, take it and the ammunition. Make every shot count.'

Hal stared at him. Finn offered Hal his hand.

'To hell with it,' Hal muttered and grabbed Finn in a bear hug.

The door slammed open.

'Plunkett's here,' Patrick announced.

In the corridor two stretcher-bearers headed for the Pearse living quarters. Slung between them, covered by a grey blanket, was the skeletal Mr Plunkett. Eyes, opaque with pain, stared out of darkened sockets, refuting the man who was want to dart the hallways, his cloaks flowing and bracelets jangling. But, as his agony-filled eyes settled on Finn, the mouth smiled and a bloodless tongue licked cracked lips that moved noiselessly but with purpose. Finn thought they formed the words, 'Éire go bráth'.

Mr Plunkett vanished into the room. Mr Pearse emerged.

'Lads, have you plans for today?'

'No, sir.'

'Then I'd be grateful if you didn't stray. I might need a favour later.' Mr Pearse ducked back into the room.

'What's that about?' Patrick asked.

Finn shrugged. 'Christ knows.'

It was late afternoon. They were lolling on the easy chairs in the common room, cards out. Finn had just drawn a full house. Mr Pearse appeared in the doorway. Finn pulled a handy copy of the *Evening Mail* over the deck.

'Lads,' Mr Pearse said, tactfully ignoring the game he'd interrupted, 'Can you follow me?'

The headmaster led them to the basement. The press, its work on the proclamations of an Irish Republic done, rusted in the corner. The basement had been transformed into a dungeon complete with prisoner. Bulmer Hobson, Fianna founding father and secretary to the Volunteers, sat tied to a chair, blind-folded and gagged.

'Jesus Christ,' Hal exclaimed.

Mr Pearse snapped his eyes on Hal and tutted. 'Mr Hobson is, temporarily, our guest,' he explained, 'I'm arranging for transportation to more suitable accommodation.' Suitable for what, Finn wondered. 'And would be grateful if you could keep Mr Hobson company. This is official IRB business, boys.'

Five voices chorused, 'Yes, sir.'

Mr Pearse halted at the stairs. 'Perhaps you may wish to procure a rifle from the Fianna store.'

'Yes, sir,' the five repeated.

When Mr Pearse had gone Charlie threw his arms in the air. 'Bloody hell!'

'This is fecking mad.' Hal scratched his head.

'I'll get a gun,' Patrick offered.

'Don't bother.' Finn produced his revolver.

'We can't leave him like that.' Freddie indicated the bound man.

'Mr Pearse said to guard him,' Charlie pointed out.

'We could take off the blindfold and gag though?' Freddie suggested.

'Alright,' Finn agreed, tightening his grip on the gun.

As soon as the gag came off Mr Hobson began protesting. The five 'gaolers' let their prisoner ramble on, becoming increasingly incoherent, alternating between demands and pleas. Finn recalled how calm Mr Connolly had been when the IRB held him.

'We're gonna sit here all night, so, listening to that shite?' Hal demanded. It was almost teatime.

'Why don't you three get some grub,' Finn suggested, 'Freddie and I'll stay. When you're done you can relieve us.'

'Righto,' Hal said and the three left.

Mr Hobson continued to rant. Freddie whispered to Finn: 'Do you know what this is about?'

'Maybe,' Finn said, 'Mr Hobson?'

Addressed by a boy waving a gun, Mr Hobson fell silent.

'Did you tell Professor MacNeill about the orders for the Rising?'

'I abhor violence,' Mr Hobson spluttered, 'I'm a pacifist.'

'That's just a posh word for cladhaire*, isn't it?'

Finn didn't know where it came from but he suddenly felt sickened by Mr Hobson. Perhaps it was because he'd nearly ruined things last night or because he couldn't see war was their only option. Perhaps it was because Finn was missing his second meal of the day over this.

'On Sunday we'll kick the British out of Ireland and parade through Dublin free men,' Finn said, 'but I doubt you'll be seeing it.' He pulled on the chain around his neck, dangling St Colmcille in front of Mr Hobson's wide eyes. 'Do you know who this is?' Mr Hobson nodded. 'He was prepared to die for the Gael. Are you?'

Finn pressed the gun muzzle against the man's temple, cocked the hammer with his thumb and lay his finger weightlessly on the trigger; the slightest pressure would fire the weapon. Mr Hobson panted, sweat beaded on his forehead.

'Finn, don't be an eejit,' Freddie cried.

Finn glanced behind, saw Freddie's face, the fear in it, and dropped his arm, flicking the safety catch on. Handing Freddie the gun, he stalked out.

Upstairs Finn leant against the wall, his legs trembling.

'Finn, Pat says he's a prisoner in the basement. What in God's name's going on?' Mary Brigid demanded.

Finn's tongue snagged on the dry roof of his mouth. Certain Mary Brigid, Mrs Pearse and Miss Margaret knew about the Rising he forcibly ejected the words, 'It's for Sunday,' then staggered to the front door.

As he stepped outside a cart drew up, driven by Michael Collins; Finn recognised him from yesterday's pow-wow at the

---

* coward

safe house. Next to him were two others who were also familiar; one was Sean something; the other was Mrs Clarke's brother, Ned, who nodded his head to Finn in mutual recognition. Collins climbed down, doffed his cap to a mute Mary Brigid who had trailed Finn to the entrance, and, recognising Finn, spoke.

'You've a prisoner for transportation.'

'In the basement,' Finn said and trudged back downstairs.

Ten minutes later Mr Hobson was gone and Finn was fighting the urge to vomit as he stirred the stewed prunes and cold custard Mrs Pearse served for tea.

After supper, as it was Good Friday, Mr Pearse called everyone into the study hall chapel. Assembled were the three Pearse women, Willie, Misters Colbert, MacDonagh, Slattery and Plunkett, who was pushed in a wheelchair, and the remaining Red Branch. They were on the second verse of 'Up from the grave He rose' when Mary Brigid, who, from her position at the piano, had a clear view into the rest of the hall, screamed, clashed the keys, and jumped up, overturning the piano stool.

Finn swung round to see a man of military bearing, wearing the dress uniform of the Volunteers. He was middle-aged, with a fine moustache wound to two sharp points; he brandished a revolver. Finn's hand flew to his belt but his gun was in his trunk where Freddie had stowed it.

Mary Brigid trembled by the piano, a hand covering her mouth. No one moved. Mr Pearse cleared his throat.

'Michael O'Rahilly. A pity, you've missed my sermon.'

'Never mind your blasted sermon, Pearse, you devil. You hear this: the man that kidnaps me will have to be a quicker shot than I or he'll die in the attempt o' it.' He flourished the gun. 'And I'll charge you to address me properly, as chieftain of my clan, you scoundrel.'

'My apologies, The O'Rahilly.' Mr Pearse bowed his head. 'And I'll charge you to not threaten my family and students with a deadly weapon.'

O'Rahilly, registering his shocked audience, holstered his gun.

'Begging your pardon, Mrs Pearse,' he said, 'But I feel it my duty to inform you your son is misguided in his plans.'

'I assure you to the contrary; our plans are meticulous,' Mr Pearse interrupted.

'Meticulous they may be but they're still the plans of a poet and an idealist. One who'll get us killed, so he will,' O'Rahilly declared.

Mr Pearse set aside his hymn sheet. 'Could I impose upon you to accompany me to my office for further debate?'

'As you wish, Pearse.' O'Rahilly removed the gun from its holster. 'After you.' He waved the barrel and, at gunpoint, Mr Pearse led the way.

'Good God, Mother,' Mary Brigid exclaimed when both men were gone.

'Willie, perhaps you should join them,' Mrs Pearse said, standing.

'I think Pat'll have everything under control, Ma,' Willie said, 'And I wouldn't want to give The O'Rahilly the impression we were attempting to take him prisoner.' Turning to the boys he added, 'To your rooms please, lads.'

From the dorm window Fin watched the Good Friday sun setting. It was three hours before Mr Pearse placated the irate O'Rahilly and they emerged to part with a curt handshake on the Hermitage steps. With that settled Finn crawled into bed and slept deeply.

Holy Saturday 22 April

Finn surveyed his small company of Na Fianna. Their equipment was laid out on the drill hall floor; rifles and ammunition, regulation issue knives, food rations, water canteens, mess tins, field dressings, phials of morphine and syringes, matches and, added at Freddie's suggestion, maps of Dublin.

Promptly at 09:00 hours Mr Colbert arrived and inspected every item. Then he asked if any boy wished to withdraw. No one did.

'It leaves me to give you your orders,' Mr Colbert concluded, 'I need three volunteers to accompany Mr Slattery to the Phoenix Park Magazine Fort. He has a charge we need laid to signal the start of the Rising.'

Three hands shot in the air. One was Donald MacCabe's and Finn was pleased he hadn't sent Donald home for being underage.

'Mr Pearse has requested the following members go with him to the GPO; Devoy, O'Hanlon, Barrett, Blackwell and Healy.'

Finn grinned; he'd hoped they'd be deployed together.

'The rest of you will join me at Watkins Brewery under the command of Mr Eamonn Ceannt. And no fooling with the contents of the barrels there.' Mr Colbert's tone was stern but he smiled. 'They said we were drunk in '98; they'll not say it this time, bejesus. Righto. Ádh mór ort*, boys. Dismissed.'

The platoon didn't move. Perturbed, Finn faced his troop.

'Didn't you hear the order?' he said, trying to imitate Mr Colbert's bark.

'Three cheers for Captain Devoy,' Charlie cried, 'Hip hip hooray!'

Every member shouted with all the air in their lungs. Finn used the moment to steal a last look at them, wondering if he'd remember enough to sketch them later, just as they were then.

---

* Good luck

After lunch Finn mooched through the Hermitage, glancing at each clock he passed. The third time he entered the common room, where Freddie had a newspaper on his knees, Hal was sharpening the already keen blade of his knife and some of the other Fianna boys, including Patrick and Charlie, were writing, he was greeted by frustrated frowns and one loud tut.

'Haven't you anything to do?' Patrick moaned, scribbling on his paper, 'Every time you come in I go wrong.' He balled up the letter and threw it at Finn's head.

Finn ducked out without answering and ambled towards the art room.

The door was closed. He knocked, heard a mumbled reply and entered.

Willie Pearse was at an easel.

'Finn, come give me your opinion on this.'

Finn recognised the cottage at Rosmuc, huddled against the Connemara hills, the wide blue sky above and the cool deep lough in front.

'Have I a mistake here?' Willie indicated the bottom right corner.

'It looks fine, sir.'

'If you say so, then it does.' Willie began daubing hints of red and orange on the horizon.

Finn stared, entranced by the elegant brush strokes. Although every facet of the painted Rosmuc was true to life the artwork had created a mythical world of possibilities. There was magic in the painting and the painter. Finn expected Cúchulainn to charge down the hillside.

Willie's voice broke the spell. 'You like it?'

'Yes, it's...álainn*.'

'Aye, not bad from the brushes of someone with only a modicum of talent,' Willie said.

'You're very talented, sir.' Finn shook his head. 'I don't know how to explain but you make things look better than they are, sort of super-real.'

---

* beautiful

'Idealised, maybe?' Willie mused, the brush chewed between his teeth, 'Perhaps because I'm forever painting things in a favourable light. Lord help me, Finn, that's an apt epitaph: here lies Willie Pearse, artist and idealist. He painted nought but what he dreamt.' Willie laughed.

Finn didn't. 'Will we be alright tomorrow, sir?'

Willie tilted his head, viewing the painting on a slant. 'Sure, some good will come of it.' Finn could see only the side of his face, the eye bright, the smile fading. 'I will bear testimony with my life.' Willie was quoting a line of his, as Ciaran, from Mr Pearse's *The Master*.

The lines that followed, those Finn's Daire had replied with, rushed up to Finn, 'What will that prove? Men die for false things, for ridiculous, evil things. What vile cause has not its heroes? Though you were to die here with joy and laughter you would not prove your cause a true one.' The words were so deafening in his head, Finn wasn't sure he hadn't said them aloud in the scornful tones of the Celtic warrior-king. But Willie just smiled and gestured with his brush.

'I think someone's wanting a word.'

Donald was sheltering in the doorway.

'I didn't mean to interrupt,' he said as Finn went to him.

'That's alright,' Finn replied, 'We're done.'

Donald shifted from one foot to the other, knotting and unknotting his hands.

'What is it, Donald?'

'I was wondering if there's time for me to join this IRB of yours?' He threw Finn a sly glance.

'How d'you know about that?'

'I heard yous talking about it yesterday,' Donald admitted.

After the Bulmer Hobson/The O'Rahilly fiasco, they'd been in the common room, gassing. Finn cursed himself for not noticing Donald but people often didn't.

'Alright. But you don't have to.'

'I want to.' Donald folded his arms. 'I'll feel better dying for the cause if I've sworn myself to it.'

'Bloody hell, Donald, steady on,' Finn forced a smile, 'There's not to be any talk of dying. But if you're set on it, then fine.'

Finn swung by the common room. Charlie and Freddie were both there; Charlie reading and Freddie bouncing a ball.

'Busy, lads?' Finn teased.

'Extremely,' Charlie grunted, 'Will you fecking stop that?' He hurled the book at Freddie.

'Oi, that's my bleeding book,' Freddie snapped.

'Can you leave off throttling each other 'til later?' Finn waved them over. 'I'm taking Donald down the road.'

'To the…?

'Yep.'

'Good man, yourself, Donald.' Charlie grabbed Donald's hand and nearly shook the arm off him.

Mr Clarke led them into the parlour where Finn explained his mission to Mr MacDermott who sat at the table, his eyes fixed on a newspaper in front of him. He didn't answer Finn.

'Sean.' Mr Clarke slapped Mr MacDermott's shoulder. 'Leave that. We've time for this, haven't we?'

'Of course, sorry, Finn.' Mr MacDermott reached for the Bible and proceeded to hastily swear Donald into the IRB.

'Now, I'm afraid, Finn, you'll have to leave.' Mr MacDermott offered Finn a slack handshake and hustled them outside.

Finn shrugged at Donald. 'He's not normally like that. I hope you…'

But Donald was glowing. 'That was grand,' he murmured.

'What the hell's up there?' Charlie asked over Donald's head.

'Did you see what he was reading?' Freddie replied.

'Nope.'

'This morning's *Irish Independent.* I've a copy at school.'

The headline read 'German submarine lands spy. Suspect captured by Kerry Police'.

'Is this to do with us?' Charlie asked.

'Jesus, Finn, tell us what the feck's going on,' Hal snapped.

Finn paced the room. 'I'm not sure. We were waiting on some guns from Germany. They were to be landed in Kerry. Maybe…'

'Does this mean no weapons?' Charlie asked.

Finn pressed his forehead against the cool glass of the common room window. 'It means no extra weapons.'

'Have we enough?' Hal asked.

Finn didn't know.

Only Donald was unperturbed; they left him by the fire, giving an invisible comrade the IRB handshake.

Finn forbade them to say anything about happenings in Kerry to the rest of the Red Branch and their table was unusually lacklustre at teatime, even Hal struggling to eat. When the tension became too much Finn excused himself.

He went outside for a smoke, sheltering against the Hermitage's grey flank. There wasn't any wind but it took three matches to get the cigarette lit. Finn was drawing his first drag when he heard a motorcar. Dropping his cigarette into the flowerbed, Finn shuffled round the corner and saw Mr O'Rahilly in the driver's seat and Professor MacNeill clambering from the passenger's side.

'Wait for me, Michael. I shouldn't need long to put an end to these shenanigans,' the professor said.

O'Rahilly cut the engine as MacNeill mounted the steps two at a time.

Finn crept along until he reached Mr Pearse's office window. It was closed. Mr Pearse was at his desk. There was a knock, Mr Pearse's murmured voice then another, too delicate to be MacNeill's. Finn guessed it was Mary Brigid. He flattened himself against the brickwork as a chair was scraped across the floor. The two voices faded. Finn chanced a look. The room was empty; Mary Brigid must have taken Mr Pearse to MacNeill. Praying they would return to the study, Finn raised the sash with fumbling fingers and retreated.

'What's on your mind, Eoin?'

'This.'

There was a rustle of papers.

'Shall I take your silence as admission that all you told me yesterday of promised weapons to ensure the Volunteers are adequately armed etcetera was a further pack of damnable lies?' MacNeill demanded.

'I admit no such thing.'

'But this.' More rustling. 'And I've confirmation of what's printed there from two Volunteers, arrived from Kerry, who inform me the arms have not and will not be landed for the ship lies scuppered at the bottom of Tralee Bay, after your men failed to meet it. So much for your twenty thousand guns and a million rounds. As for Sir Roger, he's taken by the local constabulary and there is no armed force coming to your aid from Germany, just two puny specimens who are, no doubt, languishing with Casement in the Kerry gaol. See sense. This Rising's an insanity; I will not allow it.'

'I don't need your permission,' Mr Pearse said.

'The Volunteers do.'

'The Volunteers, Eoin, do not take their orders from you.'

'They certainly do.'

'The IRB faction, at least, will disobey any countermand you issue.'

'On their heads and yours be it.'

There was a long silence. Finn thought MacNeill had left.

'For the love of Mary, why, Pat, are you so insistent when the way ahead is utterly ruined?'

'You know my reasons; I've no need to restate them. In fact, I've nothing more to say to you. We've used your name and influence for all their worth. Now we don't need you any more, Eoin.' Mr Pearse's voice made Finn shiver despite the evening's warmth. 'It's no use you trying to stop us. Our plans are laid; they will be carried out.'

MacNeill made a snorting sound. 'So well laid, these godforsaken plans, that the usually imbecilic Kerry constabulary have brought them to ruin already. Know this, you damnable fool: I will forbid any mobilisation of the Volunteers and do everything in my power to ensure that order is obeyed. This Rising is a dead letter. Contact me if you come to your senses.'

The door slammed. Finn sank to the ground, tulips and daffodils bobbing around his buckled legs. MacNeill's words crowed in his ears: this Rising is a dead letter.

Easter Sunday 23 April

In the dorm five boys donned their battledress; olive green shirt, navy britches, green jumper and slouch hat. They jostled at the mirror, checking hats had the correct slant, and helped each other belt, buckle and strap correctly. Unable to disobey his father's orders, Finn slipped the American, British and German identity documents into his pocket. The *Táin* Cathleen had given him for his birthday sat on his nightstand next to the photographs of his victorious junior hurling team and himself and Freddie as Cúchulainn and Ferdia. He slipped the photos from their frames and slid them between the pages of the book which he added to his pack along with the Bible his mother had sent. Lastly he raised St Colmcille to his lips and kissed him as he'd seen men do to crucifixes, for luck: the luck of the Irish.

Hal shouldered his rifle. 'Why'd you suppose we're meeting at Liberty Hall?' he asked, referring to the orders Mr Pearse had given after morning prayers.

'Aye, didn't Colbert say we'd be going straight to wherever we were stationed for the Rising?' Patrick said.

Finn was loading his revolver, Mr Pearse's unusual conclusion to matins echoing in his ears, 'I could not hope for a happier destiny for any one of you than to die in defence of some true thing. Sure, for to die will be a very big adventure indeed.' Finn snapped the barrel shut and tucked it down inside his belt where it sat against the small of his back. He pulled his jumper over the bulge and faced them.

'There's something I need to tell you but I'm telling you as your friend, not your commanding officer.' He removed the hat that sat proudly on his fair curls.

Freddie, Charlie and Patrick exchanged furtive glances; Hal said:

'I don't give a hoot, whatever's happened, or is happening or might happen: I'm going.'

'Let me say my piece first. Then decide.'

Hal shrugged, went to his bed and began raking through his nightstand.

Finn cleared his throat. 'That article, about the spy and the German submarine,' he paused.

'We know about that,' Freddie said.

'There's something else.' Finn spat the next word. 'MacNeill.'

'What's that bloody shite done now?' Patrick asked, half grinning.

'He found out about the weapons not coming and he doesn't think we've a chance so he's planning to issue a countermand to the Volunteers.'

Freddie removed his glasses, pinched the bridge of his nose. 'That's bad.'

'What does it mean?' Charlie asked.

'Some of them mightn't turn out,' Finn admitted.

'How many? Christ, all of them?'

'No! The IRB lot will. I don't know about the others.'

Hal had hold of a textbook; he flung it across the room. It struck the wall with a bang, exploded and showered Finn's bed with white leaves.

'What the fucking hell's he done that for?'

'Because,' Finn said, 'he's a coward, doesn't want our deaths on his conscience. Anyway, you know everything so make your minds up 'cos we've about three minutes 'til the off. If you're coming.'

Finn refaced the mirror and replaced his hat. He saw Hal's reflection scoop up the scattered pages of his textbook and make a game of throwing them into the wastepaper basket. Freddie was staring through the window. Patrick appeared to be having a serious problem with his top button. Charlie wasn't visible. Finn's breath caught in his throat. He squeezed his eyes shut.

Something warm and solid landed on his shoulder. Finn opened his eyes.

The mirror reflected Charlie, standing behind him, hand on Finn's shoulder, a grin on his freckly face.

'Alright, mate?' he asked.

'Aye, grand,' Finn replied. He pressed his fingers into his eye sockets before spinning round and grabbing Charlie into a tight hug.

*

The St Enda's company set off, Mr Pearse and Willie, Mr Colbert and Mr MacDonagh in front with Mr Slattery and Mr Plunkett, aided by Michael Collins, trailing at the rear. The boys marched in pairs, making up what they lacked in numbers with the proud angle of their heads, the wide pace of their strides and their enthusiastic rendition of the Fianna song, accompanied by Donald's ebullient piping.

As the column passed the gatehouse Mr Murphy appeared in the doorway, framed as though posing for a photograph. He wore his gardener's overalls and boots, the crust of mud on them hard and dry. He clutched an ancient shotgun, the kind farmers keep for rabbits and rooks.

'Have yous room for another?'

'We have, Michael,' Mr Pearse replied, 'Come join our merry adventure.'

Mr Murphy nodded, shouldered the shotgun and fell in. They strode on, through the gates, for Dublin and victory.

Sandwiched between his headmaster and his company, Finn was both leader and follower as he led his lads but trailed his commander, now Commandant, not Mr, Pearse. He recalled the times they'd marched in similar formation, to parade through Dublin or display at a county fete. Today had always been the goal but it didn't feel like it was real. It wasn't much different to those other times.

They took to the centre of the road; people on the sidewalks stopped to cheer the spectacle, men doffing their caps, women and children waving. Finn noticed a girl wearing the Roto nursing uniform and thought of Cathleen. He hadn't seen her since their night at the safe house. He didn't know if he'd ever see her again.

Mr Pearse led them through the quieter streets on the Liffey's south bank and over the river to Liberty Hall. The banner declaring service to Ireland still hung boldly above the entrance. Some Citizen Army lads in uniform milled about on the steps. Finn hoped there were more inside.

The soldier on the door saluted Mr Pearse.

'Mr Connolly's expecting you, sir.' He pointed out a room inside.

The St Enda's warriors filed into the building. Finn brought the lads to attention, gave the salute to Mr Pearse then commanded them to stand easy.

From the room the soldier had indicated a uniformed Mr Connolly emerged.

'Pat, sweet Jesus, have you seen it?' He charged forward, waving a *Dublin Sunday Independent* with others bundled under his arm.

Mr Pearse frowned. 'Whatever's the matter, James?'

'This! Here, I've copies.' Mr Connolly handed the papers round.

Finn secured one, and, beyond Mr Pearse's sight, began skimming. He found the cause of distress on page five:

'Owing to the very critical position, all orders given to Irish Volunteers for tomorrow, Easter Sunday, are hereby rescinded and no parades, marches or other movement of Irish Volunteers will take place. Each individual Volunteer will obey this order strictly in every particular. By Order of Professor Eoin MacNeill, Chief-of-Staff.'

The paper was leaden in Finn's hands.

Mr Pearse had also done reading. He folded the newspaper and slapped it against his palm. 'I see the professor is a man of his word. Have you heard from any of the companies?'

'A few commanders have telephoned for clarification,' Mr Connolly said, 'I told them to disregard it entirely.'

'Will they?'

'I've no notion, Pat.' Mr Connolly worried his eyes with a thumb and forefinger. 'To make matters worse he's had that bloody fool O'Rahilly driving around all night, delivering his countermand far and wide. My Nora ran home from Dunngannon in the wee hours to tell me she'd seen it herself: a great mass of Volunteers readied to fight, only to be told to stand down. It's chaos, so it is. Jesus, if there's not to be a Rising may an earthquake swallow Ireland whole.'

'Calm yourself, James,' Mr Pearse replied, 'Finn, find a room for your lads, settle them, and come to me.'

'Yes, sir.'

Mr Pearse gestured to Mr Plunkett and Mr MacDonagh, 'Shall we?' All four disappeared into Mr Connolly's office.

Countess Markievicz stamped down the central staircase. Mr Colbert intercepted her.

'Countess, have you the facilities for making our lads tea?'

'Of course. Good morning, Captain Devoy,' she said, saluting Finn before leading Mr Colbert away.

Freddie sidled up to Finn who gave him the paper and waited in black silence while Freddie read. When he'd finished he tucked the paper under his arm and fell wordlessly back into the ranks.

Finn bade his small band follow him through the building in search of a suitable room. He found one on the third try, a large library furnished with reading desks, chairs and two sofas, the walls lined with books. The boys bunched up at the doorway and Finn had to coax them inside. They drifted around the vast room in twos and threes, tiny rowing boats lost at sea.

Mr Colbert and the Countess arrived carrying trays loaded with teapots, cups and plates of biscuits. The Countess beckoned to the boys and plied them with refreshments. Finn approached Mr Colbert.

'What should I tell them, sir?'

'They're your men, Finn.'

'But, sir…'

'On the eve of battle men must trust their leaders and their leaders must trust themselves.' Mr Colbert crossed to the table and helped himself to a ginger snap, leaving Finn alone.

Madam Markievicz bustled over and handed Finn a cup. 'Keep your mettle up, young man,' she advised sternly and turned away.

Finn strode up to Freddie. 'Give me the paper.'

Freddie, juggling his cup and saucer, handed it to Finn.

Finn mounted the fireside flagstones.

'Company, fall in,' he shouted, adding, 'Bring your tea.'

The lads gathered. Donald jostled for space at the front, gained it and set unblinking eyes on Finn. Finn cleared his throat and read MacNeill's damning issue to the background noise of tea slurped and biscuits crunched.

'This announcement is by someone who thinks there shouldn't be a Rising at all. If any of you are of the same mind finish your tea and leave.'

Donald raised his arm. He spoke with surprising volume.

'What do you think, Captain, of the Rising?'

Thinking of Cúchulainn, Finn said without hesitation, 'I'm for it.'

Charlie threw a glance to Hal who caught it and nodded. They stepped forward to flank Finn on either side. Freddie and Patrick followed, forming a line of five boys that faced the rest of the room. Donald stepped forwards next and the scramble began, every boy taking his place alongside Finn until only Mr Colbert and Countess Markievicz remained facing Finn. Mr Colbert winked at him. The Countess, smiling her approval, went to the tea things.

'Anybody for more?'

Their purpose reaffirmed, the boys accepted the offer with relish; Finn struck out in search of the IRB Supreme Military Council, satisfied his men, at least, were behind the Rising. He met Willie in the hall.

'Pat's asking for you. Top of the stairs, first left.'

The room was bleak; no curtains, bare floorboards and stripped of furniture save a large table and eight stiff chairs. Finn noticed the number because he saw the empty one reserved for himself and felt his cheeks flush.

'Finn, thank you.' Mr Pearse indicated the chair; Finn sat.

The roundness of the table meant no one was at the head. Finn found himself opposite Mr MacDermott who regarded him with those intense eyes.

'I take it, Finn, you are appraised of our situation.'

'Yes, sir.'

'Have you formed any opinion on the situation?'

'Yes, sir.'

Mr MacDermott smiled. 'Would you kindly share it with us?'

'The Rising should go ahead, sir.'

Mr Clarke banged the table. 'Indeed.'

'On this we agree,' Mr MacDermott said, 'The issue is when to commence; as planned today, or tomorrow, giving us time to countermand Eoin's damn countermand.' Underneath the table Finn picked at a raggy fingernail. Mr MacDermott continued. 'Our vote has three in favour of today and three for tomorrow.'

Finn scanned the room. Mr Connolly met his eye.

'I'm undecided, Finn.'

'Don't fret, Finn, I'm not burdening you with an official IRB vote,' Mr MacDermott explained, 'But I would be glad to hear your views, as someone with a company of men who are readied for action today. To say nothing of your close involvement with our grand adventure. I'm sure a bright lad like you will have words worth hearing.'

Around the table the seven members of the IRB Supreme Military Council waited to hear him speak. Finn thought he might puke his porridge. He addressed Mr Pearse.

'What do you think, sir?'

Mr Pearse smiled. 'You first, Finn.'

'Can I have a moment, sir?' Finn asked Mr MacDermott.

'Certainly.'

Finn settled into his chair. Another night tossing sleeplessly, chased through half-dreams by the enemy or the order given and them taking the city before nightfall? But another day and more men called to fight? He sat forward. 'If we're ready today then we'll be all the readier tomorrow.' He looked to Mr Connolly, 'I'm sorry if that's no help, sir.'

The older man smiled. 'You're a smart lad, Finn, brave enough to speak your mind. For that you have my respect.'

'Aye, and for your honesty and your part in our endeavours our thanks,' Mr MacDermott added. 'I think we'd better vote again, gentlemen.'

Finn paced the landing, knowing that behind the closed door seven men were making the most important decision of their lives and Ireland's.

Willie climbed the stairs. 'Is there word?'

'They're voting again.' As the sentence passed Finn's lips the door opened.

Mr Pearse emerged, his face flushed, his eyes bright. He laid a hand on Finn's shoulder and offered the other to Willie. 'Tomorrow at noon.'

*

It was decided the Red Branch should return St Enda's, Mr Pearse arguing it was best for the lads to sleep in the comfort of their dorms than camped on the floors of Liberty Hall. Finn would have preferred the rough hard night. To have left school in such expectation only to return having not struck for independence made him cringe.

Mr Connolly and Countess Markievicz came to wave them off. Mr Pearse paused on the steps next to Mr Connolly, gazing into the distance, a dreamy expression on his face. Finn swivelled his head, following the line Mr Pearse's eyes tracked to the far-off Wicklow mountains, their peaks purple and regal.

'If necessary we can fight on in the mountains,' he murmured.

Mr Connolly clapped a firm palm on Mr Pearse's shoulder, waking him. 'You'll fight in Dublin, Pat,' he barked.

Finn saw a smirk flicker on the Countess's lips. Mr Pearse blushed and squirmed from under Mr Connolly's touch.

Finn gave the order and the brigade moved off.

They were greeted by a surprised Mary Brigid and stoic Mrs Pearse. Nothing was said about their return and they were made welcome with a hearty dinner of stew, champ and treacle pudding. Mary Brigid suggested a singsong and they spent the evening around the piano, belting out rebel songs and banishing the day's frustrations.

They had just made the decision that their voices could take no more when Mr Pearse, who had been locked in his study since dinner, appeared.

'Finn, your father's on the telephone.'

Finn stumbled up and followed Mr Pearse to his office.

'Father?'

'Finn. I've had a telegram from your end. There's been a change of plan, I gather.'

'Yes, sir.'

'The documents I gave you,' his father continued, 'You have them safe?'

'Yes, sir.'

'Keep your American passport on you at all times, do you hear?'

'Father?'

'Goddamn it, Finn, you're to carry that passport. It's essential now.'

'Sir.'

'Your mother sends love. We'll see you soon, God willing. Goodbye, Finn.'

'Father.' Finn clipped the word short and banged the receiver down.

'Is everything well, Finn?' Mr Pearse asked; his words were trapped in the slamming door as Finn stormed from the office.

Trembling with anger, Finn pulled the British, German and US documents from his pocket. The treacherous one was uppermost, its seal showing an eagle clutching arrows in one talon and an olive branch in the other: desirous of peace but ready for war. Finn crossed to the fireplace in the entrance hall and flung all three into the empty grate.

Easter Monday 24 April

A blue cloudless sky spread spring warmth on them but Finn shivered as they marched, their pace plodding. There was no singing today. A sneering voice in Finn's head told him he was a fool for throwing away his passport. Glancing to his right, he saw Hal, arms swinging, shoulders firm, a hard knot of muscle bulging along his jaw. Finn tuned out the voice. This was what he was always meant to do.

At Liberty Hall they were greeted by a crowd of soldiers massing in the street. Mr Pearse halted the St Enda's company; Mr Connolly came forward. The two men moved off a few paces; Finn gave the at ease command and surveyed the scene. It was nearly eleven o'clock but still fewer than half the Dublin Volunteers had massed. Although supported by the Citizen Army, Finn calculated there were too few men for the actions they'd planned; positions that were to be defended by dozens would have to manage with a handful.

Hardly any of the Volunteers who had mobilised wore uniforms or carried rifles. Most of the rag-tag mob were armed with whatever they had grabbed on the way out; sledgehammers, pick-axes, crowbars, shovels, the odd shotgun. One young Citizen Army lad strutted about with a wooden leg in an improvised holster. Some were even armed with pikes like those Finn had seen in etchings of the 1798 rebellion. The long poles topped with cruel hooks were fearsome and invoked the *Táin* but they weren't guns. Cúchulainn, with his gae bolga, wouldn't have looked amiss in their ranks.

'Pat, we've no choice. We've got to issue them else it'll be true to say we're going out to be slaughtered.'

The raised voice was Mr Connolly's. Finn saw Mr MacDermott had joined the two-man huddle; Mr Plunkett, helped by Michael Collins, and Mr Clarke were heading over.

'What's that?' Hal, who was beside Finn, jerked a thumb at the men who were talking at once and gesturing frantically.

'Christ knows.'

Mr Pearse shouted above the clamour. 'Anyway, there's not time to get them; they're at the safe house.' With that he turned from his co-conspirators, stamped three steps in Finn's direction, stopped and folded his arms. A deep furrow marked his brow.

'Look out,' Hal hissed and dropped into formation.

A tooting horn distracted them from the fracas. Barrelling down the road at top speed was a motorcar, The O'Rahilly at the wheel. Finn quietly cursed.

The brakes screeched. The rear wheels slipped on an oil patch. The backend skittered. O'Rahilly wrestled the mechanical beast, pulling it to a halt, skew-whiff to the pavement before leaping up and bounding to Mr Pearse.

'The O'Rahilly.' Mr Pearse bowed his head but didn't doff his hat. 'What can I do to help you this fine morning? Sure, I've a rather busy day ahead.'

''Tis I come to help you.' O'Rahilly clicked his heels together and saluted. 'I've come to throw my lot in with yours, if you'll have me.'

'You wish to join us?'

'Aye. I've helped wind the clock, I might as well be there to hear it chime.'

Mr Pearse smiled. 'If you wish.'

'I do.' O'Rahilly grabbed Mr Pearse's hand and pumped it.

'Grand.' Mr MacDermott stepped forward. 'You can be of service to us immediately. We need to collect something. May we requisition your motorcar, with you driving, of course?'

The smile dropped from Mr Pearse's face.

'I've told you, Sean, we're not issuing them.'

'Pat, this is no time for chivalrous notions of warfare. The men need weapons. I'm head of the council; I'm telling you we're using them.' Mr MacDermott scanned the assembled ranks. 'Finn, direct The O'Rahilly to the safe house. In the bedroom are some crates. Bring them here. Déan deifir*!' Mr MacDermott pulled a key from his pocket.

'I forbid you to go, Finn,' Mr Pearse said.

'In what capacity are you forbidding him, Pat? As his headmaster? Hardly a position relevant today. Or his commanding officer? In which case I outrank you and forbid

---

* Hurry

you to forbid him,' Mr MacDermott said, jangling the key at Finn.

Mr Pearse scowled. Finn sighed, plucked the key from Mr MacDermott's fingers and boarded the motorcar. O'Rahilly gunned the engine and Finn found himself sitting on a throbbing beast. It lurched forward and they sped down the road, Finn holding his hat with one hand and hanging on with the other. In less than fifteen minutes, jiggled and jarred, they were flung from their seats as the car slammed to a stop outside the safe house.

Recognising the crates as the ones he'd helped stack, Finn understood the row. Mr MacDermott had sent him for the old-fashioned guns, the ones that were too brutal for Christian Mr Pearse.

With the crates loaded, O'Rahilly whipped the motor into life and they stampeded towards town. As they approached St Enda's Finn twisted in his seat to snatch a glance at the entrance he had passed through so many times. The gates appeared. A figure loitered by them. The figure moved in a swish of auburn hair and grey skirts. Finn shouted and was hurled forward, smacking into the dashboard, as Mr O'Rahilly span the steering wheel hard to the right and stamped on the brakes. Finn sat up, rubbing his ribs, and peered behind for a body in the road.

'Finn, thank the Lord. I saw the motorcar. Are you going to Pat?' Mary Brigid's voice fluttered. Her hair was loose, her head bare and her jacket done up wrong. She clawed at the car door.

'Miss Pearse, what the devil are you doing?' Mr O'Rahilly barked.

'I must see Pat.' Her face was white, her eyes red and Finn could see silvery tear tracks on her cheeks.

'Miss, we've urgent business. We…'

But Mary Brigid was already clambering in amongst the guns and bullets.

'Help me, Finn,' she said, her voice less shrill.

O'Rahilly tried again. 'We can't…'

'Aye, you can.' She plonked herself on a crate and folded her arms in the same defiant gesture Finn had seen barely half an hour ago.

'We need to get back, sir,' he prompted.

O'Rahilly shook his head but fired the car and drove off.

Liberty Hall was bustling when they arrived. Several horse-drawn drays had appeared plus two motorbikes and a hansom cab. Finn couldn't be sure but he thought the numbers had swelled too. Darting green figures hurried among the Volunteers as the Fianna handed out armbands marking the men as soldiers. In a quarter of an hour they would set forth to take Dublin in their Sunday best.

The motorcar still rolling, Mary Brigid jumped from her perch on the crates and dashed to Mr Pearse who was engaged with Mr Colbert and Mr Ceannt. She bowled into them and threw herself at her brother, clasping his neck.

'Pat.'

'Mary Brigid, what are you doing here?'

'I've come to take you home.'

'Home?'

'Aye, Pat. Come home. Forget this foolishness.'

A crowd flooded the car. Finn struggled free from the mob that began unloading the crates and handing out guns like they were newspapers.

'A dheirfiúir bhig♣, don't fret, a stór*.' Mr Pearse stroked her hair. 'We'll be home soon enough, when Ireland is free.' With those words he lifted Mary Brigid from around his neck and held her at arm's length. Willie, having heard his sister, joined them.

'Mary Brigid,' he said, 'Go home to Mother.'

'Not without you both,' she grabbed her brothers, one in each hand, 'This is madness. I've come to help you see sense.'

'If you want help us go home and pray we take the day,' Mr Pearse said.

♣ little sister

* darling, my dear

He raised her whitened knuckles to his lips and kissed her hand. At his touch Mary Brigid crumpled; her sobs drowned the chattering men and snorting horses. Those loading their new guns became statues instantly petrified. The only sound was Mary Brigid's heart breaking. She collapsed against Mr Pearse who held her in his arms while Willie caressed her hair and murmured in her ear. They reverted to their simplest form: two brothers caring for their sister. Then Mr Pearse nudged Mary Brigid gently from him, kissed her cheek and moved away. Willie kissed her too, and said something final to her. He stepped back as well, leaving Mary Brigid hugging herself, shaking and sobbing.

Mr Connolly gave the order; the men fell in. Finn counted fourteen columns, each headed by a commandant and captains. Amidst the throng of grey suits and khaki uniforms he picked out the robin's egg blue of Mr Murphy's overalls. He looked like a sliver cut from the sky.

Finn's Fianna troop was split as Mr Colbert had said, three gathering around Mr Slattery for the Magazine Fort operation. Freddie, Hal, Patrick and Charlie attached themselves to Mr Pearse's company, destined for the GPO. Finn knew he must go to them but Mary Brigid stood alone, shaking and watching with mute horror as the thing she dreaded most happened. Finn headed for her.

'Mary Brigid.' He laid a hand on her sleeve. She started as if awoken from a nightmare.

'Finn, please, stop him.'

'He's doing what he always wanted.'

'And what's that, to die?'

'If he has to, yes, for Ireland.'

Her bloodshot eyes glistened. Her lips trembled. 'Is that what you want too, Finn, to die? For God's sake, you're a boy.'

'So was Cúchulainn.'

She shook her head. 'Cúchulainn's a legend, Finn.'

He flashed her a tight grin, 'So we will be, after today. Here.' He fished in his pocket for his handkerchief. 'I'm sure you don't need it but I'd be a proper git if I didn't offer.' He squeezed her arm and smiled again.

Mary Brigid took the handkerchief with a mechanical movement. A whistle sounded. A cry went up. Finn hugged her and jogged to his company.

The Irish Republican Army marched out.

As the cavalcade approached the GPO people stared and pointed, forgetting their bank holiday business as they watched what appeared to be another Volunteer parade. Finn's heart was trying to escape his chest; his lungs screamed for air; his mouth dried up while his back oozed sweat. He fidgeted with the strap of his rifle. They were seconds away from entering the GPO, firing shots and taking the building. And they'd do it watched by a holiday crowd. He tightened his grip on the rifle and sucked in city-stale air.

'The GPO, charge!' Mr Connolly yelled.

The company surged forward, bounding up the steps. Mr Clarke drew his revolver, fired a warning shot and burst through the doors shouting:

'Everyone out! Now!'

The Volunteers stomped into the cool dark interior and swooped on police constables and British soldiers who were dotted around inside posting letters or queuing for stamps. The opposition, startled and outnumbered, surrendered their weapons and submitted to being bound and corralled with only minor scuffles. No one understood what was happening. Finn noticed a woman at the counter.

'I need two penny-halfpenny stamps and, bejesus, I'm going nowhere 'til I've got them.' The woman slapped her palm down.

'Missus, please, look!' The harried clerk jabbed towards where Michael Collins was stuffing a dazed soldier into a telephone box.

'I've been waiting for fifteen bloody minutes and I'll be buggered if I'm going without them,' she screeched.

'In that case you can help your bleeding self.' The clerk vaulted the counter, slid along the polished wood, jumped and made a break for the doorway, now jammed with fleeing customers.

''Tis a fecking disgrace,' the woman yelled, 'I'll report you for this.'

Finn reached behind the counter for the 'position closed' sign. 'I think you better go,' he said, making sure she saw his rifle, 'unless you want to fight with us.'

'Who the bleeding hell do you think you are, laddie?'

'Captain Devoy, Red Branch. This building is under the command of Commandant Pearse of the Army of the Irish Republic.'

'Blow me! Alright, I'm away,' she said as Finn took her elbow and pointed her at the door.

Having got the British officer in the telephone kiosk and grabbed Hal and another two Volunteers, Collins shouted to Finn, 'You, with me,' dashed to the back of the room and shoulder-charged a door marked 'staff only', crashing into an office.

Seated around a table, playing gin rummy, were six men in postal uniforms, their collars open, their jackets flung over their chairs and their caps tossed on the bureau behind. When the door banged, believing they were about to be caught playing cards instead of patrolling the parameter, the official guard of the GPO leapt from their chairs.

'You can't come in here,' said an older man with sergeant's stripes on his sleeve. He reached around to the bureau where two objects sat: his hat and his rifle.

Finn saw the movement. So did Collins who raised his Mauser pistol and a single shot cracked through the air. The sergeant, cap in hand, was spun by the force of the bullet that struck him in the shoulder-blade.

'Nobody else move. You are prisoners of the Republican Army of Ireland,' Collins shouted.

The rest of the guard froze. Half way between standing and sitting, one man held the awkward position, his eyes fixed on Collins.

'Don't shoot us,' another yelped, 'We're unarmed.'

'What?' Collins barked.

'See for yourselves,' the man begged.

'Check,' Collins ordered.

The wounded man had collapsed; a dark red pool seeped through his shirt and gushed down his arm. Seeing the blood, Finn remembered Richard and Sean. His stomach lurched. He dodged from the sight to pick up a rifle that was leant against the wall. He snapped open the breech.

'Well?'

Finn peered into the barrel. 'Empty, Lieutenant.'

'So's this 'un,' Hal said, holding aloft another gun.

'Fuck. Jesus. These buggers are worse off than us.' Collins pushed his cap from his head and ran a hand through his mousy hair. 'Right,' he faced the man who had revealed the armed guard of the nerve centre of Irish communication was without ammunition. 'You, help him up.' Collins indicated the stricken man who was reseated in his chair, his face bloodless and twisted in pain. 'Don't worry, we'll get you a medic. The rest of you are prisoners. Tie them up.'

The two Volunteers went about Collins's order. Hal and Finn stood holding the useless rifles.

'You might as well get back out there. I'm sure we can handle restraining half a dozen unarmed guards,' Collins snorted, waving Finn and Hal from the room.

With the rifles in their hands Finn and Hal retreated.

'He's a quick shot,' Hal said.

'Too quick, maybe.'

'We weren't to know.'

In the main counter area, as the remaining civilians were ushered to the exit, preparations for a siege were underway. In the middle of the room, directing proceedings, were the five members of the Military Council who were stationed at the GPO, now GHQ, for the Rising's duration; Misters Pearse, Connolly, Plunkett, Clarke and MacDermott. Finn hoped Mr MacDonagh and Mr Ceannt were likewise making ready at their garrisons: the Castle and South Dublin Union.

Under Mr Clarke's orders, soldiers smashed glass from the windows with whatever they had brought, the sledgehammers proving particularly useful. Finn spotted the Citizen Army lad shattering a pane with the heel of his wooden leg. Three Volunteers wrestled a table to a window, tipped it on its side and pushed it against the shattered glass, singing while they worked. Mr Pearse wandered about, dazed, bumping into Volunteers, hampering their attempts to secure the building. Finn had to dodge him twice and would have collided with him the third time if not for Mr Clarke who was standing by, directing the men.

'For God's sake, will someone get that man an office, a desk, paper and a pen and set him to writing,' he muttered and Finn saw a Volunteer manoeuvre Mr Pearse aside.

'Where've you been?' Charlie came across to Finn and Hal.

Finn just shrugged.

'Well give us a hand. We've to go outside and pass these round.' Charlie pressed copies the proclamation on them. Seven names had been added at the bottom since last Finn read it. The document was either Ireland's declaration of independence or the suicide note of the signatories.

They followed Charlie towards the entrance. A grinning Patrick whipped past them going the opposite way.

'Where're you off?' Hal called.

'Got to hang these.' Patrick held two rolls of fabric.

Finn took one and Hal the other. Unfurled, one was the traditional gold-harp-on-green flag of Ireland but with the legend 'Irish Republic' embroidered beneath. The other consisted of three vertical bands of colour; green, white and orange. That was the one Finn held. He was struck at once; it was the sky from his painting 'Green Dawn at St Enda's' laid on its side.

'What's this?' he asked.

'New Irish national flag,' Patrick said.

'What's with the colours?' Hal asked.

'Green for us, orange for the other lot and white for peace between us, so Mr Pearse was saying.' Patrick snatched it back and darted for the staircase to the roof.

Outside Finn spotted Charlie at the bottom of the steps. He was about to go down when Mr Pearse appeared beside him. Mr Connolly came to stand on Mr Pearse's other side. Mr Pearse carried a large copy of the proclamation. He unrolled it, readying to read it to the Dubliners who, realising from the sound of gunshots and the sight of the GPO windows being smashed that this was no parade, had gathered to gawp.

'Mother Mary, give me strength.' Mr Pearse crossed himself. 'You'll have to excuse my nerves, Finn.'

'Yes, sir,' said Finn, surprised his headmaster had noticed him.

'Will you stay and watch the crowd? You can tell me how they take to it,' Mr Pearse said.

'Alright, sir.' Finn stood at ease.

Mr Pearse cleared his throat. His audience, some of whom may have known him but probably struggled to recognise him in his crisp green uniform, waited with, if not eager anticipation, at least idle curiosity.

Mr Pearse began to read, 'Poblacht na h-Eireann. The Provisional Government of the Irish Republic to the People of Ireland.

'Irishmen and Irishwomen: In the name of God and of the dead generations from which she receives her old tradition of nationhood, Ireland, through us, summons her children to her flag and strikes for her freedom.

'...She strikes in full confidence of victory.

'We declare the right of the people of Ireland to the ownership of Ireland and to the unfettered control of Irish destinies... Standing on that fundamental right and again asserting it in arms in the face of the world, we hereby proclaim the Irish Republic as a Sovereign Independent State, and we pledge our lives and the lives of our comrades in arms to the cause of its freedom...

'... In this supreme hour the Irish nation must, by its valour and discipline, and by the readiness of its children to sacrifice themselves for the common good, prove itself worthy of the august destiny to which it is called.

'Signed on behalf of the Provisional Government, Thomas J. Clarke, Sean Mac Diarmada, Thomas MacDonagh, P. H. Pearse, Eamonn Ceannt, James Connolly, Joseph Plunkett.'

Busy studying the crowd's reaction, Finn caught only snatches of the proclamation. He didn't realise Mr Pearse was finished until he felt, at his elbow, the movement of Mr Pearse lowering the parchment. The audience muttered and gaped. One old man scratched the grizzle of stubble on his chin. A small girl, holding her mother's hand, started bawling when she realised her ice-cream had slid with a splat to the pavement. Caught too tightly in the grip of the moment to notice these details, Mr Pearse shook Mr Connolly's hand.

'Thanks be to God, Pat, that we've lived to see this day,' Mr Connolly said, 'For 'tis a grand day for Ireland and a great day to be Irish.'

'Aye,' Mr Pearse agreed, 'Finn, will you find somewhere to display this?' He gave Finn the proclamation. The edges bore his damp fingerprints.

Finn left the shelter of the GPO and ploughed into the stunned crowd. He found Freddie busy doling out copies of the proclamation.

'I'm to display this. Any ideas?'

'Nelson's Pillar?'

'Righto. Thanks.'

Finn found a couple of heavy stones, weighted it down and stepped back to admire the words of his leader.

Charlie joined him. 'Cheeky git.'

'What?'

'That old codger.' Charlie pointed to the man Finn had seen scratting his beard while Mr Pearse was reading. 'I offered him one of these,' Charlie flapped the sheaf of proclamations, 'and he said he'd take a dozen because they'd be worth a fiver when they've hanged us.'

'Never mind that. Look!'

On the GPO roof the Union Jack was gone and the two flags of the new Irish Republic flew triumphantly. Finn grinned as his 'Green Dawn' sky fluttered above Dublin.

They left the crowd to ponder developments and retreated to the GPO fortress. Patrick reappeared with the Union Jack scrumpled in his fists.

'What shall I do with this, sir?'

'I'll take that.' Mr Clarke snatched the enemy flag, produced a lighter and touched the yellow flame to a corner. Fire-tongues licked up. Mr Clarke dropped the burning rag and towered above it until it was tatters of charred cloth which he trampled to dust. 'Bastards won't be flying another of those while I've breath in my body.'

*

News of the Rising spread through Dublin; men and women began arriving at the GPO, bringing whatever they thought useful, and bidding Mr Pearse or Mr Connolly to let them stay. All were welcomed, including two Swedish sailors who, hating the British, pledged themselves for the duration or until their ship left port, whichever came soonest.

For the few causalities, mostly cuts caused by breaking the windows, Mr MacDermott established a medical quarter in the rear office where the guard had been shot. He suggested they send to the hospitals for medical personnel sympathetic to their cause and requested a runner to go to the Rotunda, which was closest.

'What about Cathleen?' Hal said, 'Would she come?'

'Cathleen?' Mr MacDermott asked.

'She's a friend of mine,' Finn mumbled, unable to prevent his face flushing at an intimate memory.

'If she's a friend perhaps she'll help?'

'I'd rather she didn't, sir.' Finn ducked Mr MacDermott's resolute gaze. 'I'd not like her to get hurt or into bother,' he finished lamely.

'Sure, Finn, that's very chivalrous but would you ask her anyway? I wouldn't want us excluding any who're willing to support us.'

Dressed up though it was, Finn heard the order.

'Why'd you mention Cathleen?' he snapped when Mr MacDermott had left.

'I thought she might want to help,' Hal protested.

'Yeah, she probably will.' Finn stomped to the door and was reaching for the handle when the heavy wood panel flung towards him, knocking him to his backside.

Framed in the doorway, silhouetted against the afternoon sun, was young MacCabe.

Finn struggled to his feet. 'Donald, I thought you were at Phoenix Park.'

Donald's lips moved but no sound emerged. His hair and face were peppered with soot; there were tear-streaks down his cheeks. A wet red line ran across his forehead, clotting in the black dust.

'He shot him, Finn.' Donald's face crumpled as he dry-sobbed.

Finn scanned the room. 'Charlie, here.'

Charlie dropped the end of a table he was manoeuvring and both lads studied the shivering wreck that used to be their company piper.

'Donald.' Finn touched his shoulder. 'What's the matter?' He did his best to adopt a soothing tone.

'In the back… he went for the alarm… shouldn't have… fell through the doorway… red everywhere.'

'We need to get him somewhere quiet,' Charlie hissed.

Sheltering Donald between them, Finn and Charlie walked him upstairs and into a store room. Finn upturned some crates and seated Donald on one. He and Charlie pulled others near, sat and leant forward. Finn lit a cigarette, took two quick drags then offered it to Donald.

'My auntie says I'm not to.'

Finn patted his knee, relieved to hear him say something intelligible.

'You'll feel better. Here.'

With shuddering fingers, Donald managed to get the cigarette to his lips. Finn and Charlie waited until they saw colour flush beneath the grime on Donald's cheeks.

'Now, Donald,' Finn said in his best mother's voice, 'tell us what happened.'

'We went to lay the explosives. The guard's away. His wife and bairns were there. We told them to evacuate. The oldest lad ran for help, banged on a neighbour's door, so he did. A Volunteer shot him.'

'Was it you, Donald? Did you shoot him?'

'No.'

'That's alright then.'

'But he's dead. Shot in the back. As the door opened. He fell on her, the neighbour, and she screamed and there was blood all over her white apron. Really red, it was.' Donald's face puckered again.

Charlie said, 'You'd rather shoot than be shot, wouldn't you?'

Donald nodded.

'Look.' Finn slapped the younger boy's knee. 'He shouldn't have been raising the alarm; he had to be stopped. This is a war, MacCabe. Pull yourself together or I'll send you away to school.'

Donald shook his head. 'No! I'm staying. I'm in the IRB now. You're not making me leave.' His voice reached top C.

'Alright, but no more of this. Stay here until you feel better. Report to me later.' Finn gave him another cigarette.

They left, Charlie closing the storeroom door on a huddled Donald.

'Bloody hell,' he said, 'Shot in the back.'

Finn cut him off, 'Let's not think about it.'

They were on their way downstairs when shouts rushed to meet them.

'To your posts.'

'Man the barricades.'

'Don't shoot 'til they're within range.'

'Wait for the signal.'

Men jostled for space at the broken windows, kneeling behind the furniture barricades and taking aim.

Finn jumped the last three stairs with Charlie right behind. They squeezed in next to Hal who said:

'Cavalry charge. Here we fecking go!'

Finn peaked over their table. At the far end of Sackville Street a line of horses, mounted by soldiers in battledress, pawed the cobbles.

'Wait 'til they're in range,' Mr Connolly repeated as he dropped into place further along their makeshift battlements.

The room fell still. Finn heard a tiny buzzing. His eyes darted for the fly but he couldn't spot it. The buzzing continued, getting louder, closer. He wiggled a finger in his ear. It wasn't a fly; the buzzing was in his brain, lodged behind eyes fixed on the approaching target. He was taking aim to shoot at a cavalry charge by the British Army.

The cavalry colonel raised his sword, dropped it and bellowed, 'Charge!' The horses galloped, blackening the air with the sound of thunder.

A shot cracked out. Another followed and a third then several more, like dominos collapsing.

'Bloody eejits,' Hal muttered, 'They're not close enough.'

'Damnit, I said, wait. Wait!' Mr Connolly yelled above the cackling of rifles.

Now the horses were close enough. And the men on them. Finn sighted along the barrel. His trigger finger juddered. His whole arm stiffened with nerves. His chest tightened with a breath he couldn't let go of. Finn lower the gun, lifted his hand from the trigger, shook out the cramp and retook his hold. He aimed, lower this time, and fired. A chestnut bay stumbled, its unseated rider fought to get out of the path of rampaging hooves. Next to Finn, Hal fired. A soldier span out of his saddle, catapulted through the air and landed facedown. Street dust clouded up round him.

Hal jumped to his feet, punching the air. 'Woo-hoo! Did you see that? What a fucking shot!'

Finn yanked him down. 'You'll get your head blown off doing that.'

'Sorry, Captain,' Hal smirked. He reloaded but smoke and dust obscured the line of fire. When it cleared half a dozen horses lay felled; the rest of the column had scattered every way but towards the GPO.

'How many did we get?' Mr MacDermott came along the line.

'Not as many as we should have,' Mr Connolly grumbled.

That didn't matter to Hal, who crowed about his shot. Finn stared through the window, not listening; the chestnut bay was on the ground, struggling to get up despite the pink rip in its flank. A man knelt beside the horse, stroking its neck.

'Sir, I've shot a horse,' Finn blurted.

'Well done, Finn.' Mr MacDermott patted his shoulder.

'But, sir, it's not dead. It's in pain. What shall I do?'

'Do, Finn?'

'It's not right to leave it suffering, sir.'

'Perhaps you'd better go out and finished the job,' Mr Connolly offered.

Mr MacDermott raised his eyebrows at Mr Connolly. 'Go out to dispatch a horse,' he scoffed.

'Aye,' Mr Connolly said.

They eyeballed each other for a grim minute. Finally Mr MacDermott said, 'Can you provide cover?'

'With pleasure,' Mr Connolly replied, 'Go on, Finn, I'll keep watch but I doubt after that display there'll be much protesting from the Brits. They're probably away home for tea and crumpets.' He snorted, raised his rifle and positioned himself against the doorframe, gun trained on the street where the man continued trying to comfort the writhing horse.

With a retching feeling in the back of his throat, Finn counted himself down the steps and paced across the road. As he got within earshot the man glanced up.

'What do you want?'

'I've come to help.'

'Veterinarian are you?' he snapped.

'No,' Finn gulped, 'It was me that shot the horse.'

'What's a lad like you doing mixed up in this carry-on?'

Wordlessly, Finn removed the revolver from his waistband.

'Gonna put him out of his misery, are you?'

Finn nodded. The man stood. The horse rolled its head back. Finn saw despair in the animal's face. Eyes squeezed shut, he pulled the trigger, heard the bang as the bullet exploded from its chamber, felt the gun's kick, smelled the acrid burning and forced himself to look. The horse's eyes were still on him but it didn't see Finn now. He remembered Richard's last words, 'William, le do thoil*.'

He should have shot the horse clean first time.

'Isn't one war enough for yous?' The man stalked off, leaving Finn holding the smouldering gun.

For the rest of the day the GPO was busy but quiet, at least of military action. Men marked their own corners. Duties; sentry, cooking, first-aid, were assigned and Mr Clarke inspected the weapons. Two Volunteers had accidentally discharged their rifles, shooting themselves, fortunately not fatally, and it was revealed that the cavalry charge had been the first time many

* please

of them had held, let alone, fired a gun. Hal, still gloating, was drafted in to hold a training session for novice riflemen.

By early evening Finn was wondering if that was it. The British had launched one attack; it had proved costly and they'd decided Ireland wasn't worth the bother. Then a telegram boy knocked timidly at the GPO door and held a quivering envelop to Michael Collins who was on guard.

'For the commander-in-chief,' the boy stuttered, 'From Baron Wimborne.' He fled the steps, tangling himself with his bicycle in his eagerness to ride off, and fell, a comic mess of spokes, legs and handlebars. Fumbling, he remounted and peddled furiously to safety.

Collins gave the letter to Mr Pearse.

'What's that, Pat?' Mr MacDermott asked.

'Nonsense from on high,' Mr Pearse laughed. He climbed a post office counter. 'I have here something that will cheer your hearts, lads,' he shouted, 'We've won for ourselves the grand title 'Foreign enemies of the King'.'

A jubilant holler erupted.

'And that being so,' Mr Pearse continued, 'The Governor-General of Ireland gives us a free hand for he warns His Majesty's loyal citizens to abstain from 'conduct that might interfere with the action of the executive Government'. Sure, no man would describe us as loyal subjects. Therefore the warning pertains not to we ourselves. We are free to enjoy our rebellion.' Mr Pearse balled up the letter and threw it to the men. Whistling and jeering, they bounced it around in a mad game of hot potato.

Later Freddie crawled to where Finn lay in his sleeping bag. He set a ball of paper on the floor by Finn's head. 'Thought you'd like to know what it really said.'

Finn unscrewed the ball.

'The sternest measures are being, and will be, taken for the prompt suppression of the existing disturbances and the restoration of order.'

Tuesday 25th April

Finn went alone to the Roto. He wore the civvies he'd packed and travelled during morning rush, when he wouldn't be noticed.

The receptionist peered at him through half-moon spectacles. 'Can I help?'

'I'm looking for Cathleen Murphy. She's a nurse here.'

'What ward is it she works on?'

'I don't know,' Finn admitted.

'Young man, this is a busy hospital. I've no time to spare on such as that,' she snapped.

'What's the matter Miss Moorehead?' a passing nurse asked. She smiled at Finn and the icy receptionist.

'I'm looking for Cathleen Murphy,' Finn repeated.

'Cathleen, aye, she works with me. You must be Finn,' the nurse replied, 'I'm Elizabeth O'Farrell.' She offered Finn her hand. 'I'll take you to her. Thank you, Miss Moorehead.'

The receptionist sniffed.

Finn followed Nurse O'Farrell through the whitewashed corridors, upstairs to the second floor and onto ward fourteen.

'You'd best wait here, Matron's a bit sticky about people entering the ward,' Nurse O'Farrell said.

She went through the door. A minute ticked by; the door reopened. Cathleen emerged, sleeves rolled to her elbows, a stain on her apron and a strand of hair escaping from beneath her cap. She pressed herself against the closed door,

'If you've come to tell me it's begun my da already sent word.'

Finn shook his head.

'What then?'

'Mr MacDermott sent me.'

'Who's he, one of your lot? High up, is he? What's he sent to me for?'

'We're after doctors and nurses.'

'You've casualties?'

'A few but…'

'You're expecting more. At least you've the sense to be prepared for the worst,' Cathleen sighed.

'That's why I'm here,' Finn stammered, 'But I don't want you to come. I just thought you'd know others who might.'

The door inched open. Nurse O'Farrell's head appeared.

'Everything alright, Cathleen?'

Cathleen held herself stiff. 'Aye, Lizzie.' She fixed Finn with her eyes. 'I'm coming.'

'No, you're not!' Finn said, 'Just ask some others.'

'Ask what?' Nurse O'Farrell interrupted.

Cathleen ignored her. 'I meant it, Finn, about keeping you safe myself.'

'Safe from what?' Nurse O'Farrell demanded.

'I've come from the GPO,' Finn said in a low voice.

'The insurrection,' Nurse O'Farrell whispered. She moved Cathleen aside. 'Do you need medical supplies?'

'We've some bandages and whatnot but we're needing medics to help us with the wounded,' Finn explained.

'Can you manage until tonight?' Nurse O'Farrell asked, 'I'll put in some leave and come when my shift's finished.'

'Thank you.'

'I'm done now,' Cathleen said, 'Give me a minute to get my stuff.'

'No!' Finn repeated, 'I don't want you involved.'

'You've no say in this,' Cathleen snapped, 'and I bet your Mr MacDermott won't turn me away.'

Finn cursed the order that had sent him to Cathleen.

'Cathleen, please.' He reached for her hand and pressed it between his.

She yanked herself free and fled through the ward doors. Finn kicked the wall, the toe of his boot striking a dirty smear in the whitewashed surface.

'What's that poor wall done to you, so?' Lizzie rebuked.

'I don't want her to come,' Finn said, 'What if she…?'

'And what if you…?'

'It's my choice.'

'And hers.'

'She's only coming because of me.'

'And isn't that a grand reason?'

Finn slumped against the wall.

'I guess this isn't the first row yous have had about this.'

Finn studied the black and white floor tiles.

'You'll keep each other safe,' Lizzie added, 'and when this is done you'll have a fine story to tell your wee'uns. I'll be along later.'

Cathleen re-emerged from the ward clutching a bag.

'I've grabbed some dressings and bits and pieces,' she said to Lizzie, 'but if you get the chance maybe you can feck some morphine and iodine.'

'Aye,' Lizzie replied, 'See you after.'

Finn scuffed along the corridor behind Cathleen. In the street he stopped to light a cigarette with shaking fingers.

'Where's mine?'

Finn gave her the one he'd lit and lit another for himself.

She caught his arm. 'I said I wouldn't if you didn't. You are so I am too.'

'I don't want anything happening to you.' He scowled. She mirror his expression. He threw his arms around her, crushing her starched skirts against his wrinkled civvies. The tang of bleach clung to her hair. He breathed the fumes as though they was his last gulp of air.

'Finn, stop. People are looking.' She wriggled free and twined her fingers through his. 'Come on.'

Returning to the GPO Finn hoped to be greeted by the sight of a well-oiled military command. When he'd left that morning, GHQ was under the cool control of Mr Clarke and Mr MacDermott. Mr Clarke was talking of adding to their supply of homemade grenades, having discovered he wasn't the only IRB member with explosives experience. Mr Plunkett had been studying communiqués from other posts. Things had seemed in hand. But as Finn opened the door he was nearly knocked on his arse by a sprinting Volunteer carrying an armful of dressings. Another Volunteer with a bucket, water slopping from it, raced past coming the other way. They converged on a table with men clustered around it. Others loitered nearby, their faces pale, drawing on cigarettes.

'What's going on, Finn?' Cathleen asked.

Charlie materialized from the huddle at the table, spotted Finn and froze. Finn dashed to him.

'Is someone hurt? Cathleen's here. She might be able to help.' Finn waved Cathleen forwards.

Charlie chewed his lip. 'She's too late. It's MacCabe, poor kid.'

Cathleen gripped Finn's arm. He towed her along, battling through the crowd.

Donald was on the table, his face white, his eyes closed. A tiny smile lingered on his mouth. His hands were folded across his chest. Under them, red seeping between the fingers, was a scrambled hole.

He should have sent Donald home yesterday.

Finn ran, onto Sackville Street, over to Nelson's Pillar, and vomited his breakfast next to the proclamation.

'Are you alright?' Cathleen had followed him.

'It's my fault.'

'Charlie said it was an accident.'

'He shouldn't have been here.'

'You mustn't blame yourself.' She stroked his neck but he dodged from under her touch.

'Go away, will you?'

Cathleen crossed to the GPO and stayed on the steps, watching him. Finn paced around the pillar. Their first fatality was one of his lads. Finn kicked the flagstones beneath Nelson.

A Volunteer approached. 'Commandant Pearse wants to see you.'

'Tell him to go to hell.'

'I fecking will not.'

The Volunteer about faced. Reluctantly, Finn followed.

Inside Mr Pearse was waiting. He drifted towards Finn.

'A sad business, Finn, but that one so young should be prepared to give his life for Irish independence reminds us how great is the cause for which we fight. Take comfort in that, Finn.'

Finn thought of Donald's real reasons for fighting.

'I'll write to his people, tell them he died for Ireland,' Mr Pearse continued.

'No!'

Mr Pearse flinched.

'I'll do it. Sir,' Finn said, adding, 'He was under my command. It's my responsibility.'

'As you wish.' Mr Pearse made to leave but stopped. 'There's a roster for sentry duty. Check when your turn is, Devoy,' he said stiffly.

'Yes, sir.'

His shift on the roof was later but Finn swapped it with the next man up. He climbed the stairs and settled under the new Irish tricolour, an old exercise book he'd packed on his knee. The first pages were filled with algebraic equations. Finn turned to a blank sheet. The sun blazed overhead, dazzling on the whiteness. Finn chewed his pencil. In the street below the corpses of three horses from yesterday's cavalry charge lay rotting. Suddenly, two lads sprinted from a shoe shop, their arms laden with boots. As they skirted the horses a black cloud buzzed up. Finn knew he should challenge their looting. He crunched on the pencil, spat out a splinter, and scrawled, 'Dear Miss MacCabe,'. By the time he signed off, 'Yours with deepest regret, Captain Devoy,' the page was shadow-dark under the sinking sun.

Inside Finn was accosted by Willie Pearse. 'Pat has something to show you.' Willie led Finn to where Mr Pearse was ensconced in a small office with Mr Connolly.

'Have you finished your letter, Finn?' Mr Pearse asked.

Finn placed the paper, torn from his exercise book, in front of his commandant. Mr Pearse scanned it.

'Willie, will you see this is typed and sent to St Enda's; they can forward it. Finn, I'd be grateful if you'd read this.'

The document was headed, 'The Provisional Government to the Citizens of Dublin.' A phrase struck Finn. '"The valour, self-sacrifice and discipline of Irish men and women are about to win for our country a glorious place among the nations," he read aloud.

'I hoped you'd like that,' Mr Pearse said.

Finn raced to the end. The document was signed on behalf of the Provisional Government by P H Pearse, Commanding in Chief of the Forces of the Irish Republic and President of the Provisional Government.

'Sure, you're overwhelmed by events, Finn.' Mr Pearse drew towards him the paper which had fluttered from Finn's fingers. He came round to Finn, laid a hand on his shoulder. 'That we have such loyal lads with us is a joy to my heart.'

Finn awoke from his daze slumped against the wall outside the office. The King was dead, at least as far as Mr Pearse was concerned: long live the President.

Wednesday 26 April

The sun warming him, Finn wound his way through Dublin. Mr Plunkett had warned him to watch for British snipers but no shots pierced the sky as Finn strolled along in his Fianna uniform, a dispatch in his pocket.

At Trinity College Finn was about to step out by the university's majestic entrance when a flank of British soldiers marched along. Finn flattened himself against the brickwork until they tramped round the corner then reconnoitred the scene. In reply to their actions at the GPO, a Union Jack emblazoned the college flagpole. Coupled with the patrol, it confirmed the dispatch he carried was more urgent than Mr Connolly thought when he sent Finn to deliver it to the 'IRA Dublin' outposts. Finn retreated and, using a roundabout route, navigated his way to the city's south east quarter, the paper in his pocket growing more insistent with every stride.

Finn emerged onto Northumberland Road, went to the corner house, number twenty-five, and hauled his aching body up the steps using the wrought iron handrail. He knocked on the bright blue door.

A voice called, 'Who's there?'

'Captain Devoy; I've come from the GPO with a dispatch from Commandant Connolly.'

'Grand but come to the cellar window; we've barricaded the door,' the voice replied.

Finn retraced his steps and took the flight to the basement. When he got there a face was peering through the glass. The eyes were clear, the complexion fair and the expression jolly. The commander of this post was maybe only ten years older than Finn. He raised the sash and stuck his grinning face through the opening.

'Captain Devoy,' he said, 'of the Fianna, I see. Lieutenant Malone, Irish Volunteers, cyclist corps.'

He saluted and Finn returned, unable to suppress a smile: the Volunteer cyclist corps! Irish from handlebars to spokes.

'Come in, if you'll manage this window. It's the only way now and we'll be boarding it up later, in case we come under fire,' Malone explained.

Finn passed his haversack through then climbed into a basement filled with domestic jumble.

'You've a dispatch for us?'

Finn gave him the letter and began unpacking the supplies he'd brought while Malone read.

'I see we're to expect trouble from the Brits today.' Malone's voice hardened but his face kept its cheery countenance.

'I've seen some already by Trinity,' Finn said.

'If they're landing at Kingstown, they'll pass this way for sure and we'll be waiting for the blighters,' Malone declared, 'Will you take tea?'

Finn agreed and was treated to a tour of the fortifications while the brew stewed. In the sitting room he met the other three members of the third brigade. They welcomed him between slurps of tea. Finn perched on the sofa, scrutinised by a stern family portrait, while Lieutenant Malone revealed the locations of the other Mount Street positions. Chat turned to holidays; Malone had spent three summers jaunting around on his bicycle. He planned one day to cycle across America and quizzed Finn about the best sights. Midmorning, tea drunk and friendships born, Finn had to go.

He climbed out through the window. Malone passed through his pack, saluted Finn and offered his hand.

'Let's give them hell,' he said, grinning.

'Let's,' Finn replied, finding Malone's good cheer contagious.

From there Finn went to Carrisbrooke House, the schoolhouse, parochial hall and, lastly, to Clanwilliam House. Situated on the city side of the Grand Canal, across Mount Street Bridge, this was Mount Street's final defence. It was lunchtime when he arrived at the three storey Georgian property that occupied the entire block. The ground floor windows were boarded over and those on the upper floors had furniture bracing the panes. Finn walked up the garden path and rang the bell.

'I'll be damned, Finn Devoy,' David Reddin said as he opened the door, 'How the devil's yourself?'

'Hallo, David,' Finn said, 'Didn't know this was your post.'

'Last minute reassignment. What're you doing here?'

'I've a dispatch.'

'Righto, you can give it to our section commander.'

David led Finn into the parlour where, reclining on a chaise longue, sipping tea, was a stern middle-aged man with his arm in a sling. Seeing Finn, he set the cup in its saucer and stroked the moustache that bristled above his nose.

'Who's this, Lieutenant?'

'Captain Finn Devoy, Fianna Éireann, Red Branch, and a good pal of mine. He's come with a dispatch. Finn, this is Section Commander Reynolds.'

Finn saluted.

'Tráthnóna maith duit*, a Chaptaen♦,' Reynolds said.

'Tráthnóna maith duit, a dhuine uasail♣,' Finn replied.

Reynolds noted his Irish with a curt nod and offered up his palm. Finn passed over the now dog-eared envelop. Awkwardly, Reynolds removed the note.

'Better stick the kettle on, Reddin. If this is right, there'll not be time later.'

'What does it say, sir?'

'We're to repel the British advance at all costs.'

The last three words made Finn shiver.

'You'll stay for a cup, won't you, Finn?'

David's face beamed like he was asking a mate to a spiffing party. Shrugging off Mr Connolly's orders to return post-haste, Finn agreed.

While David made tea Commander Reynolds subjected Finn's Gaelic to a more thorough examination. Finn was passing easily when Reynolds abandoned the impromptu exam as David brought in tea and the rest of the Clanwilliam squad; Patrick Doyle, Richard Murphy and the Walsh Brothers, Thomas and James. David was filling cups when a loud bang rocked the building, spilling their teas.

---

* Good afternoon

♦ Captain

♣ sir

'What the bejesus…?' Doyle jumped to his feet, upturning his teacup.

'I believe,' Reynolds said, 'that was the firing of a rifle.' He eased himself to his feet. 'Man your posts.'

Finn faced the commander.

'You've a choice, lad,' Reynolds said, 'Go now, before the buggers get here, or stay and fight. I take it you've ammunition for that.' He indicated Finn's rifle.

'Yes, sir.'

'Well, quick lad, you've no time for thinking.'

'Stay, Finn. It'll be good craic♥, the two of us together,' David said.

'I'll stay.'

'Fine.' Reynolds issued orders with jerky words. 'You, round the back,' to Tom Walsh, 'Make sure they don't trap us in. You,' to Doyle, 'the side window. Keep Percy Place clear, that's the exit for number 25. Murphy, front room. Jim, cover the blasted canal. You two,' to Finn and David, 'upstairs with me. We'll keep them from getting up Northumberland Road.' Throwing off his sling, Reynolds sprang from the room, his feet pummelling the stairs.

Finn and David stared at each other.

'Reddin, Devoy, get your arses up here, now!'

Reynolds's yelling was accompanied by a volley of shots. Finn and David charged from the room, got jammed together in the doorway, struggled free and rushed the stairs, tumbling onto the landing.

Reynolds stationed David in one bedroom, Finn in another and took the landing himself so the road approaching Mount Street Bridge would be peppered with suicidal crossfire. All three waited, soaked by a tense silence.

The view from Finn's window covered Northumberland Road as far as the corner house from where Malone and his merry band of three were attempting to repel an entire British company. They seemed to be coping; the street was littered with bodies. Finn peered through the smoke, raking through the debris of men. Some crawled for cover in hydrangeas or

---

♥ fun

behind pillar boxes. Others, like mackerel netted and beached, flip-flapped on the cobbles. With his rifle stock, Finn smashed out a pane, shouldered his gun and cocked it.

From the landing Reynolds cried, 'Hold steady 'til they're within range.'

Finn took a deep breath and exhaled slowly.

The British regrouped. Bayonets drawn like swords, as though they were on a medieval battlefield, they charged Northumberland Road in clattering confusion. Shots flew from every Volunteer post. A soldier mounted the steps of number twenty-five and pounded the barricaded door with the butt of his weapon. Finn pictured Malone's smiling face, and aimed. The soldier shoulder-charged the door behind which a cheerful Malone was fighting off the legendary British Army. Finn drew the trigger towards his heart. The chambered round exploded and whirled through the sheer midday sun. The soldier was flung against the railings, teetering there a second before falling, out of sight, into Haddington Road. Finn rubbed a hand over his sweaty brow and reloaded with trembling fingers.

Line upon British line attacked the Volunteer posts. Finn fired again and again, at many targets then at one as the flanks thickened, becoming a single gigantic bull's eye. He picked holes in the British mob, leaving it mouse-eaten. His weapon began to burn his hands but Finn couldn't stop; he was inside a bubble, crouched at that second floor window shooting men floundering in flowerbeds below.

As suddenly as it started, it stopped. Cracks and bangs were clipped short. Smoke rose, exposing the dead and wounded. For the first time since taking his position three hours ago, Finn moved from the window. Reynolds was in the doorway.

'We need to regroup.'

Finn stumbled downstairs. David was already there, his face pale, a sheen of sweat filming his cheeks. Doyle, Murphy and the Walsh brothers ran in. Tom had a purple bruise on his cheek. Jim caught Finn staring and laughed.

'His bloody rifle recoiled. Don't worry, he'll live, won't you, Tommy?'

His brother, shamefaced, nodded.

Reynolds ordered they cleaned their weapons to prevent jamming when they laid down the next barrage. Finn had to help David with his. It stayed quiet.

'Tabhair spléachadh ar seo*.' Reynolds waved them to the window.

The street was awash with khaki figures: behind lampposts; crouched by railings; lying along low walls, their bulky packs betraying them; in the shrubbery and, most of all, in the road, a sickening khaki-mush carpet. Finn blinked. Like some hideous sludgy river, the mass moved. The throbbing body of men, now one glupey, half-digested mush, churned as if stirred inside a giant stomach. Finn gagged.

The bell rang, jarring the seven occupants of Clanwilliam House.

'What the blazes? Murphy, see who the devil's at the door.'

Murphy went out. The rest stayed in the parlour, coiled and cocked.

They heard Murphy ask, 'What is it you're wanting?' and a mumbled answer.

Murphy returned. 'It's a doctor, sir. He wants a ceasefire so the wounded can be removed.'

Reynolds scratched his head. 'Bring him in. He's libel to get shot standing on the step.'

Murphy disappeared, reappeared towing a man in a white coat and carrying a white pillow case daubed with a red cross, the paint glistening wetly.

'Are you in charge?' he asked Reynolds.

Reynolds saluted. 'Section Commander George Reynolds, Irish Volunteers.'

The doctor raised his hand as if to salute, thought better, and lowered it.

'What the hell's going on?'

'Under the command of Padraig Mac Piarais,' Finn noted the Gaelicisation of Mr Pearse's name, 'Commander in Chief of the Army of the Irish Republic,' Reynolds intoned, 'we're

---

* have a look at this

trying to do away with those blighters out there.' He folded his arms, wincing from the pain of his old injury.

'You've no authority,' the doctor began.

'I've written instructions to hold this position.' Reynolds fished in his pocket.

'I don't give a damn about your orders. There are men writhing in agony. I demand a ceasefire so my colleagues can get them to safety.'

'Granted,' Reynolds said, 'Sure, we're not animals. The British however…'

Gunfire shattered the silence.

'But I have your word?' the doctor pressed.

'Aye, my word.'

'Fine.' The doctor pirouetted on his heels; the door slammed.

'Murphy, fortify that door,' Reynolds ordered, 'Keep those pompous jackeens out.'

'Aye, sir.'

Finn stared through the window. Paddling in the khaki mulch were several white figures waving Red Cross flags.

Reynolds ordered the garrison to their posts.

'I don't trust these limeys. They'll take advantage of our Christian mercy. Be vigilant, lads.'

Murphy, Doyle and the Walsh brothers left. Finn hung back.

'I'm out of ammunition, sir.'

'There's more there.' Reynolds indicated a box on the hearth.

Finn raked through it. There was none to fit his small-bore rifle but plenty for the revolver tucked against his spine. He took a box of that.

'That's not for a rifle,' Reynolds barked.

'I know, sir. I have a revolver too.' Finn produced it.

'Jesus, we're better off than I thought if Commandant Pearse is issuing six-shooters to boys,' Reynolds retorted.

A shrill whistle pierced the air.

'Here!' Reynolds ordered.

Finn and David sprang to the window. A fresh wave of men charged Malone's stronghold despite two nurses remaining on the battlefield.

'What do we do, sir?' David bleated.

'Shoot but for God's sake miss the medics.'

Reynolds opened fire with his own revolver mid-order. Finn dropped into place next to him, with David on his other side. They stopped shooting only to reload. The column of men was mown like barley. A second column came forward to be scythed to the ground and a third. They came and came, waves on the sand. When the smoke cleared doctors and nurses resumed their bloody ministering.

Squatting under the windowsill, Finn struggled for breath. Cordite filled the room, torturing his lungs. He reloaded, his fingers practised and quick, and was ready to return fire when explosions flashed around the parlour. He shrank closer to the wall. The room came to life: chunks of plaster and wood leapt from walls and furniture; china danced off its shelves, hurled itself to the floor and shattered; a portrait above the fireplace convulsed as bullets ripped the canvas; the piano played a discordant melody as shrapnel struck the keys.

'Christ, they've a machine gun,' Reynolds muttered.

Murphy rushed into the room. 'Sir, it's on the church spire.'

'So shoot the bloody thing.'

'It's a church, sir.'

'I don't care if it's God's country-fucking-retreat, shoot it for Jesus' sake or we'll be shredded,' Reynolds bawled.

Murphy ran out. More machine gun blasts tore into the room.

For the rest of the afternoon, at twenty minute intervals, a whistle sounded, the British moved troops along the road and Volunteers fired, erasing each column only for another to replace it.

By early evening, rearmed with grenades, the British inched up the road, lobbing Mills bombs like cricket balls as they came. Finn's head throbbed, his arms ached, his eyes stung. He wanted a drink, a cigarette, five minutes of total silence. As he thought it, it happened. Finn closed his eyes, allowing the peace to soothe him.

A huge explosion exterminated the stillness. Clanwilliam House shuddered from rafters to foundations. Finn thought their position was breached. A towering pillar of black smoke, streaming from an upstair window at number twenty-five, revealed it, not them, had been hit. As the smoke swarmed skyward, Finn saw thick yellow-orange tongues of fire lap the building; he thought of amiable Malone and his men, trapped inside. On the steps a soldier was again trying to penetrate the homely fortress. Panicked, Finn fired; missed. The soldier disappeared through the door.

'They're in across the street,' he yelled.

'Hold your positions,' Reynolds called, 'For Jesus' sake keep firing on Percy Street; it's Malone's only escape.'

More khaki figures poured into the road. The barrage from Clanwilliam House repelled each wave only to see it restored and reinforced when the gun smoke thinned. The machine gun continued chattering. The sitting room walls, so punctured by bullets, let in shafts of golden sunlight, dust swirling in the shimmering rays.

Doyle rushed into the sitting room. 'The feckers're on the bridge.'

Murphy followed him. Reynolds barked for Murphy to get the Walsh brothers down as well and all seven fired on the bridge. The soldiers retreated as plumes of smoke obliterated the sinking sun.

'Clean your weapons,' Reynolds shouted, 'It might be the last chance we get and God knows we need them working now.'

They did as ordered, cursing as panic made eager fingers stutter over the task.

'Jesus, they're on the bridge again,' Doyle cried.

Half a dozen grenades smacked into the front of the house with rhythmical 'duff-duff-duff' sounds. Finn dropped facedown onto the carpet; it prickled his cheeks. The machine gun ta-ta-tatted again. For several minutes the seven could only lie prostrate, arms covering their heads, as bullets snapped and bit inches above them.

'We need to draw their fire,' Reynolds said, 'Murphy, Jim, get upstairs.'

The two Volunteers crawled from the room on their bellies. Jim's boots reappear immediately. Finn looked up. Jim was soaked.

'The stairs are shot away and they've gone through a pipe.'

'Can you get up there?' Reynolds asked.

'Aye, but not quickly.'

'Do your best.'

Jim ducked out.

'Doyle, get next door and keep firing on Percy Street,' Reynolds shouted.

Doyle crawled towards the doorway, made it and leapt to his feet.

'To be sure, this is a grand day for Ireland, isn't it just, boys?' he cheered.

'That it is,' Tom replied.

'Didn't I never think I'd see a day such as this? Shouldn't we be grateful that the good God has let us be part of a fight like this?'

The last word warm on his lips, a bullet struck Doyle's forehead, his legs buckled, he fell and didn't get up.

'Christ.' Reynolds rubbed his eyes. 'Clear that doorway.'

Finn and Tom scrambled over to Doyle. Finn heard Tom mutter an act of contrition as they dragged him aside. David made a crouching dash for it. A moment later he reappeared with a dressmaker's dummy which he propped in the far window. He had barely dropped for cover before Doyle's replacement was honeycombed by bullets. The dummy's dress, a blue cornflower print that reminded Finn of his nursery bedspread, began to smoulder.

From outside a voice hollered, 'Surrender.'

'Bollocks will I,' Reynolds chuntered, firing through air choked with fumes in the approximate direction of the voice. Reloading, he said, 'I'm away upstairs to see how they're fairing. You three stay here; fire all you can at them.'

Finn, David and Tom retook their places at the window to see another platoon massing on the bridge. They fired; the men disappeared behind an advertising hording. They emptied their weapons at it but couldn't tell if they hit anyone.

Reynolds returned with Murphy, a smear of red on his chin. Murphy threw his rifle across the room and snatched Doyle's dropped weapon. Finn saw the stock of Murphy's own gun was split to the barrel. Without a word Murphy sprinted back to reinforce Jim upstairs.

More soldiers swarmed the bridge. More Mills bombs struck the house. More explosions crumbled the brickwork.

A shout of, 'Fire, fire!' came down.

'I'll go.' Tom got up, leaving Finn, David and Reynolds to loose another volley on the troops crossing Mount Street Bridge.

The Brits advanced with fearsome recklessness; the thunder of gun fire obliterated all other sounds. Finn blasted, reloaded, blasted, reloaded and realised he was on his last six bullets.

There was a bang in the hall. Finn whirled around. Both Walsh brothers were there, their faces soot-black and streaked with sweat.

'The fire?' Reynolds asked.

'In the bedroom. We can't put it out,' Jim gasped.

'Where's Murphy?'

'Dead,' Tom said. He snatched a vase off the sideboard where it had miraculously escaped the hundreds of bullets that had strafed the room, dumped the daffodils onto the carpet and swigged from it.

'Bejesus, they're here,' David shouted.

Finn span back to the window as a grenade slammed into the frame, rebounded in the face of the private who'd thrown it, exploded and spattered his brains onto the geraniums. Nearby glass shattered and army-issue boots pounded the front steps.

'Surrender!'

'Haven't we've done all we can? Come on, lads.' Reynolds got to his feet. There was a sound like elastic twanging. Reynolds collapsed. Jim Walsh sprang to grab him but was too far away; the commander hit the floor. Jim and Tom knelt by Reynolds. David made to join them. Finn grabbed his arm.

'Bloody hell, David, keep shooting.' Finn fired two more rounds.

'Is he dead?' David gasped between recoils.

Finn checked over his shoulder. Jim had Reynolds's head on his lap. A large red pool had spread across the carpet but Reynolds wasn't dead. Tom held the vase to his lips, helping him drink. Jim bent forward, his mouth close to the ear of his commanding officer; his lips moved urgently.

'Is he?' asked David again, not daring to tear his eyes from the scene outside which, when Finn looked, was one of khaki bodies mounting the railings, scaling the wall and aiming rifles at Clanwilliam House.

'He is,' Tom said.

'What do we do?' David asked.

'You're the lieutenant, hadn't you better tell us?' Jim asked, resting Reynolds's head on the rug.

'Righto.' David faced them. 'We're getting out. Downstairs, now.'

They dashed from the room. On the way Finn swiped a box of bullets. They jostled on the stairs, tumbling into darkness. Every basement windows except one had been boarded and the door barricaded. Overhead soldiers' boots thumped.

'We'll have to go through that.' David pointed at the tiny unbarred window.

Tom sprang onto a chair, cracked the glass with his rifle stock and hauled himself through the gap. One by one they dropped into the back yard, vaulted the garden wall and regrouped in the alley behind.

'Find somewhere to hide,' David ordered, 'If you can, tomorrow head for Liberty Hall.'

'Steady around Trinity,' Finn warned, 'It was crawling with Brits earlier.'

'Grand,' Jim groaned.

'Fine,' Tom said, playfully shoving his brother. 'See yous later.'

They split into two pairs and ran in opposite directions.

Finn and David weaved along side roads, jumped garden walls and trampled through flowerbeds. Only when they'd left Mount Street far behind did Finn dare stop. Spying a narrow alley, he darted for it. David followed. Panting, they leaned against the cool stonework in silence. Finn's heart drummed. He sank to the floor and set about two essential tasks; lighting a cigarette and reloading his revolver.

'You want one?' He offered David the cigarettes but he was too breathless to speak.

In silence Finn finished with the gun.

David recovered. 'Where're we heading?'

'GPO, unless you've a better plan?'

'Will we make it?'

'Once we cross the river it'll be easy.'

There was more silence. Finn wanted to get going but sensed David about to speak.

'That was a bad business,' David muttered.

'We gave a good show of it.'

'I guess. Bloody waste though, don't you think?'

'What d'ya mean?'

'The way their officers kept sending them out for us to pick them off. Some were just lads.'

'Like us,' Finn said.

'Aye, but we've a purpose. And they're getting killed because of it.' David brought his hands to his face, inspected then dropped them and scrubbed his palms on his trousers, trying to rub off the gun residue that blackened them.

'Don't forget why we're doing this, David: for Ireland.'

David rose. 'Jesus, don't preach to the choir.'

Finn stood also. 'Sorry. I meant it's worth it.' He held out the revolver. 'If anything happens to me keep going.'

David sagged against the wall. 'Thanks for staying today, Finn.'

Finn exhaled his relief in a cloud of cigarette smoke, flicked the butt into the gutter and gave David his hand.

'No bother.' They shook. Finn was surprised at the warmth and strength in David's grip. 'We best go.' He tucked the gun in the front of his trousers.

'Yeah.'

Checking first, they stepped from the alley and went west along the quay, heading for the bridge Finn had crossed hours ago with the simple task of taking a dispatch.

Conspicuous in their uniforms and out past the British curfew, they kept to the shadows. Ahead the twin headlights of a motorcar shone, blocking their route to the bridge.

'We'll have to try further up,' Finn said.

They wound through the maze of streets by Trinity. Dread strangled Finn as they neared the college. They emerged from Moss Street. If they could make the dash they'd be only a couple of turns from the river and safety.

'On three,' Finn hissed, 'One, two, three!'

They leapt across Moss Street like they were jumping the Grand Canyon and landed in the side street opposite.

'Who's there?'

Finn felt David stiffen next to him; his own body was tight with fear.

'You are breaking the curfew. Identify yourselves.'

The voice, with its clipped tones, English accent and commanding volume, was a soldier's but the thick night had prevented him seeing their uniforms and shooting.

'Shite! What do we do?' David whispered.

Finn pulled the gun from his belt. He knew firing so close to a British garrison was risky but if his bullet found its target there might be chance to run for the bridge. Slowly, they began to turn.

A light blinded him. A shot fired out. David yelped. Finn whirled to him. David's hands were clamped to his stomach. The torch's white beam showed red running through his fingers.

'Finn.' He sank to his knees, clutching his wound.

Finn knelt beside him.

'David. Jesus, David.'

David held his gaze. He tried to speak. A trickle of blood dribbled from between his lips.

'David, don't.'

David's whole body convulsed. He toppled, facedown, legs splaying behind him.

'Hands up,' said the voice.

Beyond fear, Finn stood, holding his gun by his side, out of sight.

'I said, hands up!' the voice shrieked.

Light swung round the alley; Finn glimpsed their attacker. The soldier, a second lieutenant, was tall and thin, with an angular face and hooked nosed. From beneath his cap lank dirty-blonde hair showed. He wore the crest of the Royal Irish Fusiliers. He looked older than Finn would have pictured him but then Finn remembered he was older than he'd once claimed. The moment was an echo of the last time they faced each other; Finn recognised him easily.

'Keane.'

The torch veered onto Finn.

'Devoy,' Alasteir sneered, 'I knew you'd be mixed up in this but I never thought, when my father had me deployed here to help kick you Paddy bastards back into your bogs, I'd be lucky enough to get my hands on you.' Alasteir thumbed the hammer of his revolver, readying to fire.

Bile filled Finn's mouth. He spat it into the gutter.

He should have killed Alasteir when he'd had the chance.

Alasteir continued, 'Father'll be proud; I'll get a medal...'

He had the chance now.

Finn raised his weapon: bang. The torch clattered to the ground, the light snapping out. Finn fired again, heard Alasteir's body smack into the cobbles. He let his arm drop and, motionless, listened for the clack-clack of hob-nailed boots. None sounded.

Finn crept forwards. Alasteir lay on his back, staring with sightless eyes at a night sky that was a funny burnt orange colour. His face was spackled with blood. There were two neat holes in his chest. With his Fianna knife, Finn cut 'T', for traitor, in Alasteir's forehead. There were no regrets this time.

He went to David. He'd survived Mount Street to be killed in a fight that wasn't his. Finn wanted to get him to the GPO but reality checked him. He made David comfortable, sitting him against the wall then took his Bible from his shirt pocket but the print blurred into a watery jumble so he recited Cúchulainn's words, 'I care not though I live but one day and one night if only my name and deeds live after me.'

Finn vowed they would. He tore his captain's badge from his shoulder and rested it on David's clasped hands then fled into the night.

Thursday 27 April

To reach the GPO without encountering anymore Brits, Finn detoured along the Liffey's southern bank via several alleyways, a route that took him near Mr Colbert's post at South Dublin Union, on the city's western perimeter. He considered stopping there but fearing to find they too had fallen, kept on for the GPO, crossing the river west of the Four Courts and taking more backstreets in an easterly direction.

Around midnight Finn staggered onto Henry Street and brayed on the GPO side door. A sleepy Volunteer wrenched it open and Finn stumbled inside. He longed to sleep away the day but Mr Connolly, who'd sent him out fourteen hours ago, demanded a debrief. Finn reported succinctly; David's killer became an unknown enemy soldier who Finn had shot in order to escape. Had Mr Pearse heard his account Finn feared he'd have felt the pressure of the confessional and was glad to have been spared that; he didn't need absolution for killing Alasteir.

In the main room things were quiet. Finding his kit, Finn unrolled his sleeping bag, lay down and fell into unconsciousness.

The gun was in his hand. He fired. The soldier fell. He kicked the body over and saw David's face smiling up at him.

Finn woke with a start. A cruel dawn lit up the GPO's ruin. Bullets had perforated the walls; debris and rubble littered the floor. Everything was filmed with grey dust. Hal snored on one side; Freddie twitched on the other. A soft hand brushed Finn's shoulder. It was Cathleen, with a mug of tea.

'There'll be breakfast in a minute.'

Finn took the mug. 'You're still here?'

'I am, so's Lizzie.'

'Where's Charlie.'

'On the roof.'

'Patrick?'

Cathleen blinked. 'They brought in machine guns and artillery yesterday. He was at the window. We tried so hard for him, Finn.'

Hal leapt up, shouting, 'Get back you limey bastards.' Realising he wasn't under attack he ground sleep from his eyes. 'Any more of that, is there?' He pointed to Finn's tea.

'I'll fetch some,' Cathleen replied.

'Has she told you 'bout Patrick?'

Finn nodded.

'He was next to me. It was quick, Finn, honest. He wouldn't have felt it.'

'Yeah.'

Between sips of tea, Finn told Hal about Mount Street, David and Alasteir.

'The shite,' Hal said.

'It's my fault.'

''S not. How the hell were you to know he'd pop up again?'

Finn was too groggy to argue. It didn't matter anyway. He couldn't retrace his steps and restart. He didn't even know where the beginning was.

It was what it was meant to be. It would end the way it was meant to end. He accepted that now.

As dawn grew into day, having no doubt breakfasted heartily on kippers and kidneys, the British began their bombardment. Shells flew in on Sackville Street. Machine gun fire strafed the building. Snipers blasted at any mad man who appear beyond the GPO's portcullis. Dubliners finally acknowledged their main street was a war zone; the normally bustling thoroughfare remained deserted.

As the gunfire intensified a line of the Abbot's from Mr Pearse's play *The King* reeled around in Finn's head, 'The old wait for death but the young go to meet it.' Stationed at a window with a panoramic view of Sackville Street, Finn kept his rifle keen, waiting for his chance.

Mick Collins rambled over. 'Anything?'

'Nope.'

Collins squatted on the floor to roll a cigarette. 'Sure, this is the most cock-a-mamee plan since your man Cúchulainn tied himself to that rock. It's not how I'd be doing it,' Collins continued, 'We should be out there, picking 'em off, not penned in, waiting to be slaughtered.'

'You want to go out there right now?' Finn challenged as a sniper fired into the road.

'Aye, we could have ourselves some fun.'

'What've you in mind?'

Collins scanned the street. 'How's your fancy for unseating that ould bastard?' He gestured to Nelson.

Finn lowered his rifle. 'Fine but make sure Commandant Pearse knows it's your crazy idea.'

'Alright, if you get the explosives.'

Collins went in search of Mr Pearse. Finn requisitioned some charges. Charlie caught him carrying them to the door.

'What're you doing with those?'

'Going to have a bit of craic with Nelson,' Finn said.

'Out there? That's bloody mad.'

'And this isn't?'

Charlie pondered, then, with a shrug, tagged along.

At the door Collins directed Charlie to provide covering fire from behind the columns of the portico while he and Finn dashed to the pillar. Finn handed Collins half the charges and a length of fuse.

'I'll go left, you go right,' Collins said, 'We'll meet in the middle; blow the fucker to Kingdom-come.'

'Don't cut the fuse too short unless you want to go the same way.'

Collins grinned, winked and sprinted into the street. Finn chased after him.

When Finn got to the pillar a white flutter caught his eyes. Crouching, he saw the proclamation he'd pinned there on Monday. He shoved it into his pocket before laying the explosives and winding a length of fuse around each charge, trailing it behind him back to the GPO. Shots whistled overhead, high enough to ignore. Finn stopped halfway to jig on the cobbles until Collins caught up. Seeing his merriment, Collins grabbed Finn's arm and they reeled each other around, two demented Irish dancers.

A single shot struck the pavement at their feet; the sniper didn't reckon much to their performance.

'That's enough.' Collins dragged Finn under cover.

Huddled in the doorway, Finn and Collins lit the fuses. The wire crackled and two fizzing sparks pony-raced each other across the cobbles and over to Nelson. There was a pause. Then bang, bang, bang, bang.

'Damn. Bugger's tougher than I thought,' Collins muttered as the smoke cleared, 'Will we have another bash, so?'

They had two more goes and a third might have done it but Mr MacDermott appeared and bollocked them for wasting ammunition; Nelson stood to fall another day.

'I think it's time we had snipers of our own,' Mr Connolly announced after lunch, 'Who thinks himself a good shot?'

Hal's arm, and one or two others, sprang up. Finn knew his aim was decent, but sniping was too safe for his liking.

'What about you, Finn?' Mr Pearse asked.

'I'm not that good, sir.'

'He is, sir,' Hal said.

'Is that true, Finn?' Mr Connolly asked.

Finn nodded. 'But I'd rather be here,' he said to Mr Pearse.

'We need our best riflemen on rooftops, Finn,' Mr Connolly interrupted, 'O'Hanlon, Devoy and Hyde, come with me.' He strode to the door.

Finn shouldered his rifle. Cathleen, catching him leaving, grabbed his arm.

'Be careful, won't you?' She pecked his cheek.

Finn stifled a snort of laughter, squeezed her hand and stepped outside.

Mr Connolly surveyed the scene. 'Reckon they're concentrated there.' He indicated buildings left and right, opposite the post office. 'So we'll counter with positions here, here,' the buildings adjacent to the GPO, 'and there,' he pointed further down the street. 'O'Hanlon, see if you can get into that shop and up to the roof. Devoy, you the same there. Hyde, take the furthest post. If so much as a King Edward spud rolls into view snipe at it.'

They chorused, 'Aye, sir,' saluted, about faced and headed for their positions, leaving Mr Connolly on the GPO steps.

Finn sprinted for his target, a newsagents. The door wasn't locked; inside he found emptied sweetie jars on the floor and the shelves ransacked. Sheets of newsprint fluttered in the draught. The till lay on its side. The drawer was open; the money looted.

Finding the stairs, Finn climbed up. On the halfway landing was a window with a clear view of the street. Mr Connolly was still on the steps, tall and proud in his uniform. Finn longed for a pencil and pad: 'A soldier before his conquest'. Mr Connolly posed a moment longer for Finn's imagined sketch, then left his shelter to stroll into Sackville Street. Suddenly he spotted something and pointed. Finn looked down the bearing. Two Volunteers advanced towards Mr Connolly who signalled for them to go back. They didn't understand; gesturing furiously Mr Connolly advanced, moving further from the post office's safe shadow. The two men realised and retreated.

Mr Connolly, satisfied, was on his return stroll when, like someone had yanked his feet from under him, he toppled, legs akimbo.

Finn scanned the rooftops. Pale smoke puffed up, revealing the sniper's position. Finn smashed the window, sat astride the sill, pressing his spine against the frame for stability. A stubborn shard of glass speared his shoulder blade. Bracing against the pain, he took aim, firing two shots.

Mr Connolly lay motionless in the road, not far from Monday's now rancid horse carcasses. Finn cursed the sniper who had murdered Mr Connolly. But Mr Connolly wasn't dead. Using his arms, dragging his legs, the injured man began hauling himself towards the GPO. Finn yanked free of the jagged glass, feeling flesh tear and warmth bleed out, pummelled down the staircase and flew to Mr Connolly.

The man's face was twisted. Sweat dripped off his brow. His knuckles were white and his fingertips bloodied from inching himself forward.

'Sir!'

'Finn, thanks be to God. Can you help me? It's my ankle.'

White splinters of bone flecked the pulpy mass of skin and muscle shredded by the bullet's impact.

'Is it bad?'

'Let's get you inside, sir,' Finn said, 'Can you stand?'

Several rounds struck the pavement and ricocheted off. Finn yelled, hoping someone in the GPO would hear. An artillery cavalcade drowned his words.

'Don't worry, Finn,' Mr Connolly said, 'I can manage. Get under cover.'

'No.'

'I'll not have you endanger yourself for me, Devoy. That's an order.'

'Then you'll have to court-martial me for disobeying it, sir.' Finn smiled. 'Give me your arm, please.'

Mr Connolly, who was taller and heavier than Finn, rolled onto his side and, looping an arm under his shoulders, Finn heaved him to his feet. Limping and hobbling, Mr Connolly cursing the pain, they staggered for the GPO. A few feet from their objective, three Volunteers scrambled to their rescue; Mr Connolly was carried inside.

Finn sank onto the steps, panting. Sweat soaked his uniform and a chill ran through him. His wound throbbed. He fumbled in his pockets.

'Would it be one of these you're after?' Mr Clarke offered his packet of Players.

Finn reached for them.

'Maybes I'll join you.' Mr Clarke stiffly folded himself in half and sat beside Finn. 'I wouldn't be surprised if there's not a medal in that. Happen I'll recommend it myself.'

'I'd rather you didn't, sir.'

Mr Clarke stared at Finn. 'Aye, isn't Cúchulainn saying bravery's just another form of madness. Wouldn't be right giving a medal for that.' Mr Clarke laid a hand on Finn's arm. 'Don't you lose your head, lad. You've a long way yet, so you have.'

Finn's back thrummed with pain. He went inside, hunting for Cathleen, finding Lizzie O'Farrell near the backroom offices, now the medical rooms. Her nurse's pinafore was rumpled and stained. Her head was bare and brown curls sprang loose.

'Are you busy?'

Her arms were full of bandages. She laughed. 'Fairly. But if you're…'

'Could you have a look at my shoulder?' Finn turned.

'A Thiarna Dia*! Come with me.'

They went along the corridor. Several of the doors leading off it were open; Finn glimpsed white flashes as medics darted about. Lining the hallway were wounded men waiting their turn.

Lizzie found an empty room and bade Finn removed his shirt. There was a ripping sensation; he fought the urge to swear. 'I'll clean it.' There was a clink of glass and a cool touch on his skin that heated up sharply, the iodine stinging his raw flesh. 'Needs stitches.'

Finn glanced over his shoulder. 'Well?'

Lizzie said, 'We're not trained.'

'I don't care.'

'Alright. It'll hurt, mind.'

'Worse than the iodine?'

She laughed. 'Depends how steady my hand is.'

Lizzie pricked and tugged at the jagged cut. Finn felt his skin drawn tight, stretched to tearing. His eyes watered and every muscle was clenched against the raw stabbing that emanated from his shoulder and wormed down to his toenails and up to his eyebrows. He didn't know if he'd even got the sniper.

'There,' Lizzie said, 'Not bad, I'd say.'

The door opened.

'Lizzie, we're needing help with Mr Connolly.' It was Cathleen.

Finn twisted round. His shoulder screamed. He gasped.

'Finn. Are you alright?'

'Just a few stitches,' Lizzie explained.

'What's happening with Mr Connolly?' Finn pushed his pain aside.

---

* Goodness gracious

Cathleen rolled her eyes at Lizzie. 'That bloody eejit.'

'What?' Finn demanded.

'We've a medical student helping,' Lizzie said, 'Ten years and he still hasn't qualified.'

'Helping?' Cathleen snorted, 'He's attempting to put Mr Connolly under with chloroform so weak it wouldn't render a flee unconscious. I'm going to ask Mr Pearse to let Captain Mahony, that British Army doctor, help. Brit or not, he knows his business.'

They left. Finn picked up his shirt. Surprised to see it soaked with blood, he tossed it in the trash and went in search of a spare.

As the day marched on the barrages grew more frequent and deadly. The building was riddled by machine gun fire and sniper bullets; explosions rent Ireland's capital, reducing four and five storey buildings to kindling as the British honed their aim with the heavy artillery. When the first two shells hit, one down the street and one across it, the entire garrison flung themselves to the ground, cowering, but, as more came like aftershocks of an earthquake, they stopped only long enough for the roar to ripple away and the GPO to finish shuddering before picking up conversations mid-sentence, swallowing their tea or reloading their rifles.

At quarter to six, the GPO took a direct hit. A mighty boom thrashed the air. Dust and smoke fogged the room. Chunks of plaster and masonry pelted down. Nurses, wounded, Volunteers, commanders and prisoners, were scrambled together on the parquet flooring.

Finn staggered to his feet, squinting through choking smog at chaos let loose.

'Fire!'

'Man the hoses.'

Finn scrambled to where one of the building's several hoses hung. He uncoiled and dragged the floppy snakeskin over rubble, furniture, bodies, to the blaze. Grabbing a stunned Volunteer Finn bellowed above the din. 'Hold this.' He pressed the hose into the soldier's sooty hands, raced to the fire point and span the valve. Water spurted from punctures made down the length of the hose by rogue bullets. Only a dribble reached the nozzle.

'Get some buckets.' Mr Clarke had mounted a counter, trying to co-ordinate the fire-fight as flames flickered and danced.

Buckets were grabbed; a chain-gang formed. For three-quarters of an hour they fought a new enemy, beating it back, leaving the ruins to smoulder.

'Wish we had some bangers. We could have ourselves a camp-fire tea,' joked the Volunteer next to Finn.

Finn didn't laugh. Sackville Street was ablaze with a bonfire epic enough for the burning of a monstrous Guy Fawkes, roasted not at the stake but at the post.

That night the GPO reverberated with boots stomping, men shouting, fires heckle-crackling, machine guns cackling and long-drawn shell shrieks. Nobody slept. Faces, coated in black ash, flashed past each other obeying urgent orders. Prisoners and Volunteers alike fought the many fires bled into one, eating the building whole. The medical rooms were chock-full of men with searing burns. Nurses scurried with dressings, morphine, water, more dressings, iodine, more morphine. Mr MacDermott and Mr Clarke tried for order. Helped by Michael Collins, Mr Plunkett dragged himself from his sickbed to assist. Mr Connolly, paralysed with pain, watched with horror as the garrison was devoured. Mr Pearse wrote memoranda.

Finn thought if there was a hell it wasn't worse than this.

Friday 28 April

Dawn was tardy, black fumes hiding the rising sun until it was high.

The fires finally under control, the garrison breakfasted on hunks of dry bread and sooty water, the last of their provisions. Finn, Hal, Freddie and Charlie congregated in a corner with their rations. Charlie had been on the fire-fighting frontline most of the night and was blacker than a minstrel. Hal had both hands bandaged; he'd grabbed a fallen metal strut, not realising it was white-hot. Freddie had a deep gash above one eye where shrapnel had struck him. The ragged cut on Finn's back was smarting. He'd burst the stitches dragging a Citizen Army lad from the flames. The shirt he'd borrowed from Charlie was ruined; Cathleen had to redress the wound without stitches. The lad hadn't made it.

Hal met Finn's gaze. 'Sorry lot, aren't we?'

'I bloody say,' cursed Freddie.

'What next?' Charlie asked.

'Think we're about to find out.' Finn jerked his head to where Mr Pearse stood amid the ruin.

'Thank you for your efforts last night,' he began, 'I assure you that all you do is not in vain. At this moment the flag of free Ireland flies triumphantly over Dublin.'

'Here we fecking go,' Hal muttered.

'Inspired by our splendid action the manhood of Ireland are gathering to offer up their arms and their lives, if necessary, for this most holy cause.'

Finn thought 'if necessary' a redundant phrase.

'To have such grand men and women standing by us is testament to the mettle of we Irish.'

A cheer smothered Mr Pearse's next words.

'…given our current position I ask the women who have served us valiantly to hasten their exit.'

The cheer died. Cathleen's eyes locked on Finn's. He went to her.

'I'm staying,' she said.

Finn led her to an alcove.

'You aren't.'

'I'll not leave without you.'

'You must. You shouldn't have come at all.'

'It was my decision.'

'But made because of me. You've got to go.'

Cathleen fingered the chain around her neck. 'You're not my commanding officer.'

Finn pressed his forehead to hers. 'Just as well or this'd be highly irregular.' He kissed her soft mouth. 'I love you. I want you safe.'

'Come with me.'

'You know I can't.'

He drew her closer and kissed her again. 'Just go.'

She shook her head. 'This is what you want, isn't it, to be left to it? Left to…' Tears spilled down her cheeks.

'Please, Cathleen,' Finn coaxed.

She unfastened the chain and pressed the locket onto Finn, gripping his hands. 'I'll go if you take this and promise to bring me it back.'

Finn knew it was the only way to get her out. He had to save her this time, be the laoch* she didn't want. 'Alright.'

'I mean it, Finn.'

'I promise,' he lied, 'If I've done everything I can and there's nothing left, and if I can, I'll come.' He kissed her once more and led her towards where the other women were queuing for the signal to go. Lizzie joined them.

'You're leaving?'

Cathleen dropped her gaze.

'Of course she is,' Finn said.

Lizzie leaned forward and embraced Cathleen. 'Slán leat♥.'

Cathleen glanced to the door. 'Lizzie?'

Lizzie shook her head. 'I'll stay for Mr Connolly.'

Finn saw guilt in Cathleen's eyes and cursed Lizzie.

'Aye, that poor man. I should have thought. I'll stay too.'

Lizzie caught Finn glaring at her. 'It's little enough we can do for him, not enough work for two.'

---

* hero

♥ goodbye (to a person leaving)

'But why should it be you stays?'

'Because you've promised me you'll go,' Finn said crossly.

'I'll take it back and the necklace too.' Cathleen held out her hand for the locket. Finn clamped it in his fist.

'You're going. It's settled.'

'Let's let God settle it.' Cathleen turned to Lizzie. 'Have you a coin?'

'I haven't.'

Cathleen frowned. 'Finn, give me your saint.'

Finn's hand flew to his St Colmcille medallion.

'Isn't this the only fair way of it? Give it me, Finn, quick or we'll both miss the chance to leave,' Cathleen reasoned.

Finn saw the line of women filing through the door was growing short. He fiddled with the catch and slid the saint into Cathleen's palm.

'Call, Lizzie.'

Lizzie glanced at Finn. Finn scowled.

'Head's I go, tails you.'

Cathleen's thumbnail flicked the medallion; it jingled to the floor. Lizzie's skirt rustled as she bent down, snatching it up before Cathleen had chance.

'Tails it is,' she declared, handing Finn the saint. He nodded his thanks. Then she gave Cathleen a dashed hugged and retreated.

Finn drew Cathleen into his arms, clinging to her as the queue dwindled.

'You promised,' she murmured.

'So I did,' Finn replied.

He pushed her towards the queue's straggling end. Cathleen moved up with it. When her turn at the door came she cast Finn a last look and was gone.

He was fastening Cathleen's locket and his own chain around his neck when Hal called out on his way to the improvised medical rooms.

'Finn, lend a hand.'

Mr Connolly was reclined in bed, his injured ankle swaddled in bandages. Five Volunteers clustered around him.

'I want you to move me into the main room,' Mr Connolly instructed, 'Sure, I'm no use in here.'

As they half-carried, half-dragged the metal-framed bed into the fray, Finn wondered where it had come from. They settled it among the piles of rubble; Mr Connolly's aid-de-camp, a dutiful nursemaid, fluffed his pillows. Mr Connolly sighed and picked up the six-penny paperback that rested on the blanket.

'Has anyone a cigarette?' he enquired.

Finn produced the Players Mr Clarke gave him; someone else produced a light; Mr Connolly inhaled deeply.

'Aye,' he sighed, 'a book such as this,' he patted the murder mystery, 'plenty of rest and an insurrection to boot. This certainly is Revolution de luxe!'

Morning became afternoon; the circle of fire, flames and bullets ringing the GPO tightened. Businesses generations old collapsed in avalanches of debris. Swathes of red-orange light lashed the sky. Thunderous explosions rumbled and roared ceaselessly, punctuated violently when the oil works opposite the GPO ignited, propelling thousands of oil drums heavens high via Sackville Street. Finn was on his way to Mr Pearse with the latest report when the blast's savage howl stopped him. From an upper floor window he gaped and marvelled as drops of burning oil rained a fiery torrent.

Mr Plunkett's feet shuffled up behind him.

'It's the first time it's happened since Moscow, the first time a capital has burnt since then.' His voice was choked with pride. 'A revolution to remember.'

'Have you seen Mr Pearse?' Finn asked.

'Commandant Pearse is in his office.'

Grimacing at the familiar phrase corrupted by the new title, Finn trudged off; Mr Plunkett continued admiring the view.

The office door hung half off its hinges, a result of the blasts that had dislodged the building. Finn could hear Mr Pearse inside, speaking.

'When we're all wiped out, people will blame us for everything, I suppose, and condemn us.'

'Take heart in your own words, Pat.' It was Willie who spoke now. He continued:

'What if the dream come true? and if millions unborn shall dwell

In the house that I shaped in my heart, the noble house of my thought?'

Finn detected a growing strength in Willie's voice as he recited his brother's poem:

'Lord, I have staked my soul, I have staked the lives of my kin

On the truth of Thy dreadful word. Do not remember my failures

But remember this my faith.'

'Aye, *The Fool,'* Mr Pearse said, 'My own words. My own folly. My own poor faith.'

'Not poor, Pat, merely tested,' Willie said.

Mr Pearse sighed. 'Perhaps after a few years people will see the meaning of all we tried to do. You know, Emmet's insurrection is as nothing to this. Dublin's name will be glorious forever because of us.'

Finn was about to knock on the crooked door when Willie and Mr Pearse stepped through it. 'Coming to report, sir,' he stammered. His next words were annihilated by two clamorous crashes, the loudest so far; more of Dublin's vanguard businesses were toppled.

Waves of destruction broke over them and rolled out across the city. In the GPO below voices raised in song.

'Soldiers are we, whose lives are pledged to Ireland.'

'Listen!' Mr Pearse clapped his hands. 'Our brave boys are singing to us.' He bounded onto the landing and craned over the banister, adding his own voice to the joyous chorus.

'Come on, Finn,' Willie said, taking Finn's arm, 'Sing with us. There's nothing else for it.'

The GPO became a blazing mountain of debris. Men fell and no one picked them up; if they were dead so much the better. A hellish heat made the water from the hoses emerged as clouds of steam. Flames writhed and cavorted all around.

In the centre of the room, still in bed but having abandoned his jolly book, sat Mr Connolly. His head swivelled left and right as men succumbed to wounds, smoke and dehydration. The O'Rahilly was with him. Finn and Hal passed them with four more buckets of rapidly evaporating water.

'Another?' Mr Connolly yelled.

'Aye,' O'Rahilly bawled.

'Jesus, we'll run out of men afore we run out of bullets.'

'Just appoint someone who can think on his feet.'

'Finn.'

At the sound of his name Finn whirled around.

Mr Connolly beckoned.

Finn set down the self-emptying buckets and went over.

Mr Connolly grabbed Finn's hand. 'We're suffering many casualties. I'm out of, that is to say, am in need of another commander. You are he.'

'What?'

'Commander Devoy.' Mr Connolly pumped his arm now. 'You may direct the men of this garrison as you see fit.'

'No. Sir, I…'

'You can do it, Finn.' Mr Connolly made the matter final by saluting.

Finn, in reflex, saluted back.

The O'Rahilly pressed something into Finn's hand. 'Get that fixed on.' It was a commander's brooch.

Finn saluted again and staggered to his buckets. They were empty of all but a film of moisture. He picked them up anyway and walked, in a trance, after Hal.

'Where've you been?' Hal wiped sweat from his brow.

'Getting promoted.' Finn showed the badge.

'Hell, things that bad, are they?' Hal teased, 'Sure, you're not going to court-martial me for insubordination, are you?'

'Don't tempt me,' Finn muttered, pinning the brooch to his chest. He was a hero, by rank at least, whatever else happened.

Misters Pearse, Plunkett, Clarke and MacDermott gathered the commanders at Mr Connolly's bedside. Finn stood with The O'Rahilly on his right and Mick Collins on his left. Outside the sun died but not the fires.

Mr MacDermott spoke.

'We have concluded that the only course is to evacuate the garrison, establish a temporary GHQ in an adjacent street, then make for Commander Daly's post at the Four Courts.'

Finn pictured the map. It was a long journey to make under British artillery bombardment. If they could succeed though, united, they could head west, lose themselves in the suburbs, even the mountains, as Mr Pearse once suggested. The faces around Finn, stained with the blood and dirt of battle, were closed off. He held his own as rigid as possible; Mr MacDermott continued.

'To precipitate this evacuation an advanced party will sally into Henry Street to provide covering fire. Volunteers?'

The O'Rahilly raised his hand. 'I'll lead.' He drew a notebook and pencil from his breast pocket and began to calculate. 'Thirty men should be enough.'

Having done his utmost to prevent the Rising, O'Rahilly now coolly planned a suicidal run through the Dublin warren for its benefit. Finn wasn't the only one impressed.

'God bless and keep you, The O'Rahilly, the chieftain of your clan, for joining us at our very own Gethsemane.' Mr Pearse embrace the man who, last week, levelled a gun at his head.

'I'd like to volunteer too,' Finn exclaimed.

Mr Pearse shook his head. 'It's better you stay with us.'

'But, sir, I want to.'

Mr Clarke eyeballed Finn sternly but addressed O'Rahilly. 'Ask for volunteers,' then to the others, 'Divide the men into sections. Prepare for departure. As soon as O'Rahilly's in place we go.'

'Any questions?' Mr MacDermott said. There weren't. 'Dismissed.'

Finn ran to tell Hal, Charlie and Freddie.

'That's it, so?' Hal grumbled.

'We can't do a bloody thing while every man-jack is filling buckets. Get your kits together, what's left of them, gun and ammunition. We'll see what's to do later.'

'Finn's right,' Charlie said, 'Let's go. It's far too hot plus I'm starving. Isn't there a bakers on Moore Street? With luck we'll be having cake for tea, eh?' He nudged Hal, 'Don't know how you haven't succumbed to starvation on this rebellion diet.' He shouldered his rifle.

'Cakes,' Hal said, 'Righto.' He grabbed his rifle.

'So it's true, about an army marching on its stomach,' Finn teased.

'Isn't it right that the CO buys his troops dinner?' Charlie joked.

'Aye,' Hal chimed in.

Freddie said, 'I'll have the chicken.'

'Steak for me,' Charlie added.

'Make that two, mind, I could eat two myself,' Hal moaned.

'Shall I take orders?' Finn reached as though for an order pad.

'I'll keep you to that.' Charlie winked at Finn.

All three saluted, grinning madly. Finn grinned back. He'd got Cathleen out; if he could get his mates out it would be alright.

Finn ran around, barking instructions and rallying men, twice bumping into Collins who was doing the same but less chaotically. The able-bodied helped the wounded. Prisoners were humanely released out the front, holding a tattered white flag and providing a handy diversion.

Finn assembled his kit: rounds for his rifle and revolver; his Fianna knife sheathed on his belt; the medical tin, stowed in his tunic pocket and, in his haversack; the set of civvies, his canteen, empty, Cathleen's *Táin*, the photographs still between the pages, and what was left of his rations, a bag of pear drops. His mother's Bible was now in the pocket of his second borrowed tunic.

O'Rahilly assembled his thirty across the room. Finn heard the order, 'Move out!', glanced up and spotted Charlie amongst them. He leapt up after them but got trapped behind three men moving Mr Connolly, bed and all, closer to the exit. Finn jostled around them in a clumsy dance. Charlie had reached the door. Finn yelled his name. Charlie turned, his wide blue eyes sparkling through the fumes. Finn stared into them and beckoned Charlie back. Charlie smiled, waved and passed through the doorway into Henry Street.

Falling over his own feet, Finn floundered across to the door but it was closed and Charlie gone when he reached it.

Hal slapped a hand on Finn's shoulder. 'He's promised to get the cakes in.'

'Why didn't you stop him?'

'He volunteered.'

'You should've stopped him.'

'I'm not the bloody commander,' Hal snapped, 'Hell, it'll be fine, we'll all be having tea and…'

'You say cake once more and I'll knock you on your fucking arse.'

Finn shrugged Hal off and wrenched the door open. The last of O'Rahilly's squad stampeded out of sight. Finn pounded after them. Fingers scraping brickwork, he grabbed the wall and threw himself round the corner. Machine guns sang out. Finn ducked as bullets splintered the bricks, pinning him against the wall. Buried beneath the guns' roar was the rallying cry, 'For Ireland,' and the pounding of thirty pairs of feet. Finn listened, his heart clamouring, as shots, shouts and footsteps faded to silence. From his belt he grabbed the revolver and plunged into Moore Street. Ahead was a carpet of fallen men. A final gun-crack sounded. Cordite stung his nostrils. He scoured the scene for Charlie. Halfway along the entry O'Rahilly was slumped against the wall. Finn dashed to him. O'Rahilly had his notebook on his lap and was writing on the page adjacent to his attack plans. Seeing Finn he said, 'For my wife.' His pencil slipped from trembling fingers; the last word spiralled into a miserable scrawl.

Finn raked among the bodies, hoping Charlie was already in the bakers, stuffing his face with jam sponge.

'Finn.'

The hoarse whisper was Charlie's. Finn found him lying on his back, gazing at the narrow slice of sky visible above the alley. His breathing was ragged. Blood stained the cobbles where he lay. His freckles stood out starkly against bloodless cheeks.

'Jesus, thank God. Come on, I'll help you up.'

Charlie shook his head.

Finn scrabbled for his morphine phial. 'I'll just…'

Charlie cut across him. 'Tell Hal he can have my steak.' His hand fluttered up. Finn seized it, felt Charlie squeezing and squeezed back.

'Don't be daft.'

Charlie smiled. 'Mind you kick their arses, Finn, just like…'

Finn felt the grip on his hand slacken then drop away. Hot tears scalded his face. He grasped Charlie's hand again, crushing it. Charlie lay still, his eyes open to nothingness.

A fresh hail of bullets zipped up the street, bouncing off the brickwork. Finn pressed his ear to Charlie's chest, searched for a pulse, pawed at Charlie's tunic and felt the fabric sodden with warm sticky wetness. Charlie was dead.

More bullets pinged and whizzed overhead.

Finn jumped to his feet. 'Let's have it, so! Fucking shoot me.'

Something punched him on the chest, knocking him against the wall, smacking air from his lungs, sight from his eyes. Everything fell away. He let it go.

'Oi! You! What the fuck're you doing? Get back here!'

Finn sat up. Collins was leaning into the alley, gun drawn.

'Christ, Devoy, that's an order. Get off your arse. Don't you make me come for you, you wee fucker.'

Finn groped at his chest, felt the hard edges of his Bible. He withdrew it; the bullet was buried deep in the psalms. Shoving it into his pocket, he lurched up and ran for the alley entrance. Collins grabbed his tunic, yanked him round the corner and towed him to the GPO, crashing into the door and ploughing through it. They hit the tiles, a jumble of arms and legs, Collins' gun dancing dangerously between them. For five seconds they wrestled each other. Finn was trying to get free. He didn't know what Collins was doing. Feet planted on the floor, he pushed off from Collins who leapt up.

'Jesus! Shouldn't I knock your fucking block off, you bloody eejit.'

Finn punched his fists into his pockets to keep from punching Collins, turned, spotted Hal and Freddie watching, paralysed by realisation, Hal's hands coiled into fists, Freddie's eyes shimmering behind grimy spectacles.

'Devoy, what the hell were you doing?' A panting, red-faced Collins span Finn round.

'Fuck off.' Finn shoved him. Collins staggered but didn't fall. Finn rubbed a hand over his cheeks, smearing dirt and salty water.

He should have stayed William forever. Then Charlie would still be alive.

Finn dived into the curious crowd, parting it. As the men shrank away Mr Pearse surfaced. He raised a coaxing hand to Finn who stopped beyond reach.

'Little Hound,' he murmured, his eyes misty and vague as if in the thrall of something not there, not real; a dream, a myth: a legend.

Finn saw now there were two Mr Pearses: the everyday man who worked tirelessly, his actions practical, material, done for Ireland's future good; and this other, the dreamer, who lived in and for the Ireland of long ago, an Ireland only real in the dreams of poets: Cúchulainn's Ireland.

Eyes glassy and fixed on Finn, Mr Pearse glided towards him. He stroked Finn's cheek. 'Little Hound, fear not for there is no stain on your character and no slight on your courage. The boy troop of Emain Macha could not be saved. Theirs was a proud and great sacrifice.'

The words cast a spell on Finn:

'Twas to a wild and barren place they travelled, the White Bull's homeland. There in the ford would they fight, their swords not to slash softly and their sorrows to pour forth onto the ground that would be the last bed of one.

The young warrior readied his sword, spear and shield. With these, his youthful strength, truthful tongue, pure heart and the Gaelish fervour thrumming in his breast, would he slay the old king and free his homeland.

The old king likewise readied, him to slay the gossoon who challenged his kingship. With words given him by sages and monks, words he had swallowed and made of himself, would he vanquish the boy warrior and retain sovereignty of Eire.

Into the ford they went. Into the battle they went. First they clashed with shields heavier than the rocks of Ulster's giant sea-steps. With limbs snapped like the brittle rose in winter on they battled. Next they flashed swords with blades ice-hardened in glassy Leinster loughs. With rivers of blood running from them on they battled. Lastly they hurled stabbing-spears with points sharper than the Munster cliffs. With flesh torn and hearts laid bare they broke off and threw aside their weapons.

The old king spake: If I die let it be in search of the love of the Gael.

The young warrior spake: If I die let it be in defence of the life of the Gaels.

The old king answered: Say you that you would die for the unworthy prize of mortal lives?

The young warrior beat his bloodied breast and declared: And you would die for the unworthy prize of fickle hearts.

With these words the boy warrior reached for his gae bolga, forged by the jagged Connacht mountains, and flung the death-spear at the old king. Into his chest it went. Into his heart it went.

The old king was vanquished; the old order cleansed in the ford's red flow. The heroship of the day belonged to the boy warrior. He spoke over the fallen king: Now you have I slaughtered on this Táin. You dead and I alive. Bravery is battle-madness.

Thence the young warrior faced the hills and set off in defence of the lives of Gaels.

Finn pulled the knife from his belt and lunged at the old king. He stabbed the villainous dreamer, the unreal Mr Pearse, thrusting the blade in up to the hilt; bringing it out gore-stained. Trickles of blood ran between his fingers. Finn thrust again, the blade slicing flesh and muscle, striking bone. He had to cut out the words of the old king. 'If I die let it be in search of the love of the Gael.' Finn slashed; the words fell to the floor in thick red gouts. He hacked until he'd cut out the dreamer's heart. He went to meet his own death. 'If I die let it be in defence of the lives of the Gaels.'

'That was a brave thing you did, Finn, rushing out there.' Mr Pearse was speaking in his everyday voice and stroking Finn's cheek. His touch broke the spell.

Finn jerked his face away. He was awake; the dream was over. They were poised to fall. He stared at his hand; there was no bloodied blade.

Another shell hit the rear of the GPO. The room quaked with redoubled violence.

Someone called, 'Pat.'

Mr Pearse moved off.

Finn scrambled through the ruined building. The roof was gone, the walls reduced to rubble. He headed to the central quad where, seated on a mound of crumbled bricks, he pulled out a cigarette, snapped almost in half but smokeable, and lit it with stiff fingers. He felt too old to go out again for a meeting with death.

'Finn, what are you doing here?' Willie Pearse sprang up in the fractured doorway. 'We're ready to go. Come on.'

Finn cast a final glance to the sky, hopelessly searching for a friendly shell.

Mr Pearse addressed the men by the Henry Street exit.

'When we go out there I want you to be ready to face the machine guns as if you are on parade. You have fought valiantly; Ireland thanks you.'

Volunteers double-checked rifles, shouldered kitbags and stood to attention. From the chaos, Finn unearthed Hal and Freddie.

'I want you to look for a chance to get away.'

Hal gaped. 'What do you mean?'

'I mean escape this madness.'

'You're not serious?' Freddie cried.

'I bloody am.'

'That's desertion. They shoot you for that,' Hal said.

'You're going to bloody-well get shot anyway, when they capture you,' Finn said, 'For Christ's sake, Hal, it's finished. We've lost. I'm your CO and I'm giving you a direct order: get yourselves the hell out.'

'What about you?' Hal demanded.

'Forget me. It's you I'm bothered about.' Finn grabbed their wrists.

'Screw your courage to the sticking place,' Freddie quoted.

Finn snapped, 'This isn't a fucking play.'

They pulled free of him. Hal clenched his jaw. Freddie folded his arms.

'They're all dead,' Finn shouted, 'because of this; Sean, Donald, Patrick, David. Charlie. I can't have you two ending up that way.'

Hal shrugged. Freddie dropped his gaze.

Mr Pearse, sword raised, gave the order. The door was opened; a queue of men bustled into Henry Street to face eager bullets.

Along Henry Street, down, into Moore Street, side-stepping the fallen, ducking, holding arms above heads, tensing muscles, clenching teeth, squinting eyes through acrid smoke, wailing and flailing like men in fire, on ice, clumsy, frantic, wild, crack, bang, smash, shriek, howl, scream, stutter, rattle, fump, fump, fump.

'Halt!'

The order travelled the line. Men crashed into each other. Machine guns rattled behind them, firing on the gruesome graveyard in Henry Street. Ahead boots pounded, wood splintering and crunching, as men kicked doors, sought cover in terraced houses. Freddie and Hal merged with the rabble. Finn tried to follow, shoving at the crush of men, but was jerked away. He twisted round. Lizzie O'Farrell was holding his haversack.

'Cathleen'd never forgive me if I let you out of my sight. This way.' She towed him towards a house as Mr MacDermott slipped inside it. Mr Plunkett and Mr Clarke waited on the pavement, the younger man leaning on the veteran. Lizzie and Finn entered last. Under Mr Clarke's orders, Finn wrestled a sideboard against the buckled door.

The air was putrid. They'd broken into a fishmongers. On the counter bloated maggots wriggled over last week's catch of the day.

'Don't think I'll be eating fish again, not even on Fridays,' Lizzie said as she and Finn surveyed the shop.

Mr MacDermott appeared through a side door. 'Finn, you found us.' He mopped his brow with a grubby handkerchief.

'While we're holding counsel could you search the place for anything useful?'

Finn scowled at the order; he had to find Freddie and Hal.

'I'll check on Mr Connolly.' Lizzie left the fish-rank shop with Mr MacDermott.

Finn followed through the doorway. Across the hall from the shop was a parlour, bullet-holed, smashed and dusty. He climbed the stairs. On the landing the east windows were punctured by bullets; the west windows fractured by artillery blasts. He checked the bedrooms, aged a century in a single week. In one a teddy bear sat on the bed, a bullet hole in its forehead. Finn stroked the wound, mourning the death of innocent things. The window granted a frightful view of the blazing GPO. As Finn stared the roof collapsed. Spurning the fate that had nearly been theirs, he left the bear on the windowsill, guarding, and trudged downstairs to make his report.

The Rising's bedraggled leaders clustered in the kitchen. Mr Connolly, pale and sweating, groaned quietly. The others watched Lizzie's ministrations with grave expressions.

'If only I had a dram of morphine,' she muttered.

Finn offered his medical kit.

'Bless you,' Mr Connolly said.

'Have you discovered anything useful, Finn?' Mr MacDermott asked.

Inching towards the door, Finn shook his head.

Mr MacDermott said, 'We need to consider our strategy. I propose we leave at dawn and make for the Four Courts. We need to send word to the commanders.'

Finn stopped creeping towards the exit. 'I'll go, sir.'

'Are you sure, Finn?' Mr Pearse asked.

Finn couldn't speak to him; he answered Mr MacDermott instead. 'Yes, sir.'

'Thank you, Finn,' Mr MacDermott said, 'I'll write a dispatch. You need only take it next door, from there someone can pass it on.'

Finn paced the hall. He had to find them, make them leave, get them safe.

'Finn?' Mr Pearse, framed in the kitchen doorway, waved a scrap of paper.

Finn strode up and snatched it.

Mr Pearse flinched and hid his empty hand in his pocket. 'If you see Willie please can you give him this?' He offered Finn a second sheet. 'And no foolhardy acts of bravery, please.'

Without a word Finn slipped through the kitchen and climbed the wall into the next yard. He brayed on the backdoor. It was nudged open by a rifle muzzle; a Volunteer peeked out.

Finn saluted. 'I've an urgent dispatch for your commander.'

'I'll fetch him,' the lad stammered.

'Hang on.' Finn caught his arm. 'I'm also after two of my Fianna brigade, O'Hanlon and Blackwell. If they're here send them too, tell them it's an order.'

The lad bobbed his head and retreated.

Finn leant against the house, counting bricks in the yard wall.

'Hallo, Finn. You've a message from Pat, have you?' A smiling Willie Pearse held out his hand.

Finn passed the note.

Willie read, murmured, 'Righto, Pat,' and slipped the paper into his pocket. 'You're after a word with your pals too, are you, Finn?'

Finn blushed. 'If that's allowed, sir.'

Willie laughed. 'It's a poor do if a CO can't see his men.' He made to leave.

'Sir.'

'Aye, Finn?'

A hundred different memories of Willie jostled Finn.

'Did we do the right thing, sir?'

'We did what was in our hearts.'

'But, sir, the casualties? Is it right, what we've done?'

'The doing was ours, not yours, Finn.'

Finn pictured Moore Street, bodies burying bodies, one of them Charlie's. His throat tightened, words choking him. He forced them up. 'Aren't you afraid, sir?'

Willie spread his hands. 'Whatever the Lord wants for Pat and me we'll take with good grace.'

Finn heard peace in those words, and goodbye. Something snapped inside him. A sob gulped to the surface.

Willie rested his hand on Finn's shoulder.

'It's alright to be afraid. It's conquering fear that makes you strong. Remember, Finn, being brave's not being unafraid; it's being afraid and doing a thing anyway.'

Another sob burbled up from Finn's stomach. 'We're all going to die.'

'The Lord knows what he's about.'

Finn drew the Bible from his pocket, the bullet buried in its heart instead of his. 'Does he, sir?'

Willie took the book and traced the indentation with his forefinger. 'Aye, Finn. This proves it. Those who have more to do will live to do it.'

Willie clasped Finn to him. Finn melted into the warm arms and cried.

'Anois, anois*.'

Finn swallowed the last of his guilt and stepped free of the comforting arms.

Willie gave him back the Bible, kissed him on both cheeks and shook his hand. 'Now I'll fetch those lads of yours.' And he was gone.

Freddie appeared on the doorstep. 'You can't order us to leave. We're staying to the end.'

Finn rubbed a grubby sleeve over his face, balled up his fear and steeled himself with desperate anger. 'And what the hell do you think that's gonna be?'

Freddie shrugged.

'If they capture you they'll hang you.'

'They wouldn't. We'd be prisoners of war.'

'You'll be traitors to the crown. They'll hang you with fucking pleasure.'

'Then they'll have to hang us all, so they will.'

---

* there, there

'Not me,' Finn crowed, inspiration quickening his pulse, ''cos I'm a Yank. I've only to show my passport and I'll be sent safely home, my father said so.'

The door bounced off its frame with a hinge-splitting crack. Hal pushed past Freddie and charged into the yard.

'That's what you're gonna do, so, run home to Daddy?' Hal slammed Finn against the wall and started searching him. 'Where is it? Where the fuck is it?'

'I threw it away Sunday night, at school. I'm finished doing what he says.'

Hal continued his rough frisking. Finn shoved him; Hal fell.

'I said, I chucked it and I'm bloody glad I did. That bastard, he knew he'd ballsed it but sent us out to die anyway. You've got to leave.'

Hal got to his feet. 'The fuck will I.'

'Then they'll put a noose round your neck. Hal, Freddie.' Finn lowered his voice. 'It's not fair. You don't deserve this. Please, you need to get away, now.'

Hal snorted, 'Gonna run for it and after dragging us with you, so's you don't feel guilty?'

'No!' Finn shook the punctured Bible at them. 'Haven't I tried to get myself shot? It's what I deserve, but not you.'

'Deserve?' Freddie asked.

'Yes.'

'For shooting a few limey shites? You're just having a crisis of whatsit, boyo.' Hal tapped Finn's cheek. 'This is war, Finn.'

'Charlie's dead 'cos of me. David, Patrick, all of them. As far back as Richard. I've been so fucking stupid!'

'What'd you mean?' Freddie asked.

'Letting yous get dragged into this because I'd some grand ideas from my fucking father, the big man, the unconquerable Fenian.' Finn spat the last three words. 'I'm sorry. I should've known better. It's his fault, this, but I'm to blame, me with my daft dreams of being a fucking hero.'

'Didn't we think that too?' Freddie looked to Hal who nodded.

'Sure, we all wanted to be heroes for Ireland. Hell, we still will be,' Hal added.

'No, you'll be dead,' Finn said, 'And that'll be my fault too.'

'Shite it will.'

'You've no cause to be sorry. We decided for ourselves, to fight for Ireland,' Freddie reasoned.

'But we can't win this way. It was just a dream,' Finn pleaded, 'Mr Pearse's dream, and he was seven shades of wrong. If you get away now there'll be other chances, other fights.'

'We've not done with this one yet,' Hal said.

Finn sagged against the wall. 'Go. Please.'

'How can you ask us to do what you can't? You can't, can you?' Freddie said.

Finn, head bowed, replied, 'No.' He dropped the Bible. It landed with a dull whump.

'Then,' Freddie said, 'you know why we can't either.' He retrieved Finn's Bible, gave it to him and kept his hand held out, 'Don't let's leave it like this. Cairde go brách♥?'

Finn could see the scar on Freddie's palm from the blood oath they'd sworn on his birthday. He grabbed Freddie into a hug. Hal threw his arms around both of them and they clung to each other. Finn knew once he let go they were off down different roads, parallel maybe, but never crossing. Tears scorched his eyes.

'Hadn't you best get going?' Freddie asked.

'Yeah.' Finn dragged himself away. 'Ádh mór ort*. Slán♣.'

'Ádh mór ort, Finn,' Freddie replied, 'Slán.'

'Aye, good luck to yourself, Finn,' Hal said, 'Be seeing you.'

Bible in his pocket, Finn clambered up the wall, sat astride it and gazed down. Freddie and Hal stood together, smiling and waving. Finn waved back. He understood they thought there was nothing for him to be sorry for but he still was. They stopped waving but kept smiling. Finn swung his legs around and slid into the fishmonger's yard. He pressed close

---

♥ friends forever

* Good luck

♣ goodbye

to the wall, listening. On the other side a door closed. He cursed his father and was glad he'd thrown away the passport.

Only when Mr MacDermott asked for a report did Finn realise he'd forgotten to give Willie the second note, the one from brother to brother.

Saturday 29 April

They bedded down in the parlour. Mr Connolly was in agony and Finn's supply of morphine used up. Too overwrought for sleep, the slightest noise startled them.

Finn tormented himself with thoughts of Freddie and Hal, picturing them shackled, imprisoned: hanged from the gibbet. He was glad when his turn for the watch came. All but Mr Connolly took a two hour stint as look-out. Finn's was the fourth. Mr Pearse would take the final one and rouse them before dawn to mobilise.

Finn huddled by the window, the deserted streets illuminated by blazing buildings. He was pondering whether or not it was time to wake Mr Pearse when the commandant came to sit beside Finn, his army greatcoat around him, his thinning hair plastered to his forehead.

'All quiet?' he whispered.

Finn forced himself to reply, 'Yes, sir.'

'You haven't any water have you, Finn?'

Eyes fixed on the window, Finn shook his head but dumped his bag of pear drops at Mr Pearse's feet.

'Grand.' The headmaster sucked one. 'You should try to sleep, Finn.'

Finn was about to crawl for his patch of floor when a white flicker caught his eye. He snapped back.

'Are you alright?' Mr Pearse asked.

'Look, there!'

Three figures emerged from the swirling smog; a man, woman and girl, twelve or thirteen. They shuffled forwards, The man carried a tattered white rag tied to a broom handle. His wife hugged the child to her side and trailed her husband.

'A Thiarna*,' Mr Pearse exclaimed, 'From where did they come?'

'I think from that public house.' Finn indicated the burning building, shock loosening his tongue.

'What an ordeal they've endured,' Mr Pearse lamented. 'Sean, Tom, wake up. See! Can we help them?'

---

* Good Lord

Mr Clarke crouched at Finn's side. 'They'll be right,' he said, 'so long as they've that flag.'

A mutinous machine gun laughed scornfully at Mr Clarke's reassuring words. Bullets pelted the street. The father whirled about to shield his family as the angry metal swarm dived through the air. Searing rounds pierced his flesh; he twitched and writhed: fell. His wife opened her mouth to scream. The noise was drowned by the gun's renewed mocking cackle and she collapsed, her body pulped by bullets. The child stood alone.

Finn crashed from the room, mounted the sideboard barricading the doorway and thrust his head through the narrow window above the door.

'Here,' he yelled, 'Anseo*. Abhus anseo♣. Over here!'

The shooter stopped to reload. The girl heard Finn; saw him. He wriggled further through the window and beckoned her. She stepped towards him. The gunner fired again. Shots showered her like hailstones. She dropped next to her parents. Finn pushed off from the sideboard and was half through the window when a hand grabbed his belt.

'No you fucking don't.' Mr Clarke dragged Finn from the sideboard. 'What did I say about not losing your head?'

Finn opened his mouth.

'Go on, lad, spit it out. You'll feel better.'

'Fuck. Fucking fuck it.' Finn kicked the sideboard.

'Fuck it, indeed.' Mr Clarke hauled him into the front room.

'They had a white flag,' Mr MacDermott was protesting.

Mr Clarke closed the door and leant firmly against it. He lit a cigarette and gave it to Finn who was shaking with rage.

'Sean, what's happening?' Mr Connolly heaved his wracked body into a sitting position.

'There's been a…' Mr MacDermott began.

'Are we under attack?' Mr Plunkett reached for his gun.

---

* here

♣ over here

'We're not, Joe. Christ, the limey fuckers.' Mr Clarke left his guard at the door to go to the window.

The door sprang open. Lizzie was there, a hot compress in her hands, her face blanched.

'I should go out,' she said, eyes transfixed on the fallen girl, 'I might be able to…'

No, lass,' Mr Clarke said, 'There's nothing you can do.'

Finn took her trembling arm and led her into the kitchen, away from the sordid exhibition of the murdered family.

'Maybes you can find some tea,' he suggested, knowing she needed to work, not think. He left her searching the cupboards.

In the living room the five leaders were at the window.

'Mother Mary,' Mr Pearse murmured, hands worrying the hair from his head, 'What have I done?'

'Not you, Pat: we. And with just cause,' Mr MacDermott said.

'The cause was sound, aye, but the method horribly, oh, fatally, flawed,' Mr Pearse replied, 'The proof lies there.' He gestured to the pitiful scene then sank to the floor, cradling his head in his hands and rocking back and forth. The other commandants looked on, aghast.

The hate and fear that had twisted inside Finn since his murderous vision in the GPO faded. He wanted to comfort Mr Pearse: anois, anois.

'It's near dawn. We should make our move,' Mr Clarke muttered.

'The sooner we get to the Four Courts the sooner we can continue,' Mr Plunkett added.

'Continue what, Joe?' Mr Pearse sprang to his feet. 'The killing of more innocent Dubliners? This is the end, can't you see? Look, there!' He jabbed his finger towards the fallen family. 'We must, we've no choice, we will, surrender.'

'Surrender? That's a crime against those who've fought and died with us this week,' Mr Clarke declared.

'A far greater crime to allow women and children, children, Tom, to die,' Mr Pearse retaliated.

'Not by our guns, Pat,' Mr Plunkett said.

'But firing because of our actions.'

'Proving the Brits are desperate. This shows the world what cowardly bullies they are. It adds weight to our cause,' said Mr MacDermott.

'But no credit to our consciences if we fight at the expense of the innocent. 'Tis for them we're fighting,' Mr Pearse argued, 'and our duty to protect them,' he corrected himself, 'my duty, as president of the provisional government, to protect every Irish citizen.' Mr Pearse stood tall now. Finn longed to cheer him.

'Every bullet we fire takes us closer to that day when Ireland will be freed from British rule. We must fight on, Pat,' Mr MacDermott argued.

'If there was a guarantee we could fight without further loss of life I'd be agreeing, Sean, but there isn't.' Mr Pearse folded his arms. 'We've done enough to focus the world's eye on Ireland's troubles. By continuing we condemn ourselves to barbaric atrocities. We must surrender. It's the Christian thing.'

'We should vote.' Mr Clarke looked to Mr Plunkett and Mr MacDermott who both nodded, their 'aye' to fighting already cast.

'There's no need,' Mr Pearse replied, 'As president it's my decision.'

'Bollocks is it,' Mr Clarke replied, 'We vote.'

Mr Pearse said, 'Voting is pointless. There's no justification for continuing. The Rising is ended. To save lives we must do the honourable thing and surrender while we hold at least the moral high ground.'

There was a tense stand-off. Finn feared shots might be loosed. He rested his hand on his revolved. He would defend Mr Pearse. 'If I die let it be in defence of the life of he who loves the Gael.'

'I agree with Pat,' Mr Connolly said, 'No men could've done more than we and to try is to reduce ourselves to recklessness.'

'Thank you, James,' Mr Pearse said, 'It's settled. We surrender.'

Relieved, Finn exclaimed, 'Maith thú*, sir.'

---

* well done

The five commanders looked to him. Mr Pearse pushed through the others and put his hands on Finn's shoulders.

'Are you alright, Finn?'

'Yes, sir. It's the right thing you're doing, sir.'

Mr Pearse gripped Finn's arm. 'I shall never forget you and your deeds. Isn't it for lads like you that we've plunged ourselves into this so great abyss? I'm glad we tried, Finn. For the rest I can only beg the Lord forgive my mistakes.' Mr Pearse faced his comrades. 'Do chum glóire Dé agus onóra na hÉireann*.' Word by word his hand gripped Finn's arm ever more ferociously. He stared at his fellow commanders, challenging them.

Mr MacDermott reached out his hand. 'Aye, Pat, and won't we be glorious and honourable to the end?' The two men shook.

Mr Clarke draped an arm around Mr MacDermott's shoulders. ''Tis a grand thing today to be Irish,' he said, 'and in such fine company, too. Éire go bráth♣.'

Mr Plunkett limped over and rested a hand on Mr Connolly's shoulder while gripping Mr Clarke's free arm with the other. 'Isn't it a little thing we give in ourselves for the greatest thing of all: the nationhood of Ireland,' he added.

'Aye,' Mr Connolly said with a grin, 'Poblacht na hÉireann♦'

Finn looked around and saw, by the laying on of hands, they were united. He met Mr Pearse's gaze. With a shy smile and a shake of the head Mr Pearse released Finn.

'A thousand thanks, Finn,' he murmured, then, addressing the others, 'How am I to go about the surrender? Perhaps I best take it myself.'

Finn, elated by the moment that had righted his world, said, 'I'll take it, sir.'

---

* for the glory of God and the honour of Ireland

♣ Ireland forever

♦ the Republic of Ireland

'No.' The word was sharp, final. Mr Pearse added, 'You've done enough, Finn.'

Lizzie, who had been lingering in the hall, stepped forward. 'Let me; I'm a nurse in uniform; if I carry a white flag too they wouldn't dare shoot me, not in daylight.'

'That's courageous of you, Lizzie,' Mr Pearse said, 'But will it be safe?'

'It will.'

'If you're certain… Now, I'll need paper and a pen.'

As Finn watched Mr Pearse at the task of writing the surrender of the Irish Republican Army and ending the Easter Rising a strangely familiar finality settled over him, as if he'd already said goodbye to the men of the Supreme Military Council. The surrender meant their deaths, he knew. Mr Clarke's eyes found Finn's and Finn understood he too foresaw the surrender's outcome. He drew Finn aside.

'You've fought bravely this week, lad, and managed to keep your head. You're not to think this is the end. We've struck the first blow for freedom and Ireland will never lie down until the job's done. Remember, there are others in a position to carry on after us. One of them, perhaps the most important now we're so placed, is at Richmond Avenue, number 67. If you've the chance you might mind to pay her a visit and give her this from me.' Mr Clarke removed his wedding band, pressed it into Finn's hand and returned to his comrades.

Finn slid the ring onto his middle finger. Feeling the unfamiliar metal band hot and heavy against his skin, he fled the tragic scene.

In the backyard he crouched by the stinking bins and lit a cigarette.

'Have you another?' Lizzie squatted next to him, 'Mother Mary, it reeks here.' She laughed but Finn heard mad fear in the rise and fall of her voice.

'It's my last but we can share.' He passed her the cigarette.

'It's for the best,' Lizzie said.

'Yes.'

'What'll happen to them?'

'They'll hang.'

'All of them?'

'As many as the British can find lengths of rope for,' Finn said.

'What about the Volunteers?'

'I'm betting they'll be for hanging every one.'

'They can't,' she cried.

'They'll try.'

'Aren't you afraid?'

'Terrified,' Finn admitted, 'but it's better that than running away. I'd rather die a hero than live a coward.'

'Maybes you should go, for now at least.'

Finn said, 'My friends are dead or as good as. Why not me?'

'What about Cathleen?'

'She'll get over it.'

'Shite she will. You should go for her sake.'

Finn met Lizzie's eyes. She didn't blink.

'She deserves better,' he muttered.

'She wants you.'

'She's daft,' Finn replied, 'I've done terrible things. If you knew you'd tell her she's best off without me.'

'Sure, Finn, you've done grand things too. Like the way you saved Mr Connolly. You're a hero.'

'Like hell am I.'

'And what's a hero, so, Finn? Some bugger with a sword and a horse?'

Finn thought of the cavalry charge. 'Maybe.'

Lizzie shook her head. 'I've met some real heroes this week. They're ordinary, except,' she paused, 'they're not afraid of doing what has to be done.'

Finn raised his eyebrows.

'Like Mr Pearse,' she added, 'the surrender. For all he's done that's what makes him a hero.'

'Yeah,' Finn agreed, 'It is.'

'So you'll leave?'

'And go where?'

Lizzie gazed at the cigarette's glowing tip. 'The hospital. We've hidden soldiers before. You'd be safe there 'til you'd a chance to get away.'

'I don't want Cathleen mixed up in this anymore.'

'Don't be an eejit. She loves you.' Lizzie pulled a key from her pocket. 'The nurses' quarters. Cathleen's in room fourteen. Finn, please.'

'It's not fair. Why should I…?'

'It's doing what needs to be done. For Cathleen's sake if not yours.' Lizzie pressed the key into Finn's palm. 'Anyways, you owe me a favour for my trick when we flipped your saint.' She winked at Finn who felt himself the rope in a tug-o-war. Which way was he to fall?

The backdoor swung open, revealing Mr Pearse.

Lizzie squeezed Finn's fingers, melding the key into his skin. 'Give my love to Cathleen.' She rose and went into the house, Mr Pearse stepping aside for her.

Finn stood up, the key's teeth biting into his flesh like a venomous viper. Mr Pearse came into the yard.

'Finn, I'm needing to speak with you.' The headmaster's face was aged beyond its six and thirty years. 'Do you remember when you arrived at St Enda's, I asked what your dreams were? I don't think you told me but I recall telling you mine.'

'To be a hero,' Finn said, 'like Cúchulainn.'

'Like Cúchulainn,' Mr Pearse echoed, 'Do you remember what else I said? There are many ways to be a hero, Finn. This is the way I chose for myself but your way isn't mine. I've asked too much of you, more than I'd any right to. For that,' he paused, 'Tá mé iontach buartha♥.'

Finn thought of Freddie and Hal, how they wouldn't let him apologise for actions they'd chosen. 'You shouldn't be sorry, sir.'

Mr Pearse continued, 'But I'm going to set things right between us, Finn.' He reached into his pocket. 'This is yours.' In his hand was Finn's American passport. 'Rescued by me from the fireplace. I prayed you wouldn't need it but couldn't risk you being without it. I know, Finn, what this means for you and I understand you not wanting to take it but you must. I wish you to use it.'

'Sir, I have to stay here with you. It's my duty.'

♥ I'm really sorry

'Your duty to me is ended. There remains only one thing for me: to give my life. I will not allow you to give yours also. That would be too great a sacrifice.' He forced the passport on Finn.

'I can't, sir.'

'You must, Finn. My way is death; yours, life,' Mr Pearse smiled, 'Give yourself the chance of it.'

The passport scorched Finn's palm. 'Sir, everything we've fought for?'

'Was priced too richly for our pockets. Too many have paid. But not you. In the future there may be more you can do but that will be of your choosing and you must choose carefully, Finn. Search your heart and do nothing that you cannot wholly give yourself to.' To underline his words Mr Pearse unpinned the commander's brooch from Finn's lapel. 'So we part as we met, as master and student, perhaps even friends?' He blushed and ducked his eyes away from Finn's.

Finn nodded. 'Friends, yes. Sir, will you take this, please.' Finn unfastened St Colmcille from his neck. 'For the love of the Gael.'

'Aye, Finn, for the love of the Gael.' Mr Pearse's expression was serene. 'Go raibh maith agat*.'

'Tá fáilte romhat♣.'

'We've some Army business that'll keep us busy a while.' Mr Pearse stroked St Colmcille. 'I expect afterwards things will be such that we shan't see each other again. Do you understand I'm giving you an order, the last of too many?'

'Yes, sir.'

'Grand.' Mr Pearse pocketed the saint. 'Well, slán♦, Finn.'

'Slán, sir.'

They saluted each other, shook hands, shared a final grin and Mr Pearse disappeared inside. Clutching his passport and the key, Finn waited a minute then followed.

---

* thank you

♣ you're welcome

♦ goodbye

In the hall Finn overheard the commandants debating what terms of surrender to seek, Mr Pearse insisting they demand guarantees for the lives of the Volunteers. Finn knew the only guarantee for Mr Pearse and the other signatories was that they would die heroes for Ireland. Collecting his haversack, he returned to the kitchen.

In the dim light of a worried dawn Finn prepared to hide in plain sight, as Mr Plunkett had taught him. He changed into his civvies, the wound on his back tearing and stinging, and tucked Cathleen's locket beneath his jumper, the metal warm against his skin. He put his American passport, *Táin,* Bible, the proclamation from Nelson's Pillar and, hoping there might be a chance to somehow deliver it, Mr Pearse's note for Willie in his pockets. His uniform dumped on the floor, his revolver tossed on the draining board among the dirtied tea things, Finn went into the backyard. The day promised to be cloudy and dull.

He peaked into the alley, thinking of Freddie and Hal. Wishing they were with him, he darted down the entry and onto Parnell Street. The Rotunda Hospital lay across to his right. The area would be chock with soldiers; he had to be convincing. Arms swinging, whistling 'Jerusalem', Finn sauntered off, making a game of vaulting toppled walls and scrambling stone mounds that obstructed the footpath.

Peering between the ruins, Finn spied the front of the Roto and a patrol of British soldiers marching on the GPO. His hand flew for his gun; he rebuked himself for the reflex, stepped into the street, resumed whistling and watched the soldiers parade by. The captain regarded Finn with a keen glare. Finn grinned and waved.

'Going to sort the beggars out, are yous?' he called.

The captain faced front and the battalion tramped out of sight. Hoping his throbbing back hadn't bled through his jumper, Finn dashed across the road and around to the hospital.

He found the nurses' quarters and let himself in using Lizzie's key. Signs directed him to Cathleen's room. Two nurses passed him. One asked the other who she thought he was but Finn moved out of earshot before the reply.

He found room fourteen, knocked, waited, knocked again.

'I'm coming.'

Cathleen, in her uniform but minus the cap and cape, opened the door. She gasped, stared at Finn and crossed herself. 'Are you dead?'

'Not so far,' Finn said with a grin.

'Well for Jesus' sake, get inside before someone sees you.'

Cathleen ushered Finn into the small room. A single bed pressed one wall, a chest of drawers the other, a mirror hung above. The curtains were drawn, the filtered light a cheerless grey.

'I won't stay if…'

Cathleen threw her arms around him and shook with dry sobs of relief. Finn buried his face in her hair, felt it sticking to his wet cheeks. Only when her clawing hands raked the wound on his back did he shy from her touch.

'What is it?'

'Nothing, just my back.'

'I forgot. Is it alright?'

'Sore.'

'Let me see.'

Finn dropped onto Cathleen's unmade bed. 'Later.' He rested his elbows on his knees and let his head droop. 'It's over. They're surrendering. Mr Pearse made me go.'

'Oh.'

'Lizzie said I should come here.' He held up the key.

'I see.' Cathleen sat next to him and laced her fingers through his. 'And didn't you promise as much.'

'What if they come looking though?' He stood.

'We can hide a rebel as well as a soldier, can't we?'

'This is different, Cathleen. I'm not a deserter; I'm a traitor.'

'Ah, sure, you're nothing but a poorly lad with the fever.'

Ward forty-seven was the contagious diseases ward. John Tuohy, the doctor in charge, was he who'd first proposed hiding deserters. He was also a Volunteer but a critical patient had kept him from turning out on Easter Monday. When Cathleen explained Finn's situation he was glad to fox the

British again and falsified the paperwork admitting Finn as a case of scarlatina, quarantined in a private room overlooking the gardens where the Volunteers had first been recruited.

His wound resown by Dr Tuohy, Finn sat at the window in a hospital gown, remembering that day. Clutching Mr Pearse's proclamation, he wondered what, if anything, would survive of the hope they had felt then. The parchment became heavy in his hand. He slipped it inside his passport and picked up Mr Pearse's note to Willie.

Calm had fallen on the city for the first time in a week. Dull clouds threatened rain. Dirty smoke from smouldering fires smeared them with black smuts. But, as the room faced away from the heart of the fighting, the violence of the last few desperate days was hidden from view. Swaddled in stillness and wondering if these would be the last of Mr Pearse's words, Finn unfolded the note.

Dear old Willie,
God bless you for all your faithful work to me during the days of our lives. There are not words to tell of my love for you. No one can ever have had so true a brother as you. Do not grieve for me but know that I make this sacrifice, which God has asked of me, proudly and cheerfully. I hope and believe that you and the St Enda's boys will be safe. If this deed I have done has not been sufficient to win freedom, then others will win it by a better deed.
Pat.

P.S. I have written a little poem, below, which seems to say all there is to be said on the great grief of parting from those dear to me. I would like it added to the poems of mine in MS, in the large bookcase.

Beneath was written:

'The Wayfarer'

The beauty of the world hath made me sad,
This beauty that will pass;
Sometimes my heart hath shaken with great joy
To see a leaping squirrel in a tree,
Or a red lady-bird upon a stalk,
Or little rabbits in a field at evening,
Lit by a slanting sun,
Or some green hill where shadows drifted by,
Some quiet hill where mountainy man hath sown
And soon would reap; near to the gate of Heaven;
Or children with bare feet upon the sands
Of some ebbed sea, or playing on the streets
Of little towns in Connacht,
Things young and happy.
And then my heart hath told me:
These will pass,
Will pass and change, will die and be no more,
Things bright and green, things young and happy;
And I have gone upon my way
Sorrowful.

P. H. Pearse.

Fingers shaking, Finn placed the note with the proclamation, between the pages of his passport, lay on the bed and cried.

Finn awoke. Flat grey hospital paintwork filled his eyes. He curled round himself, wishing the same blankness would fill his mind too.

He'd been like that a while when the door opened. Finn shut his eyes as Cathleen's scent wafted in. She tiptoed across, stroked his forehead and sighed. Finn fought the urge to flinch, heard her move to the window and draw the shade. The door opened again; another set of footsteps padded in.

'How's our patient?' asked Dr Tuohy.

'Asleep. Can't we move him to a room not overlooking that abortion?'

'It's an unnecessary risk.'

'I suppose. It's just awful what they're doing down there,' Cathleen said.

'I'm sure they'll move out before nightfall. Perhaps our patient will sleep through it.'

'I hope so. You don't think they'll come for him?' Cathleen asked.

'I doubt it. The Brits have their hands full with that lot. Well, I'll be about my rounds if you need me.' Dr Tuohy padded out.

Carbolic soap and lavender overwhelmed him; Cathleen was close again. Finn kept his breathing steady and his body motionless, praying she would leave. A moment later she did, closing the door softly.

Finn leapt to the window and ripped away the blind. The Rotunda gardens were filling with companies of surrendered Volunteers. They queued in the street, shoulders sagged, eyes down, waiting to be corralled. Some, as they were shepherded through the gates, lifted their heads, straightened their spines. The British, seeing a man with spirit, cut him from his ranks with their bayonets then kicked, punched and shoved him. If he fell there was hair pulling, steel toecaps in his bollocks and whacks with a rifle stock until an officer called a reluctant end to the beating. Once on his feet, the Volunteer was slapped, prodded and poked. His pockets were emptied, his armband ripped off and trampled before he was forced, facedown, onto the damp grass to await his fate. Finn watched, sickened, as the wrecked Republican Army survivors were interned and abused. He scanned the faces, searching, fearing equally to find and to not find.

He picked them from the blurred crowd hovering at the Roto gates, Willie Pearse leading, Hal and Freddie behind. They crossed the threshold together, Willie half turned, speaking to Hal and Freddie. A British soldier with lieutenant's stripes halted them, interrogating and noting details on a pad. As Willie answered the lieutenant's head jerked up. He tossed the notebook aside, grabbed his pistol and levelled it at Willie. Willie raised his hands. The lieutenant jabbed the barrel of the gun at Willie, apparently barking orders. Willie placed his hands on his head and dropped to his knees. Two more soldiers rushed over; one, from the cap he wore, was a captain. He also pulled his gun on Willie. A crazed laugh bubbled in Finn; if only they knew they held an artist and teacher at gunpoint. The captain had Willie frisked, his hands bound. They dragged him away from Hal and Freddie who stood white, frozen and vulnerable. The lieutenant pointed to something on the ground. Freddie bent stiffly to retrieve it; the lieutenant snatched it as though touching Freddie would contaminate him. Then he puffed himself out, licked a finger, flicked a page of his restored notebook and resumed questioning and jotting. Finn blinked away hysterical tears, losing Freddie and Hal in the crowd.

After that Finn charged himself with spotting those he knew. It became a warped game; you won by losing. Tom Clarke was the first declared, the white of his flesh marking him clearly. He had been stripped of his uniform and dignity, another tactic, Finn supposed, to break the Sunday soldiers who, armed with pikes and patriotism, had held off, for almost a whole week, one of the greatest imperial armies. The sky that had been threatening all day, broke then and rain obscured Finn's view so he opened the window. Icy drops stung his face. Finn shivered, fixed his gaze on Mr Clarke and twisted the wedding ring he'd been entrusted with. Finn was determined to deliver it and the message that Mrs Clarke was waiting on, that she was to finish the job her husband had started twenty years ago in the Fenian Brotherhood. Poor Mr Clarke, the man beside him was doing his best to shelter his naked neighbour. As Finn watched, the man lifted his face to the blackened heavens. It was Michael Collins; another point to Finn.

Next he found Misters Colbert and MacDonagh. They were sitting close, their heads turned from each other whenever a guard passed but Finn knew, from how they leant together when no soldier was in earshot, that they held a whispered conversation. He imagined their words:

'This is a bad deal, Tom.'

'Aye, Con.'

'How long do you think they'll keep us here?'

'Long enough to make it miserable.'

'What then, Tom?'

'Gaol.'

'And after?'

'Let's not speak of it.'

'Righto.'

'Still, 'twas a grand show we gave them, eh, Con?'

'Indeed it was.'

'Don't suppose you've an idea what happened to Finn?'…

As the light faded Finn thought he glimpsed Eamonn Ceannt but wasn't sure. Countess Markievicz, Mr Connolly and Mr Pearse remained conspicuously absent. Finn didn't know if the fearless Countess was even alive. He imagined her going down shooting from the hip like a wild west gunslinger. He hoped that wherever Mr Connolly was he'd been dosed with morphine. Mr Pearse, Finn could only picture in his study at school.

The sun slunk away. The rain became a downpour. Finn stayed by the window, staring into blackness, the scene below, of the Roto gardens mulched with the remains of the Army of the Irish Republic, branded into his memory. He let every detail scar his mind's eye, commanding himself to never forget the sight of the fate he'd been spared by Mr Pearse.

It was later. Finn was still at the window.

'I brought you some cocoa.'

'I don't want it.'

Cathleen put down the tray and drew the window blind.

'You're wasting your time.'

'What do you mean?'

'I can still see them.'

'Drink this.' She held out a mug. 'Finn, this isn't your fault.'

'You're right there.' Finn span round. Cathleen jumped back, spilling the cocoa. 'It's my father's.'

Cathleen mopped at the spillage. 'What?'

'Aye, this is what he wanted.' Finn gestured to the window.

'Don't be daft. Your da didn't want it to end like this.'

'But he knew it could, and started it anyway.'

'He must've thought there was a good chance,' Cathleen said.

'Not good enough.' Finn threw his passport to Cathleen.

She picked it up. 'I don't understand.'

'It's my way out. He knew I'd need it. But there's no way out for those beggars. They'll be hanged.'

Her hand flew to her mouth. 'No, Finn.'

'What else?'

'But this doesn't mean anything.' She waved the passport.

'It means he knew he'd bollocksed and wanted to be sure I'd be safe, running away, like he did and his father before him. He's a fucking coward but I'm not.' Finn yanked up the window shade, threw open the window and leaned out. 'Éire go bráth*! Poblacht na hÉireann♣!' The words rang out into the cold empty night.

'Finn, for Jesus' sake, you'll have the whole bloody British Army up here,' Cathleen shrieked, tugging on his gown

'Aye, good enough.' Finn shrugged her off and shouted, 'Long live the Republic. Three cheers for President Pearse.'

Cathleen sobbed and clawed at him but Finn's immunity made him reckless. His anger made him determined. His freedom made him wild. He sang:

'We'll sing a song, a soldier's song,
With cheering rousing chorus,
As round our blazing fires we throng,
The starry heaven's o'er us;
Impatient for the coming fight,
And as we wait the morning's light,
Here in the silence of the night,
We'll chant a soldier's song.'

As he reached the chorus voices below joined in.

'Soldiers are we whose lives are pledged to Ireland.'

The voices gained strength and number.

'Sworn to be free.'

---

* Ireland forever

♣ Republic of Ireland

They threw every note of their Irishness into the anthem which rose up, filling the night with Gaelic hope and defiance.

'Tonight we man the bhearna bhaoil♦

In Éireann's♥ cause, come woe or weal

Mid cannons' roar and rifles' peal,

We'll chant a soldier's song.'

Finn became choirmaster, leading his choristers in the most glorious hymn. Below hundreds of voices answered, adding their faith to his.

Around the Rotunda house lights flicked on, illuminating the Volunteers, shivering on the wet grass, singing the fierce words of 'The Soldier's Song'. The Rising might be quashed but Irish spirits weren't and, Finn knew, would never be until Ireland was free.

'We're children of a fighting race,

That never yet had known disgrace,

And as we march, the foe to face,

We'll sing a soldier's song.'

Finn shouted the words of the second verse, his voice crackling, his throat sore. Windows across the square opened. Folk leaned out to listen and sing.

The British captains started hollering, 'Shut up! Stop this racket at once.' Soldiers began moving among the Volunteers, kicking and striking. The singing grew louder. A single shot spat into the night, punctuating the chorus in an unnatural place.

Finn craned out further and called the British to account with the third verse:

'Sons of the Gael! Men of the Pale!

The long watched day is breaking;'

There was another gun crack. Finn kept singing. More people hanging from their windows lent their voices; the song surged.

'Up there!' Two soldiers beneath his window pointed at Finn. 'It's him, there.' Faces peered up, Volunteers and British.

♦ gap of danger

♥ Ireland's

Finn waved and sang on. There was a hurried movement, blurred by the darkness. They were coming but the voices, strong now, sang the chorus one last rousing time.

Finn ducked inside and started dressing.

'What're you doing?' Cathleen grabbed him, trying to undo his shirt.

'They're coming. Go.' He brushed her aside. 'Don't worry. It's grand. Just leave.' He pulled his jumper over his head, snatched Cathleen's hand and bundled her through the doorway.

'Finn.'

'Now!' He snatched the passport from her, kissed her, slammed the door and slid home the bolt. He sat to lace his boots and wait.

Outside the Volunteers were repeating the chorus. As it faded footsteps pounded along the hallway.

'Are you sure it's this floor?'

'Yes. Which room?'

'Here?'

The door rattled.

'Locked, sir.'

'Get it open, Corporal.'

'Sir.' A boot thumped the door.

'You in there, open this bleeding door.'

Finn stayed sitting on the bed. The boot thumped harder. The door splintered. Two British soldiers and an officer rushed in. The soldiers grabbed Finn's arms and hauled him up.

'What's your name, sonny?' It was the same captain who'd arrested Willie.

Finn presented his passport.

The captain grabbed at it, swore and slapped the document against his palm. 'A Yank, eh?'

Finn nodded.

'You're not above the law, you know. Arrest him.'

'For what?' Finn demanded.

The captain stuttered then barked, 'Treason against the King.'

'How can it be treason if I'm not the King's subject?'

'Disturbing the peace, then,' the captain said.

'So you're gonna arrest everyone who sang?'

'Look here, I could have you charged with inciting a riot,' the captain blustered.

'What riot?' Finn asked.

The captain fixed Finn with stone-grey eyes. 'You're something to do with that lot out there, sonny.'

Finn remembered Mr Pearse's note to Willie folded in the back of his passport with the proclamation. 'Arrest me,' he challenged, 'and my father'll get his New York lawyer on the case; you'll be sending me home first class, courtesy of His Majesty.'

The captain ruffled the pages of the passport. Finn braced for the inevitable.

'What the devil's going on?' Dr Tuohy appeared, scowling at the broken door.

'Who are you?' the captain demanded.

'Who are you?' Dr Tuohy returned.

'Captain Lee-Wilson, British Army.' The officer extended a civil hand.

Dr Tuohy rebuffed it. 'Well, as the doctor in charge I insist you leave. There are seriously ill patients on the contagious diseases ward; I won't have them alarmed.'

At the words 'contagious diseases' the corporal and private exchanged nervous glances.

'This supposed patient of yours is causing a disturbance.'

'How's he doing that from up here?'

'Singing,' Lee-Wilson snapped.

Dr Tuohy smiled. 'And naturally such criminal behaviour warrants the smashing of that door and the upsetting of my patients.'

Lee-Wilson puffed his chest. 'I have prisoners to marshal; it's my responsibility to keep order. The singing of seditious songs is a clear attempt to incite further rebellion.'

'If you're concerned with keeping order in Dublin you should move those men indoors where your appalling ill-treatment cannot be witnessed. You're lucky it's only singing that people are about,' Tuohy replied, 'Now I insist you leave me to minister to my scarlet fever patient.'

'Scarlet fever! By heck, that's bad, that is, sir,' the corporal exclaimed.

Lee-Wilson had grown steadily redder. At the outburst of his junior officer he exploded. 'Good God, man, don't be a fool. Scarlet fever my arse!' He rounded on Dr Tuohy, 'Your superiors will hear of this insolence. As for you, my Yankee friend, I won't forget your face, or your name.' He scrutinized Finn's passport. 'I know you're involved in this damned insurrection; don't think because of this,' he shook the passport, 'you're getting away with it.' He hurled the passport to the floor and stomped out, his subordinates scurrying after him.

Dr Tuohy waited until their footsteps had faded.

'Christ, Finn, you could have blown the whole thing. Damnit, the man next door's AWOL from the Irish Guards.'

Finn retrieved the passport. 'Sorry,' he said, 'but I had to.'

'I don't think you can stay here much longer.'

'I'll be gone in the morning if that's soon enough.'

'I can't see them coming back tonight,' Dr Tuohy sighed, 'but Finn, no more singing for Jesus' sake, seditious or otherwise!'

Sunday 30 April

Finn sat by the window all night. In his mind a painting formed, a triptych, the left panel showing the Rotunda on the day they recruited the Volunteers, the middle showing tonight's agony and the right depicting the gardens adorned with a grand memorial to their sacrifice. He didn't know if he'd be able to complete such a piece without his art master's help but he wouldn't let his fear keep him from trying.

Just before dawn Cathleen arrived, wearing her day clothes.

'Dr Tuohy says you're leaving.'

'Yeah.'

'You were stupid last night. I was really cross with you.'

'Sorry,' Finn shrugged, 'At least I proved Mr Pearse right.'

'What?'

'There's more than one way to be a hero.'

Cathleen screwed up her face.

Finn sucked in air. 'Through this whole thing I've felt like everything happened because of me.'

'Of course it hasn't.'

'But that's how it felt. If my father wasn't who he is, if he hadn't sent me here, if I hadn't joined the Fianna and the IRB, if I hadn't met any of you; like it was meant to be this way. Only I don't know what's supposed to happen next. I thought I'd be killed. Mr Pearse saved me.'

'If you believe in destiny can't you believe yours is to live?'

'That's not what I deserve.'

'Aye, it is. You must have bigger, better things to do with your life.'

'What?' The question rang around the room, the final strike of the hour.

'I brought you some things; clothes, food, cigarettes, money, not much, but what I've got.' She handed him a bag.

'Thanks.' Finn dropped in his Bible, *Táin* and passport, the proclamation and Willie's note still between the pages.

'Will you go home?' Cathleen asked.

'I am home,' Finn replied fiercely.

The silence was an invisible wall between them.

'I don't want to say goodbye,' she said.

‘Neither do I. So we won’t.’

‘Alright.’ Her face relaxed.

Finn’s heart throbbed. This was his last chance. He took the locket from round his throat. ‘I hope you’ll keep it this time,’ he said as he fastened it about her neck and kissed her cheek.

She nodded.

‘Will you come back for me?’

‘If I can but I’ll not make a promise I mightn’t be able to keep.’

‘That’s fair,’ she said.

Finn drew her into his arms, held her close, kissed her, then turned her loose.

‘I love you.’

‘I love you too.’

She stepped back, eyes locked into his, opened the door and seemed to fall through it, sucked into a vortex.

Finn returned to the window. They were all gone or going. He’d have to go soon, too, but not until he’d waved the others off and said the goodbyes they couldn’t hear.

The sun was still low on the horizon when the British started kicking Volunteers from ragged sleep, jolting them awake to the misery of reality. With limbs stiff from the long cold night they staggered to their feet. Ordered into columns, Lee-Wilson ambled among their ranks, inspecting. Abruptly he stopped, pointed to a Volunteer. A private stepped forward, his rifle ready. Finn squinted against the sunrise. The private grabbed something from the Volunteer; he held on to it and there was a scuffle. Lee-Wilson struck the Volunteer. He fell but quickly raised his face to Lee-Wilson, shook his fist and spat, earning himself another blow. It was Mr MacDermott; they were fighting over his cane. Lee-Wilson snatched it, snapped it over his knee, pivoted on his heel and strolled away. Finn kept his eyes on the crumpled Mr MacDermott. Two Volunteers helped him stand and, when the column marched out, supported the crippled IRB leader as best they could.

When the Rotunda was emptied Finn set off.

*

Richmond Avenue was peaceful and tree-lined. No.67 was tucked in the corner. As Finn neared it he saw the milkman on the step. Closer still and he recognised Mrs Clarke hovering inside the doorway, arms folded.

'Nonsense, they wouldn't surrender!'

'I saw them myself this morning in the Rotunda Gardens, surrounded by British soldiers,' the milkman replied, 'and it's damn cool you take the news.' He thrust two pints into Mrs Clarke's hands and stomped down the steps.

Finn waited until he was gone before approaching. Mrs Clarke leapt at him.

'Is it true, Finn?' Before he could answer she hurried on, 'I see from your face it is. They're to be executed and I'm to put things in motion. Please, come in.'

Finn followed her inside, slipping the ring from his finger.

'Mr Clarke asked me to bring you this.'

She took it. 'Do you need money, Finn? I have IRB funds for those in need. I can see you get home to your father.'

Marvelling at her resolve and concern for him in an hour so dark for her own family, Finn said, 'Thank you, Mrs Clarke, but I'm fine.'

'What will you be doing now, so?' she enquired.

Finn pictured a clean canvas onto which anything could be painted and knew he must do as Mr Pearse had said, choosing the subject matter, fixing the perspective and deciding on the colours for himself.

'I'm not sure.'

'Well, if there's ever any help you're needing, Finn, I'll be happy to provide it if 'tis in my power to do so.'

'There is one thing, Mrs Clarke: don't tell anyone you saw me today.'

'Not even your family?'

Finn nodded. 'I would prefer it, I mean, it might be better if, my father can be…'

Mrs Clarke smiled knowingly. 'You wish to set your own course, influenced by no one.' She patted his arm. 'Your right and your responsibility.' Mrs Clarke sighed. 'Your mother would be proud to know what a fine young man you have grown into.'

Finn bowed his head. Perceptively, Mrs Clarke rushed on:

'Trust yourself, Finn, your own heart knows the way forward.' She squeezed his arm. 'And don't forget you have friends willing to assist you.'

She held the door for him and Finn stepped out.

The gates of St Enda's Park were barred by an army truck and two soldiers who blanked him, seeing not a rebel, the enemy, but a boy. As he sauntered by Finn grinned; he'd outfoxed Lee-Wilson again.

He scaled the north wall, near his grove of trees, the stitches on his back straining, and tramped through the wood to the Hermitage.

An army car, a corporal in the driver's seat, was parked on the drive. As he watched, Mrs Pearse and two officers emerged from the Hermitage. The car drove off. Mrs Pearse lingered on the steps, as if waiting for someone. Finn stepped through the trees.

At first she didn't see him. Her eyes were tearful and vacant. He drew nearer; she noticed him and smiled. When he was in earshot she called out:

'Pat, where've you been this past week? I've been worried sick, so I have. You know you're not to go off without telling me where you're biding.'

Finn climbed the steps. 'Mrs Pearse, it's me, Finn.'

She dabbed her eyes with a black handkerchief. 'Where's Pat? You haven't lost him in the woods? You boys are always getting into trouble, playing your games. Is Willie with him?' She peered over Finn's shoulder.

Finn nodded. 'Yes, Willie's with him.'

She smiled.

Mary Brigid appeared. 'Mother, come in, it's cold.' She steered her mother indoors.

Finn climbed down off the portico. Mary Brigid returned.

'She's confused. It's the shock, I expect.'

'Yes.'

'It's a while you've all been gone. Only a few days, I know, but somehow a lifetime,' she continued, 'I bet lots has happened. What's happened, Finn? Tell me.'

Finn glanced away.

'I'm sorry. Come in.'

'I'd rather walk, if you can manage it.'

'I can.'

When they were a good way from the house, Finn sank onto a fallen tree. Mary Brigid perched beside him. He told her what he could remember of the week's chaos, making sure she knew the surrender was her brother's decision. At this Mary Brigid buried her face in her hands.

'Praise be he saw sense in the end.'

Finn slipped the two loose sheets from between the pages of his passport. 'I have something for you. Actually, it's for Willie but I couldn't get it to him.' Finn handed her the note. 'And there's this. It's the one he read from on Monday.' Finn gave her the proclamation.

She held one in each hand. 'Thank you. I'll see Willie gets this when he's home.'

Finn let her keep that hope.

'I'm glad you came,' she added, 'I've been longing for news. The British won't tell us a thing. They've searched everywhere, wrecked Pat's study. He won't be able to find things when he gets back.' Her last word was clipped short. She met Finn's gaze. 'You mustn't blame yourself. It wasn't fair of Pat to you involve you.'

'I was involved long before I came here.'

'I don't understand.'

'My father,' Finn stopped, 'It doesn't matter. We did what we thought was right, Mr Pearse especially. He's a hero.' Finn squeezed her hand. 'Don't let anyone say otherwise.'

She nodded and brushed away a tear. 'You were always Pat's favourite.' They stood.

'I'll have to see to Mother. You'll be away home.' She nodded at the passport in his hand.

Finn traced the path through the trees to St Enda's, his home for five years, and wondered if he'd ever have such a thing again. 'I don't know where I'm going.'

'Then you must stay here,' Mary Brigid said, 'Until you've decided.'

'It wouldn't be safe.' The words were underscored by the rude arrival of another military motorcar. Finn shrank back among the trees. 'Not much of a hermitage now, is it?' he scowled.

'Hermitage,' Mary Brigid echoed vaguely. The next word leapt from her lips. 'Rosmuc! Wasn't Pat forever saying it was the place to away to if you'd need of sanctuary?' She seized Finn's hands. 'Go there, lose yourself.'

Finn was already lost, clinging to a tiny raft bobbing in a vast ocean; the Connemara cottage was the only land on the horizon. He'd be as well to make for it.

'Alright but you mustn't tell anyone I'm there, not even my father.'

'Why ever not?' Mary Brigid demanded.

'If you telephone or cable the message might be intercepted. I don't want you getting into trouble,' Finn argued, 'Plus, it's time I was settling things for myself.'

'You feel yourself too much in his light?'

'Aye.'

Mary Brigid's mouth quivered. 'This isn't the end of it, is it, Finn?'

He dropped his gaze. 'I don't know what it is, perhaps a beginning.'

'Sure, 'tis a hard thing you're choosing.'

He raised his eyes to hers. 'But my choice to make. Please, Mary Brigid, try to understand.'

She sighed, hugged him. 'Take care of yourself.'

'I will.' Finn hugged back fiercely.

She let go and slipped away through the trees. Finn watched until she was gone and he alone: free.

There was a heavy military presence at the station. Finn blagged his way onto a train heading west, hid in the guard's van until they escaped the city then sat staring at the horizon, waiting for Galway's ragged hills to rise from the land.

The trek from Maam Cross to Gort Mór was further than he remembered; Finn kept his mind busy recalling the features of the Connemara landscape as Mr Pearse had once named them. Finally he spied the cottage's yellow thatch and headed up the lane towards it. The tiny house brooded over the lough's dark water. Finn felt unwelcome, an intruder. He had to break a window to get inside.

A film of dust shrouded everything. The air was chilled. The cottage had been empty since his visit with Mr Pearse last summer. Finn fetched turf from the outbuilding, got a fire going and set about nursing the cottage back to life. Huddled by the hearth, Finn unpacked the food Cathleen had provided; bread and cheese, apples and a chunk of fruitcake. He hadn't eaten since Saturday but knew he should ration his supplies; he ate frugally and settled in the fireside chair where he'd spent innocent nights drawing, reading and listening to Mr Pearse's stories.

For two days Finn clung to the cottage, leaving only to collect peat and draw water from the lough. He kept busy polishing the windows, scrubbing the flags, knocking down cobwebs, readying it for whoever might come after him.

Scaring dust from a shelf in the second bedroom, Finn spotted a volume, the words '*A Boy in Eirinn* by Padraic Colum' on the spine. Mr Colum's story of Finn O'Donnell and his namesake, Finn MacCoul, had made it into print. Remembering the effect of the story on his wretched younger self, Finn whipped open the cover. On the title page were two dedications, one typed, the other handwritten. The first read, in Irish and English, 'To a Teacher of the Irish Youth P. H. Pearse.' The second said 'To Willie, my good friend and first fan. Long may St Enda's be filled with boys who like my work. Padraic.' Finn grinned and vowed to read it later.

On Tuesday evening, while eating his last slice of fruitcake, Finn read from cover to cover, glad to lose himself in the cheery children's tale. The last line declared, 'And there in that country of bog and little fields Finn lived until he grew to be a man.' Finn wished all stories could end so well.

Wednesday 3 May

Finn awoke with a jolt, his eyes springing open, his heart throbbing like it would burst. His ears rang with the echo of a gunshot. He lay as though dead, his breath puffing in staccato white clouds; the cottage was cold as the grave. He chased off the nightmare and sat up. He was in Mr Pearse's bedroom, on the bed, *A Boy in Eirinn* on the coverlet beside him. He remembered with a shiver the hollow ache that had made him sleep there last night instead of his familiar room beneath the thatch. He'd built up the fire until it blazed, cheering him; it had died in the night. The grate was filled with frost-white ash. A draught blowing down the chimney stirred the fine dust, drawing it up the lum, vanishing it like the memory of a dream. Finn struggled outside.

Across the lough the sun rose in a haze of orange light. Finn lit his last cigarette. He knew what had awakened him. Mr Pearse was dead. He kicked a tin pail from the doorstep. It fell with a clatter, skidded along the path, lost momentum and rolled in half-hearted arcs.

Finn stood there long after his cigarette was burnt down, watching the orange dawn fade and the sky fill with St Patrick's blue. Beneath it Ireland spread her arms, welcoming him home, offering herself to him: Cúchulainn's country, his now. He had only to choose it.

Inside the cottage Finn found a notepad. He sat where Mr Pearse had penned his feverish oration for O'Donovan Rossa. The words came in a torrent.

Dear Mr & Mrs Devoy,
I regret to inform you of the death of your son, William 'Finn' Devoy, who was killed in action in Dublin on Saturday, 29th April, fighting for the Forces of the Irish Republic who were engaged in trying to free Ireland from the tyranny of British rule. His tragic death marks him as a courageous young man and his loss is keenly felt by those who fought alongside him.
Yours with deepest sympathy,

*

Finn printed the words in an anonymous hand, signed an ostentatious but illegible signature, left the letter undated and folded it into an envelope addressed in the same plain handwriting. A second note, addressed to Mrs Clarke, he scribbled in his own hand, asking her to post the other from Dublin. His heart, he assured her, did indeed known the way.

He left *A Boy in Eirinn* by the hearth, tidied the cottage, swept the grates and stacked turf. He scouted out some essentials; a set of old clothes, matches, a canteen, a knife, half a bar of soap. In the pantry, he found a familiar rucksack, the letters PWF scratched on the leather flap. Rubbing away tears, he packed the haversack with what he'd gathered and what he'd salvaged of himself; the Bible, *An Táin,* the school photos still pressed between the pages, and the passport, kept as a reminder of who he wasn't. He donned the shabby greatcoat and cap that hung by the door and which Mr Pearse had worn on stormy days. From the storehouse he took a bicycle and freewheeled down the lane, leaving himself behind.

In Rosmuc village Finn bought rations and posted his letter. As the postmaster dropped the envelop into a yawning sack a spasm of grief stopped Finn's heart. His mother would soon be mourning him; her pain ached inside Finn's chest. He lamented her sorrow but was no less certain of his choice for it. This was his way.

He had died a hero's death. Now he would live a hero's life. Finn mounted the bicycle and rode for the Twelve Pins.

Half-way between Doire Iorrais and Cashel he encountered a lad his age, trying to haul a cart from a ditch with only a stubborn donkey for help.

'Would you need a hand there?' Finn asked, dismounting.

'What do you think?' the lad snapped, his face pink and sweaty.

Finn pitched in and, after much cursing and heaving, they freed the cart.

'Thanks.' The lad mopped his brow and offered Finn a cigarette. 'Where're you heading?'

'Nowhere,' Finn replied.

'On the lam, eh?'

Finn shrugged.

'Ah, that's your business, so it is.'

'Aye, but I'm not in a rush so I'll help you with that.' Finn gestured to the cart's buckled wheel.

'That'd be grand,' the lad said, 'I've to get back to the farm quick-smart or me old man'll skin me. We're shorthanded as it is, with our Joe away.'

'Your brother?'

'Aye, he's in France. I'm Fergal.' The lad offered Finn his hand, 'and what will they be calling yourself?'

Finn caught sight of the rucksack, 'PWF: Pat and Willie forever'.

'Patrick William Finnighan. But call me Paddy.'

'Right your are, Pad.' They shook. 'If you're after helping me you'd best come home with me. Ma'll be glad to feed you for getting me out of a fix. If we get on now we'll be in time for supper. She makes a great stew, does Ma.'

'Sounds grand.'

'It's a piece of luck, meeting you out here,' Fergal added.

'I don't believe in the stuff.'

'Don't you now? Not even the luck of the Irish?' Fergal asked.

'I don't indeed. Luck and fate, it's bollocks.'

'Aye, happen you're right,' Fergal mused, 'Sure, that poor lot in Dublin this past week haven't had any of the fecking stuff. Were you hearing about that?'

Finn dragged on his cigarette. 'I was.'

'My da says they'll hang the lot of 'em.'

'He's right there.'

'Ain't fair, if you're asking me,' Fergal said.

''No,' Finn said, 'Not fair at all.'

May 1913

'By Way of Comment' from *An Macaomh* Vol. II No. 2

It has been sung of the Gael that his fighting is always merry and his feasting always sad… And it is a true impression, for the exhilaration of fighting has gone out of Ireland, and for the past decade most of us have been as Fionn was after his battles – 'in heaviness of depression and horror of self-questioning.' Here at St Enda's we have tried to keep before us the image of Fionn during his battles – careless and laughing, with that gesture of the head, that gallant smiling gesture, which has been an eternal gesture in Irish history… I know that Ireland will not be happy again until she recollects that old proud gesture of hers, that laughing gesture of a young man that is going into battle or climbing to a gibbet.

What I have just written has reminded me of a dream I had nearly four years ago. I dreamt that I saw a pupil of mine, one of our boys at St Enda's, standing alone upon a platform above a mighty sea of people; and I understood that he was about to die there for some august cause, Ireland's or another. He looked extraordinarily proud and joyous, lifting his head with a smile almost of amusement; I remember noticing his bare white throat and the hair on his forehead stirred by the wind just as I had often noticed them on the football field. I felt an inexplicable exhilaration as I looked upon him, and this exhilaration was heightened rather than diminished by my consciousness that the great silent crowd regarded the boy with pity and wonder rather than with approval – as a fool who was throwing away his life rather than as a martyr that was doing his duty. It would have been so easy to die before that silent unsympathetic crowd! I dreamt then that another of my pupils stepped upon the scaffold and embraced his comrade, and that then he tied a white bandage over the boy's eyes, as though he would resent the hangman doing him that kindly office. And this act seemed to me to symbolise an immense brotherly charity and loyalty, and to be the compensation to the boy that died for the indifference of the crowd.

This is the only really vivid dream I have ever had since I used to dream of hobgoblins when I was a child. I remember telling it to my boys at a school meeting a few days later, and their speculating as to which of them I had seen in the dream: a secret I do not think I gave away. But what recurs to me now is that when I said that I could not wish for any of them a happier destiny than to die thus in defence of some true thing, they did not seem in any way surprised, for it fitted in with all we had been teaching them at St Enda's. I do not mean that we have ever carried on anything like a political or revolutionary propaganda among our boys, but simply that we have always allowed them to feel that no one can finely live who hoards life too jealously: that one must be generous in service, and withal joyous, accounting even supreme sacrifices slight. Mr J M Barrie makes his Peter Pan say (and it is finely said), "To die will be a very big adventure," but I think that in making my little boy in *An Rí* [Pearse's play *The King*] offer himself with the words, "Let me do this little thing," I am nearer to the spirit of heroes.

P. H. Pearse

We know their dream; enough
To know they dreamed and are dead;

Easter 1916 by W. B. Yeats

Killed on IRB business

Sean O'Malley 31st Oct 1915 St Enda's College for Boys

Killed in Action

Donald MacCabe	25th April 1916	GPO
George Reynolds	26th April 1916	Mount Street
Dick Murphy	26th April 1916	Mount Street
Patrick Doyle	26th April 1916	Mount Street
Michael Malone	26th April 1916	Mount Street
David Reddin	26th April 1916	Townsend Street
Patrick Healy	26th April 1916	GPO
Charlie Barrett	28th April 1916	Moore Street
The O'Rahilly	28th April 1916	Moore Street

Executed by firing squad

Patrick Pearse	3rd May 1916	Dublin
Tom Clarke	3rd May 1916	Dublin
Thomas MacDonagh	3rd May 1916	Dublin
Joseph Plunkett	4th May 1916	Dublin
Edward Daly	4th May 1916	Dublin
William Pearse	4th May 1916	Dublin
Michael O'Hanrahan	4th May 1916	Dublin
John MacBride	5th May 1916	Dublin
Eamonn Ceannt	8th May 1916	Dublin
Michael Mallin	8th May 1916	Dublin
Con Colbert	8th May 1916	Dublin
Sean Heuston	8th May 1916	Dublin
Thomas Ceannt	9th May 1916	Cork
Sean MacDermott	12th May 1916	Dublin
James Connolly	12th May 1916	Dublin

Executed by hanging

Roger Casement	3rd August 1916	London

MIA; presumed dead

William 'Finn' Devoy	29th April (?)1916	Unknown

Further Reading

Interested readers are directed to the following texts which were drawn on in the writing of *Green Dawn*:

- Campbell, Christy, *Fenian Fire*, (London: Harper Collins Publishers, 2002)
- Clarke, Kathleen, *Revolutionary Woman,* (Dublin: The O'Brien Press, 1991)
- Colum, Padraic, *A Boy in Eirinn*, (New York: E. P. Dutton & Company Publishers, 1913; facsimile reprint edition La Vergne: Kessinger Publishing, 2009)
- Coogan, Tim Pat, *1916: The Easter Rising*, (London: Orion Books Ltd., 2005)
- Crowley, Brian, *Patrick Pearse: A life in pictures,* (Cork: Mercier Press, 2013)
- Hutton, Mary, *The Táin: An Irish Epic Told in English Verse,* (Dublin: Maunsel and Co. Ltd, 1907)
- Kinsella, Thomas, trans., *The Táin*, (Oxford: Oxford University Press, 2002)
- MacLochlainn, Piaras F., *Last Words*, (Dublin: The Stationery Office, 1990)
- O'Brien, Paul, *Blood on the Streets,* (Cork: Mercier Press, 2008)
- Ó Buachalla, Séamas (Ed.), *The Literary Writings of Patrick Pearse,* (Dublin: Mercier Press, 1979)
- O'Farrell, Mick, *A Walk Through Rebel Dublin 1916*, (Cork: Mercier Press, 1999)
- Pearse, P. H., "By Way of Comment" *An Macaomh*, Vol. 2 No. 2 (May 1913)
- Pearse, P. H., *The Coming Revolution,* (Cork: Mercier Press 2012)
- Pearse, P. H., *Short Stories*, ed. by Anne Markey, (Dublin: University College Dublin Press, 2009)
- Skinnider, Margaret, *Doing My Bit for Ireland,* (New York: The Century Co., 1917; facsimile reprint edition by Forgotten Books, 2012)
- Sisson, Elaine, *Pearse's Patriots*, (Cork: Cork University Press, 2005)
- Stephens, James, *The Insurrection in Dublin*, (Gerrards Cross: Colin Smythe Ltd., 2000)